FINAL APPEAL

FINAL APPEAL

REMIGIUSZ MRÓZ

CROOKED
LANE

NEW YORK

Published in the United States by Crooked Lane Books, an imprint of The Quick Brown Fox & Company LLC.

Crooked Lane Books and its logo are trademarks of The Quick Brown Fox & Company LLC.

Library of Congress Catalog-in-Publication data available upon request.

ISBN (hardcover): 978-1-63910-804-6
ISBN (ebook): 978-1-63910-805-3

Cover design by Nebojsa Zoric

Printed in the United States.

www.crookedlanebooks.com

Crooked Lane Books
34 West 27th St., 10th Floor
New York, NY 10001

First Edition: February 2024

10 9 8 7 6 5 4 3 2 1

*"For my Parents,
this one,
the previous one,
and all the next to come"*

PROLOGUE

Joanna Chyłka entered the visiting room and sat down opposite her client. She looked at him in silence for a moment, thinking of the sentence he was facing.

Life, with a chance of parole after twenty-five years.

It didn't sound good: frankly, a terminal diagnosis would have sounded better. An hour in a prison cell feels like an age, but an entire life? If the Polish justice system still had the death penalty, this guy's head would already be on the block. And he'd probably be grateful for it.

Chyłka watched him closely, trying to get a feel for who she was dealing with. First meetings were always difficult. Defendants distrust lawyers instinctively, at least until there's a glimmer of hope that the lawyer really intends to do their damnedest to get them out of the mess they're in.

She had been prepared for the worst, but hadn't expected it to be this bad. In the past she'd defended any number of socio-, psycho- and this-that-or-the-other-paths, but none that she had ever found this disturbing.

"I see you're not exactly pure as the driven snow," she remarked, poring over the documents laid out on the table.

He'd been charged with article 148—murder with exceptional brutality. And if ever Chyłka felt a criminal charge hit the mark, it was now—although it would have been even more accurate to call it "murder with exceptional brutality and fuckheaded cruelty."

The prisoner stared at the metal tabletop without responding, then slowly looked up. When their eyes met, she felt she was facing pure evil.

He was guilty as sin.

"So what is it you want me to do for you?" she asked, pushing the papers aside.

Silence.

"I assume you don't want to plead not guilty or ask for leniency, because then at least you'd make an effort."

Still no response.

"Do you hear what I'm saying?"

"Yes."

There was something deeply disturbing about his voice. Chyłka felt as if someone was clawing at her soul with jagged nails. She was, nonetheless, glad that the man had finally spoken.

"Do you know how much an hour of my time costs?"

"More than it should, I'm sure."

He looked deep into her eyes. Joanna felt a wave of heat pass over her.

"But you don't have to worry about that," she said. "Your daddy will pick up the bill, won't he?"

No response.

Officially, his father was a respected businessman, a ruthless player in the corporate world. Privately though, he was a drunk who never knew when to stop. It was only thanks to Chyłka that he had never been convicted of that series of sexual assaults on girls crossing the Russian-Polish border in the Masurian forest.

"He must be proud of you," she added.

"I'm sure he is."

"He's renounced you on camera on at least five different TV stations. And yet he's paying for your defence. Is that why we're wasting time? Is that how you want to get at him? That's pretty weak, you know. Pathetic."

More silence. Deep down, Chyłka knew her cheap jibes wouldn't get him to open up—nor would any other gimmicks for that matter. This scum, who had murdered a young girl and her boyfriend, then sat in his flat with their bodies for ten whole days, wouldn't be easily manipulated. It wasn't that he had the mental strength; it was just that people like him lived in a world of their own, and the conventional methods didn't work.

"OK, let's cut the crap," she said finally.

"You're the only one talking crap."

She cleared her throat.

"What is it you want from me?" she asked, laying her clasped hands on the table. She leaned slightly towards him to show she wasn't scared. "I'm here to work. And how I do that work depends on you."

"How about against the wall?" he suggested, leaning back and purposefully eyeing his crotch.

She wasn't especially surprised; as a criminal lawyer she had to put up with all sorts of sexual bluster. They said women pathologists needed a thick skin to deal with decaying corpses all day, but in Chyłka's opinion it was women lawyers who drew the short straw. You saw a corpse, you went home and forgot about it: a bottle of wine would wash away the memory. But she knew from personal experience that when a defendant spits in your face or openly masturbates while looking you straight in the eye, that's harder to erase from your mind. Some days you could be treated to the most perverse and perverted synonyms for penis, vagina, or sexual intercourse, and the next day you'd be back to face the same person again, with a broad smile, because after all, this was your client.

"Carry on like this and you'll be the one up against the wall," she said after a pause. "I'm sure there are plenty of inmates at Białołęka prison who'd be happy to sort you out."

Silence. Not even that hit home.

"Don't you want to tell the world why you killed them?"

It was her last-ditch effort. Most psychopaths liked to boast about what they had done, implying it had some sort of deeper meaning. But this one just stared at her blankly.

"So it was all a fit of rage, huh?" she asked, flicking a cigarette out of the packet. She turned the packet towards the prisoner. "You know the media are still looking for a motive? But so far, it's just speculation. The prosecutor's office hasn't a clue, let alone the police. And your father claims he didn't know the victims, so there's nothing connecting you with them." She paused. "Nothing, apart from your fingerprints on the murder weapons, and biological evidence on the bodies."

Weapons. A chill ran down her spine as she used the plural. Normally, killers used only one weapon. If they stabbed the victim, they didn't suddenly stop and choose a different knife. If they were choking them, they didn't risk loosening their stranglehold while they fetched a hammer to crush the victim's windpipe.

But that was what had happened.

The killer had alternately strangled, stabbed, and beaten his victims. It was nothing to do with torture, according to pathologists; his intention had always been to kill. He had, however, repeatedly stopped at the last moment, as if he was having second thoughts. As if he was dissatisfied, and wanted something more.

"You're one fucked-up psycho."

"Undoubtedly."

Chyłka knew she'd get nothing more from him that day: only time would loosen his tongue. He needed to spend time in custody, to reflect on his situation, and then—no, even then she couldn't count on any radical change. People like him cooperated with lawyers for only two reasons: either they were proud of what they had done and wanted the lawyer to help them tell the world, or they wanted an acquittal, so they could go out and murder again.

Unfortunately, her job was to secure the latter.

PART 1

1

THE YOUNG MAN stood outside the Skylight building, looking up at the glass façade. He sipped the latte he had just bought at Coffee-heaven and took a long drag on his cigarette—probably the fifth he'd smoked in the last hour.

Kordian remembered when the undeveloped area opposite the Palace of Culture and Science had been bleak and empty—valuable land at the heart of Warsaw, squandered. Now there was an office building there, attracting major Polish and international companies eager to site their headquarters next to Golden Terraces, the bustling shopping complex through which thousands of people passed daily. One of the companies was the law firm where on that very day, Kordian Oryński was due to start work as a legal trainee.

Żelazny & McVay was a limited partnership company, a paragon of Polish-British collaboration and, as is often the case, several firms had had to go out of business before it could secure its spot on the twenty-first floor of the Skylight. It had been holding its own in the legal rankings for quite some time—somewhere just below Dentons and Domański Zakrzewski Palinka—but standards were getting ever higher, and Żelazny & McVay's owners were looking forward to toppling the competition in the coming year.

The firm had branches in ten provincial capitals and employed well over a hundred lawyers, as every aspiring trainee was required to know before stepping over the threshold of the Skylight building. They would then be given a brochure detailing how to work twelve hours a day without resorting to amphetamines or other stimulants.

In truth, Kordian didn't need that sort of information in print; he knew exactly what was involved. Once he had drunk his latte and finished his cigarette, he'd be entering a different world. A ruthless, devious, dangerous world of manipulation, multi-million-dollar scams and other intrigues.

Well, that was the theory.

In practice, he expected to be given a desk in some small cubicle and a pile of old documents, and to spend hours breathing in dust from years of ancient paperwork.

And still, he couldn't wait to get started.

"You're causing a stench." He heard a woman's voice behind him.

"Sorry?" he said, turning around.

"Put the cancer-stick out. You're causing a stench." The voice belonged to a woman of around forty, and, try as he might, Kordian couldn't tear his eyes away. Her well-fitting jacket and tight skirt didn't help.

"I can't see a no smoking sign," he said.

"It's right here, in front of you."

Then, to the young man's amazement, the woman pulled out a packet of Marlboros and lit one. She inhaled with pleasure, blowing the smoke out in his direction. For a moment Oryński wondered if she was from some sort of psychiatric institution.

"Something wrong?" she enquired.

"What are you . . . ?"

"Where are you heading to?" interrupted the woman. "No, hang on, don't tell me, let me guess. You're not shitting yourself, so it can't be any of the big-name companies. Perhaps you're with the insulation guys? Or no, I know." She took another deep drag on her cigarette, looking at the lower part of the building. "You're the new intern at the United Arab Emirates Embassy."

Kordian said nothing.

"Allahu Akbar," she added, nodding her head encouragingly.

"Really? The Embassy's here in this building?" he asked in astonishment.

"Uh huh," she nodded, then frowned. "Then . . . EDF perhaps?"

"No, Żelazny & McVay."

He tried, but failed, to keep the pride out of his voice. The woman smiled, then bowed her head, as if in reverence.

Kordian realised the smile was more one of pity than admiration, and that this woman most probably worked there herself. When he saw the look of commiseration on her face, he knew he'd hit the nail on the head. He felt his shirt stick to his back, although the weather wasn't particularly warm.

"Take your glass of milk and follow me," said the woman, scowling at the steaming latte. Kordian was glad he hadn't gone for his favourite white chocolate mocha. He hastily crushed out his cigarette with the sole of his brand-new shoe and followed her.

They rode the lift to the twenty-first floor in awkward silence. Kordian didn't even try to start a conversation, convinced he'd sink even lower in her esteem. He sighed with relief when they stepped out of the lift and into a narrow corridor. A long row of plaques bearing the names and job titles of Żelazny & McVay employees confirmed he was in the right place. *A career take-off strip*, he thought.

"Have we already offered you a position?"

"Sorry?" he exclaimed. "Yes, yes, I've already been taken on. I've spoken to Mr Żelazny, I'm doing a traineeship here in Warsaw and . . ."

"I guessed you weren't doing it in Gdańsk," growled the woman, who had stopped at a door with a gold plaque inscribed "Joanna Chyłka, Senior Associate."

"Do you know what to do next?"

"Yes, ma'am," replied Oryński, sounding so obsequious it made him cringe. "That is . . . no, not really."

"Yes or no?" she asked, shaking her head. "Go to reception. Over there," she pointed. "Get Anka to give you your Hooker and Snooker voucher, then go to . . ."

"My what?" asked Kordian. Had he misheard? Probably not, but she looked so serious that maybe he had.

"Your Hooker and Snooker voucher," she repeated, opening the door to her office. "It's tradition, for our newbies. You get this bit of paper, which you put on your desk. If you lose your first case, your boss gets to treat you as their whore for an evening. If you win, you can have a nice game of snooker together. Understand?"

He didn't understand at all. Żelazny & McVay was supposed to be a serious company modelled on New York law firms, or like in the TV series *Suits*. But this was more like a dumbed-down version of *Boston Legal*. Not what he had applied for.

"Sure," he nodded.

"So, shift your ass, go to reception," Joanna advised, entering her office. "And pray you don't get a mentor as stroppy as me."

CHAPTER

2

STANDING AT ANKA the Receptionist's desk, Kordian wondered if he should risk making a fool of himself and ask for the voucher. There was a lot at stake. If he got it right, he'd come across as brilliantly prepared, totally clued up about Żelazny & McVay's corporate culture. If he went over and said, "Good morning, I'd like a Hooker and Snooker voucher, please" and had judged it right, people would talk about him as the bright new boy who knew all about the firm's traditions even before his first day. If on the other hand, Chyłka had set him up, he'd be a laughing stock.

"Good morning. I was here yesterday," he said meekly, hoping this would explain everything. Clearly, all guns blazing wouldn't have been the right approach.

The receptionist narrowed her eyes and wrinkled her nose.

It occurred to Kordian that every time he opened his mouth, he was breathing out fumes from the Davidoff he had just smoked. He should have thought to chew some gum on the way over—the extra-strong sort that burned out your insides—but he'd been so distracted by that crazy woman that he didn't even have time to think.

"Oh, yes," replied Anka indifferently from behind the reception desk, then fell silent.

He wondered how many newbies like him stood in that spot every week. Probably around ten, of whom only one or two would make it through; the rest would decide that staying on to work from dawn till dusk and be pushed around was simply not worth it.

He cleared his throat, deciding that he had better speak, because Anka the Receptionist was saying nothing, and what little interest she had was rapidly vanishing.

"I've come for the voucher," he ventured.

"The what?" asked Anka, frowning. Then, "Go to the second room on the left, the one marked HR. They've got the paperwork."

Kordian nodded and smiled, although he thought he had done all the paperwork the previous day. He walked off towards HR, pleased that he had not mentioned the hooker thing after all. He had taken the middle path—perhaps that was the way to survive in this place.

He knocked on the door marked HR, glancing quickly down the corridor. It was so bright it could have been a hospital. Everything was ecru in colour—that is, not really any colour at all. There were a few plant pots dotted around, but they were full of weeds, with no flowers in sight. Sunlight flooded the space, reflecting off the glass walls wherever he looked; the overall impression was one of dazzling brilliance.

It was a good few minutes before someone opened the door. Kordian had imagined the room as a hotbed of evil, full of people devising ever more ingenious ways to force colleagues out of their jobs. Not easy in a law firm where most employees were familiar with employment law, where everyone knew that if you simply claimed not to have seen your dismissal notice you'd be untouchable; that if the notice wasn't delivered, it was null and void. He wondered whether companies such as Żelazny & McVay outsourced the firing of employees—but then again, the bosses probably liked to retain control over everything that happened within their walls.

"Oryjski?" asked a man in a suit so tight you could see his ribcage.

"Oryński," the young man corrected him.

"Come in and sit down. I haven't got all day."

It was time to get a grip, Kordian decided. That lawyer was one thing, but he wasn't going to let this pen-pusher intimidate him. He sat down on the chair in front of the desk, crossed his legs, folded his arms and looked up expectantly.

The clerk knew that look all too well. He had seen it in the eyes of all those would-be legal heroes who felt they were about to set the world on fire now their studies were finished and their official training had begun, and that the world was their oyster.

Perhaps it had been their oyster once, years ago, when the commercial, energy, and new technologies sectors were crying out for good lawyers. But now there were no new areas left to exploit.

"Sign here, here, and here," he said, pushing several documents towards the young man.

"OK," Kordian replied, leaning over the first sheet of paper. The clerk raised his eyebrows.

"What are you doing?" he asked.

"Reading."

"You're supposed to sign them, not read them," grumbled the clerk, taking a gulp from his Starbucks mug. He glared at the silent Kordian. "Oh, just do it, neither of us has time for this."

"I need to read it before I sign," retorted Oryński, but with little conviction. The clerk shook his head and sighed. For a moment they both sat in silence.

Not wishing to make a fool of himself, Kordian signed where he had been told.

If he had looked more carefully at the text, perhaps he would have noticed that his mentor was to be Joanna Chyłka. Perhaps then he could have done something to change the arrangement, or thought twice before signing. Perhaps then fate would have prevented him from descending into the maelstrom, into events which were to change his life.

"Excellent," grunted the clerk, gathering the papers into a slim stack. He tapped them several times on the desk and put them into a file with Kordian's name on it. "You'll be working in the room for interns."

"Sorry?"

"Normally, trainees work in the office with their mentor, or next door to them, but that's not what your mentor wants."

"So I'm to sit . . . now hold on a moment, this must be a mistake," Kordian objected.

Dark thoughts filled his mind. Memories of long hours cramming for exams, burning the midnight oil, taking anything and everything that could possibly help him get through those papers . . . and all of that to sit with interns? He'd have been better off going for the quiet life in some measly law firm in the suburbs.

He had chosen the legal behemoth Żelazny & McVay because they offered something unique: they had a knack for injecting new life into the driest of laws. In theory, every legal trainee had a mentor. In practice, however, few mentors even knew what the trainees looked like, and trainees rarely had anything to do with the people officially looking after them. But he'd been led to believe that things were different at Żelazny & McVay. Here there was supposed to be genuine cooperation between mentor and mentee.

Suddenly, he realised exactly who his mentor was.

"Did I get Chyłka?"

"Well, aren't you catching on nicely!" said the clerk. He cleared his throat, opened a drawer, pulled out yet another piece of paper and placed it before Kordian with a flourish. "Your Hooker and Snooker voucher. And now, to work. I hear your first client's a psychopath."

3

"COME IN!" CALLED the lawyer whom the Dean of the District Bar Council had appointed as mentor to the unfortunate Kordian Oryński.

She knew exactly who was knocking on her door, as everyone else was well aware that she was unavailable before noon. Always, absolutely, unconditionally, unavailable, with no exceptions. Joanna spent those morning hours poring over points of law, legal papers, and books. It was a very effective *modus operandi*, because not only did she get the worst of the work done at the start of the day, it also put her in an agreeably aggressive frame of mind for the rest of it.

"Good morning," said Kordian, crossing the threshold.

"We've already dealt with the niceties."

Kordian did not recall their earlier encounter having anything to do with niceties. Nevertheless, he plastered on a smile and held his hands behind his back.

"What are you standing there for, like some sort of dork?"

"I'm waiting for instructions."

"Sit down," said Chyłka, and the young man sank heavily into the chair in front of her desk.

Not very comfortable, he thought. This was obviously a place intended for work only, not for meeting clients. No law firm, especially not Żelazny & McVay, would expect the geese laying their golden eggs to roost on such hard perches.

"OK," she began. "So tell me, what exactly are you doing here?"

Assuming Chyłka was asking why he had chosen Żelazny & McVay rather than any other law firm, he took a deep breath and straightened himself up; but before he could launch into his set-piece reply, she set him straight.

"No, I mean why are you bothering me during working hours?"

"B-b-but . . ."

"W-w-why are you stuttering?"

"But . . . when can I bother you?"

"After twelve," she retorted, picking up a packet of Marlboros and skilfully flicking out a cigarette—she'd clearly had years of practice. "I work until noon. After that, I only pretend to work. Meetings with clients, negotiations with the other party, trials. Sheer pleasure, if you're into blood-and-gore horror stories. But if you're not, I guess, you wouldn't be trying so hard to get into criminal law, right?"

"Ma—"

"That hipster in HR should have told you, but now you know, so remember it well. Your mentor, Joanna Chyłka, is not to be disturbed until noon, because that is when she works. Like a dog. Is that clear?"

"Cl—"

"Great. In that case, let me give you some more advice. If you go downstairs, you'll find the Hard Rock Cafe. That's the place to relax."

"That's not really my scene."

She glowered at him.

"I prefer different music," he added.

"Such as?"

"Will Smith."

"Who? That actor?"

He nodded weakly.

"No," she said. "Definitely not."

"What do you mean, 'no'?"

"No, Will Smith is not the type of music you should be listening to," she said. "Firstly, the guy is a Hollywood star, not a musician. Secondly, it's not real music, it's a poor imitation, rap or hip-hop or whatever it's called, I never know the difference. Thirdly, if you really have to, listen to Eminem or even Donatan or something. Or better still, don't. Forget about them. Listen to Iron Maiden."

For a moment they were both silent. Kordian gazed around the office. "In my presence, you won't listen to, you won't hum, you won't even mention any pseudo-artistic rapper. Iron Maiden, period. And for tomorrow, find out which historical figure they sing about for eight minutes straight. I'll test you."

He nodded, completely confused.

"Cat got your tongue?" she asked, flicking ash into the ashtray. "Surprised I'll be testing you on Iron Maiden? But I will. I mean it. In fact, as your mentor, I consider it my duty."

Kordian pulled out his packet of cigarettes, but Chyłka immediately raised her hand.

"Don't make a stink in here."

"But Ms Chyłka, you're smoking."

"Yes, but I'm smoking Marlboros, and you've got some old shit."

He looked at the pack of Marlboros on the desk, and Joanna passed him the lighter.

"Thanks Ms Chyłka," he said, lighting the Marlboro.

"And stop being so formal," she said. "I don't ever want to hear you call me Ms, Miss or Madam—it makes me feel as if I'm running a brothel. Is that what I look like to you, er . . . er . . . oh, what was your name?"

"Kordian."

"Really? Tough luck," she replied, breathing out smoke. "You can call me Chyłka, like everyone else. And never, ever call me, or refer to me as Jo, Jojo, Joanne, or any other variation. My name is Joanna."

"May I call you Joanna?"

"No, that's for family only. To you, I'm Chyłka."

Oryński swallowed hard. It crossed his mind that this might all be tactics to discourage him, to prepare him for the worst and then show him that it actually wasn't so bad.

"OK, that's all from me," she said, pointing to the door. "And never knock on my door before noon again."

Kordian got up, took a final deep drag, and put out his cigarette.

He walked to the door, but then turned round, still clutching the handle. He realised he still didn't know what he was supposed to do.

"So what should I do next?"

"I told you. Get out of my office. Go to the newbie-burrow, make yourself useful," replied Joanna. "The newbie-burrow is where all the interns and novices go, and you'll get your orders there, soldier. Now move. Move!"

"Yes, sir," grunted Oryński, opening the door. And then, as a parting shot, "But I thought we were supposed to meet a client?"

"We? As in you and I? This is your first day, and you want to meet a client?"

"That's what they said in HR. . . ."

"OK, it's all right. No problem, you can come with me."

She looked pointedly at the door, and Kordian quickly followed the non-verbal instruction. He stood in the corridor, totally bewildered, thinking that this wasn't going to end well. He knew that in terms of mental health, lawyers suffered more than most. They were exposed to all kinds of depravity, and many had long forgotten the meaning of the word empathy. But to encounter this madwoman right at the very start? It didn't bode well for his future career.

Only yesterday he had imagined himself walking proudly down the bright corporate corridor, stylishly decorated in ecru. Now it seemed he was shuffling down a tunnel painted end to end in shit beige.

When he eventually reached the newbie-burrow, he found it to be faceless and dehumanisingly corporate—just cubicles, zero privacy, virtually no living space.

A battery farm.

He had thought places like this only existed on TV and in movies, but clearly they also appeared in real life. None of the young people took any notice of his arrival, which didn't surprise him much. They were all busy giving their employers the mandated 110 per cent—although there was no good reason why they should. The interns were probably slaving away for nothing, the trainees for a pittance. Their only reward was a word of praise, or some certificate or other. At the end of the day, the firm would only employ those who came top in their exams, or excelled in some other Human Resources-devised assessment.

Ultimately, Oryński decided, thinking about it was as pointless as the work those young people were rushing about to do. He looked around for a vacant cubicle.

There was only one. As he approached it, he noticed the sticky note bearing his name, misspelt as "Oryjski." He knew exactly who had written it.

The young lawyer took off the label—a poor substitute for all those gold plaques in the corridor. *My time will come,* he thought. *Even Chyłka probably started off like this.*

As he sat down at the desk, he saw another note by the keyboard, detailing his login and temporary password. He speedily accessed the Żelazny & McVay internal database, and, opening the "current cases" tab, read the heading "Jo Chyłka." Clearly, Joanna had issues with the IT guy.

In any normal company, a few people would already be gathered around his cubicle—they'd be chatting about the firm, making long introductions, telling jokes and stories and giving valuable advice. Here, however, nobody stopped work, not even for a moment.

On the other hand, it gave him a chance to get acquainted with the case he'd be working on. And as soon as he read the first line, his heart started to race.

The accused was called Piotr Langer, or rather Piotr Langer Junior, because his father had the same first name. Anyone involved in the law, consulting or real estate development, would have heard of Langer Senior. His name came up often, mostly linked with lucrative investments. He knew his business inside out too, which was why his company retained teams of the sharpest lawyers, advisers, and brokers.

His son, meanwhile, had been relatively unknown until just three months ago, when one of his neighbours had had to call the police. Apparently, the stench coming from Langer Junior's flat had been so unbearable that when they arrived, two or three of the policemen involuntarily tossed their breakfasts back up for all to see.

They hadn't needed an injunction—Piotr Langer Junior had opened the door personally, dressed in a light blue dressing gown, and politely let the police officers in. But within seconds he was lying on the floor, a policeman's boot in his back.

"Zordon!" The cry went up across the newbie-burrow.

Oryński took no notice. He was lost in thought, reflecting that he'd soon be looking straight into Langer's eyes. Unlike Chyłka, here was a real psychopath, someone who had spent ten days alone with two corpses. He didn't cut them up into pieces, he didn't put bits of them in the freezer; he just sat there with them, as if he'd forgotten he had killed them.

Kordian couldn't help but imagine what it had been like: two corpses in the living room, decomposition in full swing. Once the sphincters had given out, the smell would have been appalling. The bodies would have begun to discolour as livor mortis set in; and then there would have been the insects. The living room window had been left ajar, and all manner of bugs would have come swarming through, looking for a feast and somewhere to lay their eggs.

"Zordon!"

It would have been a gruesome sight, and the stench would have been overpowering. And yet Langer sat there for ten days, then opened the door to the police as if nothing had happened.

"Zordon!"

Only now did Oryński recognise the voice. He turned and saw Chyłka striding towards him.

"I've been calling you," she said.

"My name is Kordian."

"Zordon, Kordon, whatever," she snapped. "Get your things, we're going to see the client. Unless the very thought is making you feel faint? You look as if you've seen a ghost. Would you like me to hold your hand?"

No one else in the newbie-burrow seemed to be taking any notice, but Oryński was sure that later on, over a beer, they'd be picking over the whole exchange. On top of that, he had acquired a new nickname, Zordon. He swore inwardly, and they both went to the lift.

Inside the cabin, Kordian shifted nervously from foot to foot.

"Is there a problem? Don't tell me you get claustrophobia."

"I'm thinking about the client."

"Well don't. It'll spoil the surprise."

He wondered whether he should ask the question that had been preying on his mind. He'd had no practical experience with crimes involving
dead bodies; the prosecutor had talked about them in forensic science
lectures, but had not gone into detail.

"On a dead body," he said, "how long is it before the insects appear?
That is, if the corpse is in an apartment?"

"They come in waves, within three hours if the window is open. And
in that flat, it was open," replied Joanna almost absent-mindedly. "First
to arrive are the blowflies with their shiny bodies. *Calliphora vicina* the
entomologists call them if I remember rightly. Fucking pests. They lay
their eggs in all the moistest spots: the eyeballs, around the mouth, and
down where the sun don't shine. At least that's what happens with male
corpses." She paused. "They hatch within two or three hours, and let's
put it this way: they don't leave their new home until somebody makes
them."

Kordian really did start to feel faint.

Chyłka continued to pontificate all the way to the car. She told him
that blowflies can live off a corpse for up to six months, and that this was
an accurate way to determine the time of death. Kordian listened reluctantly. When at last they got into the car in the car park under Golden
Terraces, he breathed a sigh of relief, especially as the seat in Chyłka's
BMW SUV was super comfortable. He started feeling worse again when
Iron Maiden roared out of the speakers.

4

THERE WERE NO two ways about it—Joanna Chyłka drove like a maniac. Normally, you didn't see high-end BMWs or Mercedes driving so precariously on the open road—that was left to cheaper vehicles, where damage was much less of an issue. Granted, owners of these marvels of modern technology often drove fast, but without taking expensive risks. Chyłka, on the other hand, cut wildly in between other vehicles, leaving, Kordian felt, a margin of no more than half a centimetre.

Kordian assumed the music was affecting her. If he listened to that howling all the time, he'd probably have to release the stress somehow too. He took advantage of a momentary distraction to reduce the volume.

"Don't you dare. I'm the driver and I set the rules."

"You flare up pretty easily, don't you?"

"Yes. If the music's too quiet, I stop wanting to drive, and we need to be at Białołęka by one."

Oryński watched the vehicles passing and thought Joanna could do with a CB radio, she must already have a serious collection of points on her licence. He glanced at her as she swerved sharply to avoid a car, almost banging his head on the windscreen in the process.

"Haven't they taken away your licence yet?" he asked, taking advantage of a lull between songs.

"God knows they've tried."

"And?"

"As long as I refuse to acknowledge that I need to pay a fine, it's OK," she explained, changing lanes without bothering to indicate. "As you know, the matter then goes to court, and while it's being processed the penalty is suspended. I refused to acknowledge my first penalty points in 2006, when you were probably still at school, with the hots for your favourite teacher. To date, I haven't had a single conviction."

"Not likely to anytime soon either."

"Shouldn't think so," she replied with a smile, jumping a red light between Solidarność and Wybrzeże Gdyńskie streets.

"Oh my God!" exclaimed Oryński. He had nothing against stunt-driving or making a dash for it as the lights changed, but she had crossed the junction a good ten seconds or so after the lights had turned red.

He dreaded to think what would happen if she listened to death metal instead of just heavy metal.

"That was almost green," said Joanna as she changed gear to overtake a bus from the inside, giving it just a few centimetres' leeway. "Besides, we need to pump up the adrenaline, or you'll be bored out of your wits."

"Meeting a cold-blooded murderer doesn't sound boring to me."

"You'd be surprised; he's very quiet."

"Reticent, you mean?"

"I said quiet, and I mean quiet. Unless you're just trying to annoy me. But I should tell you that if I'm annoyed, I drive like I'm bat-shit crazy."

"OK," muttered Kordian, his attention focused on the scooter they were passing. If the BMW's wing mirror had been any bigger, the rider would have had a nasty shock. "Have you managed to get him to talk at all?" Oryński asked, adjusting his seatbelt.

"Yes, he's proposed oral sex."

"I suppose it could have been worse."

"You'd better believe it," she said. "Clients are clients, but they can get incredibly abusive, with a list of grievances as long as your arm. The trial date is too late? Your fault. They sign an agreement as a result of which they lose their life savings? Your fault because they showed you the document, even though they had already signed it. Couldn't get insurance for their house? Your fault, even if you'd warned them it was built on a flood plain."

Oryński winced.

"Do we really have to talk about all this now?" he pleaded.

"Absolutely. From the client's point of view, you're responsible for everything, because no one else will listen to them. If you have a good reputation, they'll expect nothing less than miracles. If you get your client an acquittal for a murder charge after they've sold their car for less than it's worth, assuming they won't need it in prison, it'll be your fault. I'm not joking. Once a client hurled the worst sort of abuse at me and almost hit me because I hadn't warned them we'd win the case and they wouldn't go to prison."

"Amazing," he replied, stifling a yawn.

"Think what you will, but it's the truth. The moment they receive your first invoice, you're their whipping boy. They'll pester you constantly to tell them whether or not they'll win the case. But under no circumstance must you ever say you'll win. Even if you're a hundred per cent sure. Understand?"

"Uh-huh."

"Just like a doctor should never tell a gravely ill patient they'll pull through, even if intuition and experience tell him they will, you can never promise anything. If you do, get ready to change careers and become a prosecutor, because you'll have no future in this profession. Unless of course you want to set up in some far-flung corner of the world. But I haven't worked my butt off for so many years to settle for anything less than I've got."

When Joanna paused to catch her breath, Oryński decided it was time to end the sermon, and changed the subject slightly.

"So is Langer like that?" he asked.

"No, with Langer it's different. It's peculiar. You'll see for yourself."

"In what sense?" asked Kordian. He spotted a police car in front of the Grot Rowecki Bridge approach road, but the traffic police were busy with some other unfortunate driver.

"This particular client would happily ditch his lawyers."

"So why doesn't he?"

"I don't know," she replied, ignoring the traffic cops. "I get the impression that he can't be bothered. Langer Senior pays the bills, so it would be up to him to terminate the contract, but I'm sure he'd do it at once if that's what his son wanted."

"So what's this guy about?"

"I don't know. Normally, I can work out in the first interview what it is the client expects, and what I need to do to get them what they want. With this case, it's different."

This didn't sound good.

"But I'm working on it," she said reassuringly. "I just have to find out what he wants."

"Is he guilty?"

"He's certainly giving that impression."

"So he's innocent."

"You're a clever lad, Zordon."

"And he won't admit anything?"

Chyłka sighed, and explained that Langer basically gave everyone the impression he was guilty as charged, but he hadn't actually said a single word to anyone about the murders.

He hadn't said he was guilty, so he was being held in temporary custody until he cooperated. What's more, despite Joanna's strenuous efforts, there was no reason to believe he would be released soon. The state prosecution were trying hard to get him to make a statement, but Chyłka had no idea why. If she were the prosecutor, she wouldn't have bothered. The evidence was strong, and they could be fairly certain of a conviction. The only question was the sentence—it would certainly be lower if Langer admitted he was guilty.

Kordian remained silent for a while.

"Well, this is a good case for me to start with," he said finally.

"You're the one who wanted to come, remember?"

"Oh yes," he murmured.

Earlier, he had thought this was where he could really prove his worth. He already had experience of working with clients—four semesters in a students' legal advice centre, and several months as an intern in a number of smaller law firms. But he was sure now that none of this had prepared him for what he was about to encounter.

CHAPTER

5

THE GREY-HAIRED MAN with the neatly trimmed beard put aside his soya dessert, wishing it had lasted longer. Some time ago the doctor had warned him to keep an eye on his sugar intake, so he had switched to soya. This proved so successful that he had completely changed his eating habits, only to learn that soya products could also be high in sugar. But the desserts were his only addiction and his greatest weakness—and only a few people knew about it.

One of them was a Bald Man in a suit, now sitting opposite the Grey-Haired Man, on the other side of the desk.

"Well? Have you found out everything?" asked the Grey-Haired Man, pushing away the empty dessert pot.

"Yes."

"Go on, I'm listening."

The Bald Man cleared his throat, sat up straight and adjusted his jacket.

"Langer Senior has hired Żelazny & McVay to defend his son."

"I knew it," replied the bearded man, gazing into the distance. "Those people, the owners included, have done more for him than anyone could have expected. Who's got the case?"

"Joanna Chyłka."

"On her own?"

"No, she's been given a trainee. University of Warsaw graduate, average grade 4.25. Worked for two years in a students' legal advice centre, won a scholarship, but grades rather mediocre. No particular achievements. Hasn't published anywhere, never took part in moot court competitions or debates. The lecturers barely remember him. All in all, I wouldn't say he was what top law firms look for. Seems pretty average."

"So why did they take him on?"

"I wasn't able to determine that."

"Find out," replied the Grey-Haired Man, turning towards the window.

He loved the view from his office. It was one of the high points of his job, which, if truth be told, also had a lot of low points. A bit like the Langer case.

"Of course," said the Bald Man, clearing his throat again. "By the way, Chyłka saw Langer recently, and from what I've been told, it was a waste of everyone's time."

"Langer still keeping quiet?"

"Of course."

There was a moment's silence. The older man looked expectantly at the younger one.

"Is that it?" he asked at last, not even trying to hide his disappointment.

"Unfortunately, so far it hasn't been . . ."

"I'm not interested in excuses," interrupted the Grey-Haired Man. "Bring me some proper information. By tomorrow."

"Of course, sir," lied the Bald Man. "Should I also check out that young assistant?"

"No."

"But it might be worth . . ."

"He's just an errand boy. Concentrate on the woman."

"She's not easy to follow."

The Grey-Haired Man sighed softly. "What do you mean?" he asked.

"She's cautious."

"Like every good criminal justice lawyer. But you'll just have to be even more cautious."

"Of course."

The older man looked at the empty dessert pot, coughed gently, and opened the drawer. He hesitated for a moment and slammed the drawer shut. Instead, he reached for the bottle of Old Smuggler—the only blended Scotch he ever drank—standing on his desk, poured some into a thick glass tumbler and took a sip.

"Chyłka won't give up," he said, breaking the silence.

"Do you know her?"

"Langer once told me about her. She has an interesting way of working, not entirely conventional, it must be said."

"Will she be a problem?"

"I don't think so," replied the Grey-Haired Man, turning the tumbler in his hand. "Some lawyers are quite happy to jump in at the deep end if need be, aren't they?"

"Yes, some."

"Except, she's worse. She only ever wants to go for the deep end. Langer once told me that if she hadn't become a lawyer, she'd have ended up killing herself."

"I see."

"She's like the driver of a speeding train that might derail at any moment. She knows it's going to happen, but there's nothing she can do about it."

For a moment, the Grey-Haired Man was lost in thought. Then he shook his head and took another sip of Scotch.

"Isn't that the impression you got?" he asked, looking up.

The Bald Man shrugged his shoulders.

"For me, she's just a normal lawyer. One who hasn't got a clue what she's got herself into. If she understood just a fraction of what was awaiting her and that little shit. . . ."

"Don't swear in front of me."

"Of course, I'm sorry," apologised the Bald Man, somewhat confused. "Anyway, if she did, she'd be packing her bags and heading for the hills."

The thought pleased him. He felt that bit by bit, he was becoming master of her fate. It started to dawn on him just how much Chyłka's life depended on him.

"Keep an eye on her. I want to know everything."

"Naturally," replied the Bald Man, trying to hide his excitement. It wouldn't be appropriate for him to show his boss how much pleasure having Chyłka under his thumb would give him. It was his grey-haired boss who officially held all the cards, and he was simply supposed to do what he was told. If anyone was to derive any pleasure from having unlimited power over the two lawyers, it should, by rights, be his boss.

"You are to be her shadow," added the Grey-Haired Man.

"I understand, sir."

"I'm not entirely sure you do."

"I think that so far I've proved . . ."

"I expect you to sift through her rubbish and analyse every scrap of paper. Look into her bedroom, take pictures—and always have something on you that you can use to cut her brake cables if the need arises."

The Bald Man nodded respectfully, though he suspected the older man meant the brake hose. But it was unwise to correct him—and besides, these were general guidelines rather than precise instructions and it was up to him how he interpreted them.

"Am I to understand that—"

"Yes," interjected the Grey-Haired Man. "If necessary, you'll also have to get rid of the boy."

"Accident?"

"The only way," he stressed. "But only as a last resort. If things continue as they are, don't do anything. Just keep your eye on Chyłka, watch her carefully and report everything to me. If something changes and there's an urgent need to act, or if it can't wait, or it directly threatens me—then, and only then, you're to do what you must. But not in a way that arouses media interest."

The Bald Man knew that if the need did arise, he'd have to use all his skill and ingenuity to make it look like an accident. But for the time being that wasn't going to be necessary. If Chyłka and her young protégé stuck to their roles and did what they were supposed to do, nothing would happen to them.

6

Aᴀ FTER REGISTERING AND being given their passes, Chyłka and Oryński entered the visiting room and waited for their client. Luckily, they were allowed to smoke—but only because Langer's interrogating officers had given up trying to bribe him with cigarettes. Ordinarily, tobacco was a valuable currency almost invariably loosened tongues, but not in this case. So the two lawyers were allowed to bring their cigarettes in with them.

They had only just stubbed them out in the ashtray when Langer entered, in chains. The prison officers sat him down on the opposite side of the table, then one of them looked at Joanna.

"Should I stay?" he asked.

"Only if you want to do time for violating attorney–client privilege."

He mumbled something under his breath, and the two of them went out into the corridor. Chyłka turned her full attention to Langer.

"Hi, Pedro," she said, leaning towards him. "I've brought my man, my trainee, with me. His name's Zordon. Listens to rap music," and then, turning to Kordian, "Isn't that right?"

If this is what a typical meeting with a client accused of murder with exceptional brutality looked like, the work of criminal lawyers wasn't as bad as was commonly believed, Oryński thought.

"Aren't you going to say hello?" asked Joanna.

Kordian looked at the client closely. There was only one word for it: Langer looked alarming. If one word could succinctly convey the image of this man, that was it.

Piotr Langer stared blankly at the table, motionless, as if he wasn't even breathing. The dark streaks under his eyes were even more notice-able when his head was bowed. He might have seemed despondent and defeated, were it not for the atmosphere, which became electric the moment he crossed the threshold.

"I brought my assistant along because I thought you two could talk about bopping to what you both call music," added Joanna, tapping the metal table top. "No? Pity, because Zordon here is an authority on the subject, and the record collection in your apartment leads us to assume that you committed these murders listening to Kanye West or Jay-Z. I was sure you would find something in common."

Langer didn't even twitch.

"Can you hear me?" she asked, clicking her fingers in his face. Oryński hissed, a veiled protest against her rather risky behaviour.

Langer may be calm now, but it would take no more than an instant for him to turn back into the psycho who had murdered two people and sat with their bodies for ten days.

"Calm down, Zordon," responded Chyłka, frowning. "This guy is almost a vegetable. Can't you see? He's barely sentient. A hopeless psychiatric case."

"Planning to plead insanity?" suggested Kordian, immediately feeling like a prize idiot. Of course Langer wanted to plead insanity, everyone would in his situation.

"No," said a voice, to the utter surprise of both lawyers. Kordian felt his throat go dry.

"What do you mean no?" asked Chyłka.

"No, I'm not insane."

The ensuing silence made it clear that Langer had nothing more to say. The lawyers looked at each other and then at Piotr.

"Is that it?" Joanna asked.

No answer.

"Still, it's progress," she consoled herself. "A bit more, and you'll be chattering away like a diesel engine on a cold day."

Silence filled the room again. Oryński frantically wondered what to do. In the end, he decided that there was nothing worse than doing nothing.

"Maybe he's got nothing to say?" he suggested.

"Or doesn't know how to say it," countered Chyłka. "Anyway, let's look at the insanity option. The court will buy it, you only have to look at him."

"And it doesn't even bother him when we talk about him as if he weren't here," added Oryński, beginning to understand what Chyłka was trying to do.

Upsetting a murderer was neither easy nor safe. It made him anxious—Kordian felt that Langer would just have to look askance at him and it would mean instant death.

"It doesn't bother him because he's barely conscious," continued Joanna. "I don't even know what he wants from us."

Langer sighed, but did not look up.

"Nothing," he said.

"If that were the case, you wouldn't be sitting here."

"I wanted to get out of the cell."

"What for?" asked Chyłka. "You're going to spend the rest of your life there, so what difference would an extra hour make? Besides, you wouldn't have to put up with us, and I can assure you, we're just getting started. In a minute I'll have Zordon rapping a Will Smith number, then you'll know what horrific really means. Much worse than what you did to your two . . . you know, those two . . . what were their names?"

"You know perfectly well."

"It's slipped my mind."

"Relichowski. Daniel Relichowski."

"That's one," confirmed Joanna. "And the woman? That poor, innocent victim of the Sadist of Mokotów? Did you know that's what they call you?"

"Agata."

"Didn't have a surname?"

"I've forgotten it."

It seemed to Oryński that Langer was speaking almost without moving his lips.

"You've forgotten the name of the girl you stabbed with kitchen knives, strangled and stamped on, whose skin you cut pieces from? You're not particularly friendly with your victims, are you? Unless you got more closely acquainted after her death, maybe? Did you play about with her a bit?"

The expression on Langer's face did not change.

"Well? Do you like doing it with corpses, Langer?"

"No," he replied indifferently.

"He's ashamed to admit it," said Chyłka, leaning towards her colleague. "It probably started with an innocent look after he'd hit her for one last time, and then it just happened. Look at him. One look is enough to tell you he's not only a killer, but also a lecher and a necrophiliac."

"You're wrong," repeated Langer calmly.

Oryński wished Chyłka would stop taunting him.

"Were you turned on by all those flies and things swarming around her? Did you shag her as nature intended? Or did you use a condom? Come on, tell us, you pervert. Who else could you boast to? We're sworn to secrecy, we'll take the knowledge to our graves."

"No."

"OK, so we're left with the material evidence. The investigators found evidence of sexual intercourse, although with all those injuries it's hard to tell what actually happened. There's no semen, so we assume you either had a condom, or used some sort of substitute. Maybe you couldn't get it up because of the smell? Or maybe you just like using toys?"

"No."

Kordian looked on with mounting consternation. If he hadn't known better, he would have assumed Chyłka was the psychopath, and the man opposite was her psychologist or therapist.

"You're repulsive," Chyłka said. "You can't even play the part of a deranged killer properly. I'm going to get a coffee."

She got up, and without even glancing at Oryński, started banging on the door. They heard the sound of the peephole being opened, followed by the clatter of the latch and the key turning in the lock. A prison warder appeared in the doorway, let Chyłka out and locked the door again.

Kordian swallowed. The prisoner was still not looking at him—but the young trainee felt as if he was at the gateway to hell anyway.

Finally, Langer looked up. As Oryński felt his gaze, a wave of heat swept over him. He wanted to say something, but thought better of it in case all he could manage was gibberish. He needed a moment to get his emotions under control, and the terrifying fact that he was sitting just a metre away from a man who had not only killed two people, but defiled their bodies as if they were sacks of meat, didn't exactly help.

He cleared his throat.

"Why?" asked Kordian, and looked away.

"Because I could."

In fact, Kordian didn't really know what he was asking. His "why" could have applied to a number of issues, although the most logical one would be the actual murders.

"How could you?" he said, feeling as if this was some surreal theatre play. He was familiar with surrealism; playwrights such as Alfred Jarry and Apollinaire were sacred for the Oryński family, and as a child he had often been dragged along to see their works. He rarely understood what was going on—but then seemingly, neither did the actors on the stage. It was a similar situation now.

Langer took a deep breath.

"Good question," he said. "How could I? Really good. Deep. It gets right to the heart of the matter. What was the event that tipped the first domino, the one which set all the cogs in motion?"

So, are you going to tell me? Langer thought.

"If I ever find out, you'll be the first to know," he said eventually.

Somehow, Oryński felt a little more confident. For some reason, the man sitting opposite him now seemed less of a demon and more of a human.

"Are you going to defend yourself in court?"

"No," replied Piotr automatically. "And don't start asking me why, because I won't tell you. Not because I don't know, but because I don't want to share the truth."

"The truth that you're innocent?"

"I said the truth, and that's what I mean. You can't qualify truth. It has no versions, categories or variants."

This is like spitting in the wind, thought Oryński. But what else could you expect? Even if by some miracle Langer hadn't killed those people, he'd still spent ten days with them in his apartment. He was sick, no question. Unless someone had forced him to. . . . But no, that was impossible. Kordian knew this was just wishful thinking, catathymia, a delusion, a fantasy. Call it what you will.

The investigation had established that the neighbours heard no suspicious noises, and no evidence was found in the apartment to suggest anyone else had been there. Besides, Langer had not been tied up, no one had put a gun to his head, and he had opened the door to the police himself.

"If you don't want to defend yourself in court, why do you need lawyers?" asked Oryński.

"My old man pays for your services."

"Well, no one is paying me at the moment." The accused didn't smile.

"Don't worry," he said. "My father will make sure you both get paid properly in exchange for a conviction. Provided you play it down a bit, because remember, he's got his PR to think about."

This must have been a PR nightmare for Langer Senior, and Kordian doubted he'd ever be able to haul himself out. His son's actions were bound to affect him. Chyłka might be able to work miracles in court, but not even she would be able to keep a lid on the media storm that would inevitably break after the verdict was announced.

Langer Senior wouldn't be at all pleased, while his son wouldn't be at all interested.

"What about you? What do you want?" asked Kordian.

"Me? I simply exist. I'm just waiting for events to unfold."

"You could just get rid of us if you don't want to defend yourself."

"It would only make matters worse," replied Langer, gazing across the room. "The old man would find someone to replace you, someone more determined."

"Perhaps you don't fully appreciate how determined my boss really is." Kordian was expecting to see at least a slight twitch, a grimace, anything. Nothing.

"But you want to go on living, I presume?" he said. "Because you know, a word in the right ear and someone will bring you a razor."

"I've got a razor in my cell, for shaving."

"And you haven't cut yourself yet." Oryński took out a cigarette, and pushed the packet towards the prisoner. "So you do want to live."

"Same as any living being."

"And yet you want to spend the rest of your life in a prison cell?"

"No," replied Langer, helping himself to a cigarette. The young lawyer felt he was making progress. "Would anyone want that? Anyone normal, that is."

"How about someone who won't accept the help of a good attorney?"

Piotr Langer leaned over so Kordian could light his Davidoff. He inhaled with pleasure, and threw his head back to release the smoke.

"You think you're solid as a rock, but Chyłka will chip away at you until she's made a hole big enough for a stick of dynamite—then she'll blow you to smithereens."

"Maybe."

"So if it's peace and quiet you want, change your lawyer."

"That's not what I want."

"So you do want to win."

"No."

The young lawyer shook his head and rested his arm on the back of the chair.

"Come on," he said. "All I'm getting from you is contradictions. At least you could admit that you don't really know what you want."

At last, Kordian stopped feeling like a terrified trainee lawyer left at the mercy of a psychopath. He discovered he could be a skilful player, cleverly leading the accused by the nose. It was a comforting thought—which instantly vanished as Langer lowered his gaze and glared at him.

Oryński froze, realising he'd gone too far. "Take it easy now," he managed to say.

Langer threw his cigarette on the ground and stood up, knocking over the chair. Oryński made for the door, but Langer was faster, grabbing the back of his jacket.

"Open the door!" yelled Kordian.

The key rattled in the lock, not a moment too soon.

Suddenly Langer let go of Kordian's jacket and took a step back. The young lawyer pressed his back against the door, barely able to catch his breath.

Langer moved over to the table, helped himself to another Davidoff from the packet, lit it, and crossed to the other side of the room.

A warder appeared in the doorway, somewhat bewildered, Taser at the ready. Behind him stood Chyłka.

"You are free people," said Langer before anyone else had a chance to say anything. "You can do what you want. Whatever it is, I'm not going to stand in your way." Then he made his way to the door. "You've got a free hand."

The warder looked anxiously at Kordian.

"Everything OK?" he asked.

"Y-yes."

Belatedly, the warder grabbed hold of Langer, crossing his wrists behind his back. Although there was no real need for it, he handcuffed the prisoner and switched on the Taser.

"Calm down," Chyłka warned him. "Article 230 of the Prison Service Act is one of my favourites, and you're very close to violating it."

The warder glowered at her, then led Langer into the corridor. Joanna turned to Kordian with an expression of disbelief.

"I only went out for a moment," she said.

Kordian took a deep breath.

"But I'm glad you got to know each other."

She can say what she wants, Oryński thought, *but I managed to achieve substantially more than she did.*

CHAPTER

7

KORDIAN REMEMBERED LITTLE from the journey back to Złota Street, waking up only as Joanna was parking her car in the car park.

"I'm peckish," she announced as they were getting out of the car.

"You'll have to eat alone; I've lost my appetite."

"Give it a rest, Zordon. Did that little show of strength scare you?"

"No."

"Then stop whining and come with me. I know a good place."

The music at the Hard Rock Cafe was hardly soothing. The two lawyers went downstairs, Joanna leading the way to one of the many vacant tables. The sound of a screeching vocalist blared from the speakers, competing with mawkish guitar riffs; no wonder the restaurant was virtually empty.

"What would you like?" she asked.

Kordian could hardly hear her.

"A menu," he replied under his breath.

He didn't want to risk ordering anything in the dark. What did they serve in a place like this? They probably slaughtered goats then performed bloodletting rituals on an altar. Maybe cats were also involved. It would be safer to order a coffee.

"Have some Hard Rock Nachos to get you started."

"No thanks," replied Kordian, flipping through the menu pages.

"Ah, you want to get stuck in straightaway. Then have what I'm having, the Hickory-Smoked Barbecue Combo."

He glanced at the description, which seemed to suggest the combo included not only dead goat and cat, but also the odd bit of Christian clergyman. He shook his head. There was so much meat, he'd have to play squash for hours to burn it all off. And he'd be leaving the restaurant with a tornado in his belly and a decidedly empty wallet. No, this was definitely not a good day for eating that stuff.

"I'll take the grilled salmon."

Chyłka looked up. She shook her head, then checked the menu to see if such an item actually existed.

"Salmon? Are you kidding? And are you having a nice healthy salad with that?"

"No thanks, just the grilled salmon will do.".

"What kind of a man are you?" she asked. "A good slab of meat will give you the strength to wrestle with clients and prosecutors. What I saw today was such feeble pussyfooting that for a moment . . ."

"You were watching?"

"Hmm?" she mumbled, as if she hadn't heard.

"Were you watching?" he repeated, louder this time. You'd need a megaphone if you wanted to have an actual conversation in this place.

"What do you think? I couldn't leave you alone with that criminal. In fact, I'm surprised your underpants were still clean when you left. Or were they?"

"At least he talked to me."

"Birds of a feather."

Kordian smiled to himself, then they placed their orders and went to the other room to light up. The wall of smoke was almost impenetrable, as it always was in smoking rooms, regardless of the time of day or popularity of the restaurant. Oryński hoped they would be able to smoke in silence, or at least to talk about something other than Langer. But the silence lasted only a matter of moments.

"So what do you think?" asked Joanna.

"It's too loud here."

"You're a funny bloke, Zordon," she said with a smile. "I meant about the client."

"I don't know what to make of him," he replied, ignoring the jibe.

"Not good enough." She inhaled, looking at him expectantly.

"I get the impression he didn't do it," he replied.

"That's pretty obvious."

"What?"

She shrugged her shoulders.

"I thought I was the only one giving in to wishful thinking."

"Don't get too excited, that's only two concurring opinions," she said, extinguishing her cigarette. She headed for the staircase, so Kordian quickly stubbed his cigarette out in the ashtray and followed her. "Two defence lawyers with the same opinion is still a far cry from convincing the judge. But Langer doesn't look like the kind of son-of-a-bitch who would have killed two people like that."

"And yet . . ."

"Yes, I know. He sat with those corpses for ten days. It doesn't really fit."

They went upstairs, and soon their food arrived; an American meat feast for Joanna, and grilled salmon with garlic sauce and green vegetables for Kordian. He looked at it warily, not quite trusting it to be edible.

"Maybe someone locked him in there after the murders?" he asked, chewing on a piece of fish.

"Perhaps, but we definitely won't be basing our defence on that."

Oryński put down his knife and fork, noticing that Chyłka had turned serious. They were clearly getting to the heart of the matter if she'd switched to full professional mode.

"Have you got any other ideas?" he asked.

He was hoping that any moment now she'd astound him with her insight. He was hoping to take more away from his time at Żelazny & McVay than just a line on his CV. He wasn't expecting to be offered permanent employment—he knew his limitations. The firm had several trainees, and only one—if any—would be invited to stay on. Oryński had never considered himself a high-flyer, and if his university grades were anything to go by, he wasn't alone in this opinion.

"No, I haven't," Joanna replied, spearing a piece of chicken richly covered with barbecue sauce.

"Nothing at all?"

"What do you want me to say?" she replied, her mouth half-full. "You've seen the documents; you know perfectly well what the problem is. We have absolutely nothing to work with."

"So how are we going to defend him? Are we really going for insanity?" Kordian felt it was probably a stupid question, but he had to ask it, and now he braced himself for the expression on Chyłka's face.

"Only if we want to make fools of ourselves," she replied. "But you saw that Langer reckons he's of sound mind. And he'll prove that in court at the first opportunity he has."

Kordian thought for a moment. "In that case, we could argue that someone else had done the killing and somehow planted Langer at the scene of the crime. He could have been drugged, completely unaware of what was going on and . . ."

"Toxicology showed no sign of any intoxicating substances," chanted Joanna in an official monotone.

"OK, then perhaps he was held somewhere else while the corpses rotted in his flat. Then, under cover of darkness, they put him in there, unconscious and totally oblivious. And that's why he opened the door to the police in the morning."

"Just like that?"

"Well, I think so," replied Kordian, pleased with his idea. "You'd have to ask the neighbours if any of them saw Langer enter or leave the apartment during that time. After all, he couldn't have just sat there for ten days without doing any shopping, could he? Remember, he's a bloke, he wouldn't have had anything more than a couple of beers in the fridge, or a packet of instant noodles in the cupboard. And he wouldn't have had stuff delivered—for obvious reasons."

"My, you're on a roll, Zordon," replied Chyłka, and returned to her meat orgy. Oryński's salmon lay on his plate, getting cold.

"We should also check out the garbage disposal firm," he added. "Maybe we could see if they took any rubbish away from his place."

"Brilliant idea," she retorted with her mouth full. "If you're Sisyphus, that is, and need a futile task."

"At least I'm trying to find a solution."

"Well, think something up that'll counter the DNA evidence, wise guy. You've forgotten that they've found. . . ."

"Evidence schmevidence," he said. "Professor Filar wrote that not even DNA evidence is always enough to convince a judge. Nothing is certain in . . ."

"Ah, there I must interrupt you, my rising star. As your boss, I was educated in these matters a long time ago, so spare me your words of wisdom. Of course, no evidence in the world is one hundred per cent irrefutable, but in the face of the biological evidence they've found, your speculations will hold up about as well as a chocolate fireguard."

"But . . ."

"Mind you, Filar is the master. Listen to him, read his publications, learn from him, and if you get a case involving sexual offences, be sure to study every word he's ever written."

"But . . ."

"But back to Langer. Yes, go on," She gestured for him to continue while she got stuck into a piece of beef.

"The bodies were in his flat, which would have been full of his hair. No wonder some of it found its way onto the victims."

"Well, well," replied Joanna. "Now I'm at a loss for words. I'm so impressed, I'm going to leave the rest of my meal," she said, deliberately cramming an extra-large piece of meat into her mouth.

Kordian smiled wanly. *It would have been OK,* he thought, *to talk his theories through with another trainee, but not someone as experienced as Chyłka. She had probably thought of all this the minute she'd been handed the case.*

For a moment, Joanna ate in silence, then gazed around the room as if looking for someone. Eventually, she ordered a small beer. Oryński declined a drink, preferring to stay sober whilst on duty—at least on his first day.

"The biological traces are a serious problem," she said after a while. "On top of that, his fingerprints are everywhere."

"It'd be strange if they weren't," Oryński replied, having another go at his grilled fish. "After all, he would have been using knives and a hammer for other reasons, not just to murder people."

Chyłka nodded, but he noticed that her thoughts had drifted away. These were idle speculations—in the eyes of the judges and lay judges, Langer's guilt would be incontrovertible.

Maybe we should just accept that we had absolutely nothing, Kordian thought. *This was a hopeless case.*

8

THE TWENTY-FIRST FLOOR of the Skylight was full of the usual hustle and bustle. There were lawyers running in and out of offices, calling out through open doors, hurtling down corridors, urging the photocopiers to work faster and yelling at their personal assistants.

Even the Hard Rock Cafe had been calmer, thought Oryński.

He walked at Chyłka's side, looking vainly to see if there was someone in charge of all this commotion. More lawyers were bellowing about approaching deadlines, and two couriers collided head on in the middle of the corridor. If not for their lightning reflexes, the letters they were carrying would have landed in a heap on the floor.

Kordian listened to all the instructions being yelled out.

"Do this! Do that! Only ten hours until the deadline! Run down to the post office! Have you got me Supreme Court verdict eighty-three of the fifth of June? Get me that prosecutor's number! Get me info on this, info on that. . . ."

He'd had enough.

"Żelazny wants to see you," someone said to Chyłka in the midst of the whirlwind. Joanna pressed ahead through the rowdy crowd without slowing.

"Hey, Jakobin, have you got me the info about that judge?" she asked, stopping a short, fat man in glasses.

"Yes, it's on your desk."

"Chyłka! That slander woman phoned, she left a message on your voicemail," a girl shouted, leaning out of the office they were passing.

"Thanks," Joanna shouted back, again without slowing her pace.

Eventually they managed to break free from the bedlam. They were almost at the end of the corridor, next to the office of another trainee—but one who was officially called an associate. Seeing the plaque on the door made Oryński feel as if someone had spat in his face. This trainee had their own office, a good position, respect, and a decent salary—while Kordian was stuck in the newbie-burrow. Even a mediocre plate of salmon in a bar restaurant blew a considerable hole in his budget.

Joanna knocked on the door opposite. It was only a formality, because she walked straight in without waiting for an invitation. A disoriented Kordian followed her in. He didn't even have time to read the plaque on the door to know who they were visiting. He knew it wasn't Żelazny though, because his office was further back.

"Kormak, I need to know about our client's neighbours," she said.

"Huh?" asked a skinny man with small, round glasses.

He reminded Kordian of Elton John, but several decades younger and several dozen kilos lighter. This one was probably not gay either, judging by the way his eyes gravitated to Joanna's cleavage.

"Sorry, forgot the introductions," Chyłka said. "Zordon, this is Boney—well, everybody calls him Kormak—and Kormak, this is Zordon. Get to know each other, exchange Pokémon cards or whatever it is you do."

"Why do they call you Kormak?"

Chyłka answered for him, frowning and pointing to the Cormac McCarthy novel lying open on the desk.

"Boney always has one of McCarthy's books on the go. Hence, Kormak. But never mind that now. Let's get to the matter at hand: I need details about my client's neighbours. Piotr Langer. Junior, of course."

"I know who he is, Chyłka," replied the skinny Elton. "The Old Boys pay me to know what's in the works."

Old Boys was the standard nickname for the owners of Żelazny & McVay—"Old Rusty" for Żelazny in honour of his name, the Polish for iron—and simply the "Old Man" for McVay. The pair worked abroad for the most part, and weren't always that interested in what was going on in Poland. They rarely made an appearance in the Warsaw office, and when they did, it was usually for something serious. So the imminent meeting with Żelazny did not fill Joanna with optimism.

He was bound to suggest they should back off a bit with Langer's son, Chyłka thought. Piotr Langer Senior was paying the bills, and would want the case closed as fast as possible, with no room for appeal—provided, of course, Piotr Junior didn't cause any problems.

"By the way, Old Rusty is looking for you."

"I know," said Joanna, "and for now, I don't care. Just get me whatever you can on those neighbours."

"Why can't you just go for a walk around the estate?"

"Because I haven't got a Central Bureau of Investigation badge in my pocket which I can flash around so people will tell me everything I want to know," retorted Joanna in one breath.

She walked up to the desk and looked at the book. *How many of these has he written?* Boney always seemed to be reading a different one, though perhaps he re-read them. That wouldn't surprise her. Joanna had once tried one on Kormak's recommendation, but soon lost interest. For her, Stephen King was decidedly a better read, especially in the evenings when all was dark save the muted glow of the night light . . .

"I'm not some door-to-door salesman, and I'm not going to ask my dear Zordon, because no one would want to talk to him anyway," she said. "The thing is, this is an exclusive neighbourhood, and they're probably all quite snooty. If I catch them leaving work or having a drink somewhere, maybe they'll chat to me. But at home? Forget it. They've paid good money for their homes to be their castles."

"OK, I'll see what I can do," he said. "But if it's a genuinely exclusive neighbourhood, it could be a problem."

"So tell me which restaurants or bars they go to, or send me their Facebook photos. I'll do the rest myself."

Oryński was sorry he hadn't looked more closely at the golden plaque on the door as they entered the office. He would have loved to know what job this McCarthy enthusiast did. He certainly wasn't a lawyer, because he'd have better things to do than collect information about a client's neighbours. Nor did he look like an IT specialist, because he wore a suit, and that indicated working in the field. Perhaps the firm's own private detective? Or a social media specialist? These days, you didn't need to lurk in dark alleyways, or even break into someone's hard drive in order to spy on them. Everyone uploaded so much information to the internet, you only had to know where to look. Place of residence? No problem, check Instagram, see where the photos were taken. If the GPS was switched off when they were taking pictures, you could check their jogging routes on Endomondo. Their current location? Nothing simpler, follow them on Twitter. What they looked like? No shortage of material there: Facebook alone would have hundreds of photos. Their whole professional career and phone numbers would be on LinkedIn; and look at Google Street View and you were virtually at their front door.

Everyone seemed to know all this, and yet even the biggest shysters gave themselves away online. Gone were the days when what went on tour stayed on tour; these days it was all over social media in seconds.

"I need this by yesterday," added Joanna, tearing Kordian away from his reflections.

"No change there, then," muttered Kormak.

As they left Kormak's office, Oryński glanced at the plaque on the door.

"Senior Information Specialist?" he asked with disbelief.

"Something wrong?"

"No, it's simply . . ."

"Come on," she interrupted, and they started pushing through the crowd to get back to where they had come from.

"Weren't you supposed to see the boss?"

"Later."

The office was still a frenzy of people shouting at one another, making it all the more remarkable that Oryński discerned through the cacophony that someone was calling to him.

"Zordon! There's a case for you on your desk."

The courier disappeared in the throng, so Kordian didn't even get the chance to ask what it was about. Instead, he looked questioningly at his boss.

"Go and check it out. I need to think," she said.

"But I've already got . . ."

"You haven't got anything," she said, heading in the opposite direction. "When you're with me, you're learning, but there are some things you have to do by yourself. Don't panic, it probably won't be anything important. Everybody gets some old nonsense to start with."

Kordian watched how skilfully Joanna manoeuvred through the maelstrom of people, who all seemed to have something crucial to ask her. Analysing the situation, he reached two conclusions: first and foremost, Chyłka had an exceptionally shapely backside, which in that tight skirt was as flatteringly outlined as humanly possible. Secondly, but not so importantly, her ability to negotiate the premises of Żelazny & McVay was nothing short of an art form, requiring not only knowledge but also talent.

Fortunately, it wasn't far to the newbie-burrow, and Kordian got there without any major problems. No one was interested in his arrival, and inside, the commotion was no less than in the corridor.

Not so much a battery farm, he thought, *as a lunatic asylum.*

If anyone was of sound mind when they arrived, they'd surely leave in a mental state even worse than Piotr Langer. It was hard to imagine how anyone could work in these circumstances. The lawyers had soundproof offices, but here, even simple mental arithmetic would be a challenge.

Heading towards his cubicle, Kordian noticed that most people had headphones on. Good idea. Tomorrow, he'd download a good playlist, and Big Will would help protect him from the surrounding Armageddon.

"Zordon!"

He hadn't even had a chance to sit down, and when he turned around, he saw Chyłka. Who else would it have been? She was gesturing for him to come over.

"How long have you managed without me? A minute?"

"Old Rusty is insisting that I come now. You should come with me, you'll see how big politics is played out."

"I can't, not at the moment."

"You can deal with your nonsense later, now it's time to watch and learn."

"This is my first day, Chyłka, mercy. . . ." She pointed the way to the corridor.

9

Before Kordian could do anything to avert the catastrophe, his ringtone, one of his favourite songs, blasted out as Will Smith exhorted the ladies to fiesta.

"What's that?" asked Artur Żelazny.

"S-s-sorry," stammered Oryński as he struggled to pull the phone from his jacket pocket. He was sure he had switched it to silent before he entered the building that morning, before his encounter with Chyłka.

"Don't keep your phone there, son," advised Żelazny, from behind his desk.

The massive desk reflected the status of the person seated behind it. Made of fine mahogany, it had all the trappings of legal authority: an expensive Waterman pen, brand-new unopened legal code books, and cufflinks in a gilded case.

"No, sir."

"He's not some army officer, just one of the partners," said Joanna. "And what's that musical hogwash?"

"It's from the *Willennium* album."

"*Willennium?*" repeated Chyłka, closing her eyes as if she were at the graveside of her best friend. "You put me in a bleak mood, Zordon. And that never ends well. From tomorrow, I want to hear the solo from "Wasted Years" whenever anyone rings you. That's your second task. Do you remember the first?"

"Sure," lied Kordian.

"Go on then, tell me."

Oryński scratched his head. "Was I supposed to go to the Hard Rock Cafe?"

"You were supposed to find out which historical figure Iron Maiden sing about for eight minutes straight. The test is fast approaching."

Kordian looked to Old Rusty for help.

"I don't envy you, son," Żelazny said. "But really, don't keep your phone in your jacket, it produces a magnetic field. Why keep it so close to your heart?"

"You're right, sir," replied Oryński deferentially, before he could bite his tongue. Chyłka looked at him with disapproval.

"Please sit down, both of you," said Żelazny.

Once they had settled into the comfortable chairs in front of the desk, Żelazny fixed his gaze on the trainee. It was not good form to trouble the bosses with insignificant newcomers, yet for some reason, that's what Chyłka had decided to do.

"I understand you've already signed a contract with our firm?" asked Artur Żelazny.

Oryński nodded, realising belatedly that Old Rusty was not asking out of mere curiosity, he wanted to make sure Kordian had signed a non-disclosure agreement prohibiting him from revealing company secrets.

"Excellent," said Artur, rubbing his hands. "I'm sure you'll be an asset to Żelazny & McVay."

Hearing the cliché, Chyłka yawned extravagantly.

"Why have you called me?" she asked, considering the pleasantries to be over. "And what are you doing in Warsaw? Shouldn't you be somewhere abroad, pretending to work?"

"I'm the last person you could accuse of idleness," replied Żelazny. "But we won't discuss your prejudice against all other lawyers here," he added, adjusting his jacket. "Have you been to see the client?"

"Yes."

"And?"

"And it'd be easier to talk to your own backside while sitting on the throne."

"I'm not altogether surprised," replied Artur. He was used to the fact that Chyłka did not take their differences in status particularly seriously. She was, after all, senior associate, so not far away from becoming a partner herself. In addition, they had worked together for years, so a degree of familiarity in their professional relationship was inevitable. Only up to a point, of course. When Joanna went too far, Żelazny had no problem playing the authoritarian.

"What did he tell you?"

"Nothing. I think he might be shy with women."

"Oh, without a doubt. Especially if he's anything like his father," Żelazny replied sardonically.

The firm had pulled Langer Senior out of the mire on several occasions, most recently from a situation that seemed quite hopeless. It was largely thanks to Chyłka, who always seemed able to mollify whichever girl from Belarus or Kaliningrad had been wronged this time.

"You don't have to remind me about Langer Senior," she said. "Sometimes I still wake up at night, sensing his lascivious eyes all over me."

"And Piotr Junior? What did you think?"

"I don't know, I haven't had a chance to get to know him. He only really started talking when he was alone with this young man here," she replied, making a sweeping gesture towards Kordian.

Oryński pursed his lips and nodded thoughtfully.

"So?" asked Artur, undoing his cufflinks and lining them up next to the ones that were on his desk for decorative purposes.

"No, he didn't explicitly say he'd done it. He didn't admit guilt, neither to me, nor . . ."

"No, no," interrupted Żelazny. "He's guilty beyond doubt. But what I'd like to know is will he cooperate?"

"Maybe, as a last resort. As we left, he said we had a free hand."

Artur Żelazny fell silent, taking a long look at Kordian.

"A free hand is not the same as willingness to cooperate."

"No, it isn't," agreed Kordian. "In fact, he was quite vague."

For a moment, Oryński considered adding that Langer had pounced on him like a ravenous beast craving meat. Chyłka, however, had not mentioned it, so he also decided against drawing it to Żelazny's attention.

"So he's planning to kick up a stink," concluded Żelazny. "We could hardly expect anything else."

He looked at Joanna, but she just shrugged her shoulders. "I don't have to tell you this is a high priority case."

"No," she replied.

"And you know what Piotr Senior expects?"

"Yes."

"Is that all you can say?" he asked, shaking his head.

"I am aware that Langer wants a swift, painless trial, as a result of which his darling little boy will be thrown into the slammer post-haste, to languish harmlessly with no internet or media access and pose no threat to his dear father."

Żelazny got up from his comfortable armchair and walked over to a small drinks cabinet. He poured himself a bourbon without inviting anyone to join him, and took a long, ostentatious sip.

"Listen, Chyłka," he began in a completely different tone, as if the drink had lubricated some previously seized-up gears. "I'll spell it out for you. That pervert is to plead guilty."

"Not feasible."

The boss swirled the bourbon in his glass, looking at her sullenly. "McVay thinks the same as me, so don't bother phoning him."

"Yes, but . . ."

"Whatever you have to say, I'm not interested," he cut in. "Langer is to plead guilty, the court is to rubber-stamp his declaration, the media are to be relatively silent. If there are any leaks, you are to identify them immediately. I can assign Kormak to you permanently until this case is settled."

Old Langer's clearly paying him a fortune, thought Oryński.

"Piotr Senior doesn't want to get involved at all, for obvious reasons," Artur continued. "All this has a negative effect on his commercial ventures. You know how business partners can be. Get mixed up with anything dubious, and it's an excuse to renegotiate all your deals. No, it mustn't come to that. A swift trial, a swift conviction."

"He won't plead guilty," said Chyłka.

"Of course he will."

"No, he won't."

"If he doesn't, he'll be looking at a life sentence," said Żelazny. "While if he does, he might get twenty-five years."

"He doesn't seem to care one way or the other."

"So what the hell does he want?"

Joanna pushed away a lock of hair that had somehow managed to break free from her carefully arranged coiffure. Żelazny waited for a reply, then looked at Kordian.

"I'm not going to beat about the bush," he said. "You're starting to get on my nerves. Did either of you speak to that man, or not?"

Both nodded, and Oryński came to the conclusion that the boss's surname, Żelazny, had a deeper meaning. He was indeed as unbending as iron.

"In that case, can you at least find out the sort of thing he wants? What does he intend to do? Is he ready to go to prison? Is he of sound mind? Maybe he's mad and should be restrained?"

"No, Langer seems . . ." began Kordian and then looked at Chyłka, who responded by shrugging her shoulders. "He seems calm. He's simply calm, not counting on any . . ."

"Resigned to his fate?" Żelazny interrupted.

"No, he wants truth to prevail. More or less."

"Very well, . . ." replied Artur, playing with his cufflinks like dice.

The silence was becoming increasingly awkward, and suddenly Oryński wanted to be back in the noisy corridor, where he wouldn't be able to hear himself think. Here in the stillness, everything echoed in his skull and took him nowhere.

"Your task is simple," Żelazny said at last, standing in front of the two lawyers. "Bring him to heel, just enough for him to plead guilty, get twenty-five years and go meekly to his cell. Appeal, of course, but only as a formality, so that no one will be able to accuse you of lacking commitment. Don't include anything in the appeal that could prolong the case. The appeal court will uphold the first ruling, and with that your work ends. Swift, effective and painless."

"And . . ."

"I'm counting on you, Chyłka. *No pasarán?*"

"*No pasarán, el jefe*," confirmed Joanna, and rose from her chair, gesturing for her trainee to do the same. They nodded to Żelazny and left his office.

"What's with the Spanish?"

"Old Rusty likes it," replied Chyłka, pushing through the whirlwind. "It's a tradition that before every case you say *no pasarán*, either to your boss or just to yourself."

"But it's only a T. Love song."

"It's a slogan from the Revolution, you cretin, which later became part of the catalogue of communist battle cries. It simply means, 'they shall not pass.'"

"OK."

"When we win a case, we say *hemos pasado*. We have passed. It's our tradition."

"I didn't know I'd ended up in some communist—"

"Watch yourself!" protested Chyłka. "We're all liberals here, but if you ever accuse me of lefty extremism, you'll get what's coming to you. And why are you following me around like a bad smell?"

"I thought that—"

"Go to Kormak and help him with those neighbours," said Joanna, quickening her pace.

Elegantly dodging obstacles, she reached her office and disappeared behind the door.

10

"L ANGER. VISITOR," ANNOUNCED the warder.

Without a word, the prisoner got up and moved to the cell door. The warder led him outside, stood him against a wall and, as a formality, searched him from head to toe. It was unlikely that Langer would have been given anything by the other inmates—he never even talked to them—but rules were rules. On Langer's return, the warder would be more thorough, because then he could be smuggling in secret messages.

They went through several pairs of security doors and crossed the annexe, eventually reaching the visiting room. The warder sat Langer on a chair and cuffed his wrists and ankles. This time, no one would risk having him pounce on a visitor.

On the other side of the metal table sat the Bald Man.

"Thank you," said Piotr.

The prison officer finished and left the room.

Alone, the two men looked at each other in silence. The Bald Man drummed his fingers on the metal table surface.

"It stinks in here," he said finally. "I heard that prisons have their specific smell, but I never imagined it would be so bad."

"It's much worse in the cell," replied Langer indifferently. "Several men in a tight space, and a toilet separated by just a low plywood partition. It's not pleasant."

"It could be worse."

Piotr continued to stare at the Bald Man's face. "Who are you?" he asked.

"Someone who knows you're smart enough not to ask questions you don't want the answer to."

"My father didn't send you," replied Piotr. "I know all his henchmen."
The Bald Man was silent.

"Great. In that case we have nothing to talk about, so get up and get out," said Langer, pointing to the door, "or tell me what you want."

"It doesn't matter what I want."

Langer raised his eyebrows.

"My employer wants you to cooperate."

"Well, I'm here, aren't I? That makes it pretty clear."

"You are here because you have no choice. You may not be saying anything, but you know perfectly well what we expect."

"I'm doing—"

"You're doing what you think is right," interrupted the Bald Man. "But you need to stop thinking. You must rely on us. Completely."

If the Bald Man was hoping for a reaction, he didn't get it.

"You do realise that just a word from me, and all your cellmates will have a happy, alcohol-fuelled evening tonight, doing what they want with you?"

"Keep trying."

The Bald Man smiled and shook his head. "Do you really think that if you're sent down for murder, no one will touch you? Don't be naive, Langer. You know what we are capable of and what options we have."

Piotr remained silent, looking at the floor. The Bald Man sensed victory. "That's more like it," he said. "Now listen, I have some instructions for you. Make sure you carry them out to the letter."

CHAPTER

11

Kordian's second day at work was immeasurably worse than the first.

Yesterday, he had left the office at ten o'clock, and was home around eleven. He opened his first beer just before midnight, and fell asleep at around two. And he was to report to the Skylight building at eight, so he had to get up at six.

If that was what his life had come to, he was ready to opt out. Paraphrasing Robert Frost, Kordian thought that if he worked diligently in his office for ten hours a day, perhaps one day he would become the boss—and work for fourteen hours.

Stopping outside the office building, he lit a Davidoff.

"Don't make a stench here," he heard a woman's voice say, although this time the tone wasn't scathing.

Déjà vu, thought Kordian. He turned round and greeted Chyłka with a genuine smile.

"Tell me, how many hours does a senior associate sleep?" he asked.

"As many as she likes," Joanna replied, deadpan. "Come on, don't smoke outside Golden Terraces like some lowlife. You've got an office for that."

"I don't have an office," objected Oryński. "You put me in the newbie-burrow."

"It makes no difference, there's still a smoking room."

Kordian took a last drag on his cigarette, stamped it out and followed Chyłka.

In the lift, there was an awkward silence again. Oryński sneaked the odd glance at his boss; when she noticed, she gave him a withering look.

"Didn't get enough sleep, Zordon?"

His response was a long, genuine yawn. Perfect timing. "Up all night, searching for the answer to your task?"

"What? Ah . . . yes. Didn't find anything."

"You've forgotten again, haven't you?"

"No."

"I'm not going to remind you. It's your problem."

He racked his brains for a moment, in silence. Then suddenly, somewhere in his brain, a neuron fired up.

"I was supposed to change my ringtone," he replied, proud as a teacher's pet with the right answer. 'But I haven't managed to do it yet."

"No, not that, that's just a technical thing," she said, as the lift reached their floor. "Your other task was much more important. If you don't remember it, why on earth should I think you're capable of learning the Criminal Code or the CCP?"

The Criminal Code and Code of Criminal Procedure were the last things on Kordian's mind. The events of the previous day had proved to him that his new job had very little to do with codes, laws, and charters. First, he had met a psychopath, then visited the top brass at Żelazny & McVay, and then to top it all off, he had spent hours in Kormak's office. That had been the most exhausting.

The two young men had diligently searched all the nooks and crannies of social media, but it was hard going. Kormak showed an impressive ability to multitask, being able to work and talk about the works of Cormac McCarthy simultaneously—including a not very successful Polish translation of one of his books. Initially, Kordian had made an effort to show he was listening; later, he simply pretended Kormak didn't exist.

It soon became apparent that Langer's *nouveau riche* neighbours in the apartment block valued their privacy. The pair found nothing of any use on social media.

So Oryński's surprise was all the greater when he stepped out of the lift to see the skinny man in the Elton John glasses wearing a radiant smile.

"Kordian, I've found something," he said in a low voice.

At that time of day, you could still hear what he was saying, but an hour later it wouldn't even be a murmur in the background. The two lawyers looked at him questioningly.

"That blonde," he declared. "From the same floor as Langer."

"No, I don't know who you mean," yawned Oryński.

"The one who had her picture taken in front of Christ the King in Świebodzin."

"Nope, don't remember."

"The one with the boobs."

"What boobs?"

"What a question!" exclaimed Kormak. "Shapely ones, like soft, yielding pyramids."

Chyłka shook her head in pity. Why was it that the only thing that could make a man sit up and take notice was a pair of breasts? Would things ever change?

"Agnieszka," declared Oryński. "Powirska, if I remember rightly."

"Exactly. That's her," said Kormak, nodding his head enthusiastically. "I know which gym she goes to."

"Gym?" asked Chyłka incredulously. "I thought an upmarket apartment block like that would have everything. Fitness rooms in the flats, a gym on the roof or something like that, no?"

"No," replied Kormak. "No, they don't have their own gym."

Joanna looked at the two of them, realising their minds were still firmly focused on the girl's outstanding attributes.

"Go there," she said. "Lie in wait, ready to pounce like two revolting paparazzi."

"OK," agreed Kormak, glancing at her cleavage. "But I'm going to need your necklace."

"What for?"

"I just will."

Chyłka took off her pendant, though she was not happy about it. "If anything happens to it, or you lose it, I'll rip your legs out of your arse and feed them to Old Rusty."

"Sure, sure," muttered Kormak, and he looked at Kordian. "Here, you take it."

"No."

"Come on. Grab it and let's go."

"I don't even know why we need it."

"You'll see."

Before he could answer, Joanna pressed the necklace into his hand. It looked terrifyingly expensive, but Kordian decided that it didn't matter. What could possibly happen to it? He'd keep it safe in his pocket, and whatever his Elton-John-lookalike colleague was planning, it wouldn't involve damaging it. It was fine. Everything would be fine.

"Get going," urged Joanna. "We don't pay you to stand idle."

"Nobody pays—"

"Don't worry, you'll get your cash at the end of the month."

Kordian wanted to object, but Chyłka was already way down the corridor.

Back in the lift, he thought again how far this was from what he'd expected. The paparazzi analogy wasn't completely spot on because paparazzi only took photographs, whereas he had to snoop around and sneak up on innocent people using methods straight from the Stasi playbook.

"We won't get anywhere," he said.

"Nonsense."

"If Langer's neighbours knew anything, they'd have reported it to the police a long time ago. Or the media."

"Maybe they would, maybe they wouldn't."

"Besides, running around after people and reading their posts on some stupid social media page has nothing to do with what I'm supposed to be doing as a legal trainee."

"That's life."

They reached the ground floor, and left the Skylight building onto Emilia Plater Street. Oryński lit a cigarette, and Kormak adjusted the strap of the bag slung over his shoulder.

"Parked somewhere near?" he asked.

"Are you kidding?"

"No," replied Kormak in an almost offended tone. "Other people have parking permits. I thought you did too."

"Not yet."

"So where are you parked?"

"I use the tram."

"What?" Kormak turned around and looked at his companion with disbelief. "Too tight to spend fifty zlotys an hour for parking?"

"I don't have a car."

"Ah."

For a moment both men were silent.

"So get a taxi," suggested Kormak.

"Do you think I'm made of money?"

"Man!" exclaimed Kormak. "Are you a lawyer, or aren't you?"

"Clearly not the sort you're used to," replied Kordian, looking tellingly at the tram stop. They headed off in that direction.

"And yet you smoke Davidoffs."

"You can't economise on the important things," explained Kordian. "Besides I'm not completely skint. I have money set aside; I just don't waste it on crap."

"I'm not saying a word," said Kormak, shaking his head.

Outside the Central Railway Station, they boarded tram number thirty-three, heading for Kielecka Street. They got off about ten minutes later; now it was just a matter of finding the right address.

"Where to?" asked Kormak.

"To the most impressive building in Mokotów Field."

"Mokotów Fields, I think you mean."

"Field."

"Don't think so."

"I can assure you, Kormak, it's Mokotów Field."

"Do you have to be such an arse?"

"I try not to be, but life kind of forces it on me."

"Doesn't matter. Get your phone out and Google the address."

Oryński winced.

"Something wrong?"

"Not a lot of data left. . . ."

Kormak spread his arms, pulled out his own phone and typed in the address Kordian dictated. They set off towards a modern, minimalist housing complex, walked straight past it and stopped outside a gym, whose sole purpose was probably to squeeze even more money out of the apartment block residents.

"So, I guess you've got a plan," said Oryński, as he read a poster encouraging him to try out new ways of burning calories.

"Crouching tiger," replied Kormak, pointing to himself. Then pointing to Oryński, he added, "Hidden dragon."

"Great," retorted Kordian.

"So you don't want to know the details?"

"Probably not."

"We wait here, in hiding," explained Kormak, ignoring him. "Then when you see her, you spring into action."

"Genius, not. Will it take long?"

"Could be a while, I suppose."

Two hours passed without a trace of Powirska. The pair were sitting on a bench where they could see everyone entering and leaving the gym.

"How did you find her anyway?" asked Oryński, to kill time.

"I have my methods."

He made it sound like he was getting data from CIA spy satellites.

Kordian raised his eyebrows and looked at his companion doubtfully.

"Nothing illegal," Kormak explained. "You just have to rummage through the internet. Let's imagine Agnieszka on the elliptical cross trainer right now, exercising her shapely posterior."

"So why don't we just go in?"

"Because we don't want to interrupt her. We'll catch her when she leaves. Or rather you will."

"OK," replied Oryński without much enthusiasm.

Every minute seemed to last an eternity, and there was still no trace of Powirska. A quarter of an hour later, Kordian had just about had enough. He glanced at his companion, relieved to see he felt the same.

"Clearly she's already done her stint for the week."

"In that case, we resort to Plan B," declared Kormak.

He explained his plan from beginning to end, and Kordian had to admit it seemed to make sense. There were a couple of things that could go wrong, but it was worth a try. He nodded to show that he understood, and then set off towards the entrance. The gym was pretty empty at this time of day. Through the window he could see a solitary woman slogging it out on a treadmill, looking as if she might drop dead at any moment. Kordian moved on and approached the man standing at reception. His biceps were approximately the same circumference as his head, but apart from that, he could have been a model for a metrosexual clothing catalogue.

"Good morning," said Oryński.

"Hi," replied the model with a slight smile. "Great outfit for morning training."

"This?" asked Kordian, straightening his jacket. "Uh . . . no, I was here last night. Can't do it that often," he added, patting his thighs.

He cringed to think how many times he'd made an epic fool of himself over the last two days.

"A certain girl left this here yesterday," he added, placing the necklace on the counter.

The receptionist looked at it and nodded appreciatively. Kordian knew he was taking a risk when he said he had been in the club the previous night, but assumed the receptionist was more interested in a different type of client and wouldn't have noticed someone like him.

"Expensive," commented the receptionist, as if he was surprised that anyone would bring in a find like this instead of trying to flog it online.

"It might be. But the girl was really nice."

The smile on the receptionist's face showed that he had cottoned on, and knew where this was going.

"No worries, leave it here, and I—"

"No," said Oryński, shaking his head and narrowing his eyes. "I can't do that. Man . . . give me a break," he added with a smile.

The advantage of conversing with people like the receptionist was that you didn't have to use words; it was enough to raise your eyebrows, nod your head or purse your lips. In this situation, they didn't even need to resort to these universal signals. It was obvious what he was after, and the receptionist seemed only too ready to help a brother in need.

"I'd prefer to give it to her personally," Kordian told him.

"Er . . . do you know Miss Thundershag's real name?"

Oryński had never come across the term before, and for a moment he was lost for words. But he soon pulled himself together.

"Agnieszka. And her surname . . . Powirska, I think, not sure though. When she introduced herself, I was concentrating on other things," replied Oryński, gesturing with his hands as if he was weighing up two watermelons at a market stall.

The receptionist's eyes lit up at the thought.

"Enough said," he declared, turned to the monitor and squinted at it as if he were eighty, not twenty.

"She's a member, but doesn't come in regularly. So I can't really help you much."

"And her number? I could phone her and say that I found it in the gym. . . ."

"Nah . . . can't give phone numbers, mate."

"I'm sure she wouldn't mind in this case."

"Well, I don't know."

"Come on, help a man in need," pleaded Oryński. "If I give her necklace back, I'm almost guaranteed some action, eh?"

The receptionist smiled, but shook his head.

"Dream on," he said. "But keep trying, bro, keep trying. Just try and bulk up a bit, I can see you could do with it." Suddenly he grabbed Kordian by the arm, by his flabby bicep. He grimaced as if he had touched a dead fish.

"I'll work on it when I get that number."

The receptionist sighed.

"I'm not going to leave the necklace here," said Oryński. "So it would be the lesser of two evils if you gave me the number and I returned it to her, rather than me flogging it at some car boot sale."

"OK, OK," replied the receptionist, raising his hands. "I won't turn my back on a bro on the pull. If it was just some old munter, I wouldn't pass the number on for your own good. But this chick is hot. Wait a sec . . ." he added, focused on the cursor on his screen.

Within seconds, Oryński had the number of the girl who lived on the same floor as Piotr Langer.

"And remember, at least an hour a day pumping iron. Otherwise you'll never get laid, trinkets or not, got it?"

"Got it," Kordian replied gratefully, turning towards the exit.

"Above all, you need guns. Start with the biceps, because they make the best impression. Then get working on the triceratops," added the receptionist, patting his own triceps. "And get some supplements. Without them, someone like you won't get anywhere. You need to get into it."

"I will, thank you."

"My advice would be Xtreme AnticataboliX. That's what I do."

"Thanks, I'll be sure to check it out."

"OK, laters."

"Laters," replied Oryński, and left as fast as he could.

Oryński's greatest sporting achievement was the odd game of squash—he and a few friends played on a squash court in Wyszyński Street. But it had been difficult to find time even in his previous life. Now it would be much harder. He was lucky if he had time to scratch his own backside. Still, as he left the gym, he made a solemn promise to himself: although he wouldn't go down the supplements route, he would find time to play squash at least once a week. And he would cut down on the smoking, or even give it up.

He lit a cigarette and looked around for Kormak.

"Excuse me, have you got a light?" said an unfamiliar voice.

Kordian turned around and saw a man who looked as if he'd been a bodybuilder since babyhood, starting by ripping the slats out of his cot.

"Sure."

He handed over his lighter, and the hulk quickly lit his cigarette and handed it back.

"Finished working out?" he asked.

"Me? No, just looking, because . . ."

The hulk grimaced. "You like to look?" he asked.

"No . . . I mean . . . I was looking to join."

"Do you live here then?"

"Yes, quite close."

"I live over there," said the hulk, pointing to the smart white building.

Kordian perked up. But it didn't take him long to realise he'd never seen the face before, although he'd spent hours studying the apartment block residents online.

"Have you lived there long?" Kordian asked.

"Only just moved in."

Oryński nodded. He should have expected that fate wouldn't have been that kind to him, delivering one of Langer's neighbours straight into his lap.

"Why do you ask?" inquired the stranger.

"No reason. It's just a nice building."

"Fucking awesome, I'd call it," said the hulk. "Apparently the Sadist of Mokotów lived there. Killed two people, then sat stewing with their corpses for two weeks in the bathroom."

"Ten days. And it was a different room."

The hulk didn't respond, and the young lawyer finally spotted Kormak, sitting on a bench a little further on, reading a book by his beloved McCarthy.

"Catch you later," said the hulk, stamping out his cigarette, and went into the gym.

CHAPTER

12

THE MUSCLE-BOUND BALD Man knew he shouldn't be following the trainee. The Grey-Haired Man had been clear, he was to keep an eye on Chyłka. But when he saw Oryński leaving the Skylight building with a colleague, he'd set off after them. His anxiety grew as they came ever closer to the apartment complex.

He knew he shouldn't make direct contact with the person he was following. It was against all the rules, and his boss had said to intervene only when absolutely necessary. But this situation was exceptional—the Bald Man had to know why the trainee was there. After all, he was Chyłka's errand boy, so she must have told him to go.

"Sup?" asked the receptionist by way of greeting.

The hulk eyed him up. Decent body, though not as good as his own. And those extra-tight-fitting clothes looked as if they were about to burst at the seams.

"What did that guy want?" asked the Bald Man.

"To get his dick wet, like everyone else," replied the receptionist with a smirk.

"Be more specific."

For a moment there was silence.

"And what business is it of yours?"

"I'm asking nicely."

The receptionist seemed to have no intention of cooperating. The Bald Man thought about waiting for him outside the club until he finished work, then explaining why it was unwise to avoid answering his questions.

But he decided against it, because there was no time to waste. He had to find out where Oryński and his companion were headed.

"Who do you hang out with?" he asked.

He could see that the receptionist wanted to tell him in no uncertain terms where to get off, but was biting his tongue.

The receptionist wasn't actually scared; he just saw the hulk as a potential client, and as such, should not be discouraged.

"Depends," replied the receptionist.

"That means no one," said the Bald Man. "Have you heard of the Grey-Haired Man?"

The sudden flash of interest in the receptionist's eyes confirmed that he had.

A moment later, the hulk had all the information he wanted. He gave a sigh of relief. Chyłka and Oryński were chasing their own tails. Everything was in perfect order.

13

KORDIAN WALKED SLOWLY up to the bench. Kormak raised his head, pushed up his spectacles, closed the book with the horse's mouth on the cover and put it into a compartment in his bag. Kordian noticed the words on the bookmark: "INSERTED HERE, BUT I SWITCHED OFF TWO PAGES AGO."

"Who was that meathead?" asked Kormak, pointing to the club entrance.

"Don't know, I guess he wanted to give his lungs a shot before his workout and asked for a light. He lives in the apartment block we've been trying to break into, in the virtual sense."

"I don't recognise his face."

"Because he's only just moved in."

"So never mind him. Did you get the number?"

"Yes, the necklace worked like magic."

"Then let's give the object of your desires a call," said Kormak, but Oryński had already pulled his phone out of the inside pocket of his jacket. He clearly hadn't taken Artur Żelazny's advice to heart.

He dialled the number and sat down next to Kormak with his phone pressed to his ear.

"Hello?" said a velvety female voice. She even sounded beautiful.

"Good morning, Agnieszka," said Kordian in his "official" voice.

"Good morning," she replied. "If you're calling with another loan offer . . ."

"Not at all," Kordian said. "I am a lawyer defending Piotr Langer. I would like to have a few words with you if you have time."

"How did you get hold of my number?"

"I came across it by chance, and . . ."

"Sure. Just like Obama spies on people by chance through PRISM."

For a moment Kordian wondered if he was really talking to the person whose pictures he'd seen the previous day. That girl looked more like a ditsy bimbo than someone who knew about the American surveillance programme. Or maybe she'd just liked the right page on Facebook.

"A lawyer you say? Which firm?"

"Żelazny & McVay," replied Oryński.

It was hard to hide the pride in his voice. Even more so now, because he didn't have to admit he was only a trainee.

"What do you want from me? I've already spoken to the police."

"I'd like to ask you a few questions regarding one or two issues."

"Like what?"

"Like whether you noticed anything suspicious, unusual, anything out of the ordinary."

"I've already gone over this," she sighed. "I saw nothing, I heard nothing."

"So for ten days you didn't see my client leave his flat?" asked Oryński, getting straight to the point.

"No, I didn't."

"But normally, you'd see him around? Going out to buy a newspaper, or shopping?"

"Peter, reading newspapers, are you joking? What would he want with newspapers? He had his tablet, didn't he?"

Peter, not Piotr, Kordian noticed. Why would she anglicise his name?

He glanced excitedly at Kormak, regretting he hadn't switched on the speakerphone. The way Agnieszka spoke about their client and knew "Peter's" habits was not so much a flicker of light at the end of the tunnel as the beam from a lighthouse.

"Did he ever do any shopping?" he asked.

"Yes, I often saw him in the local shop. He didn't like shopping malls, he said you met the worst kind of people there. Plebs, he called them, you know? He said half of them stank. That is, not directly. Peter was hardly ever direct. He'd always beat about the bush, you know?"

"I know exactly what you mean."

"And at our shop here on the development, they can order anything you want," continued Agnieszka. "You just have to ask them in advance."

"Did you often see him there?"

"Fairly often, because no one at our place buys food for more than a day. Why bother if you have a shop downstairs? If you want a beer, you don't buy a whole crate and lug it upstairs. You go down to the shop and buy a bottle. Or five."

"Did Langer drink a lot?" Oryński asked.

"Depends what you mean by a lot. He drank normally, same as everyone."

"Did he eat out?"

"Funny thing to ask," muttered Agnieszka. "I didn't know him that well, and I don't know where he ate. I'd occasionally see him downstairs in the pizzeria, but I don't know anything more. Is there anything else you wanted to ask? Can I get back to my work?"

Her tone suggested that there could only be one possible answer. *Doesn't matter,* he thought, *she had given him more time than he'd expected.*

"Of course, please go back to your work. Thank you very much for the information."

"You're welcome," she replied, then paused. "I'd just like to add that Peter always seemed like a decent person. A bit critical of the world, but essentially decent."

Oryński thanked her again, said goodbye and hung up. The information about Langer was worth its weight in gold, although on the other hand, whatever "Peter" had been like previously, his current circumstances were forcing him to change character completely.

"And?" asked Kormak.

"He habitually did his shopping in the local shop," replied Kordian with a smile. "Buckle up, we're joining the *nouveau riche* in their enclave."

"You talk as if you belonged to a different class."

"My family is *vieux riche.* If we can speak of riches at all."

"The first lawyer in the family?"

"Depends what you mean."

Kormak raised his eyebrows.

"Officially, there's nothing but lawyers in my family," said Oryński. "But most of them know more about getting into Parliament and how to access Poland's top politicians than about the Supreme Court."

His comment was met with silence, then the pair set off to the gated apartment complex. It was clear from first glance that no stranger would wander in by accident. The CCTV, security guards, and high fence were there to make sure it could never happen.

14

ORYŃSKI TRIED HARD to think of a way to persuade the security guard to let them in. Expensive suits were all well and good, but they in themselves could not work miracles.

On a normal housing estate, you could show the guard a pizza box and say that someone at number nine was waiting for a double pepperoni; or you could put on a red fleece and say you have a delivery for someone at number twelve. The simplest way was to get some leaflets, and beg and whine until the security guard let you in to deliver them.

Here, however, the guard would contact the apartment via the intercom to check everything was above board, and hawkers would be unceremoniously turned away. So he decided to simply tell the truth and hope the sheer gravity of the situation would do the trick.

Kordian introduced himself to the security guard, his hands clasped behind his back.

"You're very welcome to call the detention centre for confirmation," he said.

"The police have closed the apartment, there's no way . . ."

"That's the police's problem, not mine," said the trainee. "I represent my client, who is the owner of the property by law. If he wishes to have something brought from his apartment, a watch or a photograph say, that is his full legal right. The police have already taken away all the evidence they wanted."

The fact that Langer was not allowed to have any personal items in his cell was neither here nor there.

"But . . ."

"Are you recording this?" asked Oryński, pretending to be annoyed and turning to Kormak. "I want it on record that I have been denied access to a property legally owned by my client."

"Yes," confirmed Kormak, pointing his phone at the security guard.

"I'm appealing to you one last time," said Kordian. "Please open the barrier and let us in. I am not asking for the keys or the code to the door, because I have been given those by my client. I only need you to let us into the complex."

The guard looked slightly bewildered, and quickly weighed up the pros and cons. There was really only one conclusion: it was better to let them in now than to have problems later. What trouble could they cause? All he had to do was lift the barrier. They had been given keys by the owner.

He pressed a button on his console, and Oryński flashed him a smile.

On the way to the estate grocery shop, Kordian thought about how he should really be sitting at his desk drafting lawsuits, appeals, and applications, or other documents which would help him navigate the meandering twists and turns of the law.

The shop looked as if it had been taken out of a perfect homes catalogue; it was like an exclusive shopping centre in condensed form. The sign claimed that wines and spirits from all around the world were available, and the window display showed products rarely seen on ordinary shelves: Dr Pepper in various flavours, Vanilla Coke, caramel Milky Ways, Sprite Zero, Nutella Snack & Drink.

"Is that legal?" asked Kormak, pointing to the pantheon of Western consumables.

"Provided the product is on the market in the European Union or European Economic Area, it is perfectly legal. If not, they need the producer's approval," replied Oryński, walking through the automatic sliding doors.

Inside, the shop smelled of vanilla, and looked as if it had been cleaned just a few seconds ago. There was no pervading scent of salted gherkins, onions, or smoked sausage, as you'd find in other housing estate shops.

"How lovely, some new faces. Welcome!" said the portly man behind the counter, eyeing the young men. "What brings you here?"

"Piotr Langer," replied Kordian.

"So, you gentlemen are from Żelazny & McVay? Pleased to meet you."

Oryński was not surprised. The shopkeeper would know about everything that went on in the community. And you only had to Google Chyłka's name to find out who was defending Langer.

"Can I help you?" asked the shopkeeper.

"A Coca-Cola BlāK, please," said Kormak.

The shop owner took a dark bottle out of the fridge, for which he charged an extortionate sum of money, then looked expectantly at Kordian.

"I'd just like to ask you a few questions, if you don't mind."

"Of course not, I only hope I'll know the answers."

"Did our client come here often?" began Oryński, leaning on the counter. "I spoke to Agnieszka Powirska earlier, I'm sure you know her." The shopkeeper nodded enthusiastically. "She said Piotr did most of his shopping in your store."

"That is true. He valued the depth of my product range."

"Depth of range?" Kormak interrupted. "It's like calling a garbage truck a sublime model of a vehicle for the transportation of waste."

"How regularly did he come here?" asked Oryński quickly so that the shopkeeper wouldn't have time to be offended by Kormak's rudeness.

"More or less every day," replied the shopkeeper, "though there were times I wouldn't see him for a week or two. That was when he was out of town. But whenever he was in Warsaw, he did his shopping here."

"I'm primarily interested in the period about two weeks before he was arrested."

The man nodded to show he understood.

"I knew you'd ask me that. Well, in that time, Piotr wasn't here at all. Not once. The last time I saw him was perhaps three or four weeks before he was arrested by the police. He must have done his shopping elsewhere and bought in bulk . . . and that was hardly surprising. You see, sir, if I had two dead people in my apartment, I'd also be reluctant to leave them unattended."

Kordian tapped the counter. He'd got what he had come for. The fact that Langer had not done any shopping for some time gave him a good starting point. Together with the testimonies of other witnesses who could confirm they hadn't seen Piotr on the estate at the time, it could sow the seeds of doubt in the judge's mind.

"Did you know those people?" asked Kormak. "The victims, I mean?"

"Never even heard of them. I mean, I heard about them after the event, from the media. But today I can't even remember the faces and names, and I must tell you, sir, that I have an exceptionally good memory for faces, as indeed everyone should in my profession."

"Were they ever in here?" asked Kormak. "Perhaps one of your staff knew them?"

"I'm absolutely sure they weren't," said the shop owner. "If they ever came here, I'd remember them."

None of Langer's acquaintances knew the victims, which suggested that Langer didn't know them either. And that was the strange part. No murderer would pick up complete strangers in the street just to kill them in his own flat.

And yet no connection between Langer and the victims had ever been established. Both had lived in the north-eastern suburbs of Warsaw and had no reason to be in the vicinity of the Mokotów apartment complex.

"Have the police interrogated you?" asked Kordian.

"No, of course not. I just run the neighbourhood shop. Why would anyone interrogate me?"

"I'm only asking," Oryński said with a faint smile.

People often reacted to the word "interrogate" like the devil to holy water, though in reality it shouldn't have had a pejorative meaning at all. It was simply a means of determining the truth, the same as any other. Both sides were interrogated, witnesses as well as suspects, and it was the latter that gave the word its negative connotations.

"I'll take a Dr Pepper for the road," said Kordian, noting that the owner was looking at him rather suspiciously.

"Of course," he replied, reaching into the fridge again. "I can't stop drinking this stuff either. I can't wait until some country starts distributing new flavours. I know there's cherry and—"

"Thank you for all the information," Oryński interrupted.

At the cash register, the shopkeeper undercharged the young lawyer for his drink.

"I hope I won't . . . you know? I won't have to testify in court."

"You have nothing to fear, sir," Oryński assured him. "But if your statements will help Piotr's case in any way, I assume you wouldn't have anything against them being used?"

"Help him? I thought . . . Jesus, Mary and Joseph, do you think he's innocent?"

"It's my moral and statutory duty to defend him," replied Kordian, not wanting to prolong his conversation with the shop owner. He had given him information that could turn out to be crucial, so he thanked him once again, then he and Kormak headed for the tram stop. As they walked, they felt the heavy gaze of the security man who had let them in.

"That went smoothly," remarked Kormak, when they had left the estate.

"We have some material on which we can built a proper line of defence, Kormak. That's better than just smoothly."

"Chyłka will be delighted."

Kordian nodded, but his thoughts were already elsewhere. The shopkeeper's question reverberated in his mind. "Do you really believe he didn't do it?" he'd asked. Joanna seemed to be convinced, and he thought so too. But who could have framed him as the murderer? And how? The father could be ruled out almost from the start—but the world wasn't that simple.

So, who was it? And why?

Oryński had no idea. But he assumed that if they dug long enough, they would eventually find the truth.

15

C HYŁKA LOOKED UP from her laptop when she heard the knock on her door. Glancing at the clock in the bottom right-hand corner of her screen she checked the time. Four minutes past noon. She minimised the browser window, and the company logo appeared: the name "Żelazny & McVay" against a grey background, beneath which a casually drawn line ended just before the "y" in "McVay".

"Enter!"

She'd expected Kordian and Kormak to be in sackcloth and ashes because the trail of the girl so generously endowed by nature had drawn a blank. But as they stood in the doorway, the expressions on their faces told her that this was not the case. Without further ado, and without undue boasting, Kordian told her the whole story.

"So in a nutshell, we have something to work on," he ended.

"Maybe," replied Joanna. "But don't get your hopes up too high, Zordon."

"What makes you think I have?"

"You sound a bit too enthusiastic."

"Rubbish."

Chyłka leaned back on her chair.

"Have I already told you about the sacred law of legal practice?" she asked.

"Yes, unfortunately," replied Kordian. "Never tell your client that you will win the—"

"No, not that one," she interrupted. "Never identify with the client. Even if you're convinced they're genuinely innocent, never allow any empathy to arise between you. Of course, if it's just from the client's side, that's OK, but from you—never."

"But—"

"Never," repeated Chyłka. "I stress this, because you seem ready to marry Langer if the opportunity arises. The closer you are to the client, the further you are from winning the case."

"Yes, *Sensei*."

Joanna gave him a scowl, and flicked out her cigarette.

"Listen, Zordon, preaching sermons like this hurts me more than it hurts you, but you have to learn." She lit her Marlboro. "If I don't tell you, who will? Perhaps Kormak?" Then turning to the thin man, "What say you, Boney?"

"I know sod all."

"Exactly," agreed Joanna, and again turned to Oryński. "So either accept all that I say with humility and gratitude, or become the worst informed trainee in the history of the Warsaw District Bar Council. *Ponimaet*?"

"I shall cherish your instructive wisdom," declared Oryński. "And we could start with tactics in the Langer case."

"Hang on," said Kormak. "We've brought you some solid information, and we haven't even heard a 'well done.'"

Chyłka shifted her gaze from one man to the other. And for a while there was silence in her office.

"Light up, lads. You'll feel better."

"I don't smoke," said Kormak.

Oryński helped himself to one of Joanna's cigarettes.

"You should take it up," she advised Kormak. "It amazes me you've managed to stay sane in this place without it."

"Smoking has nothing to do with it."

"Certainly does," countered Joanna. "Every cigarette numbs the mind, it lowers the senses. Heavy smokers don't feel it, because the body gets used to it, but if you lit up now, you'd know what I'm talking about."

"That's great."

"Definitely. You'll have less strength to get irritated about everything around you. Some things you won't even register. A cigarette equals health."

"If you ignore the fact that it'll kill you."

"Well, yes," said Chyłka. She shrugged her shoulders and looked at Oryński. "And you, Zordon, don't you have your own? If you can't afford them, say so, and I'll make sure you don't work for free anymore."

"As far as I know, I don't."

"Never mind," she replied and waved dismissively. "Let's not waste time on this nonsense, I have some wonderful news. We've got a date for the trial, and you won't even have time to learn to tie your tie the way it should be done at Żelazny & McVay before we're working our tails off in court."

"But . . ."

"What? Surprised we have our traditions? From Senior Associate up, it's the Windsor knot, below it's the half Windsor. I don't know why McVay insists on it, but that's the way it is."

"No, I meant . . ."

"You're scared of the law court? No worries, everyone who goes there for the first time shits themselves. Best evidence of this is the stench in the toilets. Remember, never go there. Do your business before you enter the court building."

"As bad as that?" he asked with disgust.

"Imagine what half a dozen people under stress can produce . . . or better still, don't try to imagine it. And stop freaking out."

"I'm not freaking out, only . . ."

"Only what?"

"The last time I checked, we didn't have a plan of action. Now Kormak and I bring you truffles on a platter, and you don't—"

"Truffles?" Joanna shook her head. "Really, spare me your metaphors, Zordon."

"You know what I mean."

"I spoke with Langer Senior," she cut in.

Silence descended on the room. Oryński straightened himself in his chair. Kormak cleared his throat and Chyłka looked at him pointedly.

"I'll be on my way," he said, finally catching on. "If you have no further requests, I'm going to my cave."

After he left, the two lawyers sat for a while in silence.

"What did he say?" Kordian finally asked.

"What do you think he said?" she retorted. "We're to opt for insanity. We're to make him look like a complete lunatic, and secure a precautionary detention order."

"Psychiatric hospital?"

"Better than prison," replied Chyłka, lighting another cigarette. For the second time that day, Kordian decided to cut down or give up smoking. Well, that and play squash, at least once a week.

"But Peter won't go for it."

"Peter?" asked Joanna, raising her eyebrows. "So now you're on hip-hop, Will Smith terms?" Oryński didn't respond, so Joanna dismissed the subject with a wave of her hand. "I know he won't go for it," she added. "But officially, Langer Senior is the one paying the bills. And the grumpy old codger insists that we try for insanity."

"Piotr will put paid to that idea the minute he opens his mouth in the courtroom."

"Not if Daddy finds the right experts. I'm sure plenty of psychiatrists or psychologists would testify if the price is right. They might even put forward a diagnosis that Langer's refusal to confess to the crime is clear evidence that he's criminally insane."

"But . . ."

"I know that you don't agree, Zordon," Chyłka interrupted.

She got up and went over to the window, which overlooked the Palace of Culture and Science.

"I know you want to call that guy from the shop and that girl from the gym as witnesses. Unfortunately, even their testimonies aren't exactly going to change the judge's mind."

"It might not change their mind, but it might cast a seed of doubt."

Chyłka looked over her shoulder. For a moment she was silent.

"You have to accept that the client has the last word," she said.

"And that is Langer."

"Senior."

"Stuff Senior," snapped Oryński. "Our duty is to do all we can to obtain an acquittal, right? So pitching for insanity when we know he's not insane is not what we should be doing. And it's contrary to the law."

"Great, go and complain to the National Bar Association."

Kordian fell silent, he didn't care to engage in a pointless clash of words. He thought that if anyone at Żelazny & McVay had mastered the art of manipulating clients, it was Joanna Chyłka. Yet in the case of Langer, it seemed that she simply had nothing to say.

"Did you try to convince him?"

"Does the sun rise in the east and set in the west?"

Kordian took a drag of his cigarette.

"I did what I could," she said. "That guy sees things his way. He wants the matter settled as fast as possible, and if we petition for insanity without putting forward any other arguments, it'll be a fast-track trial. Expert opinion, bang, done and dusted. There won't even be anything to appeal against, because no new facts will come to light. All the facts are already known."

"Dead and buried."

"Exactly."

There was another awkward silence.

"So what should we do?"

"Nothing," answered Joanna, opening a drawer. She took out *The Attorneys' Code of Ethics* and placed it before the young man.

"I see it hasn't been opened," he muttered.

"Now it will be, because you're going to read it cover to cover," Chyłka replied, unthinkingly lighting yet another cigarette. She looked at it, frowned, and put it in the ashtray. "But seriously, look through it, then report to one of the interns in the newbie-burrow. They'll tell you what a court trial looks like and what you have to do."

"Great," replied Oryński, taking the booklet. *The Attorneys' Code of Ethics*—an oxymoron if there ever was one.

In fact, it would be a good idea to read it, because it concerned trainees as much as anyone else, and theoretically violating the Code was punishable by law. But as far as the trial was concerned, he would have preferred to watch one from the public gallery rather than hear about it from an intern who probably went to public trials in their free time for lack of better things to do.

But he knew that the boss's instructions were non-negotiable. He had already noticed that everyone was under someone else's thumb: he was under her thumb, she was under Żelazny's . . . and it was a pity that as a result of the latter, Langer would spend the rest of his life in prison.

16

CHYŁKA SKETCHED OUT the situation to her client and told him what his father expected, watching his face carefully. Like a stone mask, Langer's face did not move.

The trial was just a day away, and in that time, it would be impossible to think up anything that might tip the balance in the defendant's favour. Not when there were three adversaries pitted against the defence lawyers: the court, which was fully convinced of the defendant's guilt; the defendant himself, who was not cooperating; and his father, who was paying them.

She would probably have been able to deal with the court—not perform a miracle, but in the right circumstances she would have been able to find enough flaws in the inquest or investigation for the initial verdict to be called into question.

Chyłka had done all she could to get permission to go down that route. She'd pestered Langer Senior with phone calls, trying to convince him that bringing forward two witnesses might cast doubt, if not in the minds of the judges, then at least the lay assessors. But Piotr didn't even want to hear about it.

Now she was sitting opposite his son, trying to read his face. He was as intransigent as his father. She had told him everything he needed to know, and was waiting for his response. The prisoner stared at her in silence.

"Do you think I'm innocent?" he said finally.

His words sounded menacing, as if he was aggrieved that she'd even think in those terms.

"What does it matter what I think?" she asked.

He didn't reply.

"I'm supposed to defend you by all legal means, and I've devoted my full attention to this case. That has nothing to do with whether you're innocent or not."

"Nothing?" he asked, and took a deep breath.

"Does it for you?"

He leaned back. Chyłka tried to gather her thoughts so as not to waste the meagre opportunity of exchanging a few words with him. He was clearly displeased by the fact that they had spoken to Powirska and the shopkeeper, so she decided to stay with that.

"What did you eat for those ten days?" she asked. "And what did you drink?"

He shrugged his shoulders.

"We checked your rubbish," she lied. "It appears that the last things you threw out included empty Dr Pepper cans."

"I don't remember."

"You bought them at the local shop, two weeks before the murders. You didn't have enough food to feed yourself throughout the time you were allegedly sitting in your apartment."

Langer made no comment.

"But that's not all we've learned."

"Really?"

"Powirska and the shopkeeper will provide further evidence."

Any witness statements given by those two wouldn't solve Langer's problems, but they would open the way to calling other residents as witnesses. If it turned out that none of them had seen the accused in that period, it would give Joanna a strong card to play with.

"What do you intend to do?" asked Piotr.

"What your father pays me to do."

Langer paused to think, as if he were considering the consequences of the line she was proposing to take—consequences too far-reaching even for Chyłka to discern. But the longer he remained silent, the greater the hope he might say something that would lead her to the truth. "You have a legal obligation not to act against the accused."

"I am not acting against you. Your father wants you to plead insanity, and I have no choice. This is not about a strategy for the trial, but about the fact that you're mentally ill. I can't stop your father trying to prove it in court, can I?"

"I am not mad."

Of that, she was not exactly sure.

"It's not for me to judge," Chyłka said. "That's a job for the experts."

"I shall prove to the court that I'm perfectly sane."

Chyłka was silent.

"Insanity is not an option," he added.

"In that case, you'll get life, because I've got no other line of defence."

Piotr nodded his head.

"Unless your father pays the experts."

He responded with silence. Joanna saw that any common ground they'd managed to establish was fading fast.

"Do you want to spend the rest of your life in prison?"

No answer.

"Perhaps you have a score to settle? Maybe you want to do away with an inmate who's got under your skin?"

"No."

"Of course not," she replied. "If you did, you wouldn't have killed two people and sat with their corpses. There are easier ways to get locked up. So what are you trying to achieve?"

She wasn't expecting an answer. Although she had managed to engage with Langer earlier, she saw his interest had now all but disappeared. But she tried nevertheless.

"Will you plead guilty?"

"No."

"Will you testify that you didn't kill those people?"

"No."

"Why?"

"Because I'm consistent."

She had hoped something might change just before the trial. Now she saw she had been deluding herself.

Nothing about this case made sense. The evidence showed that he had killed those people. He didn't seem to care about defending himself, and yet he flatly refused to say anything that might incriminate him. Then there was his father, who was doing everything he could to close the case as fast as possible.

And what about the shopkeeper? Where would Langer have done his shopping during those ten days if not on the estate, in the local shop? There were plenty of shops outside the estate, but the police had questioned the security guards at the gate; they said that for ten days they had not seen Langer's car or Langer himself. So had he gone earlier to stock up at Makro or Selgros? That would mean it had all been planned in advance, and if that was the case, then the victims could not have been random strangers—and all the more reason they should not have ended up in Langer's home. Not even the most callous psychopath would assume they could spend so much time alone with two corpses. This didn't make any sense at all.

"If we go for insanity, I won't have anything to appeal against," she said. It was her last remaining argument.

She was now acting against the express wishes of Langer Senior, but it didn't really matter to her at that particular moment. Disciplinary issues were of secondary importance—her conscience was at stake.

"Do you understand, Langer?"

He nodded, almost imperceptibly.

"I don't think you do," she said. "To appeal against that would be mere formality. Even the greatest miracle worker wouldn't be able to change the ruling."

"I'm perfectly aware of that."

She shook her head, with a sense of helplessness.

"Do what the law says," he added, and the stony expression returned to his face.

Chyłka knew she would get nothing more out of him.

CHAPTER

17

TWO WEEKS AFTER starting work at Żelazny & McVay, Kordian stood outside the District Court building where Langer's case was to be heard. He was hurriedly puffing away at his cigarette, assuming he would have to be upstairs in a matter of minutes. So much for his solemn declarations to cut down on smoking. Instead, for some reason, he had switched from Davidoffs to Marlboros. At least temporarily.

He looked at Chyłka standing next to him and noticed that she was flicking a cigarette out of the packet.

"Not in a rush?" he asked.

"Relax," she replied. "Before the court reporter gets round to calling out the case, before everyone assembles, before this, before that, you'll have enough time to smoke another two. And marvel at the surroundings," she added, looking at the dingy, low-rise blocks opposite the courthouse. They made her think of bygone times. Thank goodness they were bygone—shabby façades, neglected shutters with flaking paint, and some rather unimaginative graffiti which might, in places, be called tags. In front of all this lay a carpet of crooked, broken cobblestones. Solidarity Avenue in all its glory.

A bald muscleman standing at the door to a bank next to the low-rise blocks completed the picture. He was looking directly at the two lawyers, not bothering to be discreet about it.

"Who's that guy?" muttered Joanna.

Kordian looked, but as she pointed him out a tram heading for Bank Square hid the man from view. When the tram had passed, he was gone. Oryński looked questioningly at Chyłka, but she dismissed the matter with a wave of her hand. She had no interest in scandalmongers. He was, no doubt, hoping to see a celebrity in front of the courthouse.

"Come on," she ordered, flicking her cigarette butt into the three-lane street.

On the second floor, the two Żelazny & McVay lawyers saw a host of witnesses and people interested in the case, along with a tall, burly man representing the prosecutor's office; he stood out from the crowd, and not only because of his traditional court attire. Karol Rejchert spotted Chyłka and flipped her the bird—in a way that only she and Oryński could see.

"The prosecution?" asked Kordian.

"Yup," Joanna replied. "Let's say hello."

The trainee wanted to raise his hand and respond with the same gesture, but Chyłka stopped him.

"Leave it, Zordon. A reporter will notice and all hell will break loose."

"But he—"

"He's experienced. You're an amateur."

It was the first time he'd heard her speak so belligerently, and it didn't bode well for the pre-trial confrontation. Chyłka and Rejchert eyed each other so intently it could only mean they had once been lovers, or had opposed each other in the courtroom for too long. Looking at them, they were chalk and cheese—so it had to be the latter.

"Polishing your bootees all night, Rej?" she said to the prosecutor, looking at his shoes. "If their shine could kill, you'd get twenty-five years," she added, shielding her eyes. "Without parole."

"Give it a rest," grunted the prosecutor.

"They glow like a monkey's butt."

Rejchert sighed and looked around.

"Looking for a part in the circus?" continued Chyłka.

"I like to prepare well for crushing insects in the courtroom."

"I see you're in a good mood—only lacking any wit, as usual."

"Why shouldn't I be in a good mood?"

Chyłka looked over her shoulder at Oryński and said in a stage whisper:

"Look and learn, Zordon. This is what someone with delusions of winning the case looks like."

"Delusions?" laughed the prosecutor. "Everybody knows you've let this case go."

Joanna turned back to face her opponent.

"Watch your words. I'm sure there's some official here who would treat your slanderous remarks in the courthouse corridor as an offence against yours truly."

"Get stuffed, Chyłka."

"Likewise, I'm sure."

Rejchert looked at Kordian, who suddenly felt he was guilty of all the crimes with which Langer had been charged. Only experienced prosecutors had that special glare.

"Who's that? Your secret weapon?"

"This is Zordon, my trainee."

Rejchert didn't have time to comment on the presence of this indubitable legal asset, as at that moment the court reporter appeared in the corridor and announced that the hearing of the case against Piotr Langer was about to begin. He summoned the parties, procedural representatives, witnesses and all others to enter the courtroom, then for the sake of order also stuttered out the case number. Had there been no TV cameras present, he would no doubt have skipped this formality.

The crowd of people flooded from the corridor into the courtroom. For a moment confusion reigned, but order was soon restored, after several editorial teams were forced to shed delegates.

Piotr was led in through a different entrance, and sat down next to Chyłka and Oryński, to the left of the adjudicating panel. Rejchert sat down opposite them, glancing at Joanna with glee and anticipation. He must have known that the case was his—one of those that improved the statistics without having to try too hard. The defendant had no alibi and no eyewitnesses, and all the evidence was against him.

In any case, one look at the defendant told you everything you needed to know. Once the police had uncuffed him, Langer simply stared at the emblem hanging above the empty bench where the judges and assessors would sit.

"Have you changed your mind?" asked Joanna.

"No."

She didn't have time to follow up, as the clerk signalled for everyone to rise as the presiding judge entered the room accompanied by the rest of the adjudicating panel. He cast a glance across the public gallery, sighed ostentatiously and took up his place of honour. He rattled off all the formalities, asking if all those summoned had arrived and whether there were any obstacles to the commencement of proceedings. Then he asked all the witnesses to go back out into the corridor.

18

Oryński, in charitable mood, could only describe the first ten minutes as the most boring event he had ever participated in.

And it was all downhill from there.

The prosecutor read out the indictment, which formally began the trial. Then there was a litany of instructions: the defendant was informed that he had the right to submit explanations, to remain silent, to refuse to answer specific questions . . . and so on and so on. Were it not for the fact that a man's fate was at stake, Kordian would have fallen asleep.

As the judge continued to pontificate, Oryński looked around the room and thought how it clearly belonged to a bygone age, when people would queue for hours in the street just to buy meat. The crass lack of sophistication overwhelmed you the moment you stepped over the threshold; it was enough to make even an innocent person lose all hope.

Kordian had watched the trial of Breivik in Norway—there the courtroom décor was in the latest minimalist style, with the adjudicating panel sitting on black leather seats against a grey-painted wall. The furniture was made from warm, lightcoloured wood, and the floor was ash-panelled. The lightness and elegance were in direct contrast to what Kordian was facing now.

He looked at Langer sitting next to him, and saw that he really didn't give a damn. It was as if he had gone to the cinema to see a film he'd already seen several times. Prisoners often manifest their contempt or indifference towards the justice system, but normally they do it ostentatiously. Langer, on the other hand, seemed genuinely indifferent to what was happening around him.

"Does the defendant understand the indictment?" asked the presiding judge. Apart from the judge, Langer's fate depended on four other people: three lay assessors and another professional judge.

"Yes," replied Piotr.

"Does the defendant plead guilty?" asked the judge.

Chyłka turned round and looked at Langer. Kordian did the same, biting his lower lip. From the start he had been wondering what their client would say when the inevitable question was asked.

The judge looked expectantly at the detainee. "No," answered Piotr.

The defence lawyers exchanged glances.

"The defendant may now make a statement, if he so wishes," grunted the judge. He clearly wasn't thrilled to start this trial, and it was easy to understand why. So far, the case files had grown sky-high, while it was essentially an open-and-shut case. The fingerprints, the DNA and the flat itself were sufficient evidence.

"I have no statement to make, Your Honour."

The lay assessors looked at one another in consternation, but the defendant looked as if he really didn't care.

"Then we shall proceed to questioning the witnesses," said the judge, and summoned the first of the unfortunates who had come before the court to speak the truth, the whole truth, and nothing but the truth, so help them God.

Until the last minute, Kordian had deceived himself into thinking that Chyłka would defy Żelazny and Langer Senior's wishes. But now that didn't seem to be the case.

Instead of witnesses in the witness box, they saw experts. At first glance, the psychiatrist appeared to be a courtroom veteran able to grind any delinquent to a fine powder.

"On what basis did you assess the prisoner's state of mind?" asked the prosecutor, when she had taken her place on the stand.

"I had a variety of resources at my disposal," she screeched in reply. "Transcripts of the defendant's statements, comments from his neighbours and my own observations."

"Do you consider this evidence to be sufficient?"

"In my opinion, no."

Rejchert's face turned pale. Chyłka twitched, suddenly aware that fate might have a pleasant surprise in store.

"Please explain," said the judge, frowning. At last he looked interested.

"The thing is, Your Honour, establishing sanity, insanity, or diminished responsibility is a long and complicated process. It is essential to delve into—"

"Keep it succinct," admonished the judge.

"Of course," said the expert. "In my opinion, the materials I received are not sufficient to make a clear diagnosis. Nonetheless, there is one additional factor that does allow for an unequivocal opinion."

"And what's that?" interrupted the prosecutor, taking over the questioning.

"The defendant claims to have been of sound mind when he committed the crime," replied the woman confidently.

Joanna looked furiously at Rejchert. The prosecutor winked at her, which made her realise that it had all been set up expressly to raise her hopes, then dash them.

She swore silently. She knew she could have built a decent line of defence on the earlier statement. Could, past tense. The chance was gone forever. She was hamstrung, powerless to do anything. The psychiatrist had confirmed that Langer was insane, and Langer himself would soon confirm it too. She had no room to manoeuvre.

"Thank you, I have no more questions," declared a self-satisfied Rejchert, returning to his place.

"Counsel for the defence?" said the judge, looking at Chyłka sternly. Joanna cleared her throat and straightened her jacket. Slowly approaching the expert, she realised she only had one roll of the dice. She would have to use a ploy so embarrassingly crude, that the two judges now sending her urgent glances would never forget. The next time she met them in court she would be in a weaker position than the prosecution. But she could worry about that later.

"Counsellor?" urged the presiding judge.

Chyłka nodded and forced a smile. Then she turned her gaze to the forensic expert.

"How long have you practised psychiatry?" she asked.

"Fifteen years."

"How many criminals, or rather, potential criminals, have you worked with in that period?"

"I don't understand, how is that—"

"Please answer the questions unless they are overturned," said the second judge.

The psychiatrist thought for a moment.

"It's hard to say," she replied, looking out into the distance as if she was trying to reach the farthest recesses of her mind.

"Best estimate."

"Four, maybe five."

"And did the accused in any of these cases claim to be insane when in your opinion they were of sound mind?"

"Yes."

"I ask because it seems to me that it could also work the opposite way round."

"Your Honour," interrupted Rejchert, spreading his arms. "The counsel for the defence is expressing her opinion, while—"

"Please confine yourself to asking questions," said the presiding judge, giving Joanna a hostile look. She smiled at him again, radiantly this time, and turned back to the psychiatrist.

"Is what I have said possible?"

"Theoretically, yes."

"Your honour," interrupted the prosecutor again. "I request that the question be withdrawn. The forensic expert has been summoned to assess a particular case, not to speculate about abstract theories."

"Withdrawn!" confirmed the judge.

"Your Honour, this is an important matter for—"

"Please continue," interrupted the judge. "Do you have any further questions?"

Chyłka nodded.

"To be more specific: did my client believe he was of sound mind whereas in fact he was not?"

"I don't think so."

"But it is possible?"

"In my opinion, no, not in this particular case."

"Is it absolutely impossible that it could be the case?"

"Your Honour . . ." pleaded the prosecutor.

"Please allow the expert to answer the question, counsellor," growled the judge.

Kordian listened to all of this with mounting disappointment. He had expected a sophisticated legal battle, not a verbal brawl.

"Of course, it's possible, just like it's possible that one of us will be run over by a car when we leave this courtroom," screeched the psychiatrist.

In her mind, Chyłka chalked up a minor victory. The lay assessors took notice of such things, and if she could count on anyone in this trial, it would be the lay assessors. There wasn't even the slightest chance that the judges would think the defendant was innocent.

"Do such cases occur?"

"Your Honour . . ." Rejchert chimed in again, rising from his chair; but with a wave of his hand, the judge indicated he should sit back down. The question was no longer general, but concerned a specific case, therefore the judge could not withdraw it.

"Absolutely. Just like there are cases of Stockholm syndrome, where victims start defending their persecutors. But does that mean the persecutor is innocent?"

"Allow me to ask the questions please," said Chyłka, eyeing the expert. The psychiatrist pursed her lips and sniffed, looking disapprovingly towards the adjudicating panel. "Is it possible that my client's assertion of his own sanity was actually an argument for his insanity?"

"Your Honour, this is a complete—"

"Mr Rejchert," exclaimed the presiding judge, in a tone that left him in no doubt he was sailing too close to the wind. The prosecutor raised his hands in a gesture of apology and returned to his seat. He was annoying, but Chyłka had expected nothing else.

"So what's your verdict?" she asked, looking at the expert.

"I don't think so."

"Sorry?"

"I don't think that's the case here."

"Is that your *professional* opinion?" The lawyer stressed the penultimate word, looking at the lay assessors with disbelief. She saw that she had their attention. "You don't think . . . wait. Let me get this right. This man's fate rests on your expertise, and you say you only *think* he is sane?"

"No, no," protested the psychiatrist. "He is sane, only—"

"Only you can't say that in all certainty. Isn't that what you have just told us?"

"No, I . . ."

"So tell me, is it possible, from what we've heard today that he only thought that he was sane?"

"No, I don't . . ."

She'd tangled herself up in her own words. As an expert she was now worthless, so in that sense Joanna had won.

"Let me remind you that my client has not given us any details about the crime. Is that normal, since you *think* he was sane? Shouldn't he remember the crime, along with all the details? What do you *think*?"

Every word was pushing the expert closer to the edge. She looked increasingly uncomfortable on the podium and looked nervously around the public gallery, seeking help, before fixing her gaze on the adjudicating panel. But the panel was silent, as was the prosecutor, who could have requested the withdrawal of a question on at least two occasions. But he had taken too many liberties at the start and now had to bite his tongue.

"It seems to me that . . . yes, he should. He should remember. And in my opinion, only—"

"Only what?" interrupted Chyłka, watching the judges' reactions from the corner of her eye. "If Piotr Langer claims he does not suffer from mental illness, and has no psychosis or dementia, then surely he should be able to confirm this by recounting the details of the crime he has allegedly committed? Surely this would make his claim of sanity more credible?"

The courtroom fell silent. The expert worried that everyone would notice the beads of sweat on her forehead; she wanted to wipe them off, but stopped herself just in time. That wretched defence lawyer had twisted everything round and made her look like an idiot. Never again would she agree to do anything like this, no matter how much they paid her. This was the last time she would ever agree to appear in court as a forensic expert. To hell with this stress.

"So what do you think? Should he know the details?"

"Of course, if—"

"Then why didn't he share them with anyone?"

"Perhaps—"

"No, no, not 'perhaps,'" interrupted Chyłka, noticing the prosecutor preparing to make a strong objection that would probably end the hearing. Joanna knew she was pushing the court's patience to its limit, but on the other hand, the expert was embarrassing herself. "You were asked to provide a professional, expert opinion. But by using expressions such as 'perhaps' and 'I think,' you do not allow—"

"Your Honour, this is just ranting!" protested Rejchert.

"Counsellor," cut in the judge. "Please limit yourself to asking questions."

"I am only pointing out that phrases such as 'perhaps' can be used by anyone." She looked at Kordian, who straightened himself on his chair. "For instance, I could say that perhaps my trainee is of sound mind, and perhaps he isn't. Such is the diagnosis. Perhaps my client has an antisocial personality disorder which is manifested, for instance, by him trying to convince everyone that he was of sound mind at the time he committed the crime, when in fact this was not the case. Perhaps."

Oryński smiled slightly and looked at the lay assessors. They were hers; you could see it. Her attack was merciless, but she was not rude. This was what made a good defence lawyer.

Kordian recalled one of the many wisdoms of Piłsudski: hold the balance for as long as possible, and when you can't hold it any longer, set fire to the world. It was a perfect description of courtroom tactics; now he only had to wait for Chyłka to light the fire.

"Thank you, I have no more questions," Chyłka said.

She returned to her seat and gave the lay assessors a friendly smile. The way all three of them looked at her proved to Kordian he was right.

But Kordian was far from optimistic. He recalled an article he had read some time ago about court hearings like this, where the author had said that lay assessors were no more than courtroom decorations. There was a lot of truth in that.

Lay assessors were appointed by town councils, who habitually chose residents well past retirement age. These people just wanted to turn up, get paid and go back to their own lives. This was hardly surprising, because in Poland the trial-by-jury tradition was not very widely known. Even now, there were many Poles who didn't realise that ordinary citizens were invited to participate in some criminal trials.

After a while, Kordian concluded that it didn't matter anyway. They would still need a miracle to win the case.

19

THE HEARING DRAGGED on, hour after excruciating hour. At times Oryński felt like ripping his guts out before the court, just as Reytan ripped his robes in Matejko's *Fall of Poland*. The psychologist was far better prepared for the hearing than the expert in the dark art of psychiatry had been, and Joanna couldn't unsettle her. Kordian visualised their client on the edge of a precipice, about to topple into the abyss of prison. The end of the trial was in sight—and if Kordian knew it, Chyłka must have been all the more aware of the fact.

The second expert told the court emphatically that the accused was and had been perfectly sane, as much now as when he committed the crime. She was helped by Karol Rejchert, who graciously led her by the hand during questioning, and then returned to his place on the right side of the bench like the cat who'd got the cream.

"Counsellor?" asked the presiding judge, looking at Joanna.

Chyłka remained still, biting her lower lip. She could not think of a way to rattle the woman on the rostrum. With the screeching toad it had been easy, because it had been clear from the outset that she wanted to show the defendant was guilty at all costs. She had overplayed her hand and tripped up. But the psychologist was quite different. Her answers were intelligent and she presented arguments supporting both sides of the dispute, but ultimately put forward a well-informed, well-argued opinion that Langer was deliberately making a mockery of the justice system.

"Counsellor? Questions?"

"Yes, of course, Your Honour," replied Joanna, rising from her chair. She looked at the expert, and thought for a moment longer.

"Could we refer to your predecessor's statement?"

"I'd rather not do that," replied the psychologist. "I am not here to analyse courtroom tactics."

"I'm sorry, I don't understand."

"I am assessing the current mental state of the accused, and helping to determine his mental state when the crime was committed," she replied. "What happened at this hearing earlier, when my colleague was answering questions, is of no relevance."

Her tone was measured, her facial expressions mild; there was nothing for Chyłka to get hold of. She had to let that answer go.

"Very well . . ." she said. "To recap: your colleague said that she could not confirm beyond all doubt that my client was of sound mind. You say that he was definitely sane. Have I understood you correctly?"

"No," replied the expert with a friendly smile. "The psychologist's approach to establishing state of mind is not based on empirical evidence. I cannot state anything with absolute certainty, but—"

"Therefore—" Chyłka attempted to cut in.

"But every other person in this profession will give you the same answer. Unfortunately, such is the nature of my work as a forensic psychologist, Counsellor. This is not mathematics, where two plus two always equals four."

"And so—"

"And so, to the best of my knowledge, and according to all available materials and my personal meetings with the defendant, I can state that he was of sound mind at the time when the crime was committed."

Chyłka had to concede that someone had prepared the expert very well. "Witness prep" was an art form in the United States, and lawyers in Poland were also increasingly aware how witnesses and experts should speak to benefit their case.

In addition, the woman was likeable and she inspired trust. Chyłka would have given the world to have a man up there on the rostrum, because not even the sweetest old man would make such a good-natured impression on the courtroom as that bitch. It was hard to put her under pressure, and direct, full-force attacks were out of the question.

"So why won't my client say a word about what happened? If he remembered everything and was completely sane, then . . ."

"No, I did not say that he was completely sane."

Joanna fell silent. It was one of those moments when you realise that a seemingly trivial point is of fundamental importance. Chyłka knew that with that short sentence she had lost the case.

"In my opinion, at the time of committing the offence, the accused had a partial limitation of sanity."

The die was cast. This turned all that Chyłka had won from her clash with the psychiatrist into dust. Partial loss of sanity was a safety buffer

that allowed everything else to fall into place logically—the accused did
not talk about the crime because they were suffering from an abnormality
of mind. Not completely insane, but just insane enough.

It was the bane of the defence lawyer's life: a state that was insuffi-
cient to plead for an acquittal or a more lenient sentence. Only if it could
be proved that Langer's sanity had been *severely* limited could Joanna
hope to win anything.

Chyłka stood next to the rostrum, feverishly trying to think of a way
out, but eventually she had to accept she couldn't think of anything. The
judges basically had carte blanche from the psychologist, and could do
whatever they pleased.

"Counsellor?" said one of the lay assessors, drawing the attention of
the other panel members. Lay assessors rarely spoke—most often they
simply waited quietly for the trial to end.

There was no point in asking the expert whether she was sure of her
assessment. She would repeat over and over again that nothing in psychology can be certain, and that psychology assessments always entail a
degree of uncertainty.

So she simply said thank you, and returned to her place.

Kordian passed her a card on which he had written "game over." She
nodded.

The presiding judge now called the witnesses. These were mainly
people who knew the victims and testified as to the circumstances, and
as to whether Langer knew the victims and whether they could have
provoked him in any way. What the witnesses said bore no relevance to
either party, but they were there to appeal to the lay judges' emotional
responses, which indeed they did. One woman even shed a few tears.

Just an hour and a half later, the presiding judge closed the proceedings, no doubt breaking a speed record. Langer Senior had wanted a swift
trial, and he got it.

After the closing statements, the presiding judge listened wearily to
the prosecutor, then turned to Chyłka. She knew that even her greatest
oratory skills would not work here, but she had to try.

"Your Honour," she began. "We have listened to all the experts and
witnesses, and we have considered their opinions, some very professional,
others less so. But throughout this process of determining the objective
truth—for that is the purpose of the trial—we have not heard from my
client. Apart from his answer at the start of the proceedings, he has not
uttered a single word. He does not claim to be innocent, but neither does
he claim to be guilty. He has not pleaded guilty to these charges, but if
the court wished him to make a clear statement to say whether or not he
has committed the crime of which he stands accused, he would not give
one. He would remain silent.

The presiding judge stifled a yawn. The other judge looked at Joanna with mild interest. The lay assessors seemed to absorb every word.

"I have tried to get information from him myself. Anything," she continued. "However, it's almost impossible to interact with him in any meaningful way. He talks in allegories—complete chaos and nonsense. He insists he is sane, but at the same time he denies his guilt. What does that tell us? In my opinion, he is, in some way, deeply disturbed. The psychiatrist and psychologist are unable to diagnose the exact cause, but I believe that this very fact should lead us to conclude that there is reasonable doubt as to his guilt."

She continued for a few more minutes. Kordian wasn't listening particularly hard, because he had already read the text on a computer printout. Morally and logically, it was quite a decent speech. But from a legal point of view, it did not look so good. The only chance of an acquittal would be if he were declared insane. A disturbed psyche, limited capacity, and momentary loss of control were not enough to help Langer.

As the judges left the courtroom to consider the verdict, the two defence lawyers were not optimistic.

"We would win the case if the lay assessors were the ones deciding," Kordian whispered into Joanna's ear.

"Zordon," she replied. "If we had a common law system here, I'd be so fierce that every prosecutor would withdraw from a case as soon as they heard I'd be the one defending."

Oryński nodded, sorry that fate had not allowed them to practise law in a more flexible system. Here, the panel could only rule on the basis of fixed statutory laws. They were fettered. Today's clash could only have one outcome.

"The judgement of this court in the name of the Republic of Poland is that the accused Piotr Langer, son of Piotr and Katarzyna née Gaszewska, born on the twelfth of July in the year one thousand nine hundred and seventy-eight, is guilty as charged. He is hereby sentenced to life imprisonment, and may be eligible for parole after twenty-five years."

20

That day, Chyłka and Kordian stayed in the office longer than anyone else. Neither knew what good going over a lost case would do, but both were delving into volume after volume of case files.

"When can we expect legal justification of the verdict?" asked the trainee, during a brief break.

If they were going to burn the candle at both ends, they should really have done it before the trial rather than after, but this was their way of reacting to the sheer helplessness they felt, and would never forget. "Any day now."

"And what shall we do about it?"

"What do you have in mind?" asked Chyłka, then realised what he was asking. "Ah," she said, nodding. "Nothing, Zordon. We'll stick to the psychiatric-psychological line that has brought us this far."

She paused, pursing her lips, and for a moment it seemed that she would contain her anger. But only for a moment.

"Fuck it!" she shouted, picking up the files on her desk and throwing them all in the air. Sheets of paper fluttered across the room and landed on the floor. Some landed in Kordian's lap.

There was a moment of silence.

"At least everything's in its place now," commented the trainee.

"You're right there."

"So we're going to ignore what Langer Senior wants?" he asked hopefully. "We're going for victory?"

"Forget Langer Senior," replied Joanna. "And damn it, if they threaten to disbar me, we'll get through it somehow. The chief problem is Żelazny, he'd fling us out without a second thought."

"We'll go somewhere else."

Chyłka glowered at him, then chuckled. "You think we've bonded so much we can make our exodus together? Maybe we can set up on our own? No, wait, we should tie the knot first, then you can take my name and the sign could read 'Chyłka & Chyłka.' What do you think?"

"Sounds good."

"Get serious, Zordon. Whatever fantasies you have in your empty head, it'll never happen. Not even the dramatic scene where we drop everything and leave the Skylight never to come back."

"Pity," said Oryński. "But I have plenty more images in my head, including ones that have nothing to do with law."

"Castles, dungeons, chains, BDSM, love triangles? No, thanks."

The young man drummed his fingertips on the desk.

"I meant what I said earlier," he said.

"What?"

"Stuff what Żelazny wants, and then maybe—"

"You stuff Old Rusty and you're done for," she interrupted. "No law firm would ever take you on, and if by some miracle you set up your own, you won't have access to any of the courtrooms. You know how it works. Everyone seems to be in competition with everybody else and they fight tooth and nail, but when push comes to shove, they stick together. It's the solidarity of the wolf pack. No one will allow the name of a partner to be besmirched by a mere trainee. They'll bring you down, and me with you."

"That spurs me on even more."

She shook her head. "Give me a break, Zordon. I haven't got the strength for any more banter. And what are you still doing here anyway, damn it? It's almost midnight."

Kordian turned the clock on her desk to face him. Then he got up, went to the door and stepped out into the corridor. The only light came from a small LED motion-sensor lamp at floor level. The rest of the corridor was in total darkness, the silence broken only by the murmur of the air conditioning. Oryński stepped back into the office and returned to his seat.

"We're alone," he declared.

"I already told you, it'll never happen."

"I'm only saying."

She looked at him pityingly. "You're ten years too young for me, five kilograms too heavy and . . ." she paused, grimacing, "infinitely too ugly."

"Anything else?"

"You don't eat meat. A real man has a hunter's instinct."

"I can hunt down a killer bargain at Subway."

She couldn't help smiling.

"And I'm not even a kilogram overweight. It's all muscle."

"Sure. Try your luck with Kormak," she advised.

"One day you'll appreciate me."

"It's not that I'd turn down a younger guy," she said. "If he had the right level of intellect."

"You're being exceptionally nice today. Even by your standards."

"And you seem exceptionally eager to make a pass at me, even by your standards."

She stood up and went to the window. With her hands on the window frame, she watched the rivers of red and white lights flowing along Emilia Plater Street and Jerusalem Avenue. The million-dollar question was, where were all those people heading at that time of night? At ten in the evening, it would be understandable, at eleven less so, but between midnight and one in the morning? One or two cars wouldn't surprise her, but these endless columns?

"Romantic, isn't it?" came a hoarse whisper.

Chyłka shook her head. "Sod off home, Zordon."

"I tried so hard, and I won't even—"

"Go away!" she ordered, turning to face him.

She was smiling, so his mission had been half successful, as he'd clearly cheered his boss up. Having sadly said his goodbyes, he went out into the corridor, where the motion sensors immediately lit up like an airport runway.

In the lift, Kordian realised that by cheering Chyłka up he had also cheered himself up. Standing outside the Palace of Culture and Science he took out his phone to check the time: twenty-five past twelve. The worst possible moment to leave, as the night bus left the station at quarter past and quarter to the hour.

He didn't want to spend money on a taxi—he wasn't in any hurry. If there had been a case waiting for him the next day, he'd have needed to get some sleep, but as it was, he could just as well get to bed in the early hours.

He did have certain obligations, he knew. The firm assigned minor cases to people like him as part of their training. The rejects always ended up at the bottom of the food chain. The main objective was to get the case through its first hearing with the least effort. Any second hearing would be taken over by a more experienced lawyer.

"Zordon? Too scared to go home?"

Oryński turned round to see Chyłka leaving the building and straightening her jacket.

"Want me to hold your hand?"

"You could give me a lift in that charabanc of yours."

"Mind your language!" she retorted. "My BMW X5 has as much in common with a charabanc as you have with a Calvin Klein model."

"I'll turn a blind eye to your snide comments, as I'm counting on that lift," he said, as they neared her car.

"Pity," responded Joanna. "I like a good verbal scuffle."

"I'd never have guessed."

Soon they were driving towards the Warsaw district of Żoliborz, still having digs at each other, and studiously avoiding any talk of Langer. Every subject was fair game, and the conversation never faltered. Oryński felt their conversation was getting less and less strained, which made his heart beat faster.

So somewhere in the region of Słomiński Street he suddenly asked, "Why don't you come in for a beer?"

There was an awkward silence; all the ease of the previous few minutes was gone. Oryński was angry at himself. He hadn't planned to invite her. On the other hand, he hadn't intended anything improper. It had been going well, and they weren't feeling tired. What harm could there be in just a beer—or two or three?

"It's just a casual suggestion," he added after a while.

"Too casual."

He was surprised by the seriousness of her tone.

"Don't make it something it's not," he said, wondering if he was only making the situation worse. "Can't a mentor have a drink with her mentee?"

"Maybe, but fortunately she doesn't have to."

She turned to him with a smile.

"Where to now?" she asked, as they drove into Wilson Square.

Kordian pointed to the right exit, and soon after the BMW stopped in front of an old tenement house in Mickiewicz Street. It looked shabby, even at night, and the balconies appeared to be on the point of collapse. "You live here, Zordon? Where have you brought me? Do you want someone to murder me on the staircase?"

"Don't exaggerate. This isn't east bank Praga."

"I'd rather go into a dark Praga backyard than into one of those awful places," she replied. "I must get Żelazny to raise your salary. How much do they pay you?"

"A thousand."

"A week?"

"A month."

"What?"

"A thousand a month, after tax."

"You get a thousand net a month?"

"Yes." Then clearing his throat, "Are you coming or not? We can have a beer and a laugh."

"No," she replied. "Goodbye and good luck. Hope no one stabs you on the way up. Though that salary . . . damn it. And you agreed to it?"

"Some people I know do the same thing for seven hundred. And I work for Żelazny & McVay, so that's something, right?"

"Go, Zordon, go and get some sleep," she said, shaking her head.

The young man left the BMW, and Joanna waited, looking at the dingy buildings. She wondered whether she was right not to go for that beer. Most probably yes, because she would have had to leave the X5 there and get a taxi home. But the nagging sense of frustration persisted.

Chyłka shifted into first gear and drove off towards Wilson Square. Halfway home she regretted she hadn't taken up his offer; but it was too late to turn back now.

C H A P T E R

21

CHYŁKA RETURNED THE favour a few months later by inviting Kordian to her flat after they lost the Piotr Langer appeal.

Their appeal had been based on the grounds of disproportionate punishment—essentially hopeless, but which would nonetheless have given them the greatest chance of success. If it had been up to Joanna, she would have appealed against everything that happened in the first hearing. Langer Senior and Żelazny, however, were adamant, insisting they should stick with their strategy.

So there was nothing they could do but argue that since Piotr was not of sound mind when committing the crime, he should have received a lighter sentence than life imprisonment. This did not convince the Court of Appeal, which upheld the original decision.

Chyłka had invited Kordian to her place on a whim. But they had hardly left the Golden Terraces car park when she started regretting her decision. Not that anything would happen between them—they were both sensible—but this was still a mentor–mentee relationship, and should not be taken out of the office or cross professional boundaries.

And under no circumstances should it develop into a friendship. Besides, in all likelihood, Chyłka would be the one to hand Oryński his notice. He was a bright guy and had all the makings of becoming a good defence lawyer, but Żelazny could not picture him in the firm. For the time being, he was still on probation, trying to prove his worth, but Joanna knew Old Rusty well enough to know when he wasn't kidding. Zordon was earmarked to go. It was just a matter of time.

She would still be his mentor, but their contacts would be limited to occasional meetings, and the atmosphere would be glacial.

And yet here they were, entering her flat.

"I wonder how many other men have seen this place?" asked Oryński as she opened the door.

"Not many. I deal with most of my victims outside the home."

Kordian looked around the tastefully furnished apartment. The décor was predominantly pastel, and the furniture and appliances clearly belonged to someone who didn't have money troubles.

"Make yourself at home, but not too much."

"Thanks."

"You can even switch on the TV."

"You're very gracious today," replied Kordian, sitting down on the couch. It was as hard as a rock.

Chyłka disappeared for a moment, while Oryński tried to make himself comfortable. He felt uneasy, too scared to touch anything. Eventually he picked up the remote control and switched on TVN.

"Seventy inches," said Chyłka, handing her guest a bottle of beer. Glasses were clearly unheard of in this abode. "Refresh rate of three thousand hertz, active shutter 3D system and LED, of course."

"I don't understand any of that, but I can see this is the TV equivalent of a Porsche."

"More or less," replied Joanna, clinking her glass bottle against his.

He rarely drank Beck's, not wanting to spend money on beer that tasted similar to other beers on the market but which was two or three times more expensive. However, as he took the first sip, he felt he had died and gone to heaven.

"The king will be here soon."

"Who?" he asked, looking at the door.

Chyłka frowned, pointed to the TV screen and sat down next to him. "The king of TVN. Wojewódzki."

"You watch Wojewódzki?" he asked in disbelief.

"You mean you don't?"

Kordian smiled warily and took another sip. Very soon he would cut down on or give up smoking, and spend the money he saved on better beer. A game of squash at least once a week. It was time to think about it seriously. They didn't talk about the lost appeal. And once they had settled into the uncomfortable but visually impressive couch, they didn't talk at all. Joanna switched to TVN24 and for several minutes they watched political talking heads, and then a report about yet more violence in north Africa. The last item was a story about the Kendallville hecatomb, but it didn't especially interest them. Then suddenly, the screen switched to an unexpectedly familiar sight—a famous building in Krasiński Square.

Sixty-seven columns bearing legal maxims, numerous architectural allusions to the Warsaw Uprising and the glass skyway: an image that could not be mistaken for anything else. The Supreme Court building. And then, two lawyers appeared on the screen, lawyers from Żelazny & McVay.

"You stoop," commented Joanna and tilted the bottle.

"Perhaps, a little," replied Oryński, thinking he should increase his drinking pace. So far he had been savouring the flavour of Beck's, but clearly this session was more about knocking it back than tasting. "While you are a fine-looking woman. But you walk as if you had a broomstick up your backside."

"At least I look good. Look at you. A goblin."

They disappeared from the screen, and were replaced by a reporter standing in front of the courthouse.

"Piotr L's defence claimed that his sentence was too harsh. Their chief argument was that according to the expert psychologist, the accused was only partially sane when he committed the crime, and not completely sane as the prosecution had claimed. The Appeal Court, however, upheld the rulings of the court of the first instance."

The reporter continued for a while longer, boring her viewers with insignificant details. Things only got interesting when they switched to a broadcast of Joanna just after she left the court building. The first thing she did was glare at one of the reporters who had been trashing Langer for the past two weeks; she then delivered a brief but resolute speech:

"The forensic expert confirmed that my client was only partially sane at the time of the crime. In accordance with article thirty, paragraph two of the Criminal Code, the court may in such circumstances apply a lighter sentence, even a much lighter one." She paused meaningfully, looking straight at the camera. "This means that in such circumstances, the judge may impose a sentence *below* what's stipulated in the Act. In my client's case, the lowest sentence is twelve years. So it seems to me that we all know what happened today. Thank you."

"Counsellor!"

"Is Piotr L going to . . ."

"Counsellor, do . . ."

"How do you . . ."

"Thank you," repeated Chyłka without a trace of a smile, then pushed her way through the throng of reporters with the skilful efficiency she had mastered in the office corridor. The journalists swiftly turned their attention to the prosecutor, who was standing nearby. Rejchert was beaming as if he had just won the lottery.

"Now he'll start talking about exceptional brutality and minor insanity," muttered Joanna under her breath. They didn't hear what the prosecutor said, but they didn't have to. She changed the channel.

"Chyłka . . ." started Oryński and paused, looking away from the screen.

"What?" she asked, rising from the couch. "I'm going to fetch refills. Though really that's something you should be doing."

"I'm the guest."

"You're my gofer, Zordon," she replied. "That's more important."

She returned with two bottles of Beck's, frozen almost solid.

"What did you want to say, yuppie? Now's the time, because when the king of TVN starts, you'll only be allowed to speak during the commercial breaks."

"Yuppie implies I've got a good job and earn a fortune."

"OK, I'm sorry," she replied, again clinking her bottle against his. "So you wanted to ask me a question?"

He turned to face her, putting his arm over the back rest, and asked, "What do you think about all this?"

"What should I think?" she replied, also turning to face him. Still looking at him, she reached for her Marlboros. "We weren't beaten by the prosecutor; we were beaten by our own boss and our own client. That's the long and short of it."

"I meant the ruling," said Kordian. "The way I see it, the statement you made in front of the cameras hit the nail on the head. The ruling is clearly unjust."

"It's all theatre, Zordon," she said, lighting a cigarette.

He did the same, placing the ashtray on the couch between them. "But there is something in it," he objected. "Langer should get twenty-five years at most. Even if he was completely *compos mentis,* he shouldn't get life."

"You're telling me."

"I am, but I'd prefer to tell it to a higher court."

"Great, but you should know that a ruling in the Court of Appeal ends the case. There are no further chances."

"Oh, you know what I mean. Don't nitpick."

"You're my protégé, so express yourself as my protégé should. And formulate some good ideas, not just nonsense," she advised, blowing smoke almost into his face. "Perhaps we should drag this case to the European Court of Justice in Luxembourg?"

"It'd be more useful to take it to the International Criminal Court in The Hague," Oryński replied. "That judge is really off his . . ."

"Hey," admonished Chyłka. "Remember that bit of paper you signed, the one someone inadvertently called the Code of Ethics?"

"I don't give a toss about codes of ethics. Someone's been steering this case from the start."

Joanna was silent for a moment or two. They still sat facing each other, puffing away at their cigarettes.

"Be careful, Kordian," she said eventually. "Such talk could ruin your career."

"Surely I don't need to watch what I say to you?"

"If I teach you anything in this farce we call a traineeship, let it be this: for pity's sake, don't trust anyone in the profession. There are plenty who will want to trip you up, and activating the recording function on your phone is hardly an unattainable technological innovation, is it?"

"You're paranoid."

Chyłka raised her eyebrows and nodded with satisfaction.

"So what are we going to do about it?" he asked.

"Nothing."

"But there is a way, and it . . ."

"Langer Senior does not want to take it any further," she cut in. "And Piotr . . . well, you saw him yourself. He still looks as if he couldn't care less. The whole family is a bunch of nut jobs."

"Either that or they're up to something."

"Sure, Mr Conspiracy Theorist."

Oryński shrugged his shoulders. They stubbed out their cigarettes, and he made to put the ashtray back on the coffee table. But as he held it over the glass surface, he suddenly froze, feeling the blood drain from his face.

"Breaking news," said the newsreader, who had been reporting on the eternal problem of tailbacks on Polish roads. "As you can see on our news ticker, we've just heard that famous businessman Piotr Langer has been found dead in his apartment. We have no further details as yet, but the National Police Headquarters will be making a statement in the next hour." The reporter paused, then dramatically changed his tone of voice. "Let us remind you that today a verdict was passed in the case of millionaire Piotr Langer's son, who has been convicted of murder with exceptional brutality."

Still holding the ashtray over the coffee table, Oryński turned to look at Chyłka.

"Holy shit," is all she said.

Both now had their eyes glued to the TV. That evening, Wojewódzki would have to wait.

"Rumour has it he committed suicide. In recent days, Piotr Langer is thought to have stayed at his apartment in Sopot, where a cleaner found his body an hour ago," continued the reporter. "However, this has not been officially confirmed. We'll let you know as soon as we have more details."

They showed the studio, where no doubt pandemonium reigned behind the cameras, and reporters were frantically phoning anyone who could shed light on the case. Soon Żelazny & McVay's phones would also start ringing.

The media must have known that they had struck pay dirt. Viewers couldn't get enough of the Piotr Langer case, and this development should keep viewing figures up for several weeks to come.

"I don't want any conspiracy theories from you," said Chyłka.

"You won't get any, because I haven't got any," replied Kordian, staring at the reporter now calmly reading her autocue. "There's nothing to say, we have to rely on our intuition."

Joanna remained silent.

"That guy had enough money set aside to ensure even his great-grandchildren would live the high life. If someone like that decides to take their own life, the rest of us should be jumping head first off the Marriott."

Chyłka took the remote control and switched to TVN. She would be seeing the king in her apartment that evening after all. And only when his presence on the screen was replaced with washing powders and candy bars did Oryński speak.

"Do you know what's preying on my mind? Apart from the obvious?"

"Yes," she replied. "Piotr Langer Junior will be paying our bills now."

"Who is now the one and only Piotr Langer, so the distinction is unnecessary," said Kordian, looking expectantly at Joanna.

"Let's watch the show to the end, then we'll get down to work."

Oryński didn't ask what work she had in mind; there could only be one option. To file a cassation appeal at the Supreme Court.

PART 2

CHAPTER

1

The Grey-Haired Man stared at the TV screen with rapt attention. It showed a lawyer standing outside the Skylight building, looking as if she was about to announce a ground-breaking discovery. She had organised a press conference just a week after the death of Langer Senior, although by rights a cassation appeal could be filed up to thirty days after the justification of the Court of Appeal's verdict was published. She could have waited until the very last moment, the Grey-Haired Man thought. The effect would have been greater. And she could have skipped the whole media circus thing; the more she left unsaid, the better it was for her.

"She annoys me," he announced looking away from the TV screen.

"Chyłka?" asked the Bald Man in a suit.

The Grey-Haired Man looked at him with disdain. "Who else?"

Chyłka had just announced that her firm would be filing a cassation appeal with the Supreme Court. With all the TV station cameras assembled outside the Palace of Culture and Science, it was beginning to look like another news media soap opera. The Bald Man clearly agreed.

"This'll be headline stuff."

The Grey-Haired Man nodded almost imperceptibly.

"Of the "Magda from Sosnowiec" or "royal baby" kind. Or the 'young would-be poet who stabbed her boyfriend's family to death.' You know, sir?"

"Yes, I do."

He sometimes wondered whether it was public demand that drove TV stations to cover sensationalist topics or whether the media recognised which stories would attract an audience and ran them in anticipation.

Maybe it was the latter. The media created the reality. Disgusting really, a covert method of manipulation. The Grey-Haired Man preferred simpler tools.

With the Langer case, the media had so far played their hand well. They had reported what needed to be reported, and none of the journalists were too meticulous in their research. And even if they were, the Grey-Haired Man with the neatly trimmed beard could feel safe: there was nothing that could lead them to him.

Not that it meant everything was going his way.

"I was assured it wouldn't come to a cassation appeal," he said.

The Bald Man was silent. He knew he wouldn't be able to influence any of the Supreme Court judges. There, matters could take an unexpected turn.

The Grey-Haired Man poured himself a glass of Old Smuggler, took a sip, and looked at his colleague expectantly.

"I did everything I could to—"

"I'm not interested in the process," cut in the Grey-Haired Man. "Only the result."

"Of course, I understand."

The Bald Man feared another reprimand, but his boss's attention was on Chyłka again. She was in full swing, effusing about how it was in the public interest to file cassation appeals. The Bald Man understood little of it, and assumed he was not the only one. The lawyer wasn't doing this to educate the public—she was doing it to show she knew her stuff.

"This is just PR," said the Bald Man. "She's organised a press conference as if she was running for—"

"She's trying to put pressure on the media," said a third man, a lawyer, seated by the wall some distance from the other two. "She knows she needs the public's support, because so far the client is being perceived as another Breivik or even Hitler. Everyone is interested in the case, either to see just how deep the barrel of shit is that he's fallen into, or to find out why he did it. No one is on his side, except perhaps a few complete psychopaths."

"The Supreme Court won't be interested," the Bald Man retorted.

"The Supreme Court is only interested in the Constitution and the Supreme Court Act," said the lawyer. "But it's presided over by people who are often in tune with the public mood. If there's outrage against China over Tibet, they—"

"I'm not listening to this," cut in the Grey-Haired Man.

His two guests fell silent, and he took another sip of whisky. The lawyer's presence irritated him. Until now, the Grey-Haired Man had assumed his own knowledge of the law and criminal proceedings would be enough, but now that the case had gone further, they had to take the appropriate action.

"I'm only saying they're not completely impervious to the world out-side," said the lawyer at length. "Although there's obviously the question of judicial independence. . . ."

"I said, enough."

"Of course."

"All I want from you is hard facts," said the old man, looking at the lawyer. And then turning to the Bald Man, "I need you to shadow that pair. Clear?"

Both men nodded.

The Grey-Haired Man sighed and opened the drawer of his desk. He looked at the soya dessert, grimaced, and slid the drawer back.

"And if I ever want to hear your opinions about the level of public debate or the standards of those governing the world today, I'll let you know."

The Bald Man suddenly wanted the meeting to be over. The woman who was to be his mark was still showing off in front of the cameras, and his boss was becoming increasingly tetchy.

"Take all precautions," added the Grey-Haired Man.

"Of course."

"And make sure you don't interact with these people. Other than in the circumstances I mentioned earlier."

"I understand."

The bald muscleman had no doubt that if he didn't do as he was told, the results would be tragic—for him. The Grey-Haired Man liked to have people buried in the Kampinos National Park to the north-west of Warsaw; not in Palmiry, because that had a sacred mean-ing for him. But best of all, he liked the forests out towards Bieliny, whose extensive woodlands included a former military training ground dating back around fifty years. There were plenty of good spots to bury a body.

"And make sure you behave appropriately," added the Grey-Haired Man. "Remember, you're my representative in the city."

The Bald Man felt his boss's heavy gaze bearing down on him. For-tunately, the Grey-Haired Man switched his attention to the lawyer.

"And you, tell me what you know," he commanded.

The lawyer cleared his throat.

"For now, they don't know much," he replied dutifully. "First they have to find a good reason to file for cassation. They can't just appeal against a judgement because they don't like it."

"So what will they do?"

"Either they'll argue that there was a gross violation of the law, or they'll search through the absolute grounds for allowing a cassation appeal until they find something they can use."

The Grey-Haired Man was still looking at him expectantly, so the lawyer felt obliged to explain. "There has been no gross violation of the law, so that would be shooting themselves in the foot. That leaves absolute grounds for appeal."

"Which means?" interrupted the Bald Man, beginning to get irritated. "In language ordinary mortals will understand?"

The lawyer shifted in his chair. "It's a fairly narrow range of criteria," he began. "For example, the case of *iudex inhabilis,* that is, when the judge has no right to adjudicate. The list also includes inappropriate adjudicating panel, incorrect jurisdiction, a penalty not prescribed by the law, the lack of a lay judge's signature on the verdict, a contradiction in the judgement, the absence of the accused, the absence of an attorney and similar technical issues. Generally, they have to be pretty major grounds, because cassation is an extraordinary remedy. The last resort against injustice."

"Do they have grounds or don't they?" asked the Grey-Haired Man, getting out of his chair and turning his back to the TV screen. Chyłka had just finished her long monologue, with which she hoped to show her client as a victim and not the perpetrator.

"In my opinion, they don't. Chyłka is sounding off about the sentence being disproportionate to the seriousness of the crime, but that in itself is not grounds for a cassation appeal. It would be rejected out of hand."

"Perhaps they have new evidence?"

"Even if they do, it won't be enough," replied the lawyer. "Also, questioning the grounds of an earlier judgement cannot justify cassation. Only the grounds stated in the list I just gave you can be considered."

"So there's nothing to worry about?"

"On the contrary. If a top law firm says it will file a cassation appeal, it means they probably have a plan of exactly how they'll get it to the Supreme Court."

2

KORDIAN CLOSED THE door to Joanna's office behind him and looked at her questioningly.

"Well?" he said.

"Well, what?"

"What's your plan?"

"I don't have one."

Oryński shook his head, not really surprised. For all his boss's fiery announcements in front of the cameras, he couldn't see any grounds to instigate an extraordinary appeal. Now that they had a free hand and were able to act without any constraints, the law had deprived them of the tools to do so. Meanwhile, the shopkeeper and Agnieszka Powirska were waiting to give their statements at a hearing.

"Well, perhaps a request to reopen the trial?"

"Are you mad? Straight after the case has been closed? Do you want to piss off the whole of the Polish legal establishment?"

He shrugged his shoulders.

"Every judge would curse us, and academics would write articles and treatises on the absurdity of introducing something like this to the justice system," she said, then paused. "Although actually, at least that would bring us before the Supreme Court; but then we'd have to prove a gross violation during the trial or present new facts or evidence. Unless you happen to have a Constitutional Tribunal ruling annulling the basis on which Langer was convicted?"

"Nothing to hand," muttered Kordian, sitting down at Chyłka's desk and lighting a cigarette. "But since you've announced the cassation so publicly, we'd better put something together."

"Yup."

"Does Żelazny know?"

"Not yet. Unless he watched TVN24," replied Joanna with a sheepish smile. "We wouldn't have got far, comrade, if I'd told him."

"Well, I'll be damned."

"Yes, I know, I'll be flung out on my ear, and you too," she said, sitting down in the armchair and watching Oryński smoke nervously. He must have realised that after the press conference they'd just given, his career was hanging in the balance. But what he didn't know was that he'd be asked to leave Żelazny & McVay regardless.

When her phone rang and she heard the guitar solo from "Afraid to Shoot Strangers," Chyłka knew she was facing an imminent reprimand. She glanced at the display and then turned the phone round to show Oryński.

"Old Rusty," he read.

"In person."

Joanna swiped the display and listened to the tirade in silence. She waited for the first wave of rage to subside, and then waited a little longer.

"Chyłka? Are you there?!" asked Artur Żelazny. "I'm driving to Warsaw now, do you hear? Once I get to the office, I won't make life easy for you. Do you understand me?"

Chyłka remained silent. She knew that anything she said now would be to her disadvantage. Żelazny was level-headed enough to realise that the artillery he was using was much too heavy.

"What got into you?" he asked.

"I believe my client is innocent."

"I don't give a shit!" roared her boss, so loudly that even Kordian heard easily. "You're not a child, for fuck's sake. What's innocence got to do with anything? You didn't manage to defend him, and now . . ."

Chyłka put the mobile on her desk and switched it to speaker.

"I didn't defend him because you and Langer Senior wouldn't let me use my trump card," she replied. "Now Piotr Junior has inherited everything, including the funds he'll most likely use to pay our fees. In case you're interested, I've checked, and his father didn't leave a will. His son is the only heir. You should be pleased, because you'll get an injection of cash and win the case."

"Bullshit!" Żelazny roared. "You're compromising the whole fucking firm! We're becoming a laughing stock. No, we already are one!"

Joanna fell silent again. She knew Żelazny well enough to let him talk until his anger blew itself out and he was calm again.

"All those years I've been building our reputation, for you to . . . How could you, Chyłka? How could you? Have you completely lost your mind? Can you explain it to me?"

"I have explained it."

"No!" he roared, then muttered something under his breath. "You've told me a load of crap, something I'd expect from your trainee, but not from you! Maybe he can afford to be naive, but you? You're a hard-headed bitch who—"

"And you're a limp dick," she shouted, and hung up.

She put the phone away and looked at Oryński. A smile spread slowly over her face.

"Think twice before you say anything," she warned.

"Nothing comes to mind."

"Good. Now take a copy of Waltoś and get out of here," said Joanna, pointing to the bookcase. Waltoś's *Criminal Procedure* was available in four editions: psychedelic purple, green, yellow, and most recently, a rather subdued navy blue. Every Polish law student was familiar with one of these covers.

"A hefty tome devoted to the cassation process would be better," grumbled Kordian.

"Later. First Waltoś."

"I've got no time for his twisted legal shenanigans."

Chyłka just looked at him. "Don't be silly, Waltoś is a serious scholar," she said. "Radwański, now that's another matter. I don't know if you know, but instead of writing 'editing text,' he wrote about 'a paralinguistic means of expression, involving organised written communication with graphic symbols on a two-dimensional plane.'"

Kordian shook his head. "You know that by heart?"

"We used to repeat it at every student party. It's the only thing I remember from civil proceedings."

"That's still quite a lot for a criminal lawyer."

"Hold on, I remember something else, also Radwański, I think: "Civil law does not formulate rules for conventional activities purely for the sake of intellectual gamesmanship."

Oryński pretended to look impressed.

"On the other hand, as far as the Langer case is concerned, criminal law abounds with intellectual gamesmanship," he said.

"Exactly," she agreed. "So take Waltoś and get to work."

"People are writing their PhDs on cassation, there are articles. . . ."

"Waltoś."

"I read him at university, Chyłka."

"And this time you'll not only read it, you'll understand it. Then, and only then, if you find anything useful, go for it," she said. "What's the time?"

"One o'clock."

"Excellent. See you at the Hard Rock Cafe at eight, and you'd better have prepared a concise but wide range of options. And print it out, because I'm not about to spend time deciphering your scribbles."

"Sure," he replied. "Seven hours of research, during which—"

"Zordon," she warned, looking pointedly at the door.

"OK, OK," he said getting up from his chair.

"Treat it as an intellectual game."

Without another word he took the book and marched out of the office. Heading for the newbie-burrow, he jostled his way through an ever-thicker throng of lawyers. In his cubicle, he wished he was back in Chyłka's office, where the silence was blissful and the noise from the corridor was only a muffled murmur.

He sat for a while trying to read the first paragraph of Waltoś, but came to the conclusion it was pointless. He was barred from Chyłka's office, but there was still one relatively quiet place from which he wouldn't be unceremoniously thrown out.

Minutes later he was standing outside Kormak's door. He knocked once, twice, three times. Only after the fourth knock did his skinny, bespectacled friend hesitantly open the door.

"Sorry," he said. "I wasn't expecting anyone today."

It was as if someone had come uninvited to his house, not to an office in a busy workplace. Not waiting to be asked in, and ignoring Kormak's protests, Kordian entered the room.

"I need some peace and quiet for research," explained Oryński.

"Well you won't find it here."

The trainee sat on a chair and simply shrugged his shoulders, and his host had no option but to put up with his uninvited guest.

It was not the most fruitful several hours spent in the history of the Polish bar, but by eight o'clock Oryński had managed to gather some useful information, and had hit upon a few good ideas that could help with the Piotr Langer case.

THE BALD MAN ordered a sumptuous dinner at Bistro Trójka on the second floor of the Palace of Culture and Science. The carpet under his feet reminded him of the one he'd had in his former flat in a housing block, although the restaurant itself looked exclusive enough. The carpet was probably exclusive too—it just *looked* as if it had come from some old welfare housing development.

He ordered a forty zloty starter without baulking. The Grey-Haired Man paid him well enough to dine in expensive places, even the Rondo Royal. And it was only going to get better. The more those two lawyers snooped, the greater the probability of a steep rise in his earnings. They'd reach their peak the moment his boss gave him the go-ahead to start operations.

How many people had he killed? He had no idea. He didn't count his victims; he didn't remember their faces. More often than not they were anonymous individuals whom he only saw for a moment; sometimes he didn't even make eye contact. If he could claim a speciality, it was making "accidents" happen. It didn't take much to make a car fail just when you needed it to; all you needed was a knack for mechanics, some experience in car maintenance and a good dose of inventiveness. People like Chyłka handed him everything on a plate. They parked their cars in accessible places and left them completely unattended, sometimes for twelve hours at a time. You could do anything you wanted then.

He never had to worry that his handiwork would be discovered. In a country where more than a dozen people died on the roads every day, it was easy to hide your victim in among the statistics.

If the Bald Man were to decide a car accident was the right solution to his current problem, the young man could be an issue, as he didn't have a car. He'd have to wait until both he and his lawyer boss got into that X5, or arrange an alternative "random accident." The boy spent very long hours at work every day; something bad could easily happen to him on the way to the bus stop.

Today, the Bald Man decided he'd give the trainee a taste of what was to come, and the boy would find out what it is like to be caught in the crosshairs.

His boss had stressed that he wasn't to overdo it: he definitely wasn't to kill him. They didn't need the police involved at this stage.

The Bald Man paid the bill and left a large tip. If the worse came to the worst, he would dispose of the body, and it wouldn't even cross anyone's mind that a murder had been committed.

CHAPTER

4

Sitting in the Hard Rock Cafe at the foot of the city's Skylight massif, Kordian doubted he'd ever get any work done in that place. The thumping seemed twice as loud as when he had visited before. "Zordon!" shouted Joanna. "What are you going to have? Just don't tell me you want some pretend food like salmon."

"I don't see how we can discuss anything here."

"Speak up," she demanded. "And order some meat, because you only have enough strength to squeak, and you can't conduct a conversation like a normal human being."

"Fish is meat too."

"Yeah, right," she replied. "Don't mess about, order something substantial."

He ordered grilled shrimps with vegetables and Romano cheese. He regretted it instantly, as instead of having time to calmly eat his meal, he felt his boss's gaze bearing down on him. And what's more, it cost as much as three pizzas.

"As long as the media don't find out," she said, shaking her head.

"A lot of people eat shrimps."

"I'm not talking about your sodding crustaceans."

He smiled in spite of himself.

"The media will eat us alive anyway," Chyłka continued. "They'll say that some freak is trying to mock the justice system instead of sitting quietly in prison and thanking his lucky stars that Poland doesn't have the death penalty anymore."

She stabbed one of the shrimps with her fork and examined it, then put it back on Oryński's plate.

"Have you contacted Langer?" he asked.

"Not yet. I'll visit him tomorrow."

"By then, Żelazny will have had plenty of time to talk to him."

"I bet he will."

He looked at her questioningly.

"And what would you suggest?" she asked, dipping a piece of meat into her gravy. "We can annoy Old Rusty and haunt his nightmares, but playing games with him is out of the question. Officially, Langer is a client of the firm, so there's no point trying to race Żelazny to the finishing line. Let them talk, it's not really our concern. He'll talk to him anyhow, sooner or later."

"I thought the whole point of the press conference was to announce the start of the race."

Chyłka smiled and shrugged her shoulders. "Let's call it a pre-emptive action, a *fait accompli*. There's not a lot Żelazny can do about it now."

"So, as a Senior Associate of Żelazny & McVay, you've announced in public that you're going to file for cassation, and as the owner of the firm, Żelazny's not in a position to retract."

"Well done. All kneel, Zordon has caught on."

Oryński snorted.

"Now tell me, what did you find?" she asked, urging him on.

"Well . . ."

"Wait, let's get this straight. Let's say this is a professional briefing. Talk to me as if I'm your client, as if I were an absolute cretin."

"I don't know if I can. I don't see you that way."

"Get on with it, Zordon. This is an oral exam. Go for it."

"OK. I'll start by saying that in cassation proceedings we apply the relevant provisions relating to an appeal procedure and . . . actually, I didn't find this in Waltoś, but in Grajewski, nevertheless, the Supreme Court holds the view that cassation proceedings may supplement court proceedings in a way that is comparable to a situation when—"

"Stop," she interrupted him.

"What? Why?"

"Stop, I can't listen to this," repeated Joanna, picking up her knife and fork. "You're so boring I want to stab myself."

"You told me to talk to you as if you didn't understand anything."

"Yes, but without boring me to death, for God's sake. Try telling me if cassation is applicable in our case. By the way, if you found it in Grajewski, it also has to be in Waltoś, but I'll let that one go. OK, I'm listening, but stop being boring."

"Gross violation of the law," said Oryński. "That's our only option."

"Now we're getting somewhere," said Chyłka, urging him on with a wave of her hand.

"Do I really have to explain it to you?"

"No, you have to show that you understand what it means."

"OK." Kordian cleared his throat. "There's broad scope for interpretation, because the violation has to be 'gross' and 'significant' relative to the sentence passed. So, there has to be a causal relationship between the two. But these are general provisions and not defined in any way, so the Supreme Court may interpret them as it sees fit."

"Well, OK, that's all right, though you're still pretty boring," she interjected. "But what violation would you try to prove?"

"Doda, Grajewski, and Murzynowski write that every case of imposing an unjust punishment on the accused is grounds for appealing against a 'gross' violation of the law."

"And?"

"That's all."

"You must be joking. Does this mean you haven't found anything that could be of any use to us?"

"I've got a few ideas, but even I can knock them all down; so the dimmest judge in the Supreme Court would have no trouble doing the same. If there are any dim judges there."

"Not really. They're all a bunch of badasses," said Chyłka.

The speakers were now pounding out the only Judas Priest number she liked, so she started swaying slightly to the music. Meanwhile she looked at him expectantly, hoping he might come up with something else.

"That's all," he said, shrugging his shoulders.

If truth be told, she couldn't blame him. The case was so complicated that it would probably be better to ask for the trial to be reopened. They would simply have to show that they had found new witnesses, and with them some hitherto unknown circumstances had come to light. But that would have been fudging the issue, and Chyłka preferred to be more direct. She wanted the Supreme Court to examine exactly what had happened during the first hearing: sink or swim. She wanted to go for broke.

"OK, now it's your turn to enlighten me," said Kordian. "Unless you haven't got the faintest idea of how to tackle it either?"

She was silent, still rocking from side to side. The Judas Priest track was finishing.

"Chyłka!"

"No, I haven't got the faintest idea what to do," she admitted. "I've been buried in the Code of Canon Law, and I feel like a miner who has been trapped in a collapsed mineshaft for a fortnight. I've been up to my eyeballs in adjudicating panel findings, what they accept, what they reject . . . I'm on my last legs, and I haven't found anything."

"Great," muttered Oryński. "You could have said so right away, I wouldn't have felt so guilty."

The music had stopped. Kordian was enjoying the silence.

"We need dirt," she said.

"What?"

"Compromising materials that—"

"I know what dirt means. I just can't believe you would stoop that low."

"When you're fighting pigs, sometimes you have to get in the trough."

"Not quite the right metaphor for a Supreme Court."

"You're blowing it out of proportion,' she said, in a tone that brooked no argument. 'It's simple: either we dig up some dirt or we can forget about a cassation appeal."

He gave her a wry look.

"Honestly, I've been through everything. Just like you, I've come to the conclusion that every idea that looked as if it might work can easily be refuted. Everything about the trial was as it should be, *lege artis* and all that. There's nothing we can find fault with."

"Then perhaps we should reopen the trial after all? We've got new facts, perhaps cassation is unnecessary."

"New facts?" asked Chyłka, raising her eyebrows. "Will you swear under oath that you didn't know about the shopkeeper and Powirska before?"

Kordian looked down. "We need a miracle," he said.

"A miracle or Kormak," Chyłka said. "Our skeletal friend is already working on it, trying to find something for the district court or court of appeal."

Kordian had thought that a legally binding verdict could only be appealed against in a court of second instance, but as soon as Joanna made her remark, he remembered reading something about the possibility of appealing to courts of first instance.

Suddenly it dawned on him. "The lay judges."

"A fertile field to find bumpkins."

"Do you think they might have got something wrong?"

"Not in terms of actual law, but other than that, who knows? I once assisted in a case where a cassation appeal was considered because one of the lay judges hadn't signed in the right place. Grounds for cassation, thank you very much and goodnight. The verdict was quashed, although the defendant was one hundred per cent guilty."

"And in . . ."

"And in our case, all the signatures are where they're supposed to be," sighed Joanna. "I checked. But that doesn't mean that we won't find anything. Kormak can reach out to people who, with the appropriate incentive, might be inclined to disclose certain things the judge had turned a blind eye to."

"Even if he does, that still . . ."

"Oh, Zordon, don't look so miserable," she said. "After all, it's only to get the case back into court. Once that happens, we'll do everything by the book. We'll say we have witnesses who can shed new light on the crime allegedly committed by our client. Powirska and the shopkeeper will confirm they didn't see our client at the estate, and *voilà*."

"It's that simple?"

"There's nothing simple about it, but at least it'll give us a chance to dig until we uncover the truth. Let Kormak do his work. And now I'm off home."

"What?"

"It's gone eight. How much longer am I supposed to stay at work?"

"I'm shocked."

"Then this'll shock you even more," she said, patting his back. "I'm paying, because you earn next to nothing. Go home, get some sleep. And as soon as Kormak gets a result, I'll let you know."

"OK," murmured Oryński, raising a hand in farewell.

He had no intention of returning to Żoliborz; there was still a lot to be done, and if ever he should be pulling an all-nighter, it was now. There had to be a way to get the case to the Supreme Court without the dirt and the wangling. You just needed to sift through earlier convictions: for, say, the last forty years.

CHAPTER

5

THE PLAN HAD been simple: put on his earphones, play Will Smith, and get stuck into Lex. Yet Kordian still felt unspeakably empty inside. He couldn't find a single court ruling on which to base a cassation appeal against Langer's sentence.

After almost two hours of uninterrupted work, he straightened his back. Looking over his shoulder, he saw Kormak approaching him.

"You still here?" said Kormak by way of greeting. "Come with me."

"Have you got something?" asked the trainee, rising from his chair.

"You'll see."

They passed a dozen or so trainees and interns still poring over their assignments, then headed for the McCarthy Cave.

"When do those guys in the newbie-burrow finish work?" asked Kormak once they were inside.

"They'll be getting ready to leave after ten," replied Oryński, collapsing into a chair. "Usually when one goes, the rest follow suit."

"Herd mentality."

"Better tell me what you've got," Kordian said looking at the book on his desk. This time it was McCarthy's *Blood Meridian*. He turned the book around, opened it and started skimming through.

"It's all shit," said Kormak. "Everything about this case is exactly as it should be, down to the last detail." He looked at the book. "I've only just started it, but I can already see parallels to what we're going through. Turpism."

"What?"

"Ugliness. Dirt, blood, degeneration, corpses, carrion. . . ."

"Sounds about right," said Kordian. "But you say you haven't found anything, so why am I here?"

He looked around the room, thinking he should get back to his research. But a short break wouldn't do him any harm.

"You're all right, Zordon," said Kormak. "And I want to help you."

"Thanks," muttered Oryński.

Kormak straightened his glasses. Then he unlocked his desk drawer and pulled out a small bag of snow-white powder. He placed it on the desk and looked at Kordian knowingly.

"What's that?"

"Speed. Or Gandalf the White, they call it here."

"What?"

"Amphetamines. Were you born yesterday?" said Kormak, shaking his head, then, realising Kordian still didn't understand, "a psychomotor stimulant."

Kormak watched as the penny dropped.

"And? What am I supposed . . ."

"I recommend the traditional method. Cut a line and snort. You could rub it into your gums, but I think that's stupid. You can get all sorts of problems afterwards, but once it's up your nostrils that's it. People have inhaled snuff like that since the sixteenth century, so this is just passing on the traditions of our ancestors."

"Only the product has changed."

Kormak nodded thoughtfully, opened the bag and tipped some of the powder onto the desk. He cut a line using a Golden Terraces Fitness Club card, then rolled up a small piece of paper, inserted it into his nostril and inhaled.

"Help yourself," he said, rubbing his nose.

Kordian looked at the white powder and hesitated. He knew that sooner or later the pace of work would make snorting speed inevitable. It was said that law firms and big corporations were the dealers' best customers. They always paid up front, no need for credit, and they bought wholesale. Apparently the only problem was that they were very demanding. They always wanted snow-white powder, whereas amphetamines in the capital tended to have a yellowish tinge. But there were ways to deal with that, ways that Kormak couldn't even imagine.

"Are you taking it or shall I put it away?"

Oryński considered the pros and cons. "OK, I'll have some," he said eventually.

At university it was considered almost normal for students to take stimulants. The branded products widely available in shops were a joke. If you had an exam and needed to cram the night before, there was really only one way out, and it was often taken. Kordian had tried some shit or other once or twice—and it probably really was desiccated rat shit—and the memories weren't pleasant. But a law firm like Żelazny & McVay probably attracted a better class of dealer, and he needed a powerful boost to do in one night what would normally take him a week.

He rolled up a yellow sticky note and bent over the line Kormak had racked. He sniffed deeply and swiftly, not leaving much on the desk—and what he did leave, Kormak was quick to inhale.

"OK, now I'm off to work," said Kordian, trying to stop his eyes from watering and hold back a colossal sneeze. To no avail. It seemed so powerful he feared it would rip his nostrils apart.

"Wait fifteen minutes. It'll soothe your soul," advised the bespectacled one.

Oryński sat in Kormak's room for another ten minutes or so, until he felt that overwhelming feeling . . . of what, he couldn't tell. An internal, metaphysical energy, from the very core of his being. Pure, unstoppable power. And it *was* unstoppable, like a megawave, metres and metres high, careening towards him, to carry him to a place where he could achieve anything.

That was his experience, in a nutshell—everything was within easy reach, everything suddenly seemed possible.

Back in his newbie-burrow, Kordian didn't even notice that virtually everyone had gone. He sat down in his chair, fixed his gaze on the monitor and got to work. Sometime later he saw Kormak, and wondered how much time had passed since he left his office. He couldn't even begin to guess. Events were happening at lightning speed, and at the same time everything was crystal clear and totally, beautifully logical.

He felt wonderful.

He thought about Ninja Turtles in space.

Kormak was asking him something, but Kordian waved him away. It felt like the solution to his most difficult problems was just around the corner. And he was getting everything done so quickly! He barely had to think of something, and he had it checked and sorted and was onto the next thing. The pace increased with every second.

More. He should take more. Then he'd be able to work until daybreak. But maybe it was already morning? A few hours must have passed. What time had he sat down at his computer after getting back from Kormak's? About twelve. No, no, no, it can't have been twelve. When he left, the trainees and interns were still there, so it must have been around eleven. So now it must be . . . ?

He looked around the newbie-burrow.

"What's the time?" he asked. "Go on, what time is it?"

Five in the morning? Probably. At least. And still he had nothing. There was nothing. There wouldn't be any cigarettes, there would be nothing. And everything was within easy reach.

"Aaaah!" he groaned, starting to sweat. "What's going on? Why won't this stop?"

The comedown lasted longer than the initial high. And it was painful. His strength was gone, and for a moment he thought he was going to die.

He hung his head and sat motionless for a few minutes; then he snapped out of it, summoned up the last of his strength and went back to his meandering journey through Polish jurisprudence.

It was slow going, and getting slower all the time, but Kordian finally stumbled across something that made him sit up and take notice.

"Judgement of the Supreme Court of 28th June 1977 . . . direct intention. . . ."

He read on. This was exactly what he had been looking for!

"Thank you, Gandalf the White," he whispered, forgetting that he had not discovered the judgement during his high, but after it had worn off. If he'd still been high, he would probably have overlooked it. On the other hand, without that boost, maybe he wouldn't even have got that far? It was hard to tell. Either way, he needed to get a grip and—

Something interrupted his train of thought. He suddenly realised he didn't know what to do. It would probably be best to phone Chyłka and tell her about the judgement.

He dialled her number on his mobile and waited for it to ring. She wasn't answering. This was strange, she should have been up by now.

Then again, perhaps he'd got the time wrong? He looked at the wall clock.

It was coming up to one in the morning.

He double-checked the clock on his mobile and the laptop—they all showed the same. He sighed, wrote an email to Joanna, and switched off the computer. Now it was time to recharge himself after his encounter with Gandalf the White.

He had done what he needed to do: he had found a Supreme Court ruling giving him grounds for a cassation appeal. He was absolutely sure of it, and would have probably been even more elated if he didn't still feel as if he was dying. But that didn't matter. As soon as he'd told everyone about his find, Żelazny would make him a permanent employee, and Chyłka would arrange for him to have his own office.

Still a bit dazed, he staggered out into the corridor.

6

THE BALD MAN was getting fed up with waiting for Oryński. His associate had seen the target leave the Hard Rock Cafe and head for the Skylight building next to Golden Terraces; later, he'd watched the target alone, assuming that Kordian would leave the office before eleven. Two hours had gone by and there was still no sign. The Bald Man was used to long stakeouts, but he didn't like hanging around in the city centre, right by the Palace of Culture and Science.

He sat in his black Mercedes, parked opposite the building. The main entrance was in darkness, but the pavement in front of it was illuminated. There was no way Oryński could have slipped by unnoticed, but just in case, the Bald Man also had a Pulsar night vision device. It was the size of a TV remote control, so he could keep it in the glove compartment. This time though, he spotted his victim without it.

Kordian left the building shortly after one.

There was no one else around, but the Bald Man had to act quickly. If he let Oryński get to the station, someone might see them. If there was one place in central Warsaw that always had a lot of pedestrian traffic, it was the Central Railway Station, and that was where Oryński was bound to be headed to catch the night bus.

The Bald Man grabbed the door handle. Then he froze. The target had not turned left towards the station, but right, and was now heading towards the InterContinental. The Bald Man thought for a moment, then started the car and drove out of the car park. If the target had arranged for someone to give him a lift, his one and only chance could soon be gone. Watching the young lawyer, the man slowed his Mercedes, then stopped it. Oryński had turned one way, then another, and was now turning back. It looked as if he was under the influence, though he wasn't staggering. It was obvious, even to the Bald Man. Oryński was stoned.

He smiled to himself. This was going to be a piece of cake. He drove towards the InterContinental, turned into Złota Street and slammed on the brakes right in Kordian's path. He could have jumped out of the car and knocked him out straightaway, but if someone saw him even from a distance, they would call the police.

So instead, he calmly opened the door and got out of the car.

"What's this?" exclaimed the trainee, eyeing the Bald Man. He felt a flash of recognition. "Hang on, I know you."

"Feeling OK, Kordian?"

He tried to sound like an old friend who had appeared at just the right time, as luck would have it, to give his companion a helping hand. And Oryński was clearly in need of help. He probably didn't even know where the nearest bus stops or taxi ranks were.

"I saw you that time . . . now, when was it?"

"Everything OK, Kordian?"

"Outside the gym. Damn it, I'm sure that's where it was."

"Have you taken something?" asked the Bald Man, taking a step closer. He held out his hand, as if Oryński was a sick old man.

"Who are you?" asked the trainee. "What are you doing here?"

This time, the Bald Man didn't even bother to speak.

Taking only a slight swing, he landed a powerful uppercut on the trainee's chin; Kordian's teeth slammed together and he let out a quiet groan.

Years of training in the gym and taking supplements had given the Bald Man confidence; he felt that in these situations, nobody could get the better of him. What's more, just one punch had almost felled the young lawyer.

Kordian was completely dazed. Mumbling incomprehensibly, he staggered backwards; but the Bald Man was right in front of him, and before he could protect himself, landed a brutal right hook. Blood spurted out of Kordian's nose, and his shirt was splattered with red.

The attacker opened the car door and shoved him into the back seat. Then he looked around quickly and got in behind the wheel.

He drove towards the UN Roundabout, pleased that everything had gone so smoothly. The victim would no doubt stain the upholstery red, but he wasn't particularly worried. The Grey-Haired Man's lackeys had cleaned up far worse things in their time.

It took Kordian a while to recognise the seriousness of his situation. It seemed unreal, but finally he realised he'd been attacked and was now being kidnapped. He tried to gather his thoughts, but it was hard. He knew he was in a car, but it definitely wasn't Chyłka's X5. Her car smelled of perfume, this one stank like an ashtray.

Then he noticed a strange, metallic taste in his mouth, and one by one, all his other senses returned to him. His hands were free, and sitting in front of him was his attacker, completely impassive.

As Kordian looked, his thoughts stopped racing. In the rearview mirror he saw the eyes of the Bald Man gazing directly at him. There were no obstacles between him and the driver. His self-preservation instinct warned him not to try anything as it would only make matters worse, but his fighting spirit urged him to attack.

"Sit still," said the Bald Man, "and you might survive."

But the will to fight was strong, and Kordian decided to ignore his advice.

He looked down, as if he'd given up on the idea of saving himself, then lunged forward, attempting to grab his kidnapper by the throat. The Bald Man, however, was quicker. He stamped his foot on the accelerator, the car shot forward and Oryński was thrown back. Then he slammed on the brakes, throwing Oryński forward again and smashing his nose against the front seat. He howled with pain.

"Quiet!" bellowed the Bald Man.

He stopped the car, turned around and grabbed Kordian by the shirt. With his other hand he punched him in the head.

Before Oryński managed to recover his senses, the Bald Man had jumped out of the car. He opened the back door and threw him outside.

Kordian was too dazed to get up. He felt a hard kick in the stomach, and curled up in pain. It crossed his mind that he should protect his head; he put up a feeble guard, but when the Bald Man threw his next punch, his fist went through it like it was paper.

Oryński was overwhelmed. His ears were ringing; but the Bald Man was just getting started. He mercilessly rained blow after blow on Kordian's head until the young man gradually drifted away and finally lost consciousness.

7

WHEN HE CAME to, he was lying on damp ground. The moon above him was almost full, but most of its light was lost somewhere in the treetops.

His mind was beginning to work normally again: amphetamines, the judgement, the Bald Man. His head was throbbing. His teeth were wobbly, as if he were losing his milk teeth. When he tried to catch his breath, he choked.

Before he could assess the situation, the Bald Man gave him a powerful kick in the belly. Kordian curled up again, howling with pain. The next blow was aimed at his chest, and winded him completely.

When the beating finally stopped, Oryński thought he was about to die.

"That's the pleasantries over with. Now we'll go on to the formalities," said the kidnapper. "Call me Gorzym. And remember, your survival depends on me, and me alone."

Silence followed. Kordian felt pain spreading all over his body. He began to cough, feeling as though he might cough his lungs out. Finally, in panic, he managed to gasp in some air, as if he had been under water for a long time.

"Do you understand?"

"Yes," Kordian replied, with difficulty.

"Do you know where you are?"

Oryński looked first at Gorzym, and then at the surrounding area. He had no idea where he'd been brought. Forests looked the same everywhere.

"No, I don't know . . ." he wheezed.

"You are in a forest to the east of Palmiry," said the Bald Man. "Do you want to die here, Kordian Oryński?"

"No."

"Then listen closely," said Gorzym, and crouched down next to him.

Only now did Kordian notice his attacker had a gun. He stared at the weapon. Gorzym noticed.

"It's a Walther P99, nine millimetre," he said, moving closer and placing the pistol on his lap, the muzzle facing the trainee. "Now, listen to me and remember every word I say, is that clear?"

"Yes."

"Great. I like people like you." Gorzym looked at him grimly. "Sometimes I have to spend much more time explaining things."

"Not to me," said Kordian as reassuringly as he could. He coughed, spitting out blood.

"Exactly . . . you're a smart man. You know there's no point panicking."

The few moments he'd had since the beating stopped allowed Kordian to weigh up the situation. He came to the conclusion that he was there because of Langer. And if that was the case, Langer Senior's death was no accident.

Clearly, the whole thing was far more serious than they had originally thought.

"What do you want from me?"

Gorzym looked surprised that his victim should even have to ask. The silence seemed to last an eternity. Finally, he shook his head with resignation.

He got up and aimed the Walther at his victim.

Kordian automatically shielded his face with his hand. His heart was beating like a sledgehammer, his whole body was sweating and his mouth was dry. The pain from the countless blows all but disappeared: the spectre of death overshadowed everything else.

"You really don't know why you're here?" asked Gorzym.

Oryński opened his mouth, but was unable to speak. He cursed silently and with a supreme effort, pulled himself together.

"The sentence . . ."

"What sentence?"

He gulped, tasting blood. "I've found a ruling that will allow for a cassation appeal,' he said, realising belatedly that Gorzym couldn't possibly have known this. For a moment, everything went quiet. Oryński heard the wind in the treetops. It seemed there wasn't another living soul around—even the wildlife had fled.

"Have you only just found it?"

"Yes."

"Have you told your boss?"

"No . . . well, I've sent her an email."

Gorzym fell silent again, and Kordian used this moment of calm to try and work out who he was up against in this very unequal struggle. Logic suggested the mafia. Your average thug didn't wear expensive suits or carry a gun. He didn't drive the latest Mercedes. Everything pointed to Gorzym working for some criminal underworld boss, and it wasn't a comforting thought.

Oryński looked up and saw the muzzle of the gun pointing at him. If Gorzym had wanted him dead, surely he would have killed him by now? Besides, why would anyone want him dead? Chyłka was the one leading the case, for the most part he was just a third wheel.

"What are you going to do with me?" he asked.

Gorzym looked at him. "That depends on you."

Kordian swallowed with difficulty.

"You've got one chance to get out of this."

"What do I have to do?" Kordian choked.

"Listen carefully."

The boy nodded feverishly.

"And do exactly as I tell you. Down to the last detail."

As Gorzym released the safety on his Walther, Kordian felt himself drifting away. He didn't know whether it was due to mental stress, or his injuries.

"You will be my spy, Oryński."

Again, Oryński nodded. He'd agree to anything.

"You'll be my mole at Żelazny & McVay," added Gorzym. "At least until the case is closed. Then, if everything goes well, you might become a free man again."

"I understand."

Oryński knew how pathetic he sounded. It had crossed his mind that he could tell the man whatever he wanted to hear. The minute he released him, he'd go to the nearest police station and report everything. And they'd catch him. They'd caught bigger fish than that.

"And until the case is closed, you're to look at yourself in the mirror every day and repeat: 'I'm just Gorzym's bitch.' Several times. Say it now."

Oryński mumbled something quietly.

"Say it!"

The Walther was right in his face.

"I'm just Gorzym's bitch," repeated Kordian through gritted teeth.

"That'll do."

The Bald Man twirled the pistol in his hand and took a step back. He pulled a packet of cigarettes from the pocket of his jacket, and lit one.

"You will report everything to me, no matter how insignificant it seems," he added as he smoked. "If Chyłka switches from steak at the Hard Rock Cafe to sandwiches at Subway, I want to know about it."

Clearly, Gorzym had been watching the two lawyers for some time. Kordian was racking his brains to find a connection between Langer or the murder victims and the mafia. He had examined the case from every angle, but had never come across any mafia connections. He realised there were so many things about which he had no idea.

"You will report to me, understand?"

"Yes."

"And don't say a word about our meeting."

"So how shall I explain this?" he asked, pointing to his face. "It won't take a forensic scientist to . . ."

"Tell them someone attacked you on the way home," Gorzym replied. "Dream up a convincing story, because if you don't, we'll be meeting again much sooner than you expected. If you've taken drugs, and it looks like you have, you can always say you don't remember much."

Kordian nodded.

"You'll report to me by email, I'll give you the address. But only from your home computer, or from a laptop, if you buy one you can use in the newbie-burrow."

He knew more than Oryński had realised. But how? Wiretapping was basically out of the question. Maybe his boss was a client of Żelazny & McVay? Or had Gorzym been there personally for some reason?

"Now, let's get down to business," Gorzym announced. "How do you normally get your letters to court?"

"Usually by post. Sometimes an intern takes them to the court's own registry. Occasionally, I do it, because—"

"Yes OK, we know you're one of the bottom feeders."

"So . . ."

"Your task is simple. When you've written the cassation appeal, make sure you're the one asked to take it to the post office. Or to the court."

Gorzym paused. Kordian realised he was waiting for him to nod his head, so he did.

"On your way, make sure you're delayed. Think up some sort of story."

"I understand."

"Don't keep saying you understand."

Oryński didn't know what else to say. With swift efficiency, the Bald Man took off his jacket and hung it on the back of the driver's seat.

"Because I'm not sure you do really understand."

"I most certainly do. . . ."

"Shut the fuck up."

For a short moment, Kordian foolishly thought this was just another tactic to intimidate him. But then the blows started. A hailstorm of them, landing everywhere—his face, body, legs. Gorzym was piling in mercilessly, kicking him in the ribs, stamping on him.

And deriving the greatest pleasure from it.

Gorzym liked seeing how the boy's head wobbled from side to side when he prodded it with his shoe. And then at a certain moment, the victim stopped groaning. Even when he kicked him in the crotch, Oryński didn't cry out. The game stopped giving Gorzym any satisfaction.

He looked around and decided that he couldn't leave the boy there, he'd have to take him back to a place where there were more people. So he put Oryński back in the Mercedes, and drove off.

A few kilometres later, he found himself in Izabelin. His watch said quarter to three, so he had to hurry. Soon the first residents would start waking up, ready to get to Warsaw by six to start work. Gorzym stopped at the junction of the Third of May and Kościuszko streets and dumped his cargo at the side of the road.

For a split second, he wondered whether he should make an anonymous call to the police, but decided he didn't need to. Sooner or later, someone was bound to find the boy and call the emergency services.

CHAPTER

8

CHYŁKA WOKE UP in the middle of the night and instinctively picked up her phone to check the time. She thought she had set the alarm, but wasn't sure. She promised herself for the umpteenth time that she would finally set a weekly alarm.

She cursed as the display blinded her like the headlights of a car. Narrowing her eyes, she saw that she had nearly two hours before she needed to get up. She also noticed a missed call from Zordon.

It probably wasn't anything important. Joanna put the phone down and rolled over.

But maybe he'd found something? She realised that until she knew, she wouldn't be able to sleep. She switched on the bedside lamp, pulled herself up and leaned on the headboard. She reached for the remote and turned on TVN24, then picked up the phone and dialled Kordian's number.

"The person you have called is temporarily unavailable. Please try later. Beep!"

The message annoyed her. How could they know that the person was only temporarily unavailable? What if they had shuffled off this mortal coil?

She put the phone down, sighed loudly, and fixed her gaze on yet another coach crash disaster in Europe. Not the most appropriate material if she still wanted to get any sleep that night. For Chyłka, the ideal TV programme for dropping off to sleep would have been some sort of political talk show—monotonous, calm, slow voices always had a soothing effect on her. Besides, she liked highbrow commentators, though not as much as the king of TVN.

She picked up the phone and tried again. Still temporarily unavailable. This time she felt an unpleasant shiver, as she thought of the number of times the automated voice at the other end of the line may have been wrong. But in Zordon's case, it was more probable that his phone battery was dead.

Unless someone really had attacked him on the staircase in that Żoliborz hellhole.

"For God's sake!" she muttered and tried again.

Drawing yet another blank, she decided she was making a mountain out of a molehill.

She put the phone down on the bedside cabinet and reached for her book. Joanna rarely fell asleep without reading at least a few pages. Even when she returned home very much under the influence, she would still read a page or two. In recent weeks she had been reading a J.K. Rowling novel, but it wasn't exactly gripping stuff. She'd been hoping for a murder, but all she got was gossip and internet trolling. On the other hand, it was ideal fodder for a sleepless night.

Unfortunately, not this time. Her eyelids began to droop just before five, and she had hardly managed to put the book down and switch off the light when the "Afraid to Shoot Strangers" solo rang out. In normal circumstances, she'd have cursed anyone who rang while she was dropping off, but this time she sat up immediately and grabbed the phone.

She looked at the display. Old Rusty. He never phoned at such an unearthly hour.

"What is it?" she asked.

"How quickly can you get to Bielański Hospital?"

"Depends, am I allowed to break the speed limit?" Her tone was light-hearted, but she realised something terrible must have happened.

"Definitely."

"I can be there in half an hour," replied Joanna, throwing off the duvet and getting out of bed.

"And without makeup?" asked Żelazny. "And all that other stuff?"

"Fifteen minutes."

"We'll go for the second option."

Chyłka reached into the pocket of the jacket hanging on the wall and pulled out a Bluetooth earpiece so she could talk hands free.

"What's happened?" she asked, randomly selecting an ironed blouse from her wardrobe.

"It's probably one of our employees. I don't know anything else. The police don't have any details."

"So how do we know that—"

"They got a call from someone in Izabelin, no ID, no phone and no money. His wallet was empty. But in his pocket he had a pen with our logo, so they want someone from our office to come and try and identify the poor guy. Apparently . . . well, you know. He's fighting for his life."

"So you called me. How thoughtful of you."

"Badyński is on holiday, and I'm not in Warsaw," replied Żelazny.

In the company hierarchy, Badyński was more or less on the same level as Chyłka, although Żelazny patently trusted him more than he did her. Badyński got all the sensitive cases, whereas they called on Chyłka when they needed the heavy guns.

"Are you on your way yet?"

"Hang on, let me get dressed."

"Why bother? Go as nature intended."

"In your dreams," she muttered before hanging up.

She got there in record time, though she doubted that a pen in a jacket pocket was enough to say that the victim worked at Żelazny & McVay. They handed promotional items out left, right and centre, even if it was just to a client popping in to exchange a few words with their lawyer.

Initially, it crossed her mind that it might be Zordon—and if they had found the person somewhere around the city centre or Żoliborz, she would probably have thought the worst. But Izabelin? What business would Oryński have there? Besides, his only means of transport was the night bus, which probably didn't go out that far. At least she didn't have to worry that it was him.

But everything changed when the duty doctor took her to ICU.

Kordian's swollen face was covered in dressings, but she had no problem recognising him. A transparent tube protruded from his mouth, his eyes were closed and a steady beeping sound announced that he was connected to monitoring equipment.

Chyłka stood transfixed, as if struck by lightning. When she eventually noticed the drip, she began to feel faint.

"I see this must be someone close to you," said the doctor quietly.

Maciej Roske often saw reactions such as these: first disbelief, then shock, and finally denial. It took time to realise that the person lying on the bed was someone close. Before she came into the intensive care unit, this woman had seemed tough, but now she looked like she wanted to bury her face in her hands and weep.

It was hardly surprising. The boy was in a deplorable state, and the beating he'd suffered had clearly only stopped as he was nearing the point of no return.

The doctor looked at the woman, trying to determine who she was in relation to the victim. There were three possibilities: sister, girlfriend, or wife.

"How . . ." began Chyłka, then closed her eyes and looked down. "Is he conscious?"

"No," replied Roske. "His injuries are extensive, so we've put him in a medically induced coma."

The doctor turned to Joanna. They were still standing in the doorway, and he wasn't surprised that she didn't want to go in. Her mind was still trying to process what her eyes were seeing.

"Perhaps you could tell me who it is?"

"Kordian Oryński . . . my . . . my . . ."

She buried her face in her hands and sniffed. He must think she was pathetic.

But she had no other option.

If she had been in any profession other than law, it probably wouldn't have occurred to her that if she wanted information she'd need to put on a performance. Doctors only ever told relatives about a patient's true condition. The play-acting was essential.

Besides, no one would ask a distraught relative for ID. "My husband," she said, revealing her face.

Roske was not pleased. He'd prefer to deal with a girlfriend, because then he wouldn't have to tell her all the details. Family members, on the other hand, would keep asking until they got what they wanted to know, and they usually wanted to know everything. As if a retroperitoneal haemorrhage caused by trauma to the parenchymatous organs would mean anything to most of them. Instead of pestering the doctors, Roske felt they'd be far better off saying a few prayers in the chapel. Even unbelievers—or in their case, perhaps all the more so.

"Who . . . how . . ." began Joanna disjointedly, then stopped and looked at the doctor. She began to tremble.

"That is what the police are trying to find out," replied Roske. "I can only say that you've got good grounds to feel optimistic. You husband is alive, and however trite this may sound, that's the most important thing."

"How did it happen?" Chyłka couldn't keep her voice from cracking.

"The injuries definitely point to a beating," he explained, clearing his throat. "Extensive injuries to the body, both external and internal." Roske paused, hoping the woman would nod to show she didn't need any more details.

But she was looking at him expectantly.

"Apart from the injured tissues and haematomas all over his body, which you . . . unfortunately can see with the naked eye, there are numerous injuries to the skull and ribs."

"Are any of them life threatening?" interrupted Chyłka.

Contrary to what the doctor thought, she wasn't interested in exactly how many broken bones Oryński had. A quick glance was enough to send shivers down her spine—the boy was practically immobilised by splints and dressings, some of which involved plaster. He looked more like the victim of a motorcycle accident than a beating.

"There's no threat to his life at present."

"Thank God," replied Joanna, leaning back on the doorframe. Old Rusty had said he was fighting for his life, but maybe he'd misunderstood.

She walked into the room and sat down on the edge of the bed—very gently, as if it might collapse under her weight. She placed her hand on Oryński's arm and cried silently. When she saw his closed eyes, it made her feel weak. Suddenly, all this play-acting felt soulless.

"It doesn't look good, but believe me, it could have been worse. The most important thing is that he has no internal bleeding. Other than that, everything will be fine, although it may take a long time to recover fully."

"I see," said Joanna, and fell silent. She'd suddenly realised that Kordian had probably called her very shortly before he was attacked.

"Would you like the hospital to notify someone?"

"No, thank you," she replied. "I'll take care of it myself."

Zordon's parents, or at least someone else in his family, should be informed. Or perhaps his girlfriend? Chyłka didn't know much about her protégé at all. For all she knew, he could be married and have a brood of little Zordons—the absence of a wedding ring didn't mean anything. They had never talked about private matters, and if ever they got too close to it, they quickly turned it into a joke. And she was sitting at the edge of his bed, holding his hand. Beautiful, just beautiful.

"There is one more thing," said Roske interrupting her thoughts.

"And that is?"

"Toxicology tests have shown the presence of a psychotropic agent . . ."

"A what?"

"Amphetamine. High quality, according to our specialist," replied the doctor.

Chyłka fixed her gaze on him, her mind processing this new information. Of course, lawyers took all sorts of substances: some to work more effectively, others to forget at the weekend that they had defended murderers and rapists during the week. But Zordon? Surely not.

But toxicology tests don't lie. So now, what had looked like a straight-forward beating would be seen by the police in a completely different light. Chyłka realised the doctor would have informed them. She looked at him.

"If you go out into the corridor, you'll find an officer who would like to have a few words with you," said Roske. "I hope you understand."

"Yes, of course."

The doctor nodded, then checked the monitor readings and left the room.

Once she was alone with Oryński, Joanna withdrew her hand. She sat motionless for a moment, trying to take it all in. Langer was the link; of that she was certain.

Soon she'd have to face the police officer. He wouldn't be pleased when she told him she had lied to the doctor, but she would persuade him that she was the boy's lawyer and that she'd cooperate fully. He was probably only some junior officer, pulled in from the nearest patrol.

She went over to the door and turned around to take another look. She swallowed hard. The sight of someone who'd been hurt so badly was heart-wrenching. Even if it wasn't anyone close.

9

ARTUR ŻELAZNY WAS in Gdańsk that day, where he was taking care of a lucrative contract—a client negotiating with a German company making investments in the outskirts of the city. His presence wasn't essential, but it was important; he was there to show how much they valued the client.

But he changed his mind when he'd spoken to the hospital. He called in a favour he was owed from a year or two back and got the consultant to give him the low down—the boy was brought to the hospital in a terrible state, and the doctors had to put him into a medically induced coma. They considered operating, but the X-rays showed that there was no immediate need to open him up.

Artur didn't understand everything in the clutter of words, but it was clear that for a moment the boy's life had hung in the balance.

Żelazny & McVay couldn't afford to ignore what had happened. As a company, they were constantly being assessed, fighting for their place in the rankings; and how they treated employees outside the workplace was an important factor.

"They also found traces of amphetamines in his body," said the doctor. That did it. Artur got in his car and drove off towards Warsaw. He knew the media would have a field day. There would be rumours about links with the criminal underworld, about junior lawyers being exploited and driven to the brink—and all sorts of other things. There would be numerous stories, and, no doubt, an official investigation would be launched with great fanfare: Żelazny & McVay were not exactly favourites with the prosecutor's office.

Within fifteen minutes of hearing the news, Żelazny was driving his Volvo along the A1 towards Toruń. He wasn't speeding, and reached Warsaw three hours after leaving Gdańsk. He parked outside the Skylight building and phoned Chyłka again. Meanwhile, she was at her trainee's bedside, like a good wife. Clearly, she had managed to mollify the police and hospital administration, because no one had asked her to leave.

"Go home, Chyłka," Żelazny advised her now, closing the car door. "There's not much more you can do there, because that . . . that boy . . ."

"Oryński."

"Oryński won't be waking up for some time."

"Is Kormak in?"

"I don't know. I've just got here."

"Have a word with him, tell him to check Zordon's computer."

"Whose computer?"

There was silence at the other end, so he assumed she meant the trainee. Perhaps this was a new slang word, he could never keep up. He couldn't even remember the boy—he only remembered telling Chyłka to lay him off after the trial period.

"Did you find out anything from the police?" he asked.

"Not much. Though they're quite forthcoming," she replied. "They found him in Izabelin, unconscious and robbed of all his personal belongings, so they assumed it was a run-of-the-mill mugging—until they found out that Oryński lives in Żoliborz and works in the city centre." ·

"So they know nothing."

"Nothing," confirmed Chyłka.

"What about the drugs?"

For a moment she was silent.

"How do you know?"

"I know people at the hospital. Are you surprised?"

"Perhaps I shouldn't be."

"I'll ask you again. What do they know about the amphetamines?"

"Not much," she replied hesitantly. "They don't want to talk about it."

"OK. I'm going to see Kormak, and you take the day off."

"What for?"

Good question, thought Artur. People were always sent home and told to take the rest of the day off when something like this happened. Just like in stressful situations people were offered a glass of water.

"Do what you think's best," he replied, and hung up.

He got himself a cup of coffee and headed to Kormak's room. He had often found that Kormak could work wonders, and was hoping it would happen now.

"Good morning, Boss," said Kormak, rising from his chair.

"Sit down," replied Żelazny.

"Has something happened?"

Artur explained the problem as briefly as he could. Kormak looked deeply shocked. There was clearly some sort of relationship between him and that Kordon. *Maybe they were gay,* Żelazny thought.

"How . . . but . . . how? I . . ."

"Calm down," said Artur. "When did you last see him?"

"Yesterday . . . around midnight, we were sitting here—"

"Snorting Gandalf the White?"

"Yes," admitted Kormak. "Not much, but I guess he wasn't used to it, because he looked as if he was going to collapse."

"Have a drink," said Żelazny, looking around for a bottle of water. Not seeing one, he handed the bespectacled man his coffee. So far, he had rather hoped that this Kondor, or whatever his name was, had acquired the drug from outside. Now he knew he was heading for a PR nightmare.

Other law firms were doubtless in the same boat, but no one wanted to publicise the fact that drugs were rife in their corporation. But now, for Żelazny & McVay, the milk was well and truly spilled. Clients would avoid them, at least for a while.

It was too late to disassociate themselves from the boy; now that the deed was done, that would be shooting themselves in the foot. There was no other way but to keep him on and provide him with the appropriate care—then frame him to look as if it were a personal problem and not endemic among their employees. Yes, that was a feasible solution.

"Where did you get the . . . the . . . Gandalf the White?"

"From Jacek, the one in taxes."

"Does he get it for everyone?"

"No, that's someone in HR, who gives it to Jacek in the gym, who then hands it round."

"Fuck the lot of you!" yelled Artur. "You've got an organised crime ring going."

He knew that some of their employees used amphetamines to boost performance, but had assumed they only did it outside the workplace. At least that had been the practice when Żelazny was still an ordinary lawyer.

"How is h—"

"Shut up," said Żelazny. "If you want to know, phone Chyłka." There was an uneasy silence. Artur looked at Kormak in disbelief, shook his head and got up.

Kormak realised this was only the start of their problems. "So is the shit about to hit the fan?" he asked.

"For that Zondon or whatever his name is, definitely. For you, maybe. For the firm—you'd better pray it doesn't. Follow me."

As Żelazny entered the newbie-burrow, the house of cards the train-ees had built up to enable them to work in its noisy, overcrowded conditions collapsed. First there was a murmur, then individual heads popped up from the cubicles until finally there was a whole forest of them. Paying no attention to them, Artur sat Kormak in the only available empty cubicle.

"Is that where that Gordon worked?" he asked the person working in the neighbouring box.

The intern nodded uncertainly, and Żelazny turned to Kormak. "Look through his computer. See what you can find."

Kormak got down to work straightaway. He checked the hard disk, then decided it would be better to look through his browsing history, followed by his recently opened Lex documents. The history unearthed nothing of value.

"The last Lex document he opened . . . look, it's a ruling."

Żelazny leaned over to see the screen and scanned the text. His years of poring over long, turgid legal texts helped him skip over the dead wood and get to the heart of the matter, and he quickly realised the boy had found a way that could lead to a cassation appeal against Langer's sentence.

He straightened up and thought for a moment. "Can other people see this?" he asked.

"Lex, you mean?"

Żelazny ignored the question.

"Ah, you mean the computer? Are you asking if it's possible to hack it?"

Artur nodded, taking a deep breath.

"It's always possible, even CIA and NSA databases aren't one hundred per cent secure, but I doubt anyone would bother. If you want to know their secrets, it would be easier to get one of these rising legal stars drunk."

Żelazny looked around the newbie-burrow, and all the interns and trainees instantly got back to work.

"Search this computer. Cover to cover, cable to cable," said Artur, then he turned around and headed for the exit. He had a lot to do that day. First, he'd have a word with Jacek in taxes, then find the person in HR supplying the drugs. And finally, he'd have to start the process of shifting the blame onto the hapless Kordian.

10

Nᴇᴡs ᴏғ Żᴇʟᴀᴢɴʏ's activities reached Chyłka in no time: Kormak phoned her right after he had finished pulling apart Oryński's computer. She had to admit that he'd stepped up to the plate and allied himself with the rightful side in the conflict.

"Do you think the attack had anything to do with Langer? Should I be scared?"

"Yes, and of me too, if you don't stop asking biased questions."

"But . . ."

"But Zordon was not beaten up and thrown out in Izabelin because he was in the wrong place at the wrong time," said Chyłka. "The Langer case now stinks to high heaven, if it hadn't stunk before. And I intend to find out exactly why."

"What about Żelazny? Do you think he has anything to do with it?"

"I doubt it," replied Chyłka.

Absurd question. What would the owner of a firm have to do with the beating up of one of his trainees? Of course, in a way it did look like collusion. But with whom? Langer Senior was no longer of this world, and Żelazny would gain nothing by having Zordon brought to the brink of death.

This didn't alter the fact that everyone should now be treated as a suspect.

Someone must have been watching Oryński, must have waited for him to leave the Skylight building. Perhaps the attacker had an informant on the inside, and knew when Kordian would be leaving work.

"Are you still there?"

"Yes," replied Joanna, realising she had her phone pressed hard against her ear. "I was just thinking."

"Have you got a plan?"

"Beat the whores and the thieves."

"Seriously, Chyłka. What are we going to do?"

"I'll sit with Zordon a little while longer, then you come and take my place while I go and visit Langer. Either he can start talking sense or he can forget about the cassation appeal."

"Ah yes, speaking of which," cut in Kormak, "Kordian found a ruling from the 1970s that would give you good grounds for a cassation appeal. I'll text you the reference."

Joanna looked at Oryński's closed eyes. Kormak hung up.

It seemed like a clear connection. Kordian found something, but before he could tell anyone, he was attacked. But that was just too pat, too predictable. No one would risk anything that obvious.

The whole case was raising more and more questions, and there was only one person who could answer them.

She sat on tenterhooks, waiting for Kormak. Once or twice, she wondered whether she should hold Zordon's hand or talk to him, but decided it was pointless.

Glancing nervously towards the corridor, she realised she couldn't bear to sit there any longer.

Soon she was in her X5, speeding towards Białołęka Prison. Having raced down Armia Krajowa Street, she was well over the speed limit on General Stefan Grot Rowecki Bridge, weaving in and out between the cars, cursing Langer, the law firm, Żelazny and anyone who was in any way responsible for bringing Zordon to the brink of death. She was prepared to do anything to find the perpetrators.

CHAPTER

11

PIOTR LANGER WAS brought to the visiting room in chains. He was wearing an orange prison uniform to show he was a so-called N category prisoner, and therefore dangerous. He sat down opposite Joanna and eyed her. This time, his stare didn't bother her.

"My colleague has been attacked," she began. "He's lying unconscious in Bielański Hospital."

Langer looked at her blankly. The two prison officers cuffed him to the seat, then nodded to the lawyer and left the room.

"I think his beating had something to do with us defending scum like you," she said.

He remained silent.

"You were much more talkative earlier," hissed Joanna. "And another thing: I believe it was no accident that your father's death occurred just as you were being sentenced. What do you think, Langer?"

"Maybe."

"Maybe?" She got up from her chair, and for a moment it looked as if she was going to attack him. "Maybe, I'll just go to the Prison Governor, whom I happen to know quite well, and say that I'd be most indebted to him if he could put my client in with the lowest of the low, where they'll be on his case day and night."

"Hardly likely."

She knew he was right. The orange uniform meant he was near the top of the prison hierarchy. Prison convict culture may not have been what it once was, but some things never changed. For murder, you got respect, which you paid back over many long years. For murder in the first degree, with exceptional brutality, you got a lifetime of respect, because prisoners with life sentences had nothing to lose, so they were basically unpredictable. Anyone with common sense gave life prisoners a wide berth; they wouldn't think twice about stabbing another inmate. What was the worst that could happen to them? They'd be deprived of the right to appeal for parole after twenty-five years. But after so many years, few wanted to leave. The cell was their room, the prison was their home, and the prison yard was the outside world. Prison was where they had work, friends, and more. Beyond the prison wall they had nothing; out there, after twenty-five years, no one even knew them.

Threatening him was pointless.

"Oryński has found a ruling that will allow us to file a cassation appeal."

"I've talked to Artur Żelazny," said Langer, and took a deep breath. Chyłka waited for him to go on. "He says that in my case a cassation appeal isn't justified, and he wanted me to speak to you about it."

She hadn't expected her boss to find time to talk to Piotr, but it looked like he must have wanted to kill two PR problems with one stone.

"So Old Rusty wanted you to sack us."

"More or less," admitted Piotr, adjusting himself in his chair and making a metallic clanking sound.

"And?"

"I'm not firing lawyers who are at the top of their game."

Only now did Joanna notice that Langer was calmer than she'd ever seen him. That surprised her, because despite his N status, prison life couldn't possibly be easy. The prison warders were bound to make sure it wasn't.

"If you don't fire us, I'll fire myself."

There was silence, occasionally disrupted by muffled cries coming from the cells.

"You're trying to force me to cooperate."

"I shouldn't have to force you."

She sat down and clasped her hands on the table.

"It's in your own interest to give us all the information you have, every single detail, so we can prepare properly and use it all to your advantage."

He didn't reply.

"Do you want to spend the rest of your life behind bars? Now that you know what it's like?"

"No."

"So start talking. Or you can start filling out library book requests for the next few decades. I've heard E.L. James is popular."

Langer sighed.

"Never mind," said Joanna. "I didn't come here for a book club meeting."

"Glad to hear it," he said. "But I don't understand what you want from me. For obvious reasons, I'm the last person who'd know anything about Kordian's kidnapping."

"I need to know everything, Langer. From beginning to end."

He moved his chains again.

"I want to know why two bodies were found in your apartment, who those people were to you, what were you doing there, whether you were sitting there with them for ten fucking days, and why your father is dead. Everything, understand?"

For the first time since she had met Langer, she saw something in his eyes other than the usual, unnatural calm. She saw fear. At least that's what she thought it was.

"I'm leaving," declared Chyłka, moving towards the door. "I've fucking had enough of this."

"Wait."

"Your pathetic scraps of information aren't going to cut it this time, Langer," she said. "Tell me everything or rot here for the rest of your life."

"Sit down."

For a few moments they eyed each other. She had no intention of returning to her chair. At least not until he gave her some concrete facts.

"So?"

The prisoner sighed.

"Enough," she said. "I'm leaving."

"What about Żelazny?"

"Do you think he has anything to do with it?"

He shrugged his shoulders.

"Tell me as much as you can."

"Have you got a cigarette?"

That was the first thing she'd heard him say that was halfway human. She doubted smoking was allowed in the visiting room; in detention, yes, but in prison it was hardly an option.

She looked at the camera in the corner of the room. Basically, she was free to do anything she wanted until one of the warders looked at the monitor in his cubicle. So she walked up to Langer, took out a single Marlboro from her packet and placed it between his lips. She lit the cigarette, and Piotr inhaled the smoke as if his life depended on it.

The prisoner nodded his head in gratitude.

He managed to take a few more drags before the inevitable key sounded in the lock and a prison officer entered the room. He referred Joanna to the relevant points in the prison regulations, while she contritely bowed her head, waiting for him to finish, and then promised henceforth to stay obediently seated in her chair.

"Right. Now talk," she said when the prison officer had closed the door behind him.

"In accordance with paragraph ninety of the *Attorneys' Code of Ethics,* you can't disclose anything I tell you, is that correct?" He had done his homework, but that was hardly surprising.

He had enough time on his hands, and probably read everything he could get hold of.

"I can't even send an email with the information if you do not give me your express approval for electronic transmission while being aware of the risk it involves," she recited.

"So this is completely confidential."

"Yes, Langer, I will take everything you tell me to the grave," she said. "If you need to know the basis for client confidentiality, look up *Bar Law.* Everything you need is in article six. No court can release me from my obligation to secrecy unless the case concerns money laundering or terrorism. That's it, more or less. There's also something in the *Criminal Procedure Code,* but you don't have to worry about that. Whatever you say, I have to keep to myself."

"OK."

"Unless you're a terrorist."

"I'm not," he replied, and took a deep breath. "I didn't kill those people," he said. And for the first time, Joanna didn't believe him.

CHAPTER

12

KORDIAN WOKE UP feeling like his body was on fire. If someone had asked him to describe his pain, he'd sooner shoot himself in the head than put it into words. He was experiencing a personal Armageddon which he wouldn't wish on his worst enemies.

The last thing he remembered was the Bald Man beating him uncontrollably, as if he wouldn't stop until his victim was dead.

He opened his eyes with some difficulty, and gazed around the room. He had no idea where he was. The neon light was so blinding he wanted to scream, and there was a plastic something in his mouth making it impossible to swallow.

The pain was overwhelming, and he didn't even know where it was coming from.

It took him a while to realise that someone was talking to him, touching his shoulder and leaning over him. Everything was blurred, and at first, he couldn't even make out if it was someone he knew. It was some time before he recognised Kormak.

"Are you alive?"

Kordian wanted to answer Kormak's moronic question, but could barely catch his breath. He lowered his eyelids for a moment to communicate that he could hear him, but drifted straight back into blissful unconsciousness.

When he woke again, he felt a bit better. He recognised Kormak looking down at him, and was ready for what waking up might mean. He managed to keep his eyes open a moment longer—but only a moment. Then he fell asleep again.

This scenario played out over and over again, like a broken record. Each time, Kordian struggled to stay awake a little longer, but each time his strength failed him. A few times he thought he saw Chyłka sitting at his bedside, and once she was even holding his hand.

The first time he awoke and stayed awake was a week after he'd arrived at the hospital. Luckily, Joanna was watching over him at the time, because he feared having to listen to Kormak laboriously explaining everything that had happened during his absence even more than he feared sudden death in a hospital bed.

Oryński opened his eyes. The first thing he saw was Chyłka, looking out of the window, deep in thought. He gazed at her for a few minutes, thinking that at any moment he would drift away again. But he managed to stay awake and noticed that the object in his mouth had been taken out. He cleared his throat, snapping Chyłka out of her reverie.

She looked at him with surprise, then smiled warmly, quite unlike the Chyłka he knew.

"He lives!" she said, and clutched his hand without thinking.

"Uh huh," was the best Oryński could say.

It took him another quarter of an hour to construct the first sentence. Then Joanna started telling him everything she had managed to find out. In that week, the police investigation had got nowhere. There was no trace of the attacker anywhere, he seemed to exist only in police reports and notebooks.

"The amphe . . ." he whispered.

She looked at him crossly.

"Of course they detected Gandalf the White."

He thought she was about to clench her fist and threaten him, but her hand stayed where it was, resting on his. He wondered when she'd realise.

"Have you lost your mind?" she said. "What the fuck is wrong with you?"

"I nearly died . . . give me a break."

"Don't count on getting a break from me, Zordon."

"Heaven forbid . . ."

"I felt sorry for you when you were in a coma. Now I'm going to say what I think."

He forced a weak smile.

"Besides, I'm the least of your problems. Żelazny will destroy you."

It was no more than he expected. First he'd get a dressing down from the District Bar Council, then from Żelazny & McVay. And that would be just the beginning.

"And then, of course, there are the legal ramifications," she said. "Do you know how much you could get for possession?"

"Three," Kordian replied without hesitation. "But I didn't have a gram on me . . . not even under my nose . . ."

"Well, well. Such a great lawyer. Pleased with yourself, are you?"

"I . . ."

"Only now the police don't see you as an innocent victim, but as a potential drug dealer. Someone they'll have to keep an eye on."

"I only want to . . ."

"Apologise?" cut in Chyłka. "I don't want to know. You should have thought of that before you started snorting lines with that idiot."

"You're upset."

"Of course I'm bloody upset!"

"That's why you're squeezing so tightly," Oryński replied with a broad smile.

He looked at his hand, and Chyłka instantly withdrew hers as if she'd been scalded. She got off the bed, muttering something under her breath, and stood with her back to him, looking out of the window.

"Listen," he began. "I found a Supreme Court judgement of . . ."

"28th June 1977," Chyłka continued for him. "I know, Kormak sent me the most recently opened documents from Lex Polonica. And you sent me an email."

Every time he had woken up, Kordian had worried that his discovery would be lost. He had completely forgotten about the email.

"And?" he asked.

"I think it's a good idea,"

"Have you started working on it yet?"

"Not exactly."

"I don't have the strength to drag it out of you word by word," he pleaded.

"I went to visit Langer, but . . ."

But Kordian was no longer listening. He had switched off, remembering the pale light of the moon dissipating over the treetops and the Bald Man standing over him. He had promised to collaborate, he had sworn an oath of loyalty. He had to fail to meet the deadline; he had to make sure the cassation appeal request wasn't delivered on time.

Gorzym had risked a great deal by knocking him out. Apart from the danger that Kordian could be sent from the ICU straight to the mortuary, his convalescence could turn out to be so difficult and so lengthy that he would no longer have anything to do with the case. But the Bald Man wasn't one for cool-headed calculations. There was nothing rational about that cannonade of kicks and punches; it was all part of his barbaric nature.

"Zordon?"

"Yes?"

"Did you hear a word of what I said?"

"Not really," he replied, swallowing.

He couldn't stop his mind racing. He remembered telling himself that the promises he was making were only a pretence; at the time, he kept thinking that once the beating stopped and he was free, he would go to the police.

Now everything was quite different. Perhaps Gorzym had beaten him so severely not because he was in a wild frenzy, but because he knew from experience that a victim whose life had hung in the balance would be terrified of risking the same experience again.

"Fair enough, we'll talk about it another time. Now rest."

"OK," replied Kordian.

Chyłka turned away from the window, looked at him carefully, then nodded and left the room. She deserved more gratitude from him, but Oryński had his own problems to deal with. There would be a time when she could tell him . . . actually, he didn't have the faintest clue what she had wanted to tell him."

He had no more time to ponder the question, because at that moment a doctor came into the room. He introduced himself as Maciej Roske and proceeded to carry out a detailed examination, after which he said that the prognosis was quite good—he wouldn't want to promise anything, but in this case, hope really did spring eternal.

Although Kordian was convinced that with such a whirlwind of thoughts in his head he wouldn't be able to shut his eyes for a second, he fell asleep about an hour later. He was woken a dozen or so times when nurses came in or doctors changed shifts, then the following day, Roske came again, saying it had been over twelve hours since his last visit. Time seemed to run at a different pace in here.

"When can I be discharged?" asked Oryński.

"Don't you like it here with us?"

"I don't have enough to do."

The doctor smiled and looked at the pile of magazines on the bedside cabinet.

"What, with such an arsenal of literature?" He sifted through some of the publications. "What have we here? The latest issue of *Legal Education*, well, well."

His grandmotherly tone got on Oryński's nerves, but he appreciated the effort.

"Probably not the most riveting read?" asked Roske.

"Like all specialist literature. Apparently, your *Medical Gazette* is even worse."

Maciej raised his eyebrows. "The *Medical Gazette* is great," he announced. "As long as you don't read it." He smiled, but Kordian was not overly amused. He was even less delighted by the fact that Roske sat down on the edge of his bed and picked up the latest edition of *Newsweek*.

"Let's see what you've missed out on," he said.

"Probably the same as always: wiretapping, fraud, accidents, and disappearances."

"Quite the fatalist, aren't you?"

Kordian moved his limbs, which were still in splints.

"All this stuff all over me doesn't exactly fill me with optimism."

"We'll take it off soon."

"When?"

The doctor put down the magazine. "As soon as you can put your hand on your heart and swear you're going to keep the promise you made to Gorzym."

13

W RITING A CASSATION appeal was a thankless, and not especially exciting, task. Chyłka was using her formidable skills to formulate arguments, but she knew that even if she wrote the greatest legal work ever, it would soon simply disappear under tonnes of other legal documents. If a director makes a brilliant film, people go to see it for the next fifty years. If a writer writes an outstanding novel, it is read throughout the next century. If an actor plays a part superbly, he becomes a benchmark for that role. But a lawyer? They could create a masterpiece of legal writing, but only fragments of it would ever be read by a few judges, then the whole lot would gather dust in the archives for posterity.

Even as the basis for an academic paper, it wouldn't bring the author everlasting fame. A textbook maybe? Textbook writers were cursed by students for many years after their graduation.

Joanna liked to discuss statute law, arguing with previous rulings, and even with herself. Sometimes something good would come of it; something noble even. But it wasn't something she could use to make a name for herself—or even share with someone else.

Her family wouldn't even read the first page, even if it was the best-written paper in the world. As a lawyer herself, all her friends were lawyers, and all had a justifiable aversion to legal documents. Journalists would wait for someone to translate the legalese into a digestible, newsworthy format; that left only judges, who, with a bit of luck would read the whole justification, and without that bit of luck would ask their assistants to sum up the information it contained.

Chyłka looked at her screen and decided she'd had enough. She reached for the ashtray and her cigarettes.

She had barely lit the first one when "Afraid to Shoot Strangers" rang out from the mobile on her desk. She didn't recognise the number on the display.

"Hello?" she said, exhaling smoke.

"Get me out of here!" said a voice, at once pleading and resolute.

Clearly someone had lent Zordon a phone. His own had disappeared, along with all his other personal belongings, in Izabelin.

"You sound like a general speaking to a sergeant. I don't particularly like it," she said.

"Come and get me, Chyłka. I'm not joking."

She pondered for a moment.

"I have never asked you for a favour. I'm doing it now."

His tone was serious; too serious to dismiss out of hand.

"All right," she replied.

"Hurry. I can't wait here a minute longer."

She got an earpiece and switched on Bluetooth, then grabbed her jacket and put it on, glancing at herself as she went past the mirror in the corridor.

"I'm not sure you're allowed to leave just like that."

"No one can force me to stay. You have to get me out."

"Right, and on the way, I'll phone that medical guy . . . what's his name?"

"Jacek in Medical Law, two doors to the left of Kormak," said Kordian.

Jacek in Medical Law. There was probably a Jacek in every department; there was definitely one in Taxes, and another in Commercial Law. But there were probably quite a few Joannas too.

"OK," she said. "I'll contact him, and you start packing your kit."

"Hurry."

"Calm down, it's . . ."

"I'm not kidding, Chyłka, you've got to get me out of here."

"I'm on my way," she replied, more seriously this time. "Just hold on a bit longer.

See you."

"See you," he replied.

On the way to the lift, she stopped by Kormak's room.

"Get me Jacek in Medical's number," she said, and left before he could reply.

Zordon sounded as if he was about to be dissected, or was on his way to the hospital crematorium. Although she didn't know if it was still OK to call it a crematorium, because she would only ever be able to associate that word with one thing. Out of respect for the millions murdered, she felt other uses of the word should be excluded from the dictionary. Just like people no longer named their children Adolf.

Chyłka had just got in behind the wheel of her X5 when Jacek in Medical's number pinged into her phone. She rang it straightaway, and with a screech of tyres, left her parking space.

"Yes?" said the voice on the phone.

"Is that Jacek in Medical?"

"Speaking."

"Joanna Chyłka here," she said, sounding her horn at a woman who thought she had right of way. When she saw that the woman was going to give way, she stepped on the gas pedal and darted to the Golden Terraces exit.

"Good morning," replied the bewildered Jacek. "How can I . . ."

"I need some quick advice. A patient wants to leave hospital, but he's practically bedbound, plastered up like a soldier in Emperor Qin's Terracotta Army, and hooked up to more equipment than the Star Trek sickbay."

"Did you see—"

"Come on!" she bellowed as the car sped into John Paul II Avenue. "I don't have much time," she added more calmly. "I don't watch the series, only the new Abrams films."

"Terrible degeneration of the universe. You should—"

"Will you help me or won't you?" she asked. He was starting to annoy her.

"Sure," he replied and cleared his throat. "Every patient, with the exception of minors and those who are incapacitated, has the right to request the discontinuation of medical care . . ."

"Get to the point!"

". . . and leave hospital," he ended. "The doctor has to inform them about the consequences of their decision, and the patient has to confirm in writing that they are discharging themselves. The situation is different when the . . ."

Chyłka hung up. She needed a free hand to change gear, and she already had all the information she needed.

Ten minutes later, she pulled into the hospital car park. This time she didn't think about how they were cashing in on all those people who wanted to spend time at a loved one's bedside. It was an appalling practice, extorting money from those in need—but the advantage was that there were a lot of free parking spaces. The same couldn't be said for the roads around the hospital. She parked her X5 and rushed into the building.

In the corridor leading to the ICU, she saw the person she was hoping to see. Actually, she had planned to go to Zordon first to calm him down, and was going to look for the doctor later, but since he was already there she decided to talk to him first.

"What's the matter?" asked Roske, noticing how agitated she was.

"That's what I'm trying to find out," replied Joanna, still trying to catch her breath. She wasn't exactly fit, and rarely did anything that could be defined as sport unless it was speedreading statute law or scanning court rulings in search of something useful.

"I don't understand."

"I got a phone call from my . . ." she paused, ". . . from your patient."

"Is something wrong?"

"Clearly," she said, after a deep breath. "He sounded as if he was being tortured here."

Roske paused to think, looking down the corridor towards Oryński's room. Chyłka decided that there was no point talking to him and started heading down to see Zordon.

"I know you're not family, but . . ." started Roske.

The lawyer stopped and looked at him over her shoulder.

"And there are some things I shouldn't be telling you," he stopped and shook his head. "Especially as you lied to me about being his wife."

"You're prevaricating. Almost as if you're expecting me to give you a bribe."

He looked at her with resentment.

"How could you . . ."

"If you have something to say, say it quickly," she cut in.

"I know you're close to the patient," said the doctor. "The police have tried to contact his family, but apparently he's a black sheep, or they've all died, not that it's any of my business. But you and that man with the glasses are the only visitors he's had."

"Get to the point."

"I feel someone should be told, and you'll anyway hear it sooner or later from . . . your boyfriend? Fiancé?"

"Say what you have to say, I'm losing my patience."

The doctor raised his hand in apology. If he hadn't been so focused on the role he was playing, he'd have been amused by her fury. She was like a madwoman, capable of anything. And Roske liked women like that.

"The thing is, it's not just the physical injuries."

"You mean Gandalf the White?"

"The what?"

"The amphetamines?"

"No," he replied. "I mean his mental health. The patient's mental health has suffered too, to some extent. I'm not a psychologist, I can't say exactly what happened, but there's certainly been some trauma. When he woke up and you weren't here, he'd hurl abuse at the nurses, accusing hospital staff of complicity, of being part of the plot to get him beaten up. Do you understand?"

"Yes, I understand."

"It was different when you were there," added Roske, knowing she'd be happy to feel needed. "You have a soothing effect on him, that's why I thought it might be a good idea for you to talk to him with a psychologist present. But with this situation now, I'm not so sure. Perhaps he should be transferred to the psychiatric ward."

"You must be fucking joking."

"Please don't get me wrong, I only want what's best for the patient," said Roske, spreading his arms. "Let me talk to him. You'll see for yourself that his problems go far beyond what we can deal with here."

She nodded and smiled insincerely, deciding she'd already wasted enough time. She walked past the doctor and again headed towards Oryński's room, with no intention of spending any more time on the pile of nonsense she'd just heard.

But as her initial anger subsided, she mulled it over again. Thinking rationally, she had to admit that Roske might be right. Zordon had sounded excessively agitated over the phone, and his severe beating must have had some effect on his mental state.

She quickened her pace.

14

"At last!" Kordian cried out in greeting. "What took you so long?"

"Traffic."

They looked at one another as never before. As if everything depended on that exchange of looks.

Kordian struggled to get out of bed. Joanna rushed to help him free himself from all the medical apparatus.

"Let's get out of here," he said as she took him under the arm. "We need to hurry. . . ."

"Not until you tell me what it's all about."

"You have to trust me."

"Oh no, Zordon, we're not playing that game," she protested. "You're not going to be another Langer. That's out of the question."

"I'll tell you on the way."

"No. Tell me now."

He looked at her reproachfully and wondered for a moment what he should do. He glanced nervously at the corridor, not doubting for a moment that Gorzym's messenger was somewhere nearby, perhaps even listening in on the conversation. If he said anything now, it would be signing his own death warrant.

"For God's sake, Zordon, tell me what's going on," she urged him.

He swallowed and made up his mind.

"That doctor, Roske," began Kordian. "He came up to me not long ago. He said he was sent by the thugs who beat me up. He threatened me, saying that they would do it again."

"Why would a doctor threaten you, Zordon?"

Oryński stepped back, looking at her in dismay. There was no surprise in her voice, she took in everything he said with total calm.

"Exactly," cut in Roske as he entered the room. "Why?"

Kordian took another step back. His legs were shaking.

"Please leave," said Chyłka, looking pointedly at the corridor.

"If the patient wishes to leave the hospital, it is my duty to inform him of the possible consequences. I also need his decision in writing," countered the doctor. "Otherwise, I won't be able to discharge him."

Kordian moved back a little more.

"Relax," said Roske. "No one's keeping you here by force. We just have to go through the formalities."

"So send someone else," said Kordian. "I have no intention . . . I shan't . . ." he paused and turned to Chyłka. "They're all . . ." he whispered. "They're all in it together."

Joanna looked at Oryński, then at the doctor.

"They're all in it together," Oryński repeated in an undertone, as if Roske, who was right next to them, wouldn't be able to hear. "This is something really big. I don't know what it's about, but you've got to talk to Langer."

Joanna had talked to Langer. She had found out a few things, but nothing that could explain Kordian's beating. Now she looked at him, half hoping he would suddenly smile and say that he and the doctor were just pulling her leg.

"Get me out of here, Chyłka. Do this for me."

She didn't know what to say. Everything she was seeing now confirmed what Roske had told her.

"Chyłka!"

"Relax, Zordon."

"I have to do my rounds," said the doctor. "So if you don't want to wait until I've finished, I suggest we complete the formalities now."

"We'll wait."

"No!" protested Oryński.

He hobbled towards the door, full of nervous energy. He went straight for the doctor, as if he wanted to knock him down. Fortunately, Roske had fast reflexes, and caught the patient as he started to topple.

"Let go of me!"

He tried to break free, but Roske was holding him tight. Joanna looked on in helpless despair. "Chyłka!" He was pleading for help.

She could see he was trying desperately to get away and that the doctor had stopped him, although it had taken considerable effort. Now Zordon was trying to headbutt him.

"Can . . . you . . . help me?" said Roske to Chyłka.

Oryński moved sluggishly, as if in slow motion, but he was still difficult to contain. Finally, Roske shouted something in the direction of the corridor, and three nurses rushed into the room. Seeing the doctor in danger, they threw themselves on the patient.

"Hey!" protested Chyłka. "Easy now!"

Kordian was yelling at the top of his voice as the hospital staff forced him onto the bed. He was writhing, even with his legs in splints, and Joanna was sure he'd damaged his dressings. He was still shouting when they strapped him to the bed. Then suddenly he stopped, and quietly begged Chyłka to help him.

She looked away, she couldn't watch. She felt like a complete bitch, turning her back on someone in need.

"Please come with me," said Roske striding to the door.

Chyłka followed him uncertainly, trying to ignore Oryński, who was trying to convince her he was in danger.

"What's all this about?" she asked the doctor after they had gone outside and closed the door. "When he arrived here, he was fine mentally, but now . . ." she paused and shook her head.

"As I say, this is a complicated matter. Only the psychologist will be able to . . ."

"What will happen to him?"

"That depends on his family," replied the doctor. "If you could give us any details, I'd be most grateful."

"I'll see what I can do."

Roske nodded.

"For now, I'm going to give him propofol, because it looks like he needs to calm down."

Chyłka had no idea what this was, but she had no reason not to trust the doctor.

"I'd like you to sit with him afterwards, if possible."

"No problem."

For a moment, she sat in silence, looking carefully at Roske. Her profession brought her into contact with liars and all kinds of other scum, and she could usually spot deception and duplicity a mile away. But he seemed sincere. Besides, how on earth could he be involved in a plot?

The whole Langer case was suspect—and from what Langer had told her, she had reason to believe he'd been framed. But somehow, for the first time, she didn't trust him. Likewise, she didn't believe someone had it in for Zordon.

On the other hand, mental illness was even less likely. Perhaps it was shock? After all, Oryński had been beaten so severely that he could easily have been a goner.

In the end, Chyłka decided shock was the most likely explanation. She waited until Roske had administered the sedative, then sat down on the side of the bed and placed her hand on the boy's hand. Kordian gazed unconsciously at the ceiling and seemed quite unaware of her presence. And yet, she was not planning on going anywhere.

15

Maciej Roske burst into the medics' staff room and slammed the door behind him. No one else was there, so he let loose his rage, swearing profusely. Then he took a deep breath, held the air in his lungs for a moment, and released it through his nostrils. He had to repeat the process several times before he calmed down.

Then he grabbed the phone and dialled a number he'd been given to use only if absolutely essential.

"What's happened?" the voice in the receiver asked.

"Gorzym has happened. A fuck-up has happened, which I can't clean up. The bloody thug who can't even . . ."

"Try breathing slowly and deeply."

"I have done, but when I think about him . . ."

"Tell me what happened."

"You've got to get rid of people like him," said the doctor. He was one of the few people who could talk so directly to the Grey-Haired Man. Most of his other associates had to speak to him with far more deference.

"Gorzym can be useful."

"For burying bodies maybe, but not for this sort of thing," protested Maciej. "He was supposed to explain the consequences of disobedience, not demonstrate them. He almost killed him."

"Calm down."

The doctor dutifully fell silent and breathed in and out a couple of times.

"Anyway, the young man wanted to discharge himself from hospital today. I had to give him a fairly powerful sedative."

"Can he walk?"

"Yes, instead of breaking his legs Gorzym remodelled his face."

The Grey-Haired Man was silent for a moment.

"Did you explain what's in store for him?"

"Yes. He panicked and phoned his boss."

"You obviously didn't do it very well then."

Roske knew that in the end, he'd probably get all the blame. Gorzym had some sort of hold over his boss, and made good use of it.

"If they hadn't nearly killed the boy, he wouldn't have had any reason to panic," argued the doctor. "I would have reminded him of his promises, and he would have left the hospital to do what was expected of him."

There was a momentary silence.

"Fix it."

"How?" asked the doctor.

"Speak to him. Remind him that Gorzym can turn up at any time."

"He's going to avoid me like the plague."

"You've dealt with more difficult situations."

"Yes, but . . ."

"Can I count on you?"

"Of course," Roske replied, though he had no idea how he was going to get Oryński to cooperate. The trainee had had plenty of time to think things through, he wouldn't be making any hasty decisions.

"Let him leave hospital," said the Grey-Haired Man.

"I wanted to hold on to him a while longer for a psych . . ."

"No. It's time for him to do what he's got to do."

"That might be difficult. He made a huge scene in front of Chyłka and the hospital staff."

Maciej Roske waited for his boss to respond, but he'd already hung up. He looked at his phone and swore silently.

There was nothing for it, he had to get to work. He looked at the nightshift roster and started making changes. A few minutes and several phone calls later, he had arranged to be on duty that night. He waited for visiting hours to end, then personally escorted Chyłka to the car park. He assured her that everything would be all right and that he had contacted the psychologist, who would visit Oryński in the morning.

She didn't seem happy with the arrangement, but at least she had left her protégé in hospital. If she had done as Oryński wanted, Roske's problems would have been far greater.

He limited his night rounds to just a few wards, spending a long time in the one where Oryński lay. He stood over his bed, made sure he was securely strapped in, and proceeded to wake him up. When Kordian opened his eyes, he started flailing around like a wounded animal caught in a snare.

"Lie still."

Oryński tried even more desperately to free himself, swearing wildly. Roske sighed and left the room again to finish his rounds. He looked in on other patients here and there to satisfy his professional conscience, then returned to his most important patient some ten minutes later. By then, Kordian had calmed down.

"You're in big trouble," said the doctor, closing the door behind him.

Oryński looked at him with fury.

"You've caused a lot of problems."

"Good."

"Oh, really? Do you want to play games with me?"

The boy jerked his hands and gritted his teeth.

"What have you given me?" he asked.

"Still feeling the effects? Weakness? Feeling lightheaded?"

Oryński didnt answer.

"I gave you propofol," explained Roske. "It's normally used as an anaesthetic in surgery, but in your case, I made an exception. And let me tell you, there are plenty of other exceptions I can make."

"So much for the Hippocratic oath, eh?"

The doctor looked at Kordian as if he was born yesterday.

"And you, a lawyer, saying that. Unbelievable." He shook his head. "But let's stop kidding around, because the situation is very serious. At least, it is for you."

"Go to hell."

Roske sat still for a moment, then pursed his lips and got off the bed. He walked over to the door and looked back over his shoulder.

"I can go, but you'll suffer most."

"I'll take that risk."

"We don't want much from you," continued the doctor undeterred. For now, it's only a matter of sorting this out. You only need to tell Chyłka that you weren't feeling well, that you were dazed or something. You'll manage."

"No."

"And then I'll discharge you, and we can forget all about the post-traumatic stress incident."

Oryński said nothing.

"It won't take much for me to let Gorzym into the room," added Roske. "I have keys, I can open every door. And that man has no self-control. There's no knowing what he'd do."

Kordian stared at the ceiling, breathing heavily.

"And he won't stop at you," continued Roske. "Gorzym has much more fun with women than with men."

He looked at his patient and saw how much closer he was to making the only sensible decision. He must have realised that if he didn't cooperate, they would not only make him suffer, but they'd come for those closest to him.

"Who the fuck are you?"

Roske grabbed the door handle. "I'll explain it all to you first thing in the morning."

"I don't know when Chyłka will come."

"She'll come as always, in the morning. If you do it quickly, I'll personally make sure you get discharged."

Oryński nodded without a word. He had no other choice.

CHAPTER

16

S OMEHOW KORDIAN MANAGED to persuade Chyłka that he had suffered a temporary moment of madness—the result of shock. Joanna
believed him, no doubt because she wanted to believe him, and also
because Kordian told his story with a good dose of self-deprecation.

When he had finished, Chyłka looked at him inquisitively. "I don't
understand," she said. "Are you crazy, or aren't you?"

"No, I'm not."

"And yet I get the impression that you might be."

"I've been discharged, haven't I? They wouldn't let a madman loose
on the streets."

"Maybe they had to vacate a bed on account of the current health
service crisis."

"The health service is always in crisis."

"True."

They were making their way down the corridor towards the exit.
Oryński, on crutches, looked around nervously. He was convinced that
Roske would appear at any moment and stop them leaving. But the doctor was nowhere to be seen, and they reached the car park safely. Clearly
he'd told them all they needed to know.

"Where are you parked?" asked Kordian.

Joanna pointed to her X5, and offered Oryński a cigarette. He lit it
with satisfaction, although after the long break he'd had, the first drag
made him cough.

"Where are we going?" he asked, manoeuvring himself into the passenger seat. He put his crutches on the back seat.

"To your place."

"OK, as long as it's only to get changed. After that I'm going to the Skylight."

"Oh yes? And then we're going to climb Mount Everest."

"I'm serious," he said. "I have to occupy my mind, or I'll lose it."

"You're using the future tense, and yet you really did lose it yesterday," she said as they drove into Marymoncka Street. She changed lanes several times, although the road was short. "Are you sure everything is all right with you, Zordon?"

"You're asking as if you care."

"And who else should care if not me? And Kormak?" she said. "We sat at your bedside for hours when no one else did."

"I do appreciate it. I'm genuinely grateful," said Oryński. "It would be quite different if my family . . ."

"I'm not especially interested in your family relationships."

"My father has basically disowned me. Even disinherited me."

She looked at him. "He's deprived you of your legal portion?" she asked.

"No, not in that sense . . ."

"So express yourself in precise terms, as befits a legal protégé," she told him. "Disinheritance means depriving someone of their right to a legal portion."

He nodded, not really wanting to dive into the twists and turns of inheritance law.

"In that case, he didn't include me in his last will and testament. Precise enough?"

"Yes," she replied. "Why?"

"A minute ago, you weren't interested in my family relationships."

"Well now I am. What did you do to make your family hate you?"

Kordian watched in terror as the car passed a cyclist, leaving only a centimetre between the BMW's wing mirror and the potential victim.

"My mother died a few years ago," said Kordian. "And my father thinks it's my fault."

"What?"

Kordian shrugged his shoulders.

"Now you've really got me interested. What happened?"

Kordian thought for a moment, watching the passing cars. It seemed as if all the other cars were driving a good fifty kilometres per hour slower.

"We took turns to look after her," he said. "My father and I. It wasn't easy, my father neglected his work, I didn't have time to study for tests and exams. That's how I managed to fail Roman Law and Civil Procedure."

"What was wrong with your mother?"

"Lupus."

He thought Chyłka would make a joke about it, because lupus was always the last-resort diagnosis in *House,* although no one ever really suffered from it. But she was silent, systematically overtaking successive cars. Maybe she had never watched the TV series.

"It affected her heart," added Oryński. "It was very tough on her. Basically, she was almost bedridden. It's a terrible disease."

Chyłka nodded.

"She had to take this drug for her heart condition," he continued. "One day, when I was looking after her, she took a double dose. It was enough to kill her."

"And your father blamed you?"

"He and my entire family. Once, when he was drunk, he even accused me of giving her the overdose."

"Nasty situation."

"I'll say. I doubt there are many sons whose fathers accuse them of euthanising their own mother."

Joanna fell silent, and Kordian knew she was going to ask the question all lawyers ask their clients.

"Did you do it?"

"No."

That was enough for her. They dropped the subject, and for a quarter of an hour they drove in silence. There was heavy traffic at this time of day, but Chyłka skilfully managed to avoid the biggest jams in the city centre. Then a bus turned into the left lane in front of them. Joanna swerved into the right lane and stepped on the accelerator. The X5 shot forward.

"What are you so edgy about?" asked Oryński.

Chyłka shrugged it off, but she had to admit she was a bag of nerves. Zordon talking about his mother had distracted her for a moment from the image she'd seen the day before, the recurring image of her trainee writhing on the hospital bed, screaming and screaming.

Yesterday, she was sure it would take him forever to get over it. Although the wounds on his body were healing fast, she thought the psychological damage would take much longer to repair. And yet today he was sitting next to her in the car, ready to get behind his desk in the newbie-burrow and pick up where he had left off.

And as if to prove her right, Kordian now asked, "What about the cassation appeal? Did you follow my lead?"

"Your lead? The lead that was determined by seven judges of the Supreme Court in 1977?"

"But I sniffed it out."

"Like the best bloodhound," she agreed.

"I don't particularly like the way this conversation is going," replied Kordian, resting his head against the window. "I'd prefer it if you told me if you've already got something."

"I've already scribbled half the application for appeal. Your jaw will drop when you read it."

It was a comforting thought. Her family, friends, and the judges were unlikely to read what she had created, but her trainee certainly would. What's more, he'd not only understand the text, but comment on it.

They pulled up outside Kordian's block in Żoliborz, and Oryński invited her to come in with him.

"It wouldn't be for long," he added.

"That's not much of an argument. If someone's going to stab me in the stairwell, they'd only need a second."

"Well, wait for me down here?"

"No."

"Give me a break, I don't want to stay home alone, like a dog," he said. "Besides, in case you hadn't noticed, I have a problem." He glanced at the crutches on the back seat. "I can't do the stairs on my own."

"Do you want me to take you to the toilet as well?" she muttered, opening the car door. She went to the passenger side and pulled out the crutches, magnanimously lent to him by the hospital for the duration of his convalescence. She helped Kordian out of the car and supported him as he limped towards the building. At the entrance, she looked over her shoulder at the X5 parked in the street. It could be the last time she saw her baby.

"Hmm," murmured Oryński.

"What's the matter?"

"I have a problem."

She looked at him with concern but couldn't see the problem. He was white as a sheet, there were deep shadows under his bloodshot eyes and his face was one big, bloody bruise.

But even so, he looked much better than he had the day before.

"Zordon?"

"The keys."

She swore under her breath. "You left them at the hospital?"

"Not exactly," he replied. "The thing is, during the attack, I was robbed of everything. Well, apart from that pen and a pack of tissues."

For a moment, Chyłka stared silently at the locked door.

"You imbecile," she finally said. "You could have thought of that earlier."

"I had a lot on my mind, then you started asking me about my father and . . ."

"And did these people take your ID card as well as the keys to your flat?"

"Well, yes," he admitted, clearly perplexed. "But at least I'm not registered here."

"Oh, well then I take it back," she said. "No one will ever be able to track you down now, genius."

"Can you put me up for the night?" he asked, coming straight out with it, not allowing himself to be put off.

"No, spend the night on the staircase if you reckon it's so safe."

"I don't have the keys."

"A neighbour will let you in," she replied, then she let go of him and turned away. "See you, peg leg," she added with a wave of the hand.

Kordian stood stock still, watching Chyłka walk away. When he thought about it, he realised he didn't know many people who would put him up for a few nights.

"Come on then, you moron," she said without turning around. He limped to the BMW as fast as he could.

Though locked out of his own home, he was in a good mood. He had survived an encounter with the tyrant from hell, escaped from hospital—and he was spending the night at Chyłka's.

But then he came back down to earth, remembering he was now under Roske's thumb as well as Gorzym's. He also remembered Joanna saying something about Langer. Had she visited him in prison? Did she talk to him? There was some snippet of information rattling around in his head, but he couldn't quite put his finger on it.

"What about Langer?" he asked as they were leaving Mickiewicz Street.

"What about him? she replied, slamming on the indicator.

Oryński liked talking to her when she was driving, when she was completely absorbed in manoeuvring between cars and answered questions without really thinking about it and without taking her eyes off the road. There was something almost sexy about it.

"Did you visit him?"

"I already told you," she replied, changing gears and swooping in between a bus and another car. "I visited him, and gave him an ultimatum."

"Well done."

"Shut up and listen."

Kordian looked at her intently, silently urging her to continue.

"I told him he had to be honest with us or he could look for another lawyer."

"Did it do the trick?"

"Not exactly. First he announced that he couldn't tell me everything, though to be fair, he did open up a little. He began by saying he was innocent."

"At last."

"I'm not sure what to think, Zordon," she replied, frowning. A van had just slipped into her lane and she was desperate to overtake it. "Something's not right."

"Nothing is right when you drive like that."

"I'm talking about Langer."

"I thought we'd established that he was innocent? At least between ourselves?"

"Yes, but now I'm not so sure. I didn't believe him. Perhaps it's intuition, perhaps it's stupidity, it's hard to tell."

"You're getting quite self-critical," he said appreciatively. "A bit more of this and there'll be no narcissism left."

She threw a glance in his direction and shook her head.

"What did he tell you?" Oryński asked.

"That he can't give us any leads."

"Why?"

"I don't know. He also said he can't talk about whether he's guilty, and he can't actively participate in the trial."

Kordian started picking at his lip nervously, looking at the cars she'd overtaken.

"So what *can* he do?" he asked.

"It seems he can only talk about what he can't do."

Oryński opened the glove compartment in search of cigarettes, and was surprised he couldn't find any. Then he remembered there was a strict no-smoking rule in the X5.

For a while they drove in silence.

"There can only be one reason," Chyłka said finally, looking at her passenger to see if he had worked it out too.

"Someone's got something on him," said Kordian. "But what?"

"I don't know. I tried to ask him, but he wouldn't say anything at all."

Oryński tried to piece everything together. In vain.

"But you don't believe him," he said.

"No."

"Pity, because that would make sense, Chyłka. It would be boring, but it would make sense."

"Unless he had set it all up himself. Unless he was playacting from the start, playing it quietly at first, and now claiming someone else was behind it."

"I don't think so. Too much trouble."

"He's facing a life sentence. I wouldn't have thought anything would be too much trouble for him."

"Even if you're right, it doesn't explain why he was sitting with those rotting corpses for ten days."

"Maybe he's even more depraved than you thought?"

Oryński shook his head. He longed to be in Chyłka's apartment, smoking a cigarette. He hoped it would help clear his mind, because at the moment everything was beyond him.

17

THEY SAT IN the kitchen at Chyłka's to continue the conversation, moving swiftly on from the what-ifs to the much more pressing matter of the cassation appeal and the strategy they should adopt.

When they were finished, Kordian was dead on his feet, dreaming about lying down on a comfortable bed. Instead, he got the couch, a piece of furniture whose only purpose in life was to look good. It was as hard as rock, but Joanna swept away his objections by explaining how much better it was for him to sleep on a firm surface.

She offered him a beer, which Kordian readily accepted, but by the time she'd brought the bottles from the fridge he was already fast asleep.

The following morning as they drove to work, Oryński used Chyłka's tablet to find out how you could legally open the door to your flat if you'd lost the key. The solution was alarmingly simple. You just had to make a phone call. The internet was full of authorised companies, available 24/7, who could open your car, apartment or anything else that you'd locked.

"So I could have slept at my flat yesterday, after all," he said, turning the tablet around to show Joanna the emergency locksmith advertisements.

"Uh-huh," was her only reply.

"Oh, believe me, I'm really disappointed."

"Why, were you hoping for something in the night, Zordon?"

"No, I'm disappointed with the couch."

"It cost a shed-load of money."

"It was probably more comfortable in Auschwitz."

Chyłka gave him a scathing look. She loathed people referring to World War II victims in a light-hearted way, out of context; they deserved to be remembered with respect. She decided, however, that this was not the time to explain it to her protégé.

They parked under Golden Terraces, and set off on foot down Emilia Plater Street towards the Skylight building.

As they entered the office, the usual tumult suddenly turned to silence. Everyone was looking at them. A few people started to applaud quietly, but soon everyone was clapping and cheering, and shouting words of support to Kordian. They patted him on the back, congratulated him on his fortitude—even Żelazny appeared and personally shook the trainee by the hand.

"Injured, brought back from the brink of death, barely able to walk on crutches and yet he has turned up for work," said Artur, looking around at all his employees.

"Ready for work and eager to fight," replied Kordian.

It was as if there was a hidden camera somewhere and they were shooting a Żelazny & McVay commercial.

Old Rusty invited him into his office, and the employees immediately moved away to make a path for him. Oryński limped slowly to the end of the corridor, feeling rather foolish.

Żelazny closed the door behind him, making Kordian feel uneasy. It would have been good to have Chyłka next to him, but she had gone off to her own office. Oh well, he'd just have to manage.

"I'm glad you're so keen to get back to work," began Żelazny, helping Kordian into a chair. Żelazny perched himself on the edge of the desk with his arms folded. "You really should be resting, but your presence here is testament to your fortitude."

"Thank you."

"It's important to me that you realise how much I appreciate your work ethic. And it is I who should be thanking you."

The calm before the storm, Oryński thought.

"May I call you by your first name?" asked Żelazny.

"Of course."

"Well, how can I put it, Kordian? I'm in an awkward . . . very uncomfortable situation."

Kordian had to admit that his boss was a good actor. If he hadn't known what to expect, he would have been quite taken in by Żelazny's performance.

"You'd be a hero were it not for that one thing," he said, letting out his breath in one long whistle.

"I understand."

"You'd be my hero too, son. I'd put you on a par with Leon Peiper. Have you heard of him?"

"No, I haven't."

"Yet every law student has heard of Makarewicz," said Żelazny dramatically, the pain evident in his voice.

He pronounced the word student with disdain, disgust almost, as did every veteran lawyer of his ilk. It was as if they were talking about creatures not of this world, hobgoblins living somewhere underground, fearing the light and leaving a trail of slime behind them. Warhorses such as Żelazny seemed to forget that they wouldn't have the positions they had now if they hadn't at some stage left behind their own five-year trail of slime.

"Makarewicz is remembered because his code included the penalty of death by hanging," said Kordian.

"Indeed, it did. But apart from that, it included legislation of the highest level. World Class. In my opinion, however, he doesn't hold a candle to Peiper," said Artur, standing up.

He walked around the office as if he couldn't find the right place, until he eventually sat down on the leather chair behind the desk. He unfolded his arms and put them on the armrests, looking inscrutably at Oryński.

The trainee wondered when Żelazny would stop his playacting and get to the point.

"Do you realise that if we had the same internal Criminal Code they had in those times, I'd have to administer a similar punishment?" he asked with a ghost of a smile.

"Yes."

It was hypocrisy of the worst kind, and Kordian's reaction was to be as monosyllabic as possible. He assumed he was in for the high jump anyway, so there was no point in getting involved in clever wordplay.

"Were it not for the amphetamines, I'd shower you with gold, really."

Kordian wondered why on earth he should be showered with gold—he might have been beaten up, but he hadn't rescued anyone, jumped into a blazing building or helped a damsel in distress.

"I don't know, I really don't know . . ." continued Artur, folding his arms again. "What am I to do with you, Kordian? You know that the firm's reputation will suffer?"

"Yes."

Żelazny sighed ostentatiously. "I am waiting for you to suggest something, because I really have no idea what to do with all this."

"Sir," began Oryński, trying to control his nerves. "At the moment I am just glad that I survived."

Short, clear, and to the point. He wanted to make Żelazny realise that there was more to life than just the firm, but he wasn't expecting miracles.

"What do you want me to say?" said Rusty. "I'd like you to be honest."

Żelazny looked far into the distance and nodded his head.

"Keeping you on is going to be a problem for me," he said. "At the same time, I don't want to be seen as the brute who fires employees because they're weak and need drugs to stay afloat."

"It was only once . . ."

"Don't interrupt me."

He sounded like a virtuoso distracted in the middle of a performance by a ringing mobile.

"What I feel like doing is handing you your notice now, then organising an anti-narcotics campaign within the legal community. I'd make you a scapegoat, but it's no more than you deserve."

Kordian appreciated his boss's frankness, but said nothing. "Nevertheless, I'm willing to keep you on until this case is closed. Then Żelazny & McVay will pay for you to stay at a rehab centre, and we'll say goodbye."

"Rehab?" said Oryński, genuinely bemused. "I'm not a drug addict."

"In the eyes of the media you are."

The trainee didn't respond. There was no point. "Do you understand everything I've said?"

"Yes," he replied, getting up onto his crutches.

"You don't leave until I say the case is closed."

Kordian ignored him and headed for the door. He had a little difficulty with opening it, but Artur didn't help. He didn't shut the door behind him. Hobbling slowly towards Chyłka's office, he wondered whether Żelazny had anything to do with Gorzym and his mob. After all, he was allowing him to stay on until the case was closed, which would make it possible for him to miss the cassation appeal deadline. Under normal circumstances taking drugs meant immediate dismissal.

He went straight to Joanna's office, thinking he'd soon have to decide what to do about the cassation appeal.

"Finished already?" she asked, looking at her watch.

Normally she'd be off limits to the world at this time of day, but this was an extraordinary situation. She helped him in and sat him down on the other side of her desk.

"Not a nice man," he said.

"Difficult to get on with, but at the end of the day one of the best bosses I've ever had. Perhaps not as great as McVay, but that's probably because McVay has better things to do than worry about PR blunders."

"Such as practising law?"

"Among other things," Joanna replied with a smile. "Here, look at the justification," she added, turning her laptop around.

The thirty-page document was an elegantly phrased tirade against the courts responsible for Langer's sentence. Kordian read through the text with interest, proud to note that his discovery formed the basis of

Joanna's very well-argued appeal. None of the points she made were laboured or far-fetched, which was important when writing for the Supreme Court. He was sure the judges would give this a chance.

Provided it was submitted on time.

"Very good," he said. "You can see I had a hand in it."

"Watch yourself, or you'll see my hand slapping your face."

"You watch yourself," he objected, "or you'll make me relive my trauma."

"I'll send the file to your office address," said Joanna, changing the subject and turning the laptop back to face her. "Do you need help to limp over to the newbie-burrow?"

"Can't I work here?"

"Can you see any computers here other than mine?"

"I can bring one in."

"Out of the question, peg leg," she replied. "You can go to the newbie-burrow, get a few words of praise from the cyborgs, if any of them can tear themselves away from their work, then proofread what I've written and add a few of your own suggestions. The clock is ticking, and we're on the home stretch. To battle!"

"I don't want to sit in the battery cage."

"Go away, Zordon, while you still have the use of your legs."

He mumbled something under his breath and rose slowly from his chair. Chyłka got up to help him.

"So how does all this work?" he asked on the way out. "How do they decide whether a cassation appeal can go ahead? Is there some sort of trial?"

Chyłka stopped at the door. She shook her head, then ushered Oryński back into the room. He protested quietly as she sat him back down on his chair.

"Did you read the Criminal Procedure Code?"

"A bit."

"A bit would be enough if you were working for the Tractor and Combine Harvester Law Firm in some fly-blown village in the middle of nowhere."

"It's not exactly riveting literature," replied Kordian. "What can I say?"

Joanna raised her eyebrows and sighed.

"The cassation appeal is brought to which body?"

"Are you going to test me? Seriously?" asked Oryński, with a smile that gradually began to wane as he realised she was waiting for him to answer. "The Court of Appeal, in our case."

"Well done," she gushed. "And who rules on the admissibility of the cassation?"

"The Court of Appeal."

"Wow, Zordon, you're the perfect man for this job," she said, applauding slowly. "When you were at university, did you ever think about studying?"

"Go on, have your fun," he grumbled. "But I seem to remember the Supreme Court has the right not to consider the cassation appeal if it doesn't fulfil all the criteria."

"And then what happens? Assuming we manage to pull something amazing out of the bag?"

"Is there a trial?"

"Yes. Except where a sitting takes place without either party present."

"Well, yes."

"And would that apply to us?"

"No, it wouldn't."

"Excellent! You're a star. If there was a medal for outstanding achievement in the field of shirking, I'd award it to you right now!"

"You can laugh, but I also remember that if the Court of Appeal rejects our case, we can formally complain in writing directly to the Supreme Court."

"Well, Zordon!" exclaimed Joanna, covering her eyes. "The light of your wisdom is blinding me."

He gave a wry smile and shook his head. He would enjoy needling a trainee like this too, especially if they deserved it. And he did deserve it. He should have had all this off pat, it was basic knowledge. But he did know something about the later procedures—he knew, for example, that for the Supreme Court, the scope of the case was strictly limited to the way it had been presented in the cassation appeal. There were a few exceptions, though Kordian couldn't remember offhand what they were.

"May I go now?" he asked. "I feel older and wiser."

"Go in peace and sin no more," said Joanna.

She helped him to the newbie-burrow, and left him in the tender care of the resident humanoids. Kordian dived straight into Chyłka's justification document. It was really not bad at all. And it occurred to him what a huge leap this could be for his career.

You usually had to wait years before having a case heard by the Supreme Court, because as a rule, cases were assigned to more experienced lawyers. As a trainee, Kordian's role would be little more than decorative, but it would still be something to tell his grandchildren. Only if they studied law, of course, otherwise they wouldn't be impressed at all.

Oryński looked at the address of the Supreme Court at the top of the letter. He still hadn't made up his mind.

18

E VERYTHING WAS READY a day ahead of the deadline, at least in terms of content. All they needed now was the seal of the post office or court registry. Of course, deadline with a day to spare was as much an oxymoron at Żelazny & McVay as anywhere else. There was always something else that needed doing, something that had to be completed or corrected.

Looking at the finished document, Chyłka tried to remember whether she had ever filed a lawsuit a day in advance. She couldn't recall a single time it had happened, but she certainly wasn't unique in that respect. As an intern, she'd made some interesting acquaintances thanks to the last-minute rush, with employees from other law firms also making a mad dash to get to the court registry before close of business. It was a prime meeting place for interns from all around the city: they stood in the registry queue together, left the court building together, and relationships blossomed. There was always something to talk about, cigarettes to share and gossip to exchange.

But for her, those days were long gone. As a Senior Associate, she couldn't run around the city taking documents from A to B, she had more important things to do. Besides, it would break with age-old traditions. Now it was Zordon's turn to enjoy the charms of a potential chance encounter at the court building.

He no longer needed crutches, although the doctors said he should still be careful not to overdo it. He also tired very quickly; but taking the papers to court was not a task Joanna could entrust to anyone else.

Everything was ready to go. Their arguments were sound and convincing, and Chyłka was in no doubt their case would make it through the appeal stage. In any case, the Appeal Court had no discretionary powers. If the application fulfilled the basic criteria and was not subject to the exceptions stipulated in statute law, it had to be sent on to the Supreme Court. And Joanna had checked over and over that there were no technicalities to prevent the cassation appeal from being considered. Admittedly, lawyers have been saying since time immemorial that some cases should be settled before they reached the courtroom, because once they were in court nothing was certain—but this case was different. Here, the case could not be just made to go away, at least not in the early stages. Of course, once the hearing began, anything could happen.

Joanna was pleased that she'd be facing professional judges only, and no lay assessors. She wanted to draw their attention to legal tricks and loopholes, small enough to have been overlooked, but not so small that they were little more than an irritation for the adjudicating panel. She couldn't predict the outcome but was cautiously optimistic.

Of course, there were always a few things that could go pear-shaped.

Cassations were subject to a number of regulations, the most awkward being that if something wasn't included in the original appeal document, it couldn't be considered by the court. And Langer was opening up more with each passing day, giving them new information. Now he was saying that he had never met the two victims. Oryński believed him, but Chyłka was sceptical.

Still, none of this mattered anymore. Whatever new facts he revealed, the case was closed as of tomorrow.

When the knocking on her door began, Joanna looked at her watch. Half past eleven. This was a completely inappropriate time to bother her—even Zordon was off limits now he was off crutches.

So when the knock came again, Chyłka ignored it. But the visitor let himself in anyway.

"Hi Chyłka," said Żelazny, closing the door behind him. "I know this is your research time, but I need to let you know my decision."

Joanna recognised that tone of voice. Seemingly friendly, affable even; but the message he carried was bound to be grim.

"I have to fire him," he said, sitting down on the edge of her desk.

Chyłka scowled.

"Relax. I paid for the furniture in this office."

"Have you gone mad, Artur?"

"Quite the opposite," he answered with a smile. "I've decided that now this is the perfect time to say goodbye to your drug addict. And I'll tell the media that we've had to dismiss him for reasons completely unrelated to drugs."

"And they'll believe you of course," she sneered, although she noticed he had a look of supreme confidence in his eyes. This was a bad sign.

Żelazny was highly experienced both in legal and media matters, and if he decided he could do something, he'd make sure it would happen.

"They'll wonder why I did it. A day before filing the cassation appeal, practically at the start of the trial! What a blow to Żelazny & McVay. What a blow. Why didn't Żelazny wait? In the end they'll assume the young lad has been caught with drugs again, and for his own good I'm keeping it quiet. Why else would I dismiss him now and not after the cassation hearing?"

"Have you thought about anything other than this in the last few days?"

"As my son says: hookers, coke, and—damn, I can't remember the third thing."

"Your son is fourteen."

"But he listens to hip-hop. You know how it is," said Artur and shrugged his shoulders.

Joanna got up and went over to the window. She looked out at the Palace of Culture and Science and the cars parked across Parade Square.

"You can't fire him," she said without turning around.

"I can, at any time, just like that."

He snapped his fingers.

"Just try."

"A kindergarten child is more of a threat than you, Chyłka."

"I'm simply stooping to your level," she replied, turning to face him. "And it's not a threat, but a reminder that you are not the only partner in this firm."

"McVay and those whose names don't fit on the plaque have no say in this."

Żelazny walked around the desk and sat on Chyłka's chair. He noticed the justification on her laptop screen.

"I don't want to read it," he said. "But I've heard you've done a good job."

Chyłka paused. "I'll talk to McVay," she eventually said.

"Go ahead. Shall I give you his number?"

"No need."

"Are you sure? I didn't think you were particularly close."

Where there are two bosses, there are inevitably two camps. Some lawyers were originally hired by Żelazny and others by McVay. Usually, they stayed in their respective camps and rarely had any sympathy for the other camp. The partners felt the same way. But the lawyers everyone disliked most were those who changed camps—and one of those was Chyłka.

So Artur wasn't worried that McVay might lend Joanna a helping hand. Even when she wasn't in his bad books, the Englishman was not interested in what was going on in Warsaw. He found the city repulsive, and wanted nothing to do with it. Whenever he was in Poland, he worked in the firm's Kraków branch office.

"Now I'm expecting you to threaten to resign yourself."

"I don't have to, because I'm telling you, if you fire him, I'll . . ."

"You'll do what?" he interrupted. "You'll ruin your entire career, throw away everything you've worked so hard for over so many years? For a trainee who'd be better off tucked away somewhere deep in the suburbs? Be serious."

Joanna knew many good lawyers from the suburbs, and from many of the small towns around Warsaw, but she remained silent. She knew that for Żelazny, all the barristers worth their salt were on a single floor in the Skylight building.

But he'd given her food for thought. Was she prepared to lose all she'd ever worked for to protect Kordian? Żelazny would see to it that no other reputable firm would take her on, so she'd have to go over to the other side of the barricade, to the prosecutor's office. And Kordian? He should be able to find another job in Warsaw, provided he could clear his name with regard to the drugs. With all the media fame, plus Żelazny & McVay on his CV, he was actually very employable. Chyłka doubted that anyone would be taking much notice of his university grade averages now.

That was only one side of the coin though. The other was a matter of loyalty.

"If you fire him, I'm leaving," she said.

"Too many legal soaps," he replied with a smile, leaning towards her. "*Suits, Boston Legal,* or whatever they're called? I know you all watch them, I do myself sometimes. The only thing I like about them is that they only talk half as much bullshit as we do with our clients."

Chyłka glared at him. He was becoming less and less inhibited and had a smart alec smile on his face which she knew all too well from office functions where the alcohol flowed freely.

"Get out of my office, Artur."

"I also enjoy the love interest stories in those series."

"I don't doubt it."

"I sometimes regret we can't be as direct as they are on TV."

He looked at her knowingly, so Joanna decided it was high time to reach for the most effective weapon in her arsenal.

"Article eighteen, index three, paragraph six."

"I didn't know you knew the Labour Code by heart," said Żelazny appreciatively.

"When you work in a place where going out into the corridor equals being groped by random hands, you know where to look up sexual harassment in the statute."

"Well," began Artur, "you can throw around whatever paragraph numbers you like, but . . ."

"Get out," she said.

For a moment or two he was silent. Then he sighed deeply.

"We'll get help for him," he said. "We've found a rehab centre and we have the funds to pay for it. The media will be pleased."

"Sooner or later they'll find out just how much Gandalf the White is used on the twenty-first floor of the Skylight tower. Think about it. Sacking Oryński won't change anything."

"It will. When the media campaign begins, we will be seen as a shining star, tackling drug abuse in the legal profession."

"Bullshit."

"Think what you like," Żelazny replied, heading towards the door. He took the handle and turned round. "I hope you pass on my decision with kindness and compassion. And do it today."

She opened her mouth, but nothing came out.

"Surprised? After all, you are his mentor, who else should do it?"

"I won't fire him, Artur. You know that."

He shrugged his shoulders and left her office without another word.

She didn't protest; it would have been pointless at this stage. Her career was edging towards an abyss, and it was futile to think it could be saved. For the first time in her life, she could see no way out—unless she turned her back on Zordon.

She reached for her mobile and texted him.

CHAPTER

19

WHEN HE RECEIVED the message—Her Majesty Requires your Presence—Kordian closed the commentary to the Supreme Court Act he'd been reading and went out into the corridor. It wasn't an enthralling read, but he no longer had anything else. He had battled his way through everything that could be relevant to the cassation case, and now he was learning all he could about the institution where the case would be heard. He knew, for instance, that before you could consider becoming a Supreme Court judge you had to work as an attorney for ten years: and his career path was set.

He knocked on Chyłka's door and had to stand back as she came bursting out of her office.

"We're going to lunch," she declared.

"It's only . . ."

"OK, for a snack."

A few minutes later they sat down at the Hard Rock Cafe. Joanna ordered a "snack" that would defy ten athletes who had just run a marathon. Kordian wondered whether this was a special ritual before filing a cassation appeal, or perhaps they were there deliberately, just so the loud music could get on his nerves.

"Are we here for any particular reason? Or did you just feel peckish?"

Joanna shrugged her shoulders. She didn't speak until she had finished her meal.

"Order yourself a salmon, Zordon."

"I'm not hungry. Besides, it costs half my salary."

"Order it. It'll be a consolation, because I'm supposed to fire you."

"What?"

His first thought was that the Bar Ethics Council had looked into his case. This is what he had feared most as the consequence of his amphetamine escapade. Lawyers were supposed to have each other's backs, as in every other closed community, but he had to remember that he only had one foot in their world. As a trainee, he hadn't had time to build up enough goodwill among his professional colleagues yet, and fifteen minutes of typing would be all it took for a court reporter to terminate his legal career.

He decided to order the salmon. They both also ordered a beer.

"Old Rusty came to see me," she said, putting aside her knife and fork.

"Now? Right before the cassation appeal?"

Kordian's earlier suspicions that Żelazny might be colluding with Gorzym collapsed like a house of cards. If he was fired today, he would not be able to prevent the cassation appeal from being filed in time. And that brought with it certain problems, because Gorzym would make not only his life hell, but also Chyłka's.

He was starting to get hot. The aggressive guitar riffs and furious percussion weren't helping. He felt even worse when the lead singer started screeching hoarsely out of the speakers.

"Zordon?"

"Go on, I'm listening."

"You look as if I'd cut off your privates with a pair of secateurs rather than told you Żelazny wants to sack you."

"I just wasn't expecting it."

"Then you're more of an optimist than you should be," she said as their beer was served. She started nervously swiping the dew drops from her mug. "I have to fire you because otherwise . . ."

"I can imagine," interrupted Oryński. Because he could. "So, what are you going to do?"

"Sit down with you at the Hard Rock Cafe and think up a plan, which is what I'm doing now."

She looked up, and Kordian smiled wanly. He had to admit that it was a nice gesture on her part, if a futile one. If she hadn't managed to persuade Żelazny it was a bad idea during her conversation with him, they hardly stood a chance of finding a way to influence him now.

Despite himself, he thought about the consequences of Żelazny's decision. Gorzym did not make idle threats.

For Kordian, Langer had stopped being important. He had told himself time and again he'd had a chance to defend himself twice in court, but had remained silent on each occasion. That had been his choice.

Ultimately, there was only one choice. He took a sip of beer and decided to go for it.

He would not allow himself to get fired, and he would make sure the cassation appeal was not filed on time. He'd sort out any feelings of guilt after the fact, when the dust had settled and he had had time to think everything through.

"Sorry, my mind is blank, Chyłka," he said.

"I'm also suffering from a deficit of ingenuity at present," she replied. "I used it all up writing that cassation appeal."

"Rubbish," he bridled, raising his eyebrows. "You're brimming with ideas, you just don't know how far you're prepared to go."

"What do you mean?"

"I mean that you have ideas, but you know there's a hefty price to pay for each of them."

She gave him a searching look. For a moment, with Megadeth booming out of the speakers, Kordian wondered how on earth he could make sure he stayed in the firm.

He could only think of one thing. Blackmail.

It was a universal method of dealing with difficult situations, called upon since the times of the Roman Empire, if not earlier. The problem was whether Chyłka had anything on her boss. If it had been McVay they wanted to catch out, it would have been far simpler, as both camps collected dirt about the other side all the time.

"Chyłka?"

"I'm thinking," she replied, chewing her lower lip.

Kordian fixed his gaze on her lips and waited. He managed to drink half the mug of beer before he saw the familiar flash in his boss's eyes.

"I have an idea," she said.

"I can see."

"But I need your help."

"Use me as you must. I'm all yours."

Without further ado, she started explaining her plan. When she had finished, the salmon and beer were gone without trace. They returned to the Skylight, and Joanna locked herself in her office.

20

HARRY McVAY NEVER thought he'd get a phone call from Chyłka, of all people. If anyone from the Żelazny camp was going to call him, she was the last person he'd expect. Not after their clash during the company's last social function, when the firm had been celebrating a birthday of sorts—the anniversary of its entry into the National Court Register—and McVay and Chyłka started a conversation that rapidly turned into a verbal scuffle. She was of the opinion that since almost half of UN member states still had the death penalty, it was worth considering its reintroduction in Poland. He argued that it would be a step back in the democratic development of state law.

The subject was grist to the mill of their mutual resentment. The same could be said for every subject under the sun.

McVay paused when he saw her number on his screen. He took a deep breath and swiped his finger across the display.

"It must be something serious if you're calling me," he said as a greeting. He spoke Polish with no difficulty. His mother had been born in Kraków, and had emigrated to London in the early part of the communist period. She'd had to flee, as during the war she'd been secretary to a minister of the Polish Government-in-Exile, and had been very active in politics. Polish was spoken in the McVay household, and even his father, an Englishman from Kingston upon Thames, learned to say a few words. After 1989, Harry McVay visited Poland regularly, until eventually he settled there for good, for the best reason a man could have to settle in a foreign country—he got married. His life was quite blissful.

He could basically rest on his laurels while the money kept rolling in.

"I have a problem," said the voice on the phone.

For a moment Harry didn't say anything.

"You've finally decided to take over the firm and you need my vote to oust Żelazny?" he asked.

"No . . . that is, basically . . . I don't know? Perhaps I have."

"Have you been drinking?"

"One beer."

"You sound as if you've had quite a few."

"Artur wants to fire one of my people."

"Oryński," said McVay. There was a moment of silence, indicating that he had guessed correctly. It surprised Chyłka. "I keep my finger on the pulse, my dear. Whichever way you look at it, this firm is named after me. It's my baby."

"I need your help."

"I can well imagine. Otherwise you wouldn't be calling."

Another moment of silence.

"I believe that firing him would be a big mistake," she said after a while.

"For the sake of the firm or your own sake?"

"For both."

McVay did not expect Chyłka to beg, even if she wanted something from him. Just making that phone call must have taken major courage, because she was convinced that Harry held a grudge against her. She was wrong. The Englishman was not unforgiving, even with those who had betrayed his trust.

"Is Artur determined to fire him?" asked McVay.

"Very much so."

"Then you've got my attention," he replied. "But that's not enough."

"I'll change camps."

"You've already done that once, to get promoted to Senior Associate."

"I deserved that job," she replied. "You wouldn't give it to me because you were scared you'd be accused of favouritism."

"Nonsense."

They both knew it was the truth, though Harry had needed a little more time to come to terms with it. Chyłka was a young lawyer then, he an old hand. The age difference was enough to make him look at her with greater interest than was seemly. He'd never had designs on her, but the rumours started anyway. McVay was convinced that Żelazny was spreading them.

"Transfers are out of the question," he said, "I have no intention of taking people away from Artur."

"You'd get Zordon."

"Who?"

The name rang a bell. Zordon? A character in one of the TV programmes Harry had watched with his children when they were ten. It had been a nightmare, but when the children pulled him by the hand into the living room, he hadn't been able to refuse.

"Oryński. You'd get Oryński."

"I've got him anyway if he stays with the firm," he said without hesitation. "Once Żelazny flings him out, he'll come to me of his own accord." McVay knew this was her opening gambit, a way of testing the water.

He waited for the real proposal.

"You'd get Kormak. I'll get him to move to Kraków."

"Pigs might fly," said McVay.

Kormak was not a lawyer, so officially he wasn't in either camp. The division of spoils as agreed by Harry and Artur did not include him. McVay had more than once offered him a pay rise, better conditions and a larger office if he moved from Warsaw to Kraków, but he was never able to persuade the boy. And when Żelazny found out, Kormak became the rope they tugged in opposite directions when they were having a tussle. For Harry McVay, it was a matter of honour. Getting Kormak would be compensation for Żelazny taking Chyłka.

"I'll arrange it," said Joanna.

Harry laughed.

"All right," he said. "If you pull it off, we have a deal. When does Żelazny want to give Oryński the boot?"

"Today."

"In that case, Kormak has three hours to dream of an apartment in Foch Street. Though no, wait a minute. That offer no longer stands, as he's already turned it down once. Now I can offer him a studio apartment in Nowa Huta, at best. It'll teach him that when Harry McVay makes an offer, he should snap it up."

"Come on. . . ."

"I'm serious," Harry replied. "A studio flat in a block. That's the best I can do."

"Here in Warsaw, he's got a house even a partner would envy."

"Then the only solution is to sell it and buy a similar property in Kraków," retorted McVay and cleared his throat. "It's two o'clock. Call me by four."

"But you said three hours."

"Good luck."

21

KORDIAN WAS SITTING at Joanna's desk while she talked to McVay. Initially, her face showed only embarrassment, but now the trainee also detected disappointment.

"How did it go?" he asked.

"Scumbag," she hissed. "A vile scumbag pretending to be civilised. English gentleman my arse."

Joanna summarised the conversation. Kordian had to admit that the rules by which this great law firm played were similar to those in a toddler's sandpit. These are my toys, those are yours, and this is the line that separates them. No one is allowed to take toys from the other side, but everyone tries to.

Kordian and Joanna left her office and headed for the McCarthy cave. Kormak looked up from the monitor, nonchalant at first, but then realised that the two of them arriving together did not bode well.

"We have a favour to ask you," began Chyłka. "The career of a certain desperate person depends on whether or not you agree."

"I don't like your serious tone," grumbled Kormak. "I feel I'm being put under pressure."

"This is a serious matter," said Oryński.

Joanna nodded.

"We need you," she said. "But your task will be difficult, it'll be a long and bumpy road, and I can't promise you any benefit to speak of."

"So what you have to say shouldn't really interest me," Kormak muttered.

Joanna took a deep breath and began.

Half an hour later, they left the McCarthy cave.

An hour later, a furious Żelazny burst into Chyłka's office.

"For fuck's sake, I'll sack the lot of you and that will be that!" he roared by way of greeting, not bothering to shut the door. "What the fuck do you think you're doing?"

Kordian and Chyłka were sitting on the desk. They looked determined, even a touch brazen. Their arms were folded, and they were smiling. They had placed a chair in front of them, like an interrogation room. Chyłka invited him to sit.

"Have you lost your minds?" Żelazny yelled, his face getting redder and redder, a time bomb that might explode at any moment. He shook his head and calmed down a little. "How long have you been waiting for me like this?" he asked, looking at the chair, then at the two of them.

"About ten minutes," replied Joanna.

"You're off your bloody rockers. To do something like this . . . Kormak . . . no, this smacks of mean-spirited fucking churlishness, insolence, double-dealing, and—"

"Sit down, Artur," said Chyłka.

Żelazny pushed the chair aside. He walked around his two employees and sat down in Joanna's chair. The two lawyers turned to face him.

Chyłka and her trainee had known from the start that Kormak wouldn't be tempted by McVay's offer. Even if it included a salary several times higher and the most expensive apartment in Kraków, Kormak would never leave the city where he'd put down roots.

They'd also had to rule out deception. If Kormak pretended to accept the offer, McVay and Żelazny would see through it straightaway. Their legal careers had prepared them well for spotting conspiracies.

The plan to transfer anyone to Kraków was dead in the water before it even began.

Instead Chyłka had had to go for plan B: blackmail.

Sooner or later, the Ethics Committee would summon Kordian for a hearing, and would want to know where he had got his Gandalf the White from. She told Kormak that if he didn't do as they asked, Oryński would tell them. Their professional code of conduct stopped them from naming other lawyers, but a Data Acquisition Specialist was fair game. The committee would be happy to accept his story.

It was a convincing argument.

Kormak agreed to hack Jacek from Tax's inbox and look through his deleted messages—Jacek was the one responsible for supplying amphetamines to the twenty-first floor of the Skylight building. With hard evidence that some of Żelazny & McVay's top names were involved with drugs, Kordian would have the ultimate bargaining chip.

IT were quick to notice unauthorised access to one of the inboxes. Żelazny most probably went to Chyłka's office immediately after they'd phoned him.

How had he put it? "Mean-spirited fucking churlishness, insolence, and double-dealing"? Chyłka regretted she couldn't remember his exact words. There was some truth in what Żelazny had said, but on the other hand, they would have nothing if snorting speed had not been rife. Taking drugs was risky. Everybody knew that.

"Unbelievable," fumed Old Rusty. "Kormak, of all people!"

He was seething, but who could blame him. Now that he had Jacek's messages, Kordian held all the cards. Admittedly it wouldn't hold up in court, but if the media got wind of it, it would unleash a scandal of biblical proportions. And Żelazny was fully aware of it.

He looked at Kordian and Chyłka with hatred, as if he was capable of anything.

"I promise you one thing," he said. "You're going to regret this."

Neither of them answered. They were waiting for Żelazny to get to the point. Finally, he took a deep breath, rose from the chair and headed for the door without a word.

"So?" asked Oryński.

The boss stopped.

"You're staying," he replied. "Until the case is closed."

Chyłka beamed.

"You see," she said. "You can get on with people if you want to."

Artur looked over his shoulder.

"You'll fail at the Supreme Court, and I'll make sure your careers are ruined."

He slammed the door behind him. Chyłka didn't hold it against him—quite the opposite in fact: his reaction told everyone nearby who had won that particular clash. Still smiling, she looked at Oryński. For a moment they gazed at one another in silence.

Suddenly she noticed that he had lowered his eyes to her lips. She felt the temperature in the office rise by a few degrees. Her heartbeat quickened, but in a good way.

It wasn't something she'd expected.

If she was to do anything, she had to act now. Avert it while she could, or surrender to the moment. She thought about the age difference, the staff hierarchy and the mentor–mentee relationship, and realised it was all quite insignificant in this situation.

She turned her head away before it went too far.

Oryński felt bewildered at first, but realised what he'd been trying to do. Innocent flirting or holding hands in hospital was one thing, but this. . . . On the one hand, nothing had happened, on the other, it could have started an avalanche.

Chyłka sat down behind her desk and gave a sigh of relief, which Kordian interpreted as meaning she wanted to say nothing more about the embarrassing situation. He soon found he was wrong.

"That was close," she said.

He smiled and shook his head, then sat down opposite her.

"We'd be thrown out on our ears," he said, noticing with surprise that she was avoiding his eyes. "Have no illusions, Zordon," she replied.

He wasn't sure whether she was referring to the almost-kiss or the prospect of an imminent sacking.

"Sooner or later Żelazny will dust off the heavy artillery," she said, dispelling his doubts. "McVay will never stick up for me, and you'll become a hot potato that no one wants to hold on to."

"So what should we do?" he asked.

"Nothing," she replied, shrugging her shoulders. "Żelazny will find a way to get rid of us, but at least we won't be disgraced. We'll find jobs in another firm, and if he tries to smear us, we'll rake up even more muck."

"You sound as if it doesn't affect you."

For a moment she didn't answer, still trying not to meet his eye.

"But it does, Zordon," she said. "I worked my fingers to the bone to get this position. I don't even want to think about how many sacrifices I've had to make."

"In any other firm, they'd start you off as senior partner."

They both knew it was true. Provided Chyłka left without any scandal, she'd be welcomed with open arms by any other firm in the city. If she played her cards right, this could also up her earnings substantially.

But it wouldn't be Żelazny & McVay, who were rising in the rankings and were next year's sure-fire top legal services provider.

"Besides, we could set up on our own, we've already talked about it," added Kordian. "A partnership, for instance."

"With you I could only have a limited liability partnership."

"Ouch, that hurts."

She smiled. Their eyes met, and for a moment they just looked at each other like a pair of children who liked one another but didn't know what to do about it.

Eventually, Joanna coughed and looked at the door. Oryński took his opportunity and returned to the newbie-burrow, wrestling with his thoughts. Meanwhile Chyłka tried not to go over the day's unpleasant events in her mind; they both had work to do before the approaching cassation appeal deadline. Everything else would have to wait.

22

After what had—or rather hadn't—happened, Kordian found it much easier to make a decision. Chyłka's safety and wellbeing trumped Piotr Langer's every time, that's all there was to it. There would be no cassation, but Chyłka would be safe.

The next day, Oryński reported to collect the documents from her office with no qualms or doubts in his mind. He had lost no sleep over his decision.

"Got anything for me?" he asked entering the office.

"I'm sure I can find something."

She handed him the documents. He looked at the file and wondered whether he would face legal consequences. Probably, because the Code of Ethics stipulated severe penalties for transgressions that were far less serious.

But would anyone ever see that the situation had been manipulated? He didn't really care. He was more concerned about what would happen if his mentor discovered the truth. She would hurl all sorts of verbal abuse at him, then announce their relationship was over.

"Have you fallen asleep or something? Get this down to the court registry."

"Can't I take it to the post office? A sealed stamp, just the same."

"No, better take it to court," decided Chyłka. "I'll feel safer with a court seal."

"OK," he replied automatically and took the file. He knew what she would say next.

"Look after it as if it were your own child, Zordon."

"Of course."

He smiled and went out into the corridor.

Although it was a slim file, it felt heavy. Kordian knew it only contained a procedural document, but it carried his whole future. He had no trouble making his way to the lifts—he was still limping, so the crowd in the corridor made space for him.

Having left the Skylight building, he stood outside Coffee-heaven and watched people crossing Parade Square. Some walked quickly and confidently—these were, without doubt, Warsaw residents. Others spent time looking at the Palace of Culture and Science, the skyscrapers, or other people—those were tourists, visitors or workers commuting from the villages. This image comforted Kordian, perhaps because it was a breath of normality.

"Kordian?" said a man's voice.

Oryński was startled. A wave of heat swept over him, but when he looked to see where the voice had come from, he saw a familiar, friendly face. He knew the man was called Jacek—but was he from Medical Law or Taxes? Żelazny & McVay probably had a Jacek for everything, including supplying Gandalf the White.

"Hi," replied Oryński casually. He didn't recall ever exchanging more than three sentences with this particular Jacek, but then he'd recently become a bit of a celebrity on the twenty-first floor of the Skylight.

"Something wrong?"

"No, why?"

"You look like you're at death's door."

"That more or less says everything."

"Drop you off somewhere? I'm driving to a client in Marymont."

"No, thanks, I'm going in the opposite direction."

They said their goodbyes, and Kordian thought that unless things changed, his plan would unravel. He had to convince the world that he genuinely intended to submit the documents, so everyone he met on the way was important, especially colleagues. They'd be the first to be questioned about his behaviour on the day he'd missed the deadline.

Too bad, but this slip-up right at the start served as a reminder to take more care. And, he decided, that meant coffee. He went into Coffee-heaven and ordered a white chocolate mocha to go.

Thus equipped, he headed out towards the Palace of Culture and Science, turned left and sat down on a vacant bench, placing the file beside him. It crossed his mind that with a bit of luck, someone might steal it. But then he'd have to let the firm know, and they'd have a second copy printed out in no time.

He had even considered filing the appeal to the wrong court, but that would still mean the deadline was kept. But eventually he'd decided that the simplest solution would be the best, there was no point in doing anything elaborate.

He took a sip of his mocha and pulled out a packet of cigarettes.

"Fuck me, you've healed nicely," said a familiar voice.

Oryński swallowed. Gorzym was standing right behind him. He knew he'd be under constant surveillance and had realised he might be encountering Gorzym again.

The Bald Man sat down next to him, on the cassation appeal file.

"Oops," he said. "Have I crushed something?"

Oryński said nothing, nervously smoking his cigarette.

"Do you know how you'll do it?" asked Gorzym. "Or are you still wondering whether it's worth it?"

"No."

"No, what?" hissed the Bald Man, leaning towards him. "Did I damage your jaw last time we met? Have you got problems talking?"

There was something not quite right with his jaw, it clicked when he yawned, ate soup, or chewed gum, but Kordian was not about to go into that. It was something he'd have to learn to live with.

"Well?"

"No, I don't have any doubts," he replied with difficulty, although he knew it would all get easier from now on. "And I know how to do it."

"Fucking awesome," replied Gorzym. "I might even get some supplements delivered to you, as a thank you. Which address is better, Mickiewicz or Hoserów Street? No, wait, my mistake, you don't ever go to your father's place in Hoserów Street."

Kordian was perfectly aware that he was dealing with people whose tentacles spread everywhere, so the showing off was unnecessary.

"Who are you?" asked Oryński, looking straight at Gorzym for the first time.

"As of today, your friend," replied Gorzym. "If you do this for us, my boss will be pleased. And a happy boss means an opportunity for you. Do you get it?"

"No."

"You'll be kicked out of Żelazny & McVay," explained the Bald Man. "And if all goes well, my boss will make you an offer."

"I don't understand."

"He'll take you on as a lawyer in his, er . . . firm," replied Gorzym, spitting to one side. "How much do you get now?"

"One thousand net."

"A thousand?" asked the Bald Man and looked around furtively. "With us you'll get twenty times as much. Untaxed. Why should you pay a penny to the state if all they do is use it to feed those pigs at the trough?"

Oryński had not expected this turn of events. He doubted the offer was genuine, but it made him realise just how important Langer's case was to these people. Not only had they threatened and violently assaulted him, they were now adding bribery to the list.

"A cool twenty thousand," repeated the Bald Man. Suddenly the offer seemed more real.

"Uh-huh."

"Plus a bonus. If my boss is pleased, you might even get one every month. How much would depend on how useful you turn out to be."

"What would my work involve?" asked Kordian.

Asking a question felt strange. All the more so because the Bald Man was looking at him as if they were going to be best buddies.

"I won't finish my training, that's almost a given," he said with faux naivety.

"We don't need a barrister. We have people to represent us in court," said Gorzym, resting his arms on the back of the bench.

"So?"

"You'd settle our affairs in a different way," replied the Bald Man. "There is a lot of work, and we're not so much short of brawn as of brains, if you get what I mean."

Kordian could only assume what mafia lawyers did, but made sure he looked as if he understood.

"When are you going to get it done?" said Gorzym, returning to the matter in hand.

"In a moment. What I'll do is . . ."

"I'm not interested in the details, Zordon."

Hearing the name, Kordian realised that somehow, he was being bugged. Not the office, that would have been impossible, but perhaps his home? Or his newly purchased mobile?

"If it's a good plan, we trust you," Gorzym added after a while. "Is it good?"

"Maybe."

"If not, I can help you."

"How?"

The Bald Man pointed to the entrance of the Youth Palace young people's centre, and Oryński spotted the familiar Mercedes, parked next to a fountain. He shuddered. He would sooner jump into the fires of hell than into that car.

"We could simply drive away."

Oryński could hardly believe he was having this conversation.

"No, there's no need."

"All right. But remember that sooner or later you'll have to leave town. As I see it, that's not a major problem, because apart from Chyłka you haven't got anyone here."

Oryński said nothing.

"OK, I won't hold you up," said Gorzym, getting up.

Kordian also stood up. He was still silent, although the Bald Man was looking at him expectantly. Oryński bent down, snatched up the file and handed it to Gorzym.

"What the fuck . . . ?"

Kordian patted him on the arm and walked away. At a brisk pace and without a word.

23

T HAT WAS THE first—and easiest—part of the plan over with.
Oryński walked towards Nowy Świat Street. He wanted another
coffee and something to eat, but first he had another matter to attend to.
He took out his mobile, remembering Żelazny's warning about phones
generating magnetic fields. Somehow, ever since then, it had seemed
heavier when he carried it near his heart. He dialled Chyłka's number
and, still walking briskly, waited for her to answer.

"What's up, Zordi?"

That put him off his stroke.

"Hello?" said Joanna. "Are you there?"

"I don't know how to respond to that."

"Great. In that case, I'll call you Zordi from now on."

"But . . ."

"Have you filed the letter?" she asked in passing, already preoccupied
with other things. Perhaps she was setting a date to visit Langer to let him
know everything had been taken care of and that they'd soon be fighting
in court for his freedom.

"I'm going to the court now," replied Oryński. "Also, I'm wondering
if you could give me a lift later on? It's so bloody hot."

This was taking a huge risk, like balancing over a precipice. Kordian
assumed that Chyłka would be too busy at this time of day, but if, on a
whim, she agreed, then his entire plan would fall apart.

"Chyłka?" he asked.

"What?"

"I have to go to hospital for some routine tests."

"Take a taxi, I'll refund you," she muttered. She wasn't paying much attention to the conversation, thank God.

"OK. It'll take me some time though, and I probably won't make it back to work today."

"You want the day off, Zordi?"

"I'd rather rot in the newbie-burrow than get these jabs and things."

"I hope Roske will be gentle with the enema," she said. "And stop whingeing, you've got the rest of the day off."

"Seriously?"

"Ask again and I'll change my mind."

That took a load off his mind. He'd hoped the hospital excuse would settle the matter, but things could have gone very wrong.

"I've got to go now, whinger."

"OK, see you tomorrow?"

"Yeah, see you," she said and hung up.

He looked at the phone, put it away in his pocket and walked along Marszałkowska towards Moniuszko Street. From there it was no more than ten minutes to the Starbucks in Nowy Świat. He needed a serious shot of caffeine, and the white chocolate mocha just hadn't done the trick. He needed a pitch-black, freshly brewed Pike Place coffee.

He sat outside with his coffee and a chocolate muffin, calmly watching the pedestrians and cars. He felt he was no longer part of this world; the moment he had handed over the documents he found himself in a new place, one that was difficult to define.

Was he really considering collaborating with the mafia? When they'd talked about that twenty thousand, for a moment he was. But sitting outside Starbucks, he realised it was absurd. Was he really prepared to be an in-house lawyer for an organised crime gang?

There were some in the legal community who'd jump at the chance. For most, however, it would be worse than defending a child murderer.

On the other hand, if his actions came to light, he might have no other choice. The offer had been made. If it was genuine, he'd also have to consider the fact that Gorzym was not a man who took rejection lightly. Either Kordian agreed to take the job, or they'd dump his body in the Vistula on a cloudy autumn night.

It didn't bear thinking about. Besides, now he had to think of the excuses he'd have to make in the office. It wouldn't be easy, but he had a plan he hoped would work. But it was crucial that no one said anything more about the matter today.

After the telephone conversation, he didn't have to worry about Chyłka. Langer couldn't check whether the appeal had been filed on time, and no one at Żelazny & McVay had any reason to interfere.

Oryński took a sip of coffee and sighed with relief. He was convinced he had saved not just himself, but also Joanna. He was a hero, though probably no one else would ever know. He repeated this to himself a few times.

And then he realised that he'd failed everyone miserably.

It really only sank in the following morning, when he opened his eyes and realised that the final deadline for filing the cassation appeal was gone forever.

It took him a while to get himself together—for half an hour he stared blankly at his reflection in the mirror, repeatedly rinsing his face in cold water. The previous day he had not stopped at two shots of coffee in Starbucks. At home, he had several more large cups of coffee and then started on the beer. He had hardly slept, and looked like a ghost. Standing in front of the mirror, seeing the dark circles under his swollen eyes, he was overcome with lethargy.

But there was no turning back. He had to implement the next part of his plan. Yesterday, when he was tired and stressed, it had seemed like a flash of genius. Today it just looked foolish.

He pulled a shirt he had worn two days earlier out of the laundry basket, and carelessly knotted his tie. Ten minutes later he trudged down the stairs, his heart in his mouth.

He had no idea how to start the conversation with Chyłka. Nothing, not even the best lie, could get him out of this hopeless situation. Joanna's anger would be boundless, and would last as long as the earth kept orbiting the sun.

He walked to the tram stop. With each passing minute he felt more and more like a Judas, and less and less like a hero. But he had to play out his role in front of Chyłka.

As he knocked on Joanna's office door, his heart was pounding. This was the wrong time of day to intrude on her privacy, but today that was about as relevant as the price of butter.

Kordian walked straight in.

"Will you ever learn? From morning till noon I'm busy working, and you are not allowed to pester me. When you were injured, that was an exception, because I felt sorry for you." She looked up from her monitor, frowned, and then winced. "You look as if you've been dragged through a hedge backwards. And that's a polite understatement, because you actually look more like something that's been through an animal's digestive tract."

Oryński closed the door behind him, and sat down in his usual place without saying a word. He hoped he looked like a condemned man walking up the steps to the guillotine.

"What's up?"

He remained silent, judging it to be a better introduction than anything he could say.

"Has something happened? Tell me."

"I . . ."

"Yes, you."

When she saw he couldn't utter another word, Joanna's face fell. She
knew that expression. She had seen it with clients who had inadvertently
killed someone.

"Speak, Zordon, what happened?"

"It's gone, Chyłka. . . ."

"What's gone?" she asked, although she already knew.

"The cassation appeal, deadline, everything, gone. . . ."

"How?"

Oryński looked up, just a little. Just to see if she was already furious.
But she looked quite calm, if perhaps a little incredulous.

"I'm . . . I'm sorry, Chyłka," he said. "God, I'm really sorry."

"Tell me," she repeated. "What happened?"

Kordian shook his head and winced, as if saying another word would
only make matters worse. Finally, he began to describe in painstaking
detail what had supposedly happened the previous day. He cursed and
swore, burying his head in his hands as if it was causing him unimagi-
nable pain. That, he did not have to imagine. He really did feel like
a scumbag, and the embarrassment and shame were genuine. Only the
reason was different.

He began his account with what happened after their telephone conversation. He told her he had decided to go to the courthouse via the
Saxon Garden, which turned out to be the worst decision of his life. With
the file under his arm, he felt quite relaxed, not expecting any problems.
Then suddenly, he heard footsteps behind him. Before he knew it, he was
lying face down, half conscious and paralysed with terror.

He said it all quite chaotically—at least he hoped it seemed that way.

"Perhaps there were two of them. I'm not sure. . . . When I came to,
the file was gone. I immediately thought of that Bald Man."

Kordian paused. He knew Joanna would start pelting him with questions. Why hadn't he phoned, or printed out a new copy and rushed off
to the nearest post office to get it rubber-stamped? He was prepared for it
and began explaining himself even before she asked.

Still muttering nervously, he explained that he was in a state of
shock—the trauma of his previous encounter with that thug had
returned. He was disoriented and overcome by a paralysing fear so great
that he couldn't even lift himself up off the ground. He just lay there
under a tree, covered with dirt. He lay there, waiting for them to come
back and finish him off.

"You don't know what it's like," he added. "It's as if someone put a gun to your head and was ready to pull the trigger . . . and then . . . I don't know. I chickened out, Chyłka. I simply chickened out. I wanted to phone you, get to the office, anything . . . but I was paralysed with fear. Completely fucking overcome . . ."

"Don't say any more," she interrupted. There was no bitterness in her voice, but neither was there any compassion. It was as if she was talking to one of her clients.

For a moment there was silence.

"Go to the newbie-burrow."

"Chyłka, I . . ."

She raised her hand and pointed to the door. He nodded, got up and left the room without a word. Their relationship was over.

PART 3

CHAPTER

1

THE NEXT DAY, Oryński turned up at the Skylight building after a second sleepless night. Chyłka was not at work, apparently for the first time in the firm's history. He asked around and learned that she wasn't answering phone calls or emails either.

He sat down in his cubicle, started the computer and saw something new in his inbox. It was an email from Chyłka with no subject line or message, just an attachment. The document was a form, already filled out and addressed to the Dean of the District Bar Council, a ready-to-print application to change mentors. The only thing missing was his signature. At the bottom was a reference from the current mentor, the name of the new mentor, and a promise from the new mentor to take Oryński under their wing.

Kordian swore under his breath, staring at the monitor. Clearly, there was nothing to discuss. It was a while before he could think straight. He wondered whether Chyłka had seen through his game. She would have been disappointed, sure, but this dramatic gesture with the filled-out application form was simply not her style.

"Zordon, have you dropped off?"

Oryński shook his head and saw Kormak standing by his cubicle. "What's up?"

"I hear you've been asking about Chyłka."

"So what?"

"She's just texted me. She wants me to get her an L4 sick leave certificate from one of our doctors."

Kordian had been hoping for something more.

"She doesn't need an L4 to take a day off work. She's probably got a million overdue vacation days."

"Well, yes," admitted Kormak, scratching his head. "Maybe she needs it to be done by the book. You know how it is with lawyers," he added. He noticed the file open on the screen, straightened his glasses and looked at Oryński.

"Surprise," murmured Oryński.

"Seriously?"

"Unfortunately."

"Anyone else and I'd have no trouble believing it. But a divorce between you two?"

Kordian forced a smile.

"Come to the cave and tell me all about it."

"Somehow it makes me feel uncomfortable when you call that place a cave," said Oryński. "Besides, there'll be time for explanations later. Now I have some things I need to attend to."

Kormak took the rejection without a word. He turned round and started to make his way out of the newbie-burrow.

"Kormak," Kordian called out after him. "Get me an L4 too."

"Just for today?"

"OK."

In less than half an hour, Kordian had his sick leave form. He left the Skylight building. He couldn't bear to spend another minute there: now that the news was most likely common knowledge, every pair of eyes seemed to be looking at him reproachfully.

Before he left, he printed out the application form, signed it, and put it in an envelope. Now all he had to do was to post it. Which he did at the nearest post office.

He had hardly left the post office when the phone in his jacket started playing a Will Smith song. Taking it out, Kordian looked at the display. It was an unknown number, probably a loan company who had got his number from the phonebook.

"Yes?"

"Good morning," said a friendly voice. "Am I speaking to the owner of this phone?"

"Yes," answered Oryński reluctantly. A mobile network consultant then. They were even worse than loan companies. It wasn't hard to get rid of the latter as they had acquired the number illegally and tried to avoid conflict. But with the former, Kordian could foresee a long and tedious conversation.

"May I take up a few minutes of your time?"

"I'm sorry, I'm rather busy at the—"

"Busy? I don't think so. Not now you're on sick leave."

"What?" Oryński snapped.

He stopped in his tracks in the middle of a zebra crossing. The woman behind him would have knocked into him if not for her quick reaction. She looked at him in concern as she passed.

"Who are you?" he asked, wondering whether the caller would tell him to hurry up because the green pedestrian light was about to disappear. Big Brother was watching him.

"Don't panic."

Kordian moved on. The voice was right. He shouldn't panic.

"I'm hanging up," said the caller. "I'll phone you again, from another number."

"What?" Again Oryński couldn't help himself. "Why the fuck are you calling?"

"I'm so sorry," said the caller. "I've forgotten to introduce myself. Harry McVay, the pleasure is all mine."

"What?"

"You should learn to stop saying what."

Oryński said nothing, choosing it as his best strategic option. It wasn't every day he spoke with one of the top brass. Or asked him why the fuck he was calling.

"Don't you want to know what this is about?" asked the Englishman.

"I think I know the answer to that one."

"Of course. It's fairly obvious."

"Has Chyłka contacted you?"

"Better," Harry replied with pride in his voice. "She's here in Kraków."

Kordian fell silent again—this time because he didn't know what to say.

"She's told me everything, Mr Oryński," added McVay. "From beginning to end. From the strange behaviour of your client, his blood-chilling gaze, to how you were assaulted and badly beaten up, to yesterday's failure—that is, failure to meet the deadline."

Kordian had to admit he had not expected this. Joanna was capable of many things, but to pour it all out to McVay? He was the last person he'd have expected her to turn to for help.

"You must also stop making these long pauses," advised Harry. "You're surprised, aren't you?"

"A bit."

"I am no less surprised, actually. But I'm glad she's done it."

"Yes, I'm sure that . . ."

"Because you see, I am convinced my partner is involved in the affair," continued McVay, giving Kordian no chance to get a word in edgeways.

It was the last thing Oryński was expecting to hear.

"But perhaps I should start at the beginning. Can you talk?"

Kordian looked around. Standing around outside a travel agent's at the junction of Nowogrodzka and Poznańska streets, he looked like he was selling cheap tours. So he quickly headed down Poznańska Street towards the Palace of Culture and Science.

"I won't be a moment," he said, worried he might lose some valuable snippets of information whilst trying to cross the busy road. "I'll just find a quieter spot."

"Fine. I'll call you back in quarter of an hour," said McVay, carefully enunciating every word like a true English gentleman, and hung up.

Kordian turned right. He passed a restaurant, but saw it was crowded. He wanted somewhere more secluded. As he headed towards the Rotunda, there were two questions buzzing round his head: how much did Chyłka really know, and how much of what she knew was she passing on to McVay? Had she guessed that he had missed the deadline for reasons other than trauma? Maybe, but McVay clearly also had his own ideas, since he suspected Żelazny.

Once Kordian had completed a circle and was again in Nowogrodzka Street, he remembered that somewhere nearby there was a bar serving decent Georgian food. He headed there, sat down at a small table and ordered a traditional Georgian khachapuri. He had no idea what exactly he'd get, but he didn't really care. He also ordered wine, which was served immediately. The glass was on a coaster right next to his phone, at which he was staring intently. At last, Will Smith rang out.

"Yes?"

"That was quick. Was your phone in your hand?" asked McVay.

"More or less. You said that you'd start at the beginning, but I don't even know where the beginning is."

"Well then . . . allow me to speak uninterrupted, and the time for questions will come later."

Kordian didn't even manage to answer.

"Joanna came here early this morning and spent two solid hours explaining the situation. Normally, I enjoy being in the company of beautiful women, but when they're angry, and feeling betrayed and cheated, I can think of better ways to spend my time. Besides, our relationship . . . well, you understand."

"Indeed."

"When she had finished her account of what had happened to the two of you, something occurred to me: Artur Żelazny had set up the whole situation, including your dismissal, to avoid accusations of being part of the conspiracy."

"But . . ."

"Oh, I forgot to say we also came to the conclusion that you missed the deadline of your own free will and not as a result of any traumatic experiences. You see, Mr Oryński, we think that you are being forced to work with someone who wants Piotr Langer to stay in prison. I'm assuming you've been threatened, and perhaps been told that something unfortunate could happen to Joanna. Am I right?"

Silence.

Kordian presumed that he was not talking just to McVay. Chyłka had probably made sure the speaker-phone was on.

"I understand," said Harry after a while. "You were threatened and then you deliberately missed the deadline in order to protect you both. For me, as a man, this is perfectly understandable, because I assume that the two of you have feelings for one another. In my opinion, there's nothing better than a workplace romance; it's a wonderful institution, sadly prohibited in certain American states, can you imagine? They have their unique charm. The emotions, the risk . . ."

"Mr McVay . . ."

"Oh, forgive me," Harry got back on track. "So we came to the conclusion that you were beaten up primarily to make sure you cooperated. You were to take the documents and get rid of them. Is that right?"

Again silence. Kordian did not know how to answer, because anything other than a resolute and indignant "no" would be an admission of guilt.

"You don't have to say anything, we've pieced everything together ourselves," added McVay. "Which is why I believe my partner is involved. In fact, he didn't intend to sack you until you had played out your role. It was theatre, intended to divert suspicion."

Oryński took a sip of the wine. It was good, tart as hell, but very good.

"I ought to tell you that Artur has previously made suspicious deals and acted in a way that I consider amoral. He made agreements with individuals my people were unable to vet, and that's saying something. But thanks to Kormak, we managed to get some useful information anyway. That's why we need Kormak so much. He's the only way we can source information on some of the things Artur is involved in."

Kordian took a larger sip of the wine. Until then, he had thought Kormak was too insignificant to be used in a bidding war. Now it all made sense.

"Hello, are you there?" asked the Englishman.

"Yes, I'm still here."

"Good," said McVay and took a deep breath. "After Joanna and I had put everything together, we both came to the conclusion that you are essentially rather foolish, but quite innocent in this whole situation and . . ."

"I beg your pardon," said Oryński, surprising himself by daring to interrupt McVay and using the same haughty tone.

"You may take as much umbrage as you like, but this does not alter the fact that I've been dealing with fools for decades, and I'm perfectly able to discern whether or not I'm dealing with a fool in this case," Harry continued, with a lightness as if he derived pleasure from his words. "Nonetheless, I have phoned the Dean of the District Bar Council, instructing him to tear up the letter that he will most probably receive tomorrow."

"What?"

"You're not going anywhere, Mr Oryński. You'll remain in the firm as a trainee, under the caring wing of Joanna Chyłka. Together we shall endeavour to make some changes in the firm's hierarchy, and if you're wondering about the veiled way in which I'm expressing my thoughts, I'm just going to say that I intend to use a *cast-iron* argument."

"But what about Langer's case?"

"Read article twenty-six, paragraphs one and two of the Criminal Procedure Code, which, to my infinite sadness, you insist on abbreviating to CPC. And also, the Supreme Court ruling of the 17th April, 2007. See you soon, Mr Oryński."

"But what . . ."

McVay hung up, and at that moment the waitress appeared. Kordian raised his flummoxed gaze, and she responded with a warm smile, placing the Georgian cheese bread on the table.

"Straight from the pan," she said.

The trainee followed the waitress with his eyes as she left the room, then sat for a moment, the steaming dish in front of him. He took a bite, trying to sort everything out in his mind.

Suddenly he pushed the khachapuri away, although it was exceptionally delicious. He grabbed his phone and searched the CPC article McVay had mentioned.

"Although the deadline for filing a cassation appeal is an absolute contractual time limit," he read, "it may, if missed, be reinstated at the request of either party. The request is adjudicated by the Court of Appeal. . . ."

This was no revelation, and Kordian already knew that. Next, he started searching the internet for the court ruling. McVay had not given the reference number, but Oryński remembered the month and year. That was enough.

He scanned the text, and then stopped at the significant passage.

"The precondition is to prove that the deadline was not met for reasons beyond the control of the requesting party."

Oryński raised his eyebrows, speared a piece of Georgian cheese bread with his fork, and nodded his head. Piotr Langer still could be defended in court. He had seven days to file a request for the deadline to be extended. All he had to do was prove that he'd had no influence on the deadline being missed.

2

CHYŁKA RETURNED TO Warsaw the following day, she in her X5, McVay in his Lexus, racing all the way down National Road 7. Although the boss had much more horsepower under the bonnet, her strategic manoeuvring gave Chyłka the lead, and she reached the capital first.

The journey would have been the ideal occasion to mull over recent events, but Chyłka's mind was preoccupied with juvenile racing antics. When she was leaving Warsaw the previous day, she'd been ready to rip Zordon's guts out and hang them out on telegraph poles across the country. Initially, she couldn't think rationally, because when he had appeared in her office—a beaten puppy with its tail between its legs—and told her the whole stupid story, it was as if she'd been hit on the head with a blunt instrument herself. Her talk with McVay calmed her down. It was then that she realised two things: firstly, that Zordon had lied out of concern for her, and secondly, that the deadline could be extended.

If anyone had put pressure on Oryński, this was grounds for setting a new date for filing the cassation appeal. They only had to prove that he had been coerced in some way—and that wouldn't be difficult. Beating Kordian up should have ensured victory for the other side, but it was likely to be their undoing. In addition, Oryński had met Jacek from whatever-department-it-was outside the Skylight building, and he could confirm that Oryński was about to take the file to court. No judge should have a problem with granting a new deadline for Langer's appeal.

After passing the Welcome to Warsaw sign, Chyłka flashed her lights to thank McVay for the race. She drove through the capital's streets straight to Białołęka prison.

The visit had been arranged previously, but Joanna wasn't sure whether her relations with the Prison Services were good enough to allow Harry to come in as an additional visitor at such short notice.

They parked outside the prison, got out of their cars and stretched their limbs. Chyłka lit a cigarette and looked at the grim edifice.

"I don't know if I'll manage to get you an entry pass," she warned McVay.

"You don't have to," he replied, flexing his back. "I rang them on the way."

"And?"

"And I am the partner of one of the leading law firms in this country," he replied, as if surprised he needed to explain anything.

Soon they were both sitting in the visiting room, sipping vending machine coffee and waiting for Langer. His arrival was heralded by the sound of opening locks and the clanking of chains. Two warders cuffed the prisoner to the chair and looked at Chyłka. As usual, she encouraged them to leave with a pointed glance at the door.

"Good morning, Mr Langer," began McVay, as if he was greeting a potential client. "My name is . . ."

"I know who you are," replied Langer.

"Great," said Chyłka. "That's the formalities done, so we can spare ourselves any further bullshit."

"Tactful as always," said Harry.

Chyłka looked at Langer expectantly. She had no idea how he would react to the presence of one of her bosses. Lately, he had started cooperating at long last—even admitting that he hadn't known the victims. Joanna, however, found him hard to believe.

"Well," said the Englishman. "I don't know if you've heard about what happened recently?"

The prisoner glared at him, and Chyłka recognised the former Langer. Langer the murderer. Perhaps that had been the real Langer all along, and maybe that was why she couldn't bring herself to trust him.

Whether your client was guilty or not, you had to do your job as best you could. And not just because the law required it. Even if you were defending someone like Breivik or Josef Fritzl, it soon turned into an ambitious struggle, a case of to be or not to be. It all boiled down to whether or not you could defeat the other party. It didn't matter whether it was an article 148 crime, robbery, rape or causing a traffic accident, at the end of the day it was simple rivalry. The individual themselves? His or her life? No one cared, that wasn't the aim of the game.

McVay started speaking, revealing more and more to the prisoner. The lawyers had agreed that the situation required total openness; it was hard to say if it was a prudent idea, but it was definitely necessary.

Piotr listened to the story with indifference.

"As you can see, we've got a problem." Harry summed it up. "I don't know who committed the murders, but they have no scruples, and they have a whole range of tools to help them implement their plans."

"Yes."

"What did you say?"

"Yes, I agree with you," said Langer dispassionately.

McVay looked at Chyłka, raised his eyebrows, and clasped his hands on the table. Chyłka knew he wanted more of a reaction. He'd been talking for a good quarter of an hour.

"I see that you don't take easily to new people," said the Englishman.

"Maybe."

"In prison, that's an advantage."

Chyłka coughed. "Langer . . ." she said. "I trust this man. Even more than Zordon, at the moment."

Piotr kept his gaze fixed on the Englishman. "I don't know him," he said finally.

"You'll have the chance to get to know him. I vouch for him, Langer."

For a moment, the prisoner remained silent.

"What do you want from me?" he asked eventually.

"Answers to a few questions," replied McVay. "Firstly, we'd like to find out who these people are."

Piotr shrugged his shoulders.

"I thought we were past that stage," said the Englishman, looking at Joanna.

Before she could say anything, Langer spoke. "I couldn't tell you anything, even if I wanted to."

"Why?" she asked.

"You are bound by attorney—client privilege," he said. "But he isn't."

"You can be sure . . ."

"I'd only be sure if I put your two children on the line. Amelia and Jakub, if memory serves. You might wonder how I know, but it's probably best not to think about what I could do if they undid these chains and I was able to escape from prison."

"Is that it?" asked McVay.

"Yes."

Harry yawned, opening his mouth wide and stretching. It triggered Chyłka, who yawned too. Langer, however, kept his stony expression.

"You can stop trying to catch me out," he said. "I'm not sleepy, so I won't yawn. And just because I don't, it doesn't make me a psychopath."

"You've watched too many American TV shows."

"Actually, I got it from a British one."

Joanna remembered how Italian scientists had found that yawning was contagious, something to do with mirror neurons primarily responsible for empathy and sympathy. Another theory said that if someone didn't "catch" a yawn easily from another person, it pointed to a greater chance of psychopathy.

For a few moments, all three of them were silent.

McVay finally spoke. "Well, in that case, I'll leave you two alone." He tapped his fingers on the table, took another look at the prisoner, then got up and left the room.

Chyłka immediately noted the change on Langer's face. "I guarantee we can trust him."

"Let's get to the point," Langer said. "I know who those people are."

She waited for more, but he fell silent.

"And?" she asked.

"And that's all I can tell you," he replied looking at the camera in the top corner of the room.

"That crappy set-up doesn't record sound, Langer."

He smiled wanly, as if to tell her that it didn't mean there wasn't a bug installed somewhere.

"What have they got on you?" she asked.

"Who?"

"You're in prison, what can they do to you? Put you in solitary confinement? You're in for murder, no one will touch you, even if they send other prisoners to sort you out."

"These people don't need to have anything on anyone."

"Bullshit!" she exclaimed. "And you're not scared to mention them?" she said, looking at the camera in the corner. "Maybe they'll burst into this room and sort you out themselves?"

Langer looked at the door. Chyłka knew that if she didn't calm down, the meeting would be over. She had failed to get any practical information from her client. The mere fact that Piotr knew the perpetrators did not help her in any way.

She rose from the chair and walked to the wall. Leaning her back against it, she looked at the prisoner. He sat there motionless, as if he couldn't wait for the visit to finish.

"Who are you so scared of, Langer?"

His response was more silence. Joanna focused her gaze on his face. It was unnerving, as always, and to make it even more disturbing he had started to blink nervously. The tic showed that beneath the man's ostensibly calm exterior there lurked an obsessive anxiety.

"Do you want justice?" she asked.

"Justice is to experience what you have done to others."

She raised her eyebrows. "The Bible?"

"No, Aristotle."

Before she could answer, a warder entered the room and escorted the silent Langer back to his cell.

Chyłka watched him leave the room, regretting that she had played it that way.

CHAPTER

3

KORDIAN WAITED FOR the two senior lawyers, as agreed. He was supposed to be at the entrance to McVay's Warsaw residence, but he wasn't entirely sure he'd got the right address. The building was different from the other houses in the suburban district of Elsnerów, its shape reminiscent of the bygone communist era and the façade looking as if it had last been painted when the country was overburdened with foreign debt.

But when a Lexus pulled up followed by a black X5, Kordian knew he was in the right place. First to emerge was Harry with his salt-and-pepper hair.

"Could you open the gate, please?" he said.

Oryński looked at the gate with trepidation, but headed towards it. He jumped swiftly over the fence, landing in unmown grass, and unbolted and opened the creaky gate.

As the cars drove into the forecourt, Kordian tried to catch Chyłka's eye. She, however, parked the car in front of the house, ignoring him.

A moment later, McVay approached him with a broad smile.

"Pleased to meet you, Kordian."

"Pleased to meet you too, sir."

That was a massive understatement. Many lawyers at the firm had never had the opportunity to exchange a word with either of the partners.

"How do you like my estate?"

"It's pretty good." Kordian glanced again at the house. "On the roof . . . is that asbestos?"

"I suppose so. I haven't been here for a long time, so some things might have changed."

"Isn't having asbestos punishable by law?"

"Certainly not!" snapped Harry. "What kind of country would tell its people what they can and can't make their roofs from? I could build a mud hut here, and it'd be nobody else's business. This is my land. I bought it, developed it and then . . ."

"And then handed it over for perpetual usufruct to fungi, dust mites, and wild animals," added Joanna as she approached them.

She raised her eyebrows, looking at the carcass of a mole that had given up the ghost under the fence.

"Pay no attention to the asbestos or the carcass," said McVay, patting Oryński on the back. "You'll see that inside it's quite charming."

But the Englishman was in no hurry to enter the house, so Chyłka took the initiative. She had barely opened the door when the smell of mustiness hit them.

"Forgive me," apologised Harry as he passed the other two lawyers on the porch. "I have a kind neighbour who comes to air the house once a month, but clearly that's not enough. Or maybe she doesn't bother, I don't know, I have no way of checking."

Oryński thought that a bulldozer would do more good than a friendly neighbour.

They set about opening all the windows, and once the air was a bit fresher, the Englishman invited them into the kitchen. The table was spread with a red and white oilcloth, there were transparent coffee cups in the cupboard and an old Jowita radio on the kitchen worktop. Next to it stood a clunky sugar bowl, no doubt remembering the days of the inflationary gap and food ration cards.

A time capsule.

"Where do you keep your Donald Duck comics and bubble gum?" asked Joanna warily sitting down on the chair. "Do you still do your washing with IXI powder?"

"Very funny," muttered McVay.

Oryński couldn't help but smile. Chyłka was sitting opposite him, but still ignoring him. Instead, she was looking around the kitchen as if she were looking for fungus on the walls.

"But I do have some collector's items here," admitted Harry. "Somewhere in the cellar, there's a game my children used to play constantly. Something about hens? Perches?"

"Well, Just You Wait!" suggested Kordian.

The Englishman snapped his fingers and nodded approvingly. He opened one cupboard after another, rummaging through their contents and muttering, but eventually he gave up and sat down at the table.

"I'm afraid I can't offer you anything," he said with a sigh.

"Thank God," replied Chyłka.

McVay pulled out his phone and raised it above his head, looking for a signal.

"Mobile office," he explained, shaking the latest Samsung Galaxy Note. He browsed online and ordered food from Telepizza to be delivered to Radzymińska Street.

"OK, now I feel like a proper host," he said. "We can get down to business while there's time. By the time the pizza arrives, we'll be preoccupied with more important things than the life and times of some convict stuck in prison."

"There's nothing to talk about," said Joanna. "Unless you want to listen to that traitor giving us a monologue," she added, pointing her head towards her trainee.

"I don't think that would be a bad idea," said Harry.

When the Englishman looked at him, Oryński felt the urge to thank them both for their delightful company and hospitality, make his excuses, and leave. For a few moments the kitchen was totally silent. Then finally, Kordian realised he'd have to tell them everything anyway, sooner or later.

"What I'm about to say has to . . ."

"Yes, yes," interrupted Joanna. "Everything will be in confidence, between you, us and this communist era house of horrors Harry calls home."

"Naturally," agreed McVay.

"Speak, Zordon. This is your one and only chance to redeem yourself as a human being in my eyes."

Kordian cleared his throat and began to tell them everything he knew. From his first encounter with the Bald Man outside the gym to meeting him again outside the Skylight building and their tête-à-tête on the bench in Parade Square. He remembered to tell them about the doctor at Bielański Hospital, who also turned out to be working for the mob.

When he finished, Joanna and McVay exchanged knowing looks. Oryński assumed they had already worked it all out.

"I'm tired of having to refer to them as 'those people,'" began Harry. "It makes me feel like they're elusive, even transcendental, impossible for our minds to fathom, shimmering somewhere between metaphysics and reality."

No one answered him at first.

"Maybe we could call them the Band of Pricks," muttered Chyłka.

"I'd rather call them the Collective," suggested McVay, looking around his kitchen. Its communist era feel must have inspired this reference to communist nomenclature.

"Do we have to?" asked Chyłka.

"You need to imagine the enemy as real people," explained the Englishman. "Then they become less terrifying and more real."

"OK, you might be right," she agreed. "And now can we get down to business?"

Suddenly there was an alarming sound, as if nuclear war had broken out. The crude, mechanical doorbell was hammering away in a way that made Kordian think his visits to the Hard Rock Cafe were pleasantly relaxing in comparison.

Soon three pizzas appeared on the table along with liquid refreshments—non-alcoholic, to the disappointment of the guests.

"Time to talk about specifics," said the host. "Once we get an extension to the deadline, we'll be able to implement . . ."

"If we get it," mumbled Kordian.

"If we don't get it, we'll appeal."

"If your appeal for an extended deadline is rejected, you can't appeal against it," said Oryński, chewing on a piece of excessively dry pizza. Too much flour on the base. It was good for stopping your pizzas sticking to the paper, but only within reason.

"That's true," agreed the Englishman. "But a court rejecting an extension effectively rejects the cassation appeal. And that decision can be challenged on the grounds of what was written in the official complaint. It's a rather roundabout way of doing things, but remember it, my boy, it might come in useful one day."

"One day? I think we're going to need it now."

"No," said McVay, sipping his lemon iced tea. "We'll get the new deadline. I've read your letter, and think it has a good chance of making an interesting court case."

"Interesting it certainly will be," said Joanna. "I just don't know whether it will be more interesting in the courtroom or outside it. That Band of Pricks of yours . . ."

"Collective," the Englishman corrected her.

"That Collective," she hissed, "won't stand idle. And first in the firing line will be Zordon."

"And then there's the problem with Żelazny," added Oryński, looking at McVay. "Your partner has promised to do everything he can to wreck our careers."

"He doesn't have to try hard. You're doing a good job of ruining them yourselves."

"Careful what you say," said Chyłka. "I intend to use this case to boost my career so fast, all you two will be able to do is watch my meteoric rise from below."

"One way or the other," sighed McVay, "we're a triangle now. No, that doesn't sound quite right," he added, and cut himself another slice of pizza.

The guests ate with their hands, perhaps out of habit, or perhaps because the cutlery resembled an archaeologist's find. Seeing this, Harry also put his knife and fork to one side and ate in the traditional fashion.

"Have you spoken with any of the witnesses?" he asked.

"Zordon and Kormak exchanged a few words with a neighbour and the shopkeeper. But they're pretty poor witnesses. They didn't see anything. No one knows anything."

"And after talking with us, they could both be lying in a shallow grave in Kampinos National Park," added Oryński.

"Get hold of them. Make it a priority . . ." said McVay, ignoring the comments, and paused. "Forgive me for being so officious and giving you orders, but you have to remember that this isn't just about Langer's fate, it's also the fate of my firm. It's either Żelazny or me, there's no third way. Everything hangs on this one case."

He put his slice of pizza back in the box and looked at Kordian and Joanna. They looked none too pleased.

"I don't want to put you under pressure," he said.

"Perish the thought," said Kordian.

"Just concentrate on this one task," continued the Englishman. "I'll deal with Artur and prepare the ground for our little revolution . . . our *coup d'état* if you will. And you must find those witnesses, keep them safe, and we'll prepare them for the hearing."

"Prepare?" asked the trainee.

"There is absolutely nothing wrong or amoral in a witness being prepared for the benefit of one of the parties. The trick is not to influence them to give false testimony."

Oryński looked at his boss doubtfully, thinking how much he wanted to light a cigarette. He got up and started searching for an ashtray. In one of the cupboards, he found two bowls of thick glass that seemed more suitable as urns for holding human ashes than cigarette ash. He placed the two heavy ashtrays on the table, and pulled out a packet of Davidoffs.

"I'm sorry, but please don't smoke in here," said McVay.

Kordian raised his eyebrows, and out of the corner of his eye noticed Chyłka lighting up.

"Give it a rest," she said. "You could invite every union rep from across the entire country to burn tyres in this dump and it wouldn't make any difference."

Harry murmured something under his breath and pushed the ashtray away. He looked at his employees, then took a deep breath to indicate there was something else he wanted to tell them.

"Witnesses are still the most important source of evidence. I know that we live in a world where everything is recorded electronically in a thousand different ways, but most cases are still resolved on the basis of the evidence given by witnesses. Make sure you prepare them properly."

"But is it legal?"

"I've never heard of it being penalised in any statute," replied McVay, raising his open hands. "Eat your pizza, and then to work. And then get yourselves to bed. Together. You're young, you shouldn't be arguing, you should be having sex."

Harry couldn't help but notice the expression of consternation on the faces of his guests.

"While you two indulge, I'll take care of the rest," he added.

"And the Collective?" asked Kordian, ignoring the thinly veiled allusions. "Gorzym's going to appear sooner rather than later to renew his job offer."

"Don't worry about him, I'll assign someone to protect you."

Kordian's eyebrows shot up.

"It's not the first time I've hired a bodyguard, you know," added McVay, seeing Kordian's surprise. "You won't even notice him, he'll be like your shadow on a late summer's afternoon."

"How romantic," commented Joanna.

"It'll be romantic when you two get down to work."

"Yes, sir!" she replied, carelessly saluting with a cigarette in between her fingers.

"So what are you still doing here?"

"I thought we were . . ."

"Take the pizza with you," replied the Englishman with a smile. "Now go, Langer can't defend himself without your help."

CHAPTER

4

T HE LEGAL DUO from Żelazny & McVay got into the black BMW in silence. On the way to Mokotów, neither of them uttered a word. For a moment Oryński considered making some sort of light, provocative remark, but decided it wasn't worth the risk.

They drove up to the development where Piotr Langer's apartment was, and this time they had no problems entering the premises. Chyłka had a remote control for the gate, a magnetic card for the entrance door and keys to the flat. They parked in a space reserved for residents and got out of the X5, still in silence.

They glanced at one another surreptitiously.

"Zordon," Chyłka finally said. "We're making prize idiots of ourselves."

"True."

"So let's stop this fooling around and get down to work."

"OK," he replied. That was a weight off his mind. "Who do we attack first? The shopkeeper?"

"No. The girl you tracked down to the gym. Big tits."

"Agnieszka Powirska."

"I assume you lost her number when you lost your phone?"

"That's right."

"Do you remember where she lives?"

"We never found out."

"How come?"

"We got the phone number from the receptionist at the gym, but there was no mention of her address."

"I see," she replied under her breath.

They stood by the door of the staircase leading to Langer's apartment. It would have been easy if they had the names of the residents on the outside, but that didn't happen on these exclusive developments.

"This leaves us with the traditional method," said Joanna, and phoned Kormak, asking him for Powirska's number. Soon the pair were on the phone, waiting for the girl to answer.

"Hello?" sounded a voice Kordian already knew.

"Good morning, Ms Powirska. This is Joanna Chyłka of Żelazny & McVay."

"And Kordian Oryński. We spoke over the phone some time ago."

There was a moment of silence.

"Indeed, I remember. Not a particularly nice name," she replied eventually. "You were phoning about Peter."

"That's right. We're downstairs now, in your building, by the staircase."

"My staircase?"

The two lawyers exchanged looks.

"That's right," he replied. "We'd like to talk with you, if it's not a problem."

"Now?"

"Yes, now."

"But I've got no makeup on."

Oryński grimaced and scratched his head.

"It's an important matter, Ms Powirska," added Chyłka. "But I promise you it will only take a few minutes."

"All right . . . just wait a moment."

Five minutes later, they were beginning to doubt the girl would open the door at all. Eventually, however, the magnetic lock opened. They entered, and walked up the stairs to Langer's floor.

Powirska, now powdered and coiffed, opened the door to her apartment. She looked at them and smiled.

"How is he?"

"Like a man in prison," replied Chyłka.

With a gesture of the hand, Agnieszka invited them in. They hurriedly wiped their feet on the doormat and having caught their breath, crossed the threshold. The situation could have played out in any number of ways, but being cordially invited in was by no means the one they had thought most likely. "Do sit down." Powirska pointed to the sofa and two armchairs.

"Would you like something to drink? Tea, coffee, beer?"

"I'd love—"

"No, thank you," cut in Chyłka.

"Well, I can see who rules the roost."

The girl poured herself a Pepsi and sat on the sofa. "So what are the conditions like?" she asked. "Because I know prisons are all different. You just have to look at what they're like in Norway."

"Norway would be the least of your worries," said Kordian, trying not to look at her two most outstanding attributes. "The inmates at Leoben enjoy the highest standards of incarceration. The Justice Centre has been compared to a five-star hotel with a glazed façade, spacious, modern interiors, comfortable couches and a park instead of an exercise yard."

"Really?" Agnieszka asked unenthusiastically. "That's fascinating."

"Well," started Joanna.

"It's not going too well for Langer," Kordian cut in again. "So far, it hasn't been too bad, but each day brings him closer to the line that every prisoner eventually crosses."

"What do you mean?"

"I mean a point, or perhaps rather a barrier in the mind, beyond which you start to lose all feelings. In order to survive in prison, you need to behave like a sociopath, and scientists believe that twenty-one days is enough for any recurring behaviour to become a lifetime habit. So you see . . ."

"Oh . . ."

"There's going to be another trial soon," said Chyłka, taking over the conversation. "And we would like you to give evidence, as a witness. Would you be prepared to do that?"

The question was unnecessary. If the court summoned her as a witness, she would have to agree or she'd be penalised. But Joanna wanted to prepare her, and that would only be possible if she cooperated willingly.

"I don't see why not," replied Agnieszka. "Are you sure you don't want anything to drink? Is there anything at all I can tempt you with?"

"Chyłka and I wouldn't mind a beer if you've got anything good?"

"Just shandy."

"Excellent," said Joanna, eagerly nodding her head. But when Agnieszka went to the kitchen, she turned to Oryński and made a vomiting gesture.

Agnieszka brought out two frost-covered bottles. Kordian took a swig and instantly wanted to spit it out, but kept a poker face. He noticed Chyłka had a similar expression.

"I love shandy," said Joanna after a while.

"Me too," added Kordian.

Powirska gave a radiant smile.

"What will I have to say in court?" she asked.

Chyłka turned the bottle in her hand, wondering why the girl was unexpectedly so willing to stand in the witness box. There could be a number of reasons: romance, attention-seeking, goodwill, or too much free time.

"We'll ask you a few questions, then the prosecutor will probably want to know a few bits and pieces from you," explained Chyłka. "Nothing that would intrude into your private life, but questions like at what times of day you saw the accused, how he behaved in your presence, and how he behaved among other people."

"Only that kind of stuff?" said the girl.

"You didn't witness the actual crime, so the questions will only be about background facts. General matters."

"But it can still be a bit unpleasant," added Oryński.

"Oh, yes," confirmed Chyłka, nodding her head energetically. "Kordian told me you believe Piotr is innocent."

"I simply feel that Peter would not be capable of doing it, and . . ."

"That's why the prosecutor will target you," interrupted Joanna. "It might turn out that he'll want to be a bit more aggressive. Would you be ready for something like that?"

"I'll crush him like a steamroller."

Chyłka couldn't help but smile. If Karol Rejchert had heard, he'd probably have burst out laughing.

At the thought of the prosecutor, she took a deeper swig of shandy. She really, really wanted to take him down. After their humiliation at the district and appeal courts, Rejchert deserved an ass-kicking, and that was Chyłka's intention. She doubted that the girl would get out of the confrontation unscathed, but no one expected miracles from her—she only had to survive the prosecution's onslaught for long enough.

"Excellent," Joanna said. "We won't leave you without support. We'd like to have a practice run, though, if that's OK. Of course, we're not telling you how to testify, we just want you to be prepared mentally, so that none of the questions surprise you."

"No problem."

"Kordian?" Chyłka looked at her trainee expectantly.

Oryński cleared his throat and adjusted his jacket. He was annoyed they hadn't discussed how to conduct this witness prep; now he had to improvise. He knew a thing or two about the techniques—he'd participated once or twice in moot courts during his studies, but he was hardly well versed in the subject.

But he put on a brave face.

"If you've nothing against it, shall we try it right now?" he suggested.

"Why not?"

"Informally, without microphones and cameras," he added, noting that her eyes gleamed at the words. Obviously hungry for fame.

"OK, let's do it," suggest Powirska as eagerly as if the trial was to start tomorrow.

Kordian recited the formula about speaking the truth, the whole truth, and nothing but the truth more or less correctly and then started pacing around the living room. He felt that Chyłka was amused by all of this, so he tried not to look at her.

"How long have you known the accused?" he asked.

"I dont know . . . a few years. Maybe three?"

We've got our work cut out here, thought Oryński.

"You must be careful," said Chyłka from the sofa. "If you hesitate like that, the prosecutor will rip you to shreds in front of the cameras."

"OK, I get it."

"You have to be concise, never say more than is needed to answer the question, and always look at the judge, because they are the ones most interested in your answer," added Chyłka. "If you don't know something, simply say you don't know. Never try to answer a question if you're not certain you can. Avoid vague formulations such as 'maybe,' 'a few years,' etc."

"If you can't answer at once, ask for a moment to consider," said Oryński, feeling rather pleased with himself. He had to admit he felt exceptionally good in his role as a barrister, someone *au fait* with the subject. A fully fledged lawyer.

"How long have you known the accused?" he asked once again, putting his hands behind his back and pacing around the room.

"For four years."

"Who moved in first?"

"We both moved in at more or less the same time."

Kordian stopped, raised his chin slightly, and looked at the witness meaningfully.

"Do you live alone?"

Agnieszka nodded.

"And you lived alone from the start?"

"Yes."

"As did the accused, so could we assume you were both looking for company?"

Kordian felt he had overdone it a little with the refined tone.

"Yes, I suppose so."

"Did you meet, and talk about the neighbourhood? Perhaps take the dogs for a walk, or go jogging together?"

"I don't have a dog."

Oryński looked at her.

"Sometimes we had dinner together."

That would be enough for the prosecutor to conclude that the witness and the defendant were close. This didn't totally rule her out as a witness for the defence, but given that she didn't hear or see anything and was only supposed to sow a seed of doubt, her testimony might be of little use.

"How often did you have sex?" asked Kordian, now taking his hands from behind his back, folding his arms on his chest and tilting his head to one side.

"I beg your pardon?"

"At what intervals did you engage in sexual intercourse? I mean both in the . . ."

"This is getting a bit personal," said Powirska with a smile, but shaking her head.

"As someone close to the accused, you have a right to refuse to testify," said Chyłka, deliberately making things slightly more tense.

And she had hardly finished, when Kordian continued, "I have asked the witness a simple question which has not been overruled, and therefore I request an answer."

"I . . . will I really have to answer questions like that?"

"Yes," said Oryński. "And the way you answered leads me to assume you regularly slept together."

"But that's not true," said Agnieszka and looked somewhere out into the distance. "Won't you raise objections, or something?"

Chyłka didn't answer directly. "It's important in the context," was all she said.

"So what should I tell them?"

"The truth," advised Kordian. "You face a severe penalty for giving false evidence, so I'd suggest you don't take any unnecessary risks."

"But I . . . I've got a boyfriend."

Chyłka was not surprised. She really was quite lovely to look at. *Easy pickings for all sorts of oafs and thugs,* she thought.

"Then we won't invite your boyfriend to the trial," said Oryński and smiled as sympathetically as he could. Agnieszka seemed to be wondering if she should withdraw her offer to testify.

Joanna decided it was time to tell Powirska what was what. When they made it clear to her that when she was called, she'd have to appear before the court and testify whether she wanted to or not, their work became appreciably easier. Now the poor girl treated the two of them as her best friends, not realising it was their doing that she would be called at all.

They were on their third shandy, and Oryński was ready to puke, but at least they'd got the formalities out of the way. Now it was time to get to the nub of the matter.

"Did you see him during the time the bodies were in his apartment?" asked Joanna.

"No, not once. I hadn't seen him for about a week beforehand, but we weren't meeting up so often by then."

"That doesn't matter," said Chyłka. "You were still living virtually opposite each other."

"And you didn't hear anything suspicious?" added Kordian.

Agnieszka resolutely shook her head.

"Nothing that could indicate that Langer was in his apartment?"

"No."

"And would you normally hear anything?"

"Often," she replied. Joanna's eyes flashed. "When he watched television or played music, or sometimes at night, when he brought girls home. One of them squealed like a piglet. She would often be there on Fridays, or rather Friday nights and Saturday mornings. I reckon she was a prostitute, because no one yells like that naturally. She must have trained for it."

"OK," said Chyłka, getting up off the sofa. "That's probably everything. If you remember something more . . . anything unusual, please contact me." She handed Powirska her business card, then, raising the bottle to her lips like a bugle, she downed the rest of her shandy in one.

Leaving Agnieszka's flat, they felt as if they had drunk at most a single beer, not three.

"You probably shouldn't drive, though," Kordian noted once they were out into the street.

It wasn't the most adept way to start a conversation, but at least he'd said something. Quite unintentionally, the tone was slightly provocative.

"If you're scared, you can walk on foot."

"You can't really walk on anything else."

He paused. Chyłka had stopped in her tracks, as if struck by lightning. But before he could ask her what was wrong, he saw for himself.

The X5's tyres had been slashed, and something was leaking from under the car. The bodywork was scratched along its entire length, and the wing mirrors were hanging on by a couple of cables.

"Bastards . . ." she whispered, looking around.

Then her emotions got the better of her and she found another dozen or so choice words to describe the perpetrators. Oryński didn't note down every phrase, but he did remember "broken pricks," "fucking marrows," "whoring pig snouts," and "gutless dickheads."

Having verbalised her anger, Chyłka walked up to the BMW with Oryński and began to conduct an organoleptic evaluation of the damage. They circled the car for a while before eventually moving away from the expanding puddle of petrol and taking out their cigarette packets.

"It won't go," concluded Kordian.

Chyłka glowered at him, a cigarette between her lips. She took a deep drag and shook her head, smiling.

"I was expecting a smack in the kisser sooner than see you smile."

"It'll get fixed," she replied, pointing with her cigarette to the battered bonnet.

"I was thinking more about us."

"That'll get fixed too, nerd."

Instead of answering, Oryński also smiled and looked down. This was, perhaps, the best possible answer.

"But they've got a bloody cheek," said Chyłka. "In a gated community, with surveillance cameras and security guards milling around. Can you believe it?"

"No," replied Kordian. He suspected the Collective were capable of many things, but for the Bald Man or some other thug to break into a closely guarded premises just to upset a couple of lawyers?

"The bunch of shitty . . ." began Joanna and articulated another stream of invective against those who had taken a swipe at her BMW. When the lawyers had finished their cigarettes, they flicked the butts as far away as possible from the puddle of petrol. Unfortunately, they were spotted by a security guard who happened to be passing nearby.

"Cigarette butts go in the bin," he barked.

Oryński managed to get between Chyłka and the guard.

"What's up with you?" said the guard, taking a step back. She had almost rammed straight into him, and he had nothing to defend himself with. His security guard equipment consisted of nothing more than a uniform and peaked cap.

"Are you blind, you poor excuse for a janitor?" snapped Chyłka.

Kordian raised his hands in apology and smiled at the guard in as conciliatory a way as he could. One thing they definitely did not need at that moment was a battle with the security guards. The man could radio for help, and before they knew it, they could be dealing with ten more of them, all feeling none too convivial.

"Someone has demolished our car," said Oryński quietly.

The security guard looked at him with disbelief.

"Over there, idiot," said Joanna, pointing to the wrecked car.

The man looked in the direction she was gesturing and froze. Not only was he completely lost for words, it had dawned on him that the damage could only have happened on his watch.

"How . . . when . . . but you . . . ?"

"We were gone for one and a half hours at most," said Chyłka.

She watched the security guard's reactions. He must have been worried that all the blame would land at his feet. He'd be reprimanded, his pay might be cut, and he would be moved to the outskirts of town.

Chyłka frowned. All at once it occurred to her that the Collective must have people inside the community. Someone must have let the perpetrator in, then turned a blind eye as they demolished the car.

A security guard? One of the cleaning crew? One person was enough to open the gate, and perhaps facilitate the transferral of two human corpses.

Suddenly Chyłka was ready to believe what Langer had said. Perhaps he was telling the truth when he insisted on his own innocence.

5

THE INSURANCE COMPANY required that the police be informed, so immediately after ending her conversation with the guard, Chyłka phoned to report the possibility of an offence being committed under article 288 of the Penal Code. This really infuriated the woman on duty on the other end of the line, but Chyłka couldn't help herself.

Some time later, a police car appeared at the estate, attracting the attention of all the residents. Out climbed two police officers, who swiftly carried out all the required formalities and assured Chyłka that investigations would be made.

"Is that it?" asked Chyłka with disbelief.

"Yes."

"But you've done nothing but make a few notes."

"At this moment, we cannot—"

"Interview witnesses?" cut in Chyłka. "Identify the security guards?"

The officers looked at one another.

"How about searching the site?" continued Joanna. "Finding non-human sources of information? You've got surveillance cameras, for heaven's sake."

"Madam . . ."

"You're downplaying the whole matter," she said, shaking her head. She looked at Oryński helplessly, while he pointed to a crowd of people gathered a little further on.

"We have quite an audience," he said.

The two officers looked at the ground and headed back to their car.

Chyłka cursed under her breath, but decided there would be a chance later to talk with their superiors, who might be more decisive. She turned her gaze to the onlookers. If you counted those leaning out of their windows, there must have been a good few dozen people.

"I expect there are already rumours going round about another murder," she said. "And actually, we should be glad, because now we've become local celebrities, and it should be easier to interview the residents."

"And are we going to interview anyone now? Apart from the shopkeeper?"

"In this situation, Zordon?" she raised her eyebrows and lit another cigarette. "We must seize this opportunity. Because that bloody Collective must have an insider."

"I know, or the car wouldn't have been wrecked."

"And they could have planted the bodies in Langer's apartment."

"Or killed those people in his apartment and then planted Piotr's unconscious body in there," added Oryński. "But the police have found nothing to corroborate that."

"Maybe we're dealing with rubber glove and disinfectant fetishists."

"Maybe."

"We need to interview the other neighbours," she said, looking at her X5. Mobile Care roadside assistance had just arrived, and the crew were preparing to load the BMW onto their truck.

"Did you hear me, Zordon?"

"Yes, yes, we need to interview the other neighbours," he repeated. "But do you really think they'll want to talk to us?"

"After this incident, they'll all be inviting us in for coffee and biscuits. Or possibly champagne and caviar, given the affluence of the locals."

"Well, I'm not so sure."

"Everyone will be happy to talk to the two people at the centre of today's events. They'll invite us in to find out what happened, but we'll be the ones asking the questions."

"As simple as that, eh?"

"Stop whingeing," she said. "Let's go to the shopkeeper first. Lead me to his shrine, Zordon."

They set off towards the neighbourhood shop, watched by the crowd.

"Do you think they know who we are?" asked Oryński.

"I think you're an idiot if you even need to ask."

"It's quite an important issue."

"Not in the slightest," she said. "What does it matter? They're here because they think they have another killer in their community. And God knows, they soon will, if you don't stop asking such lame questions."

"But . . ."

"Listen," she said, cutting him short. "A moment ago, I saw my poor car, my battered baby. In my mind I can still see it. Anyone who pisses me off may end up regretting it, and you are in a high-risk category."

He glowered at her and muttered something under his breath. "The shop is just round the corner," he said.

They turned the corner, but the shop wasn't there. What was more, there was no evidence that it ever had been there. Kordian decided that either he had made a mistake, or the shopkeeper was a master at covering up his tracks.

"I don't understand," said Chyłka. "Have you got amnesia?"

"Everything looks the same on this estate," said Oryński to justify himself, looking round at the surrounding buildings. "But I'm pretty sure this is where Kormak and I came."

"And I'm pretty sure you were more preoccupied with Ms Powirska's formidable assets than about thinking where you actually were."

"Do I detect a hint of jealousy?" said Kordian with satisfaction.

Chyłka glared at him. "Believe me, if I'm ever jealous, you'll know about it."

He smiled and wanted the banter to continue, but Joanna had lost interest. She had noticed a boy watching them from a distance, and waved to him.

She headed towards the child. Oryński sighed, and followed her.

"Hi there," she said. "We're looking for the grocery shop, could you show us where it is?"

"It was here not long ago," the boy answered shyly, pointing to an empty building.

"When did it close?" asked Kordian.

"I don't know. But if you want Dr Pepper, you won't get it anywhere here," replied the youngster. "Well, you could come with me and Mum to Blue City, then yes. But it isn't here anymore, and the next nearest shop is . . . oh . . . way over there." He waved his hand to the right.

"Do you know why the man moved out?"

The child frowned, as if he was trying to trisect an acute angle using Archimedes's method.

"I don't know," he replied. "But Mum says it's strange, because he had customers all the time. Everyone went to his shop."

"And did you hear anything else?"

"Mum says that maybe someone drove him out of here."

"Thanks," said Chyłka.

The boy nodded and briskly walked away. Joanna looked at Kordian knowingly. They didn't need the youngster to tell them that the Collective had taken care of the shopkeeper.

"Needless to say, he didn't leave a forwarding address," said Kordian peering through the window.

Joanna ignored him.

"Why did they remove him?" she asked. "He wasn't that important."

"Maybe he was and we didn't realise it. I guess he could have testified that during those ten days, Langer didn't buy anything from his shop. If we compare this with readings from his magnetic card, the amount of fuel he used, money withdrawn from his account, etc., we could argue that there's no way he was in that apartment."

"That would be stretching it too far."

"Perhaps not," objected Oryński. "If no one else in the community could testify that they had seen Langer in that ten-day period, the shop-keeper's testimony would be worth its weight in gold."

"Don't exaggerate. You've watched too many legal soaps on TV. Absence of evidence is not evidence of absence. And even more so in this case, because our client has already been convicted and is now doing time."

Kordian preferred to drop the subject, bearing in mind that Chyłka's emotions associated with the destruction of her car had not yet completely subsided.

They both smoked another cigarette and got down to work. They started by gathering information from the residents on the ground floor—and just as Chyłka had predicted, people spoke to them fairly willingly. Once the news spread that "the lawyer who was recently on TV" was meeting residents, doors were opened wide for the Żelazny & McVay legal duo, even before they reached the given floor.

Once they had checked every apartment, they could be certain that none of these residents would compromise their case. None of them had seen Langer during the ten days when he was supposedly hiding the bodies in his apartment, and what's more, none of them had seen him for a long time before that.

6

"AND NOBODY KNOWS where the shopkeeper moved to?" asked Harry McVay when Kordian and Joanna appeared in his hotel room at the Holiday Inn. They weren't surprised that the boss preferred to operate from his hotel room rather than his house in Elsnerów. In addition to the obvious, it was much closer to the Skylight building.

"No," replied Kordian. "He vanished into thin air, taking all his baggage with him."

"And no curtain-twitching granny saw him and asked where he was off to in such a hurry?"

"Over there? I don't think it's that sort of neighbourhood."

"Unbelievable," said McVay, rifling through the minibar. One of the advantages of having a room close to your place of work was that you didn't have to drive. One of the disadvantages was the ridiculously small size of the bottles.

"He's gone to ground," added Oryński, shrugging his shoulders.

"But you said he had quite a lot of stock," responded the Englishman offhandedly. "So it must have taken him a bit of time to get his kit together. It's unbelievable that none of the neighbours saw him go."

"All his stuff was packed and driven away by a removal company," said Chyłka.

"No doubt paid for by the Collective," concluded McVay, fishing a tiny bottle of Johnnie Walker out of the minibar.

"I'm not sure about that name," said Joanna, opening the window. She leaned out and lit a cigarette. "It sounds like a hipster band playing punk rock."

"To me, it sounds more like an Afro Collective," said Oryński.

"What in God's name is that?" she asked, taking a drag. "No, I don't think I want to know. It'd probably be something in your style, so I'd rather live in blissful ignorance."

Kordian squeezed in next to Chyłka and also tried to lean out of the window.

"I see that the make-up sex has been successful," said Harry, and didn't wait for either of them to deny it. "Excellent. In that case, I can get straight to the point. We have a new deadline. It took persuasion, a touch of blackmail and a bit of calling in old favours, but I eventually got what I wanted. I had the biggest problems with Artur, who has clearly got it in for you, young man. But all things considered, everything is OK now."

"But how did you . . . ?"

"I convinced one of the honourable judges of the Supreme Court that before submitting the appeal you were held up by . . . well, by a superior force, though not *vis major* in the contractual sense," replied the Englishman and chuckled. "Though it wouldn't be a problem anyway," continued McVay, "because I had Chyłka's written statement that the cassation appeal was well founded and, to the best of her knowledge, should be heard. So the legal side was settled. All we had to do was get an equivalent document from the procedural side and prove that our failure to meet the deadline was not deliberate. We even went one better, saying it was the result of a crime."

"But . . ."

"Yes, unfortunately," said McVay, looking at the trainee. "This will have to be handled as a criminal matter, but all in good time. You'll have to report it as a crime. In fact, you should already start doing the paperwork. For the time being, I've submitted a written statement to the effect that I have full knowledge of the affair and am able to verify it. If need be, a colleague of mine has all the right papers."

"So for the time being, I'm the culprit?"

"Yes," said Harry, shrugging his shoulders. "The court knows you are at fault. Contrary to the wishes of the client and his lawyer, you failed to deliver a procedural document. That is sufficient. The judge won't conduct an investigation personally, that's not his job. That's a job for the Crime Division, regional or district, I don't remember which."

"What can I expect to get?"

"A reprimand," declared McVay. "But due to the fact that you have good relations with your employer, and your employer has good relations with the rest of the legal establishment, you have been granted a letter of safe conduct, thanks to which you can continue to navigate the great convolutions of the law."

Kordian was a bit confused, and the Englishman's metaphors didn't help. "Can I still be part of the trial?"

"Nobody's going to stick you in jail," said McVay nonchalantly. "But that's for the law firm and the client to decide. Even with all your flaws, I've nothing against you representing Langer, and it just so happens, neither has he."

"Great," remarked Joanna. She had already heard all this in Kraków, when Harry first presented his plan to her. Back then, there had been a good many question marks, chiefly concerning favours and gestures of goodwill, but McVay was certain the matter would be settled quickly. And it had been, though sooner or later Kordian would have to appear in court not only to answer charges of negligence, but also to face the people who had threatened his life. The two cases were inextricably linked.

"So what about witnesses?" asked the Englishman, looking at Chyłka and Oryński.

"There's plenty to choose from," started Chyłka. "On Langer's staircase there are at least ten people willing to testify, including a bloke who lives directly above him and a lady who lives below. This is a modern building, so the walls are paper thin, and the neighbours constantly heard all sorts of sounds coming from Langer's apartment. He was hardly into peace and quiet, but appeared to love loud music and the opposite sex. And yet during those ten terrible days, they heard nothing."

"Nothing at all?"

"Not a dickie bird."

"How is that possible?" asked McVay, frowning. "Even if Langer didn't kill those people, someone must have heaved those bodies there. Are you saying someone entered the building unnoticed, with two corpses, placed them inside the flat and arranged the whole scene? And no one heard anything?"

"Or saw anything," added Chyłka.

For a moment they were all silent.

"Alternatively, someone could have killed them inside the flat," suggested Oryński. "It would have been considerably easier."

"Let's assume that's what happened," said the Englishman. "Then it seems even more improbable that no one heard any noise coming from the apartment. The bodies of the victims were mutilated, so much so there were problems identifying them. According to the police report, their bodies were abused over a long period of time.

Oryński refrained from asking McVay how he knew what was in the police report. He probably wouldn't have been given a straight answer anyway.

"And what about surveillance cameras?" asked Harry, but with little conviction.

"They are trained on the perimeter fence and the back wall," explained Joanna. "In theory, the security guards look after the rest of the premises, and the main gate is guarded 24/7."

"OK," said the Englishman. "And you believe the Collective have an insider there?"

"My slashed tyres are proof that they do. And bear in mind that it's not easy to get into those premises. Zordon and Kormak had considerable difficulty, and they were representatives of the law firm defending one of the residents."

"Maybe it's one of the security guards?"

"Or one of the residents," suggested Chyłka. "In fact, it could turn out that the brains behind the whole operation is someone living in the same block as Langer."

The three lawyers fell silent. Oryński looked at the ceiling, wondering what he had got himself into. The professor teaching them criminal procedure repeatedly warned them never to work for corporations. Do anything, they said, even become a tax adviser, but never join a large law firm. The lecturer had been a good person, one of the very few who actually believed the students would make something of themselves when they graduated. He had enough faith to speak of justice as if it was a value, and also spoke of having a "mission," a concept that back then was more generally associated with getting exam credits. He encouraged students to become prosecutors or judges, because out of the three evils of legal life, those were the least hypocritical and deceitful.

Slowly but surely Kordian was realising that he would have to repeat everything he had told his two lawyer colleagues before the court. Then they'd start the tedious process of determining what lay behind the legal world's favourite oxymoron: "the objective truth."

The Collective would do everything to destroy him. And its members had demonstrated they knew how to do their job.

The "Afraid to Shoot Strangers" guitar solo shook Kordian out of his thoughts.

McVay nodded in time with the music as he sang along with Bruce Dickinson. Clearly, he was no stranger to British heavy metal.

Chyłka pulled out her phone glanced at the display and pressed it against her ear. She did not look pleased. For a moment she listened to the caller, then put the phone back into her pocket without a word.

"Powirska," Joanna said in a grave tone.

"What did she want?" asked McVay.

"She won't testify. She's leaving the country, and if she's summoned to court, we'll be informed in writing," explained Chyłka, her face pale. "Then she hung up, as you can imagine."

A heavy silence that had been circling like a vulture over the decaying hope of winning the case now descended on them. The three lawyers had no doubt that someone had been advising Powirska, because leaving the country was the only possible justification for not appearing in court after a summons.

Oryński turned to the window and lit another cigarette. Joanna joined him. They all remained relatively calm, although two of their most important witnesses were now unavailable.

"Serious shit," Kordian finally said.

"Blackmail?" asked Chyłka, exhaling smoke.

"Perhaps," said Harry. "From what you tell me, she's a fairly promiscuous girl. Maybe they took compromising photographs, maybe they've put pressure on her, or maybe they've kidnapped her and taken her out of the country."

"We have to find her," said Joanna.

McVay agreed. Two cigarette butts flew out of the window towards Golden Terraces, and shortly afterwards the duo left the hotel room.

Powirska was not at home—the security guard told them that she had left the estate shortly before their arrival. None of the neighbours knew where she had gone.

Kordian was comforted by the fact that at least they were still willing to talk to them.

At least for the moment.

The following day, none of the residents would even answer their phone calls.

THE COLLECTIVE COULD not blackmail all the residents, let alone kid-
nap them. But removing Agnieszka Powirska seemed to be enough.
The news spread throughout the gated community and almost instantly
there was a general conviction that nothing good could come from being
involved in the Langer case.

People are, by nature, reluctant to testify in court; but when they have
reason to feel threatened, they suddenly don't know or remember anything
at all. Chyłka was persistent to the end. But even when residents eventually relented and answered her calls, they insisted that they shouldn't be
summoned as witnesses for Langer's own good, because they knew nothing and would say nothing or that under cross-examination they might
suddenly recall they had in fact seen Piotr during those ten days.

The situation was becoming hopeless, and time was inexorably
running out. Before they knew it, a week had passed since their visit
to Agnieszka's apartment. McVay was still in the hotel room, sustaining
himself with whisky but complaining that even single malt tasted different in Warsaw. He communicated with his business partner exclusively
by phone, to give the impression he was still in Kraków.

The date for the first hearing was set, and the Żelazny & McVay
lawyers still had nothing to support Langer's case.

They had no witnesses. Apart from the residents, there were also
security guards, but they too had all but disappeared: a different security firm was now in charge of the gated community, and it turned out
that the original guards had been "underqualified" and had therefore
been replaced. A removals truck arrived to collect Agnieszka Powirska's

belongings. Data protection regulations prevented the lawyers from acquiring the address to which the belongings were being dispatched.

For two weeks they made no progress at all. It wasn't even as if they were standing still; they were reversing towards the precipice at break-neck speed.

"All we can do now is settle out of court," Joanna said one day.

"What?" snorted Kordian. "That's surrender."

"Oh, stop it."

"Is it really that bad?"

Just two weeks earlier it had seemed like they had everything under control. Then the enemy counterattacked and everything collapsed like a house of cards.

"I'm afraid so, Zordon. We'll have to talk to Rejchert."

"And what if he double-crosses us? He'll make sure the trial goes ahead, and then he'll present . . ."

"What are you talking about?" she asked, frowning. "According to paragraph thirty-three of the Code of Ethics, our conversation has to remain confidential."

"Well, yes," he conceded. "But this doesn't alter the fact that Rejchert won't be very willing to talk to us. He's won in two instances, or have you forgotten? What's our bargaining chip now?"

She responded with silence. There were no bargaining chips, but this was their only option. Joanna arranged a meeting with Karol Rejchert. And unfortunately, if any public prosecutor could be called Chyłka's most dogged eternal adversary, that person was Rejchert.

They arranged to meet at El Popo Restaurant on Senatorska Street, where you could experience a "true Mexican adventure." Joanna chose it because her stomach was used to spicy food, and she hoped that the pros-ecutor's less experienced guts would fail miserably against Mexican levels of spice-driven heat. It would have been fun to test Zordon's capabilities too, but she decided that this should be a duel, with no third parties.

She settled down on a comfortable cushioned bench, resting her arms on the backrest and ordered a Tequila Rapido as an aperitif. She'd never had one before, but hoped that it would indeed have a *rapido* effect. The rhythmic music of a mariachi band flowing from the speakers filled her with unexpected happiness, which turned into a feeling of total despair as soon as Rejchert arrived.

"Interesting place," he said, sniffing the spices wafting from the kitchen. "I understand you're paying?"

"You're such a gentleman, Rey."

"Sod convention," he said. "I work for the prosecutor's office, while you lot have a fucking licence to print money."

"OK, since you put it so eloquently, I'm paying today. But please don't select *Caxitl Popocatepetl,* because that'd break even our budget."

And that was exactly why he ordered *Caxitl Popocatepetl,* quite unaware that this peculiar mixture of Mexican delicacies would be like placing a layer of Tabasco sauce sprinkled with ground white pepper on his unseasoned taste buds. The meal would have fed several people and cost almost a hundred zlotys, but it was worth every cent just to see Rejchert's face. A good investment to know that the prosecutor would be sitting on the throne for most of the rest of the day.

"Hot as fuck," he said, stuffing down nachos. The green sauce looked pretty innocuous, but soon he was frantically washing it down with a whole glass of water—not that it helped.

The guacamole was taking its toll. And Chyłka knew it would only get worse.

"Mine's just fine," she said, taking another mouthful.

"Why am I here? Do you want to poison me?"

"Mexican food is a serious affair; you don't fool around with it."

"Perhaps that's true. No bacteria will survive this bloody culinary conflagration," he replied, shaking his head. "So tell me, why are we having this meeting?"

"Langer."

"I know it's Langer, Chyłka. I'm not fooling myself that you've invited me here to reminisce about university days. I just can't figure out what makes you think you can get anywhere."

"We've got a new deadline, Rey."

"So what? You've got no grounds . . ."

"And our cassation appeal has been accepted," added Joanna, not letting the prosecutor get into full swing. It was the only ace up her sleeve. The prosecutor's office had not yet received the letter confirming the cassation appeal hearing, whereas McVay was informed earlier in the day by an acquaintance. If this ploy didn't work, nothing would. Simple, but true.

"I haven't received anything."

"Because you don't go to the court every day and ask the right questions," said Joanna, smiling. "I have people to do that sort of thing. They spend their whole day chatting with secretaries, clerks, and judges."

"You must have a judge," concluded the prosecutor, taking a piece of pork. It looked tasty, but he could no longer be absolutely sure. His mouth was still numb after the guacamole.

"Yes," confirmed Chyłka. "McVay is a good friend of one of the judges. Of course, if he ends up on the adjudicating panel, we'll ask for him to be excluded."

"He'd have to withdraw anyway. *Iudex suspectus.*"

"I know."

Joanna graced Rejchert with yet another smile.

No judge on that level would be allowed to adjudicate if there was even the slightest hint of potential bias. However, no judge ever went completely off the radar. They still performed their duties, still met other judges, sometimes for a beer, sometimes at a match, sometimes deliberating over some controversial new law. Sometimes their conversations concerned matters closer to home, such as ongoing trials. Therefore, even a judge who was excluded from the panel was bad news for Rejchert. If that judge had good relations with the Supreme Court's remaining twenty-seven judges, it could be a problem.

"Is that why they rubber-stamped it?"

"I don't know. Ask the Court of Appeal, because they were the ones who accepted the cassation appeal and passed it on."

"That's nonsense . . . everything in the proceedings was watertight. Flawless."

"Apparently it wasn't," replied Joanna, shrugging her shoulders.

Karol put aside the cutlery, swallowed the last morsel he had been chewing, and turned to her with a penetrating stare. Chyłka had long ago realised that only prosecutors could stare like that. Maybe there was some special postgraduate college where they were taught to do it.

"Give it a rest, Rey," she said, ordering another *Rapido*. "I have alcoholic fortifications that defend me against your gaze. Besides, it never made much impression on me, even when I was sober."

In fact, he did make her feel like a criminal. This was the quintessential purpose of the prosecutor's stare: to make innocent people feel guilty. It was enough to make an eighty-year-old ex-kindergarten teacher feel like a closet paedophile.

"What do you want?" asked Rejchert.

"Confirmation that there was an infringement."

"What kind of infringement?"

"You'll find out in good time. And I assure you it's nothing far-fetched. Otherwise, we wouldn't have a chance to humiliate you in the courtroom."

"If I'm not mistaken, I was the one bruising your arses in that court-room," replied the prosecutor, looking disapprovingly at the glass of tequila the waiter had just placed in front of Chyłka. "Are you driving?"

"Mhm," she murmured, taking a sip. She felt instantly better. "The thing is, Rey, what's happened so far doesn't count. Now, only the cassation is important, as you very well know."

The prosecutor thought for a moment. Three quarters of his meal was still in front of him, and he knew that at best he would only be able to finish the soup. It was terribly spicy, but of the two evils, it was better to eat that and put the rest in a doggy bag to take home. Maybe the wife would be tempted. "I didn't notice any infringements," he said after a while. "But if I were to confirm that the court had made a mistake, what would I get out of it?"

"The fact that Langer will stay in prison. The case will return to a lower court, and we'll do a deal. Twelve years instead of life. That's the bottom line."

Rejchert chuckled under his breath, and returned to abusing what food was left on the plates and platters. Chyłka had to wait until he reached the limits of his endurance again.

"My offer expires the moment you finish the soup," she announced. The prosecutor sat for a moment, holding the spoon halfway between the bowl and his mouth. He looked up at Joanna and started eating faster. Beads of sweat appeared on his forehead, and Chyłka felt hot just looking at him.

"You wanted to surprise me, and you succeeded," started the prosecutor. "But it doesn't change anything. You must have taken me for a complete loser if you thought you could get anything out of it. For my part, everything was *lege artis,* so you're the losers."

He wiped his lips, got up and walked over to the bar. Soon, the staff were packing the unfinished dishes into cartons, while Joanna was quietly thinking up curses. She knew that the chances of making any deal with that dickhead were slim, but her offer to settle for twelve years was her bottom line. They were supposed to meet somewhere midway, reaching an agreement that satisfied both parties. Admittedly, the court could overrule the settlement, but such cases were extremely rare.

"Thank you for a pleasant afternoon," said Rejchert, taking his food. "And see you in the courtroom, Joanna, my dear," he added as a parting shot.

Chyłka ordered another drink—something different this time. It didn't take her long to realise that not even Mexican cocktails could cheer her up. She had no idea how to win the case, and she'd never been in this situation before. Sometimes her ideas weren't all that great, but so far she had always had something.

She sighed, and sent a text to Oryński. Come to El Popo. We're getting plastered.

CHAPTER

8

PRIVATE ZORDON OF Żelazny & McVay reported for duty, raring to go. It had taken him half an hour to get from Parade Square to the National Theatre, and by then he expected to see Chyłka completely legless. But when Kordian crossed the threshold of the Mexican restaurant, he saw she was still in fine form.

"You're slower than a cross between a tortoise and a snail, Zordon," she declared as he sank into the chair opposite her. "And you're sitting in Rejchert's place."

Kordian shrugged his shoulders, not understanding what the seating arrangement problem was.

"How did it go?" he asked.

"Like shit through your nose."

"An excellent comparison, bearing in mind I'm about to eat."

"You're either overly imaginative or oversensitive," Chyłka replied, taking a sip of her drink. As someone intent on getting hammered at the speed of light, she didn't seem in any particular hurry. "I recommend Tequila Rapido. It's *rapido* as fuck."

Kordian ordered a drink and they got down to conversation. Joanna gave him a blow-by-blow account of the meeting with Rejchert, calling him the "Kim Jong-un of the Polish justice system." The outcome of the confrontation didn't especially surprise Oryński—the prosecutor was in a considerably better position, and there wasn't much Chyłka could do about it, however skilfully she manipulated him.

"So what now?" asked the trainee.

"We drink and see," replied Joanna. "Personally, I don't think we have much choice, apart from making fools of ourselves in the courtroom."

After a careful study of the menu, Kordian predictably chose salmon, although he expected it to come swimming in a sea of jalapeño peppers, and have as much to do with the fish he knew so well as an ayatollah with an Orthodox priest.

The waiter brought over his dish. It didn't look too bad, and smelled delicious. After a while, Oryński realised that the man was still standing over him, as if waiting for a tip. He looked up.

Suddenly he froze. The man standing over him was none other than Gorzym.

The Bald Man contorted his face into a smile—the situation gave him immense satisfaction—while the victim sat on his seat and the salmon on his plate got cold.

"Long time no see," he said, pulling up a chair.

Oryński looked to his mentor for help, carefully ignoring his survival instinct, which screamed at him to get up and run.

"What's all this about?" asked Joanna. You could see in her eyes that she'd realised who he was.

Kordian swallowed with difficulty. He kept repeating to himself that he was safe, that he was in a public place and if anything happened, someone would call the police immediately. It was the Bald Man taking the risk.

Chyłka glared at Gorzym. The trainee comforted himself with the thought that he was the one who should be scared.

"I don't think I need to introduce myself," said the Bald Man.

"You'll do time, you bastard," said Joanna in greeting, narrowing her eyes.

She looked like a sprinter in the starting blocks, awaiting the signal.

Gorzym raised his eyebrows and leered at her as if she were potential prey. "I like you," he said. "Roske told me that you were special. Special tits, special ass. In other circumstances, I'd take it—"

"Shut your filthy mouth," said Oryński.

He instantly felt a whole lot better, as if the weight of the world had been taken off his shoulders. His words were a feeble demonstration of heroism, but what more could he do? Chyłka smiled wanly, the Bald Man just looked indifferent.

It did not bode well.

But before they could exchange any further courtesies, Kordian spotted another meathead out of the corner of his eye, standing very close to their table. Clearly, the Collective were determined to bring the two lawyers round to their way of thinking.

Joanna reached for her phone, and Oryński felt a wave of heat come over him, as if he had drunk all the Tequila Rapido in one go. He looked up at the newcomer, and realised he may have misread the situation. The second meathead was looking down at Gorzym as if he was something on the bottom of his shoe.

"Any funny business and I'll fuck up your septum," said the newcomer.

In his mind, Kordian thanked God first, then McVay. He remembered that the latter had promised him protection.

"A bodyguard?" asked the Bald Man with a smile. "Quite understandable. Every pussy who can't protect himself should have one."

The newcomer approached Gorzym and looked at Oryński questioningly.

"Just say the word," he said.

Gorzym laughed. "If not for the Glock under my jacket, I might even be scared," he said, shaking his head indulgently. "But perhaps we should get to the point before that fish gets completely cold?"

"Go on then," said Chyłka. "What do you want from us?"

"First, I want to repeat the offer I made to you, Oryński."

The answer was silence, and the Bald Man did not wait for the trainee to change his mind.

"In that case, the offer's expired. The second matter is just as simple. Your careers are at a crossroads, and you're in danger of making an unwise choice."

"You're begging us to drop the case?" asked Chyłka.

"I expect you'll be doing the begging at some point."

A waiter appeared at the table and the Bald Man fell silent. Only now did Kordian realise they were attracting the attention of other clients and the restaurant staff. A waitress taking an order from a nearby table was so engrossed in the conversation between the two heavies and the young couple that she had to ask the guests to repeat their order.

"Would you like anything else?" asked the waiter hesitantly.

"A large beer for me," said Gorzym.

"Is that all?"

Chyłka raised her hand. "Could you spit into that beer please?" she asked.

The waiter looked confused and didn't move for a moment. Then he smiled, just a little, to ease the tension.

"Go away," said the Bald Man.

They were alone again, but the heavy silence persisted. Gorzym transferred his gaze from Chyłka to Oryński, waiting for them to broach the subject. But neither spoke.

"You think you can guess what I want to say?" he asked. "You imagine you know what I am going to tell you?"

Joanna gulped her drink and Oryński shrugged his shoulders.

"And you think that this guy here will protect you?"

The bodyguard folded his arms, and his biceps bulged.

"Pumped up with supplements, but he's also worked hard, I'll grant him that," continued the Bald Man. "There are plenty like him, but he does look better than most. They usually just work on their beer guts. But mention my employer's name and he'll run away in a panic."

"Will you get to the point?" asked Chyłka.

"Gladly," said the Bald Man. "Let's put all our cards on the table."

"Well, do it quickly, because by the time your beer arrives, we'll be gone," said Chyłka. She had no intention of staying a second longer than was absolutely necessary. Whatever Gorzym wanted to tell them, it would inevitably boil down to making a deal. Organisations like the Collective preferred to stay in the shadows and not attract unnecessary attention.

"As you know, all your witnesses have disappeared . . . hold on, you're not recording this by any chance?"

"No," replied Joanna.

"You?" said Gorzym, looking at the bodyguard. "No? Just as well, because it'd only get me seriously pissed off. And out of all you lot, only Oryński knows what that means. To make sure I stay calm, everyone should put their phones on the table."

There was a moment of consternation, but no one moved.

"OK, I'll let it go," said Gorzym. "Anyway, you can't use those things as evidence in court, can you?" He looked at Chyłka. "Under which article is that?"

Joanna thought of the twenty-third article of the Civil Code, but she wasn't about to share her knowledge with the Bald Man. Even conversations such as these had protected status, and if it could be proved that confidentiality was breached, any evidence would be rejected by the court. What the rules actually were was another question. Hundreds of pages had been written on the subject, each work offering a different opinion.

"You're not very talkative. You're forcing me to do a fucking monologue."

Now no one spoke because the waiter had returned with a mug of ice-cold beer, which he placed in front of Gorzym. This time, he retired swiftly. Gorzym downed the beer without stopping to wonder whether something had been added to it.

"Witnesses," said Oryński.

"Ah, yes. Powirska has been given a cosy apartment far away from here and, unfortunately, she's not planning to return any time soon. She's happy where she is now, and enjoying the climate. Her neighbours think she's been kidnapped, but that's not my problem. I'm not going from house to house explaining everything to them like some fucking hawker."

"Get to the point," urged Chyłka again. She was preparing to leave.

The Bald Man licked his lips.

"Our lawyer doesn't know what you've based your case on. But he's convinced you have no chance of getting Langer out of prison. Ah, yes! I know what I wanted to say."

Chyłka and Oryński looked at him expectantly.

"He's doing OK in prison, isn't he?" asked Gorzym, turning the beer mug on the table. He's in a one-man cell, probably spends all day choking the chicken, no one there to disturb him. With his orange overall, he doesn't have to worry about his arse in the exercise yard. After all, he's a high security prisoner, right?"

"What are you driving at?" said Chyłka.

"What I'm trying to say is that it can all change, and very quickly."

The lawyers didn't respond, as if they didn't care—but Gorzym knew that wasn't the case.

"If news was spread in that boarding house that Langer wasn't high security but just an ordinary lag, the boys will soon make him their bitch. They'll ride him from morning till night."

"You know from experience?" said Joanna.

The Bald Man looked at her appreciatively.

"The situation might change very quickly for him if you carry on playing games," he said. "Am I making myself clear?"

"No," replied Chyłka.

"In that case, I'll say it in words that even you can understand: Langer will be thrown into a cell with plenty of others, and we'll make sure our people have a chat with your client's new roommates. He'll take it in the mouth so often that he'll get a reputation as a master of his craft. And as for his arse. . . ."

"Enough," cut in Chyłka. "I haven't come here to listen to your reminiscences from prison."

Gorzym smiled again. "You think we've got no influence inside? Just one message will do the trick."

She didn't doubt it. The prison was its own world, and the Collective was bound to have plenty of contacts there.

"Your bosses must be quaking in their boots," she said after a while. "Does Langer know something he shouldn't? Is that why they're so scared of us?"

"As far as I know, my paymaster fears only his wife and God."

"He's trying very hard to silence us," answered Chyłka.

"You should treat this as a gesture of goodwill."

"Why are we such a threat to him?"

Gorzym looked at her indulgently.

"Why does he want us to let go of the case?" she asked.

"That's not for me to say."

"In that case, we'll have to speak to him directly. Face to face."

9

BLINDFOLDED AND JOLTING along in the car on an uneven road, Chyłka had no doubt in her mind that this was the worst mistake she'd ever made. One reckless decision had sent them on a journey from which they might not return. And all because for a moment, the amount of tequila she'd drunk had made her feel heroic. The only good idea she'd had that day was to go to the ladies' room before leaving El Popo. After so many drinks, the local roads would have been torture for her bladder. All the rest was one big mistake. To be fair, she wasn't expecting Gorzym to agree to take them to meet his boss.

Kordian sat in the car next to her, wondering more or less the same things. After Gorzym had agreed to arrange a meeting, it took some effort to convince the bodyguard that his presence was not only unnecessary, but unwanted.

The pair were blindfolded before they got into Gorzym's car; later they transferred to another car, probably an off-road vehicle judging by the suspension. It was then that their hands were tied behind their backs, with assurances that it was essential. Otherwise, the boss they referred to as the "Grey-Haired Man" would call off the meeting.

"How much longer?" grumbled Chyłka. "Zordon's about to puke."

"No I'm not," objected Kordian. "You're projecting again. And I'm not surprised, because after all that Mexican food washed down with so much alcohol, you've every right to feel ill."

"Not bad, Zordon, not bad. Before long you'll be able to record hip-hop songs full of hatred and cutting remarks. What do you call it?"

"Dissing."

"Oh, how cool. You'll be dissing about other rappers."

"On."

"What?"

"You diss on someone."

"Quiet!" said a voice from the front. It wasn't Gorzym, so there was obviously another thug in the car.

"Smash the wanker's skull in," added yet another voice. Kordian didn't want to know how many of them there were.

"Calm down," said Gorzym. "The Grey-Haired Man doesn't want anything to happen to them *on the way.*"

It wasn't all that comforting, especially the way he stressed the words "on the way."

They ground to a halt after almost an hour. Chyłka and Oryński were helped out of the car, and their blindfolds taken off. Before their eyes could get used to the light, they were led down a track, winding between trees for a kilometre or two until it reached a gravel path. Then they turned a corner and found themselves outside a fenced estate that could have been the summer residence of some head of state.

A security guard emerged from a booth next to the entrance gate. He nodded to Gorzym, and the gate opened automatically.

"Move it!" ordered one of the thugs and pulled the two lawyers over to the other side.

They saw an impressive two-storey building with a dark façade, surrounded by a garden, with a stable block on the left. It would have been idyllic, were it not for the fact that it all belonged to the man responsible for their difficulties with the Langer case.

"Untie them," said Gorzym to one of his henchmen.

The two lawyers massaged their wrists and looked around.

"The Grey-Haired Man will see you in the Japanese garden behind the house. For some reason, we traditionally call it the back room," announced Gorzym as if he were a tour guide.

They walked down a path that led them around the building. Oryński felt his heart beat faster and faster, as if he were about to meet the devil himself. The Grey-Haired Man stood with his back to the newcomers. He raised his hand, and Gorzym told them to stop where they were. Between them and him was a tiny knoll covered with neatly trimmed grass and magnolias.

Just beyond it was a small pond, and further on, a bench, in front of which their host stood.

"Before you say anything, you should know that I won't put up with any flapdoodle," he said. "Or you'll end up as fertiliser for my tulip tree." With a leisurely movement, he pointed to a tree growing nearby. "I know that this might seem strange to you, but experience has shown that angiosperms grow best on human remains."

He sat down on the bench, his back still turned to the guests.

There was a temporary silence. To say Kordian felt uneasy would have been an understatement. It wasn't even what that man was saying, but his whole demeanour.

Yet that wasn't the main problem preying on his mind.

"What's flapdoodle?"

"Don't you know?" asked Chyłka. "It's blithering."

"Talking crap," added Gorzym.

The Grey-Haired Man sighed and bowed his head.

"Flapdoodle is an onomatopoeia," he began. "It reflects the foolhardy, mindless use of words. At least that's how I see it."

"Wow," said Chyłka. "A gangster who pretends to be a professor. I knew we wouldn't regret this meeting."

Oryński opened his mouth to object, but she stopped him with a stern look.

"I knew you'd have no manners," responded the Grey-Haired Man.

"And who are you to talk about manners?" asked Chyłka with a smile. The Grey-Haired Man remained calm, but she was planning to change that very soon. "You think you're some kind of intellectual? So erudite you even know what onomatopoeia means? If you're surrounded by idiots like Gorzym, it's hardly surprising. In company like that, even Zordon would look like a sage."

Oryński opened his mouth again, but again Joanna would not let him speak.

"Who do you think you are? I bet a hundred bucks that you were brought up and spent half your life on a welfare housing estate, or in some shithole village, envying those who could read and write. Then you bought yourself a high-school certificate, and bachelor's and master's degrees. Perhaps even more?"

Kordian felt the temperature rising. Launching into an angry tirade didn't seem like an overly sensible thing to do, but since Chyłka had gone this far there was no point stopping her.

"I suppose that instead of playing outside with your friends, collecting bottle tops, enjoying a carefree life, you were worried that other people were so clever and that you were such a miserable cretin. And then you decided to make up for your inadequacies the only way you could. You built your own little gang and now you pretend to be a sophisticated mafioso figure, like some fucking Sicilian *capo di tutti capi*. Embarrassing. Really embarrassing."

"Gorzym," said the Grey-Haired Man.

From the corner of his eye, Kordian noticed the Bald Man raise his hand. Before he could react, the hand was clutching Chyłka's neck like a vice. Oryński turned to face him, ready to defend her, but was stopped in his tracks by another bodyguard.

Chyłka took a swipe, but Gorzym dodged. He laughed, and pushed her forward as if she were a sack of feathers.

She landed with full force on the knoll, but the dense grass absorbed the impact. She turned over onto her back and quickly got up. She felt grass clinging to her face, but didn't let it bother her.

"Not bad, Mr Manners," she said spitting out blades of grass.

The Bald Man was standing by, ready to take her down again.

"You have only yourself to blame," said the Grey-Haired Man, making himself more comfortable on his bench. He crossed one leg over the other and sat as proud as a pasha. "I hope you understand that my time is very limited. And precious. Far more precious than yours, Joanna. How much do you charge an hour? A hundred euros?"

She didn't answer.

"Two hundred then. Smaller firms charge a hundred."

She did indeed charge two hundred an hour, but the fact that he knew it didn't impress Chyłka. He could easily have checked on Google.

"That's barely a fraction of what I earn in that time."

"Bully for you," she replied. "Pity it involves corpses, rape, and missing children, but each to their own. Personally, I'd rather work than prostitute my integrity."

"Gorzym."

This time the Bald Man pushed Chyłka much harder.

She hit the hillock with such force that her ears rang. The Bald Man didn't give her a chance to get up. Again he grabbed her by the neck, and this time dragged her to the pond. She tried hard to break free and heard Oryński shouting threats to the bodyguard holding him back.

She realised that this time it would not end with words.

"Let go, you bastard!" she shouted.

The Bald Man grabbed her by the hair, and plunged her head in the pond.

She had just enough time before her head went under, to think that the water stank like the dirtiest part of the Zegrze Reservoir; then she could only think about trying to survive.

Just as she was starting to suffocate, Gorzym pulled her head above the surface. In panic, she desperately gasped for air and heard Kordian yelling at the top of his voice.

But she couldn't make out what he was saying, because Gorzym suddenly submerged her head again. This time she didn't have enough air in her lungs. She struggled and wriggled and thrashed out at him, and in doing so swallowed copious amounts of water. But eventually he pulled her up and threw her to the side.

She rolled around a couple of times, completely disoriented.

"Chyłka!" shouted Kordian, trying to break free from the bodyguard's grip.

She coughed violently, spitting water, then looked up. She scowled at Gorzym. Her hair was stuck to her face.

"Bastards . . ." said Oryński. "As soon as I'm free . . ."

He didn't finish because the man holding him hit him on the back of the head. Then Gorzym appeared before him, adding his own tuppence worth by punching him straight in the stomach. He doubled over, winded. For a moment he felt paralysed, terrified, dispirited. But he quickly shook it off.

"Go on, is that all you've got, motherfucker?" he said, straightening up. His voice was trembling, but he didn't care. He was prepared to take the brunt of their fury if it meant they left Chyłka alone.

Gorzym smiled and rubbed his hands with glee; but he would have to wait before he had his fun.

"Enough," said the Grey-Haired Man. "You've proved that you're not some delicate little flowers."

"Fuck you," hissed Joanna, and started coughing again.

"That's rather coarse, even for you," said the host, clearly disappointed. "But let's get to the point. You've said you were willing to cooperate if you had a chance to speak to me directly. Well, here I am, I'm listening."

"Fuck you," repeated Chyłka.

The Grey-Haired Man sighed. "How am I to take that? First you suggest you are serious businesspeople, ready to make a compromise, and now you appear to bear me ill-will."

"Ill-will?" repeated Joanna slowly as she got up.

Her body was covered with droplets of cold water. She felt humiliated and helpless, but what had she expected? They had entered the lion's den and even helped him sharpen his teeth.

Chyłka cursed her decision to come here with Gorzym. It had seemed a good idea at El Popo; she thought at last they'd get to see who was pulling the strings. But now she swore she would never touch Tequila Rapido again.

She brushed aside her wet fringe and looked at Oryński. But his gaze was actually fixed not on her, but on the Grey-Haired Man, who still had his back to them.

"Gorzym did not make us an offer," began Kordian. After all that shouting, his voice had become hoarse and croaky.

"That's not true, boy."

"Really?"

"He made you a very specific offer."

"To work for you? That doesn't count. And I don't suppose that offer was ever genuine."

"For a time it was," answered their host. "If you had carried out all the instructions and not betrayed my trust, you'd be in a far better position now. And you'd be earning far more than two hundred euros an hour."

"Tough," said Oryński calmly, and shrugged his shoulders. He'd decided it was time to put aside their pride and indignation, and try to get as much information as they could out of the man before they were thrown out on their ear. Kordian had no doubt that that was how their meeting would end. If he'd wanted to use them as a tree fertiliser, the Grey-Haired Man wouldn't have bothered to hide his face from them.

"Has Gorzym told you what the prison situation could be like?"

"Oh, he was very persuasive," replied Chyłka. "But the message you left on my BMW was even more fucking emphatic."

"Gorzym . . ."

"No, wait," interrupted Kordian, looking fearfully at the Bald Man, who was already heading towards Joanna.

The man on the bench raised his hand, stopping his subordinate in his tracks.

"Let's give the caveman behaviour a rest," said Kordian.

"No problem, if Joanna can control herself."

The Grey-Haired Man paused, signifying that he was waiting for her response. Chyłka muttered something under her breath to express agreement.

"I ought to apologise for the car," said their host. "I wanted my people to leave a mark, but not to make the car unusable. *Mea culpa* that I did not see to it personally."

"Is Langer so important that it would even cross your mind to see to it personally?" asked Oryński.

"We're not going to discuss how important Piotr is to me. Let's get back to our negotiations."

"What negotiations?"

"Gorzym has explained what your client can expect in prison if you don't comply. What more can I add?"

"We came here to—" began the trainee.

"Enough," interrupted the Grey-Haired Man. "You came here so that I could explain to you why you should not oppose me. If for one moment you thought I would give way, you're even more naive than I assumed."

Kordian wanted to parry the blow, but didn't know how without further enraging the host.

"Therefore, let me be absolutely clear. If you do not agree to drop the case, I'll make sure that everything Gorzym described will happen to Piotr."

"Good luck with that," replied Joanna.

"Do you think he'll be able to defend himself?"

"It's none of your fucking business what I think."

For a moment the Grey-Haired Man was silent, and Oryński fixed his gaze pleadingly at his partner.

"I admit he's resourceful," he replied after a while. "But not to that extent. For the last time, I'm asking you to—"

"No," cut in Joanna.

"Are you sure?" asked the Grey-Haired Man, and sighed. "I'm not hosting *Who Wants to Be a Millionaire?*, and I'm not going to ask ten times."

The lawyers remained silent.

"Then you've put your client in a very difficult situation," he concluded, pulling out a phone. He issued some instructions, which would probably turn Langer's life into one long nightmare.

"You bastards," growled Joanna.

"Perhaps," said the Grey-Haired Man, putting down his phone. "But ultimately you're the ones who sealed Piotr's fate. I gave you a choice. I even made sure that this was what you wanted—normally, I don't bother."

Neither of the lawyers responded.

Kordian wondered whether there was any chance of tracking down the Grey-Haired Man if they ever got out of this mess. He very much doubted it. The back of his head and his grey hair were useless in terms of identification. And locationwise, they could be anywhere within a twenty-kilometre radius of Warsaw.

"But since even that hasn't convinced you to drop the case, I'm forced to use another means of persuasion. I'm thinking about Magda Chyłka—although I suppose that's not what she likes to be called. Apparently, just like her sister, Magdalena doesn't like it when her name gets twisted."

The host paused, his satisfaction palpable. Joanna was controlling her emotions, and keeping her mouth firmly closed.

"I understand that Magdalena lives with her family in Piaseczno on one of the new housing estates. It's a fairly good location, bearing in mind she has a small child. The nursery is some three hundred metres from their front door. Also, the area is up and coming, which means they could live there in peace and prosperity for many years to come."

Chyłka still remained silent. Oryński was poised to intervene, but instead he sighed with relief. His boss had clearly seen sense.

"I don't know if little Daria likes it there, though," continued the Grey-Haired Man. "At what age do children start speaking? Two, two and a half? In that case, soon one of my people will be able to—"

"You touch them, you fucking bastards, and I'll rip your fucking guts out."

"Gorzym," said the Grey-Haired Man calmly.

Kordian could not react in time.

10

CHYŁKA WAS QUITE helpless as the Bald Man held her in his iron grip. She tried to headbutt him, kick him, or at least spit at him, but he knew what he was doing. When he clutched her close to his body, she smelled the sharp tang of cologne and chewing gum.

He lifted her effortlessly, slightly off the ground. When he started panting in her ear and pressed his erect penis against her, she felt sick. It took her just an instant to see what these people were capable of.

They had no intention of killing them, or even beating them as Kordian had been beaten. But it didn't mean they wouldn't do a whole host of other things to them—especially to her.

She heard Kordian shouting threats at the Bald Man. For an instant their eyes met, then Gorzym suddenly threw her back on the ground.

He whispered something in her ear and twisted her arm hard behind her back. The pain was excruciating, but for her this was the lesser of two evils. She felt that he might dislocate her shoulder—and at that moment the Grey-haired Man finally raised his hand.

The attacker let go and she fell to the ground.

"That was completely unnecessary," said the man on the bench. "You don't have to prove your courage and fortitude. We all know your temperament."

"I repeat, you touch my family, and—"

"Exactly," cut in the Grey-Haired Man. "Returning to Magdalena, you can still save her and her daughter. With Piotr, that chance was lost when I made the telephone call. If I have to make another call, the chance for your family, Joanna, will also be lost."

She was trying to gather her strength, and didn't reply. What could she say? Further threats were pointless, this man was not joking.

"It's quite straightforward," said the host. "With Kordian, I had quite a dilemma. It was hard to find a person in your life for whom you'd sacrifice everything. Normally I'd look at the family, but after what you've done. . . ."

The trainee jerked his body frantically, but couldn't break free from the bodyguard's grip.

"Then I thought, maybe a girlfriend? But unfortunately, you haven't had many, and you parted with the few you've had on rather unfriendly terms. Ultimately, I can target that skinny guy in your office, what do you say to that?"

Chyłka pushed herself up on her hands, and was breathing as if she had just run a marathon. Kordian looked at her anxiously.

"So what will it be?" asked the Grey-Haired Man. "Shall we leave Magdalena and the others in peace? Or shall I make that phone call?" He flipped the phone in his hand and waited for one of them to reply. But the response was silence. This was starting to irritate him.

"Boss?" said Gorzym. "Should I speak to them . . ."

"No. These two are clearly a pair of cold-hearted scoundrels who have no regard for their clients, or even their families and closest friends. It's interesting, very interesting. But what is it all for? What is so important that it overshadows other people's well-being?"

"They want to win their big case," prompted the Bald Man.

"Ah, if only it was worth the struggle," sighed the Grey-Haired Man theatrically. "You don't even know who you're defending."

His momentary silence suggested that he was wondering whether to tell them. Or perhaps he was just play-acting.

"You ought to know that Piotr was a serial abuser of women, hooking himself a new one every day. He'd drink himself almost senseless, then get behind the wheel of his car. I hate to think how many tragedies he's caused, and he never suffered any consequences. For him, every excess was an experience, and he wanted to repeat it over and over again, but twice as forcefully. I assume you know all this, because your client-checking system works well, like a well-oiled machine. I keep forgetting what that hapless skinny man is called, the one who gathers all the information."

"Kormak," prompted the Bald Man.

"Yes, Kormak. A strange name, but I've heard stranger. Besides, that's the least of his problems now."

Chyłka and Oryński looked at the phone in the Grey-Haired Man's hand. It was probably just a matter of seconds before he turned his words into deeds.

Kordian had had no idea that Joanna had a sister, let alone a niece. But he wasn't surprised that she'd never mentioned them.

"All right," said their host, putting the phone to his ear.

"Touch them and everything changes," hissed Chyłka.

But it was too late. The leader of the Collective had directed the whole scene from the outset, and now he was going to end it with a bang.

"Do it," said the Grey-Haired Man, and put the phone down.

Chyłka was the first to throw herself at him. Before Oryński realised what was happening, they were both on the ground. Gorzym and the other bodyguards dragged them to the pond, and started repeatedly submerging their heads in water.

The Grey-Haired Man got up off the bench.

"Have fun with them," he said. "But for no more than ten minutes. And whatever you do, don't kill them."

A quarter of an hour later, they were blindfolded, their hands were tied behind their backs and then they were thrown into the back of an off-road vehicle. But before the doors were shut, they heard the voice of the host one last time.

"Now I can officially tell you my offer has expired."

11

F OR A WHILE, the Grey-Haired Man had considered killing them. It wouldn't have been particularly dangerous for him, as the trail would only lead to one of his people. The cassation appeal, however, complicated matters. The media would cotton on that the case was about something much more than the murder of two people in Mokotów. So they had to find a less drastic solution.

Magdalena Chyłka's telephone was tapped. That was how he knew that right after the encounter with his people, she had phoned her sister. For half an hour she had complained that some thugs had attacked her husband on his way home from Lidl.

It wasn't the most discreet way of telling people that they should know their place, and Chyłka and her trainee received the message loud and clear. The jokes were over.

The next day, the Grey-Haired Man was sitting in his Japanese garden, thinking about how he would soon taste the final victory. Seated next to him was Maciej Roske, a bottle of Clos Apalta, a dry wine made from the Carménère grape, open between them. As he drank, the subtle plum flavours began to irritate him. The producer had assured him that the wine's fine tannins would suppress them.

Meanwhile, Roske was drinking very reluctantly. He couldn't believe this bottle of battery acid had cost over four hundred zlotys.

"Is that it then?" asked the doctor, placing his glass on a small wicker table.

"What do you mean?"

"You threatened them . . . and that's it?"

"It depends on what they do. If they've finally realised that the cake's not worth the candle, I don't think I need to bother with them anymore."

"They won't drop the case."

"I never expected them to," replied the Grey-Haired Man. "It would arouse suspicion in all the wrong places and would probably alert the law enforcement agencies."

"So you're hoping they'll deliberately lose the case in court?"

"They'll most probably lose it anyway."

"So why go to all this trouble?"

"I want to be certain that this will all end well."

"And do you think they'll let it?"

"Yes. They'll lay down their arms the moment they realise the threat to their loved ones is real. If they haven't already."

The host broke off in midsentence because he noticed a bodyguard running towards the Japanese garden. It wasn't normal for anyone to disturb his peace in this way. He rose from his wicker chair. Roske did the same.

"Boss!" yelled the bodyguard. "Pigs!"

The Grey-Haired Man looked at him in disbelief. There was no way the police, or any other investigative agency could have even picked up his trail, let alone tracked him all the way here.

"It's a raid, boss!" said the bodyguard.

The host immediately thought about the previous day's guests, but ruled out any connection. They had been blindfolded, they had changed cars and the off-road vehicle had weaved its labyrinthine way down local lanes and byways to make sure the lawyers would not be able to memorise the route. This was standard procedure, and so far, it had never failed.

"How did this happen?" asked Roske, his voice shaking. The bodyguard was unable to answer.

"Four police cars," he said, barely able to catch his breath. "They're at the entrance gate."

The Grey-Haired Man headed in the direction indicated. He noticed several policemen, all clearly looking vexed. Gradually, he began to calm down. This was a coincidence, nothing more; no one could have found any clues leading to his home. He had always taken all the necessary precautions, used intermediaries and paid the right people. If one of his henchmen was arrested, the Grey-Haired Man looked after his family and made sure that the hapless henchman was looked after in prison by a warder, also paid off by him. There was no one who would have spilled the beans.

Yet now there were several police cars outside his entrance gate. He thought maybe one of his men had committed some offence and they had followed him; if so, no problem: he would offer a sacrifice to the god of blue lights, and there would be peace again.

But the blood drained from his face when behind the last police car, he saw a black BMW X5 with scratched paintwork.

12

CHYŁKA AND ORYŃSKI looked at the Grey-Haired Man with some satisfaction. As he approached the entrance gate, he looked as if he was about to collapse from shock. Truth be told, he deserved a far worse death.

They had thrown them out of the off-road vehicle near the Vistula, somewhere between Bielany and Żoliborz. Even before they shook the dirt off their clothes, both had promised themselves and each other that they would not let the matter rest.

Once they had managed to wriggle their hands free from the bindings, Chyłka reached for her telephone. She handed it to Kordian, as if she wanted to show him something. He looked at the display: Eiffel Tower wallpaper. It took him a while to spot the Endomondo icon.

Almost every fitness enthusiast knew about the Endomondo app. It counted your calories, measured your heart rate, organised your workouts and monitored your progress. It also tracked your walking, running or cycling routes via GPS.

He had no idea when she had switched the app on, or how much she had managed to track. Before he could check, Joanna snatched the phone from him. Oryński noticed a characteristic expression on her face: she was exhausted, but there was a flash of triumph in her eyes.

When she handed the phone to him again, he noted that she had set the program for cycling, although the speed sometimes reached 120 kilometres an hour, which would have made training redundant. The route was very precisely marked, from El Popo to a point somewhere in the River Narew basin to the north of Warsaw, with a different route leading back to the capital. It meant that Joanna must have switched the app on just before they left the restaurant, probably when she went to the ladies. The route ended at a point on a path that ran under General Stefan Grot Rowecki Bridge.

Chyłka brushed the earth off her clothes and phoned McVay. The bodyguard they had left at the restaurant arrived no more than a dozen or so minutes later.

Now, as they were sitting in the X5 outside the home of the Grey-Haired Man, Oryński felt on top of the world.

"Chyłka."

"Yes?"

"I'm not happy."

"What?" muttered Joanna.

"I can't say I'm relishing this."

"What the hell are you talking about, Zordon?"

He looked at her and frowned. "It'd be a gross understatement. I feel like the scourge of God, like the angel of death," he said. "Like the sword of Damocles that has just slashed the throat of the Grey-Haired Man, Like . . ."

Chyłka glared at him, so he fell silent.

They watched the police officers, who looked like crazed predators baying for blood.

Kordian and Joanna had had no difficulty arranging for the police to come here. Joanna had devised a plan that guaranteed they would. First, she had asked McVay to phone any prosecutors he knew who might be interested in their case. None of them were particularly inclined to talk about grey-haired gangsters operating to the north of Warsaw, until one of the Englishman's old acquaintances confirmed that "a son-of-a-bitch of that description could be of great interest to the district prosecutor's office in Ostrołęka." She knew very little about it, other than that he was wanted for a number of offences but there was not enough concrete evidence to convict him. He was also suspected of being involved in an organised crime gang, which did not surprise the two lawyers in the least.

Next, Chyłka and Oryński filed a report with the police, and then it was only a matter of bringing in the prosecutor's office. Their report mentioned criminal threats, persistent harassment, intimidation, and physical coercion involving use of violence. Taking all these into account, the Grey-Haired Man could face seven years in prison—which bore no relation to what he really deserved.

For the moment, however, all that mattered was to get him handcuffed and into a police car.

Sitting in the BMW, the two lawyers exchanged glances then simultaneously opened the doors. They saw the man in question, with his bodyguards, walking confidently towards the gate. He would probably pretend to be shaken, shocked, and disgusted that the police were at his front door.

To some extent, this wasn't surprising. It was certainly unexpected: to get the police cars to come to this estate close to the confluence of the Bug and Narew rivers had required calling in a raft of past favours and involved tactical methods which could be perceived as manipulation. Not everything was done in good faith. This was part of Chyłka's plan, which, if you asked her, was "bloody good."

If the police officers didn't foul up, everyone would be happy. Everyone except the Grey-Haired Man.

"Can you see his face?" asked Oryński when he had got out of the car. He didn't close the door but rested one arm on it and the other on the car roof.

"I'd rather not look," replied Joanna. "Once you look into the eyes of the devil, you'll never be the same."

"Ah."

"I'm joking, come on," she said, closing the door. She walked over to the gate, which remained firmly shut. Clearly, the Grey-Haired Man intended to talk to the police from behind a metal barrier. He stopped just in front of it and put his hands behind his back, looking for all the world like a troubled homeowner looking for an officer in charge to whom he could complain. He looked at the gathering of people and waited.

Oryński could not see his face clearly from behind the metal grating, but he imagined a theatrical grimace of disapproval. He imagined the Grey-Haired Man had a convict's face, a habitual criminal who had done time more than once.

"Are you coming?" asked Joanna, looking at her companion leaning on the car. "Or are you going to hang there like bird shit on a cornice?"

"I'm coming," he replied, then shut the door and headed towards the gate.

One of the policemen stepped forward, and the Grey-Haired Man focused all his attention on him.

Outwardly, their arguments had seemed strong, but in reality, the lawyers had no concrete evidence. Langer had been roughed up by fellow prisoners in the exercise yard, Kormak only suspected that he was being followed, and Chyłka's brother-in-law was unable to identify any of his attackers.

The police had nothing much to go on, although they weren't aware of it yet.

"Good morning," said the officer as he approached the gate.

The badge on his chest and the markings on the epaulettes told the Grey-Haired Man that he was dealing with Staff Warrant Officer Szczerbiński.

"I don't understand this intrusion," said the Grey-Haired Man before the police officer could introduce himself. "I do not understand the purpose, the reason, or what you could possibly wish to gain from this. Is this Poland or Bangladesh? Do you have a—"

"Warrant?" asked the warrant officer, pulling out a document signed by a public prosecutor. "We are authorised to search these premises and secure any items for the purpose of collecting evidence in ongoing proceedings." The warrant officer handed the piece of paper to the Grey-Haired Man, who pored over the text. "We are authorised to carry out this search with or without your consent. A report will be made and a list of items confiscated will be given to you after the event. This will also tell you where and how to make a complaint should you wish to do so."

The officer recited this in a single breath, while the Grey-Haired Man rued his decision to drink wine with a doctor rather than a lawyer.

"Who ordered this?"

"The order was issued by the Head of Police and signed by the prosecutor."

Oryński was standing close enough to hear this exchange. He still couldn't see the expression on the Grey-Haired Man's face, but suspected he had turned pale. If he was the criminal they suspected he was, there would be plenty of items on the premises that would be like a red rag to a bull for the prosecution service.

And that was what they were counting on, and why they had dragged all these police officers here. They had no evidence, but they intended to acquire some.

The gangster sighed melodramatically, then folded the paper and looked up.

"It appears that your superior is doing this as a favour to someone," he said.

"I beg your pardon?"

"I know those people," said the Grey-Haired Man, pointing to the two lawyers from Żelazny & McVay. "I had a disagreement with them because of their *modus operandi*. They represent some truly reprehensible characters. Once they defended someone who famously told the most perfidious untruths about me. I tried to settle the dispute amicably, out of court, but that woman wouldn't relent." He pointed his finger at Joanna, and drew breath to indicate that he had more to say. "Recently I learned that these people are defending Piotr Langer. The murderer who took the lives of two young people in an exceptionally brutal fashion and defiled their bodies . . ."

"Please open the gate," interrupted the policemen.

"I also know that these two are planning to frame me, to set me up in some sort of game they're playing," continued the Grey-Haired Man.

"I didn't realise at the time what it was all about, because after all, that monster Langer has been sentenced and is in prison. However, when I heard that they were planning to manipulate the next stage of the legal proceedings, I knew that I would be the main reason they give for filing a cassation appeal."

"I'm going to ask you once more before I take action," warned Szczerbiński. "You have read the search warrant which authorises us to enter your premises. Please open the gate."

"Of course, of course," said the Grey-Haired Man, and paused. He gave the impression that it had only just dawned on him how serious the situation was. He nodded to Gorzym, who pulled a small remote control out of his pocket and pressed the middle button. The gate swayed and began to slide apart.

Kordian had imagined they would go in all guns blazing; the bodyguards would give way and the police would pour like locusts into the Grey-Haired Man's estate, pistols in hand, ready to shoot. But the reality was somewhat different: they entered quietly and calmly.

Nonetheless, it was enjoyable to watch. Szczerbiński's team set about comprehensively searching the property, while the warrant officer was stopped by the Grey-Haired Man, who stood in his way and had no intention of letting him pass until he had answered all his niggling questions.

"Are you allowed to intrude on law-abiding citizens for no reason?" he began.

"You're holding the reason in your hand," answered Szczerbiński. He held out his hand for the warrant, and the Grey-Haired Man obediently gave it back to him.

"That's not a reason," he protested. "That's the effect. I want to know the cause."

"You know very well," replied the warrant officer.

Now that the Grey-Haired Man had let them in, Szczerbiński had no intention of keeping up the pretence. Admittedly, they could have got in without the owner's permission, but that could have given them any number of problems: there were decidedly more bodyguards than policemen. The warrant officer nodded to the host and tried to move on, but the host grabbed him by the wrist.

Szczerbiński automatically reached for his holster. Inside it was an old P-64, more like a peashooter than a lethal weapon. Recently, faulty endcaps had resulted in a nationwide recall of police service Walther pistols and instead officers were issued with old P-64s, which had previously been used by the communist militia.

Still, it was good to have anything in the holster, it gave a sense of security. Szczerbiński knew full well he was dealing with organised crime. A massive mansion off the beaten track, in the middle of nowhere, bodyguards dressed in suits and an owner who modelled himself on Tony Soprano. There was probably at least one corpse buried in that garden.

"Let go of my wrist," said Szczerbiński calmly.

"Sorry," said the host, and did as he was told, raising his hands in apology. One of the other police officers saw what was happening, but when he was sure that Szczerbiński was in no immediate danger, continued searching.

"Am I under suspicion? Are you carrying out an investigation?"

"It's procedure," replied the warrant officer. "You can get all the details from the police station. They'll be happy to talk to you and listen to what you have to say. I am here only to search for and secure evidence."

"Evidence of what?"

The policeman handed the Grey-Haired Man the warrant again. Then he walked past him and headed towards the house, instructing everyone else to stay outside.

The Grey-Haired Man swore angrily under his breath, looking at the two lawyers standing just behind the gate. A stupid slip-up somewhere on the way had allowed them to locate his residence. But how had they done it? And who had slipped up? Everything was secure at his end. Besides, even if they had managed to locate him, how did they get the police on their side? None of the evidence linked the Grey-Haired Man with any crime. There were no grounds for the police to visit at all, let alone with a search warrant. The Grey-Haired Man looked at Gorzym. It must have been him. But while there were many things you could say about Gorzym, he was not reckless. He knew very well that a mistake could cost him his life.

He stopped his musings and beckoned the two lawyers to come closer. "Come in!" he called. "You know the way."

Kordian scrutinised the gangster's face. He expected to see a face marked by sin and transgression, but the Grey-Haired Man looked like a pretty average fifty-year-old, notable only for his dense, but evenly trimmed, beard.

Seeing that the lawyers had no intention of moving, the host headed towards them. On the way he glanced over his shoulder at the policemen, with an expression of pity.

He stopped a metre away from Chyłka and Oryński, and began to applaud quietly.

"Bravo, bravo, *bravissimo*," he said. "How did you pull it off?"

"You'll find out in court, slime ball," said Joanna, and took a step towards him.

"I'm only going to the public section in court to see the fiasco your pseudo legal exploits have unleashed," he replied. "I suppose one of your partners cashed in some favours, hence the police. But we all know you have nothing on me."

"Keep your pearls of wisdom to yourself," advised Chyłka.

The host smiled. "I see," he said. "So it was Gorzym, after all. Camera?"

"Yes, not far from the Palace of Culture and Science," said Oryński. "It recorded your orangutan sitting down next to me on the bench, and taking the cassation appeal documents away."

"I doubt very much that he would threaten you in public. There's nothing on those recordings."

"You're right, there's nothing to show that I was physically threatened," conceded Kordian. "But that doesn't matter. Your lawyer will argue that I handed over the cassation appeal papers voluntarily, but the hospital documents will provide evidence that I was intimidated."

"Nonsense."

"It would be nonsense if not for the fact that Chyłka and I were kidnapped," replied Oryński. "You're about to get your comeuppance."

He looked into his eyes, but saw only indifference.

"Really?" asked the Grey-Haired Man. "And what about the evidence?"

He didn't get an answer to his question because suddenly everyone's attention was drawn to a Ford transit van that had pulled up nearby. From it emerged several people who looked like fitters, technicians, or plumbers.

"Our specialist team," said Joanna with a smile. "Apparently, after examining our wet clothes, they can determine whether the water came from your pond. Collecting samples will only take a little while."

"What is the m—"

The Grey-Haired Man broke off, feeling his heart race, and the skin beginning to burn all over his body. This was bad. First Gorzym, now this. And if they managed to join all the dots, the problems it would cause him were quite significant. Admittedly, all the evidence was circumstantial, but all in all, the not inconsiderable human resources available to Żelazny & McVay would make full use of it.

"Are we off?" said Joanna.

Kordian looked at her as if he needed to give the matter serious thought, and then nodded. They waved carelessly to the Grey-Haired Man and got into the X5. It was a wonderful feeling, seeing the expression on his face. He stood in the gateway, gazing at the car, still with his hands behind his back. He looked defeated, though only for a moment. Once the initial shock passed, his fighting spirit would return with a vengeance.

"Do you think anything will come of it?" asked Oryński as Joanna was reversing on to the dirt road. "Will they find anything?"

"No," she replied without hesitation. "They will search and search, and then people will gather to say that valuable police resources are being wasted tilting at windmills."

"That much I know."

"So why are you asking?"

"I mean the less formal part of our undertaking," said Kordian, as Chyłka stopped the car on the country lane at the edge of the forest. She sounded the horn twice. From behind the trees came the figure of a man, who opened the back door and jumped into the car.

"Ah, now that's a completely different kettle of fish," replied Joanna with satisfaction.

"What's a different kettle of fish?" asked Kormak, placing the ruck-sack on the seat beside him.

13

ORYŃSKI LOOKED IN the rear-view mirror and saw their passenger pull a camera from the McCarthy rucksack. Kormak winked at him and said, "Nikon D800, decent camera. Costs almost ten thousand. I only have it because I need it for my work, and it has the initials of the sponsors: Ż & M."

"Did you get everything?" asked Chyłka.

"Everything," replied Kormak. "See this lens? It could capture a single hair in the beard of your Grey Man."

That same day, the set of pictures was sent to the media, along with an anonymous letter explaining a few relevant facts. When he spoke to the journalists, Kormak said he was forwarding the images without the knowledge of his bosses in the law firm and demanded that his name should not appear anywhere.

Some took the material willingly, whereas others . . . well, they held back until the first pictures appeared on the news. Then there was no stopping the avalanche. Everyone wanted to add their tuppence worth, TV stations were trying to outdo each other in assigning hidden meanings to the tiniest details, the studios invited experts to analyse the situation from legal and factual points of view. Admittedly, most of the commentary appeared in the early afternoon rather than at prime viewing time, but the case generally received a lot of air time anyway.

The photographs themselves were very eloquent. One showed the Grey-Haired Man helplessly raising his hands in front of a warrant officer as a large group of policemen entered his residence. Another photo depicted a row of police cars seen from the back and a police officer standing at the gate holding a warrant.

Kormak had done a great job. The media had been handed a villain in a well-cut suit, with a large villa and garden behind him, surrounded by a crowd of police officers. The conclusion was self-evident.

The next day's headlines gave Chyłka and Oryński a lot of pleasure. Most of the papers covered the event extensively, and one of the biggest advantages was that the police and prosecutor's office were unable to comment on account of the ongoing proceedings. This gave Kormak carte blanche to start the rumour that police had tracked down a dangerous gangster directing his criminal activities from a villa in Suladówek. And where was Suladówek? Some wilderness in the back of beyond. But the "leak" was grist to the media mill.

The police were not happy about it, but that didn't bother the two lawyers. After the story was published, the phones began ringing off their hooks. McVay was labelled a disgrace to the legal profession; by taking part in the charade, he had burned all his bridges, both with the prosecution service and the police. But it had been worth it.

From that moment on, the Grey-Haired Man was under close scrutiny. The police had not found anything on his premises, but now the journalists were on the case; they started to exert pressure on the police, and, more importantly, kept their finger continuously on the pulse.

Chyłka had achieved her goal. She had no evidence, but as the Latin legal maxim said, *manifestum non eget probatione*. What is manifest does not require proof.

She also managed to achieve something that had a direct influence on Langer's situation.

The judges who were to adjudicate his case were independent and sovereign in their decisions; but they were also people. It would have been difficult for them to ignore the media storm that had broken overnight and whipped up public opinion—all the more so as it was the public they served.

Chyłka was sure that whoever was dealing with Langer's case would already have made enquiries about the Grey-Haired Man. They would already have come to the conclusion that even if he was not as cruel and scheming a criminal as the media made him out to be, he still had plenty of skeletons in his cupboard. During the trial, Chyłka intended to show exactly what those skeletons were.

Now she was sat at her desk watching Oryński, who was twisting a ballpoint pen between his fingers and staring at the wall, his frown indicating that there was some sort of thought process going on in his brain. Just as he was staring at the wall, so Joanna was staring at him. She only looked away when Kordian shook his head and looked at her. Her own behaviour irritated her, but there wasn't much she could do about it.

He was a trainee and she was his mentor. They were working together on a case, and to make matters worse, they were very much in the limelight. If the media had the slightest hint that there was a love interest in the relationship, they'd be onto it immediately, and it would be broadcast far and wide.

"So what now?" asked Oryński, putting down the pen.

"We'll wait a little longer. Anyway, we don't have much choice."

"Do you think it'll get us anywhere?"

"Zordon . . ." she began, shaking her head. "When God created the world and decided that criminals should get a chance at a better life, He created the prosecutor. When He changed His mind and decided they should be punished, He created the investigative journalist. In my experience, one investigative journalist is worth fifteen policemen and ten prosecutors."

"And I think you have a rather warped view of creation."

"At least half of these matters will sort themselves out," continued Joanna. "Someone will shake the apple tree, and we'll stand under it and wait for the apples to fall. I think we can allow ourselves to feel just a tiny bit of inner satisfaction. And, for God's sake, you can stop pretending to be one of the Wise Men."

"What?"

"Your forehead's as wrinkled as a prune."

"I was only wondering how much this will really change Langer's case."

Chyłka looked at her watch, as if she suddenly remembered something.

"We have nothing to prove his innocence," he said. "But we have grounds for good media coverage. . . . Hey, are you listening to me?"

"I've got to go."

"What?"

"I have to go out, Zordon, so get your things and get lost."

"Would it hurt you to be a bit nicer?" he grumbled, pulling himself up from the chair. "All of a sudden, you tell me to get lost?"

"I could say something worse. You know I shoot from the hip, and I'm not scared to offend."

"OK, OK," he muttered, and opened the door. He looked at her one more time and disappeared into the corridor crowd.

A few short minutes later, Chyłka was behind the wheel of her BMW, leaving the Golden Terraces car park, tyres screeching. It usually took some effort to get the tyres on an X5 to make that sound, but the surface here made it easy.

Driving to Białołęka, Joanna thought about what she might see when she got to the prison. The Grey-Haired Man had told his thugs on the inside to pay Langer special attention. She was worried that she'd see a picture of misery, a man in despair.

She was on tenterhooks in the visiting room waiting for her client. She had once defended a paedophile; after the first night he still looked normal, but when the news about what he'd done spread, he became unrecognisable. He couldn't look up, he hobbled when he walked, and sitting down clearly caused him pain.

Now Chyłka was scared she might see the same. Only this time it would be much worse, because this time, Chyłka would know that she and Zordon were responsible.

A few moments later, a prison officer appeared, with Piotr behind him. The first thing she noticed was his calm, confident gait. He didn't move like someone doing duty as the prison slut.

He greeted Chyłka with a nod and sat down opposite her. Joanna tried to assess his physical state as much as the circumstances would allow. She noted the dark patches under his eyes, and various wounds on his face indicating that he had recently been punched, but generally his condition did not appear too bad.

Langer looked at Chyłka indifferently, and she felt the weight of his gaze. Deep in his eyes, she realised, there lurked fear.

The prison officer left, and Chyłka drew a deep breath.

"Were you badly beaten?"

"I'm alive. That's the most important thing."

"Do you know who's responsible for it?"

"Of course."

"The Grey-Haired Man," she added to be certain, looking at him inquisitively.

Langer was silent for a moment.

"How do you know about him?" he finally asked.

"His orangutan followed us until finally he made us an offer we couldn't refuse. I told him I would only talk to his boss directly."

Langer smiled. From the dark storm cloud of his face there came not rain, but a beam of sunlight.

Now Joanna could see the Langer the Grey-Haired Man had talked about. His eyes flashed beguilingly, while a dangerous smile played on his lips. It was at once alluring and menacing, a mixture that no doubt worked on the Agnieszka Powirskas of this world.

"I don't reckon it was the smartest thing I've ever done."

"Did he knock you about?"

"A bit," Chyłka admitted reluctantly. Compared with what Piotr must have been through, their encounter with the Grey-Haired Man was a mere slap on the cheek.

"He likes to present his arguments forcefully."

She nodded, and swallowed nervously. For some reason, she wanted to leave. Langer was being too friendly, too normal. She found that disturbing.

"And how about you?" she asked.

He sighed, turning to face the door, then looking at the camera. His nervous tic returned and his eyelids started twitching. Chyłka noted that his emotions got the better of him when he began thinking about surveillance.

"It's not so good," he admitted, which, in Joanna's opinion, was quite candid for him.

"Did they get to you?" she asked in spite of herself, aware that if he gave too detailed a response, she might not be able to sleep that night.

"No," he replied.

"Has anyone here got your back?"

"I've got my own back, with my orange jacket."

"I see."

He settled himself more comfortably in his chair.

"In the shower it's OK," he added. "Because there I know from which side they'll come from. It's more complicated during association. And the exercise yard is torment."

"So stay in your cell."

"If I did that, it would let everyone know I'm scared."

"So what? Sod your reputation, at least you'd be safe."

"Here, reputation is life."

Perhaps he's right, she thought. *If a high-security prisoner started showing fear, his status would soon be reduced to that of a nonce. Potential rapists would be queuing outside his cell.*

"Is there anything I can do to help?"

"No," answered Piotr. "Help from outside isn't well received."

"The only way I can help is from the outside," she replied. "But perhaps I can get the Grey-Haired Man to call off his thugs?"

"No. Keep clear of that man." For a moment, he paused. "Plenty of people have tried to get one over on him, and he even allowed some of them to believe that they had. Don't annoy him."

"It's a bit late for that now."

"Hmm?"

"We've set the newshounds on him, and now he's the main topic of conversation on TV."

"How is that?"

Joanna smiled and briefly summed up what they had done. She had expected Langer to be pleased, but she was wrong. He listened calmly, but indifferently.

"So what happens next?" he asked when she had finished.

"So far he hasn't been formally charged, but . . ."

"I meant you," said Piotr. "The Grey-Haired Man will make sure you regret it."

She fell silent. Chyłka had no intention of sharing everything with her client. Langer didn't need to know about her sister and Kormak. The silence must have worried him, because he started blinking again.

"Will you be OK?" she asked eventually, straightening up in her chair.

"When's the trial?"

His question was quite telling. Along with his nervous tic, it almost gave the impression of pleading.

"Soon," she said. "Hold on a just a bit longer, Piotr."

"I have been holding on," he replied. "But you have to understand, any chance you have of defending me is getting increasingly slim."

"I do understand. We're trying to speed everything up, believe me."

He relaxed a little.

"What are our chances of winning?"

"It isn't hopeless, but we can't be complacent either," she replied. "Admittedly, we haven't got a huge amount of extra evidence, but . . ."

"You haven't got any at all," interrupted Langer. "And as far as I know, you've lost several key witnesses."

"I have a solid defence," said Joanna. "And the Grey-Haired Man issue gives me grounds to start sowing seeds of doubt as to your guilt. At the end of the day, we have reasons to be cautiously optimistic."

She knew that she had gone too far with raising his hopes. She shouldn't have done it. On the other hand, what could she tell him? That he'd have to go back to his cell and face the constant threat of gang rape? Langer must have noticed her hesitation, because he started blinking again. Then a prison warder appeared and announced that visiting hours were over. Watching Piotr being taken out of the room, Joanna wondered whether there was any real chance of getting him out of prison.

14

THERE WAS A strange calm in the newbie-burrow. Not unlike pictures of Chernobyl with its desolate buildings and abandoned playground, the battery farm looked as if it had once teemed with life. Discarded personal belongings were scattered here and there, chairs had been moved away from desks, and occasionally there were photographs of long-forgotten people pinned to cubicle walls.

The last soldier on the battlefield was Oryński, spinning in his chair and trying to think of anything that might change Langer's fate. Some time had passed since Chyłka had visited him in prison, and the trial was fast approaching. In fact, Kordian should have been planning how to dress for the event rather than desperately searching for something that could save his client.

Selecting the right clothing was no trivial matter. Lawyers were expected to dress appropriately, not only as individuals, but as a duo. They had to match in terms of colour, and general aesthetics. It had nothing to do with vanity; experts insisted that the smallest of nuances could subconsciously affect how their arguments were perceived by the judge.

Oryński, however, decided he would leave this to Chyłka, while he focused all his attention on making a last-minute breakthrough. There was not much room for manoeuvre. The adjudicating panel was bound by the accusations put forward by the defence. In the Polish legal system, cassation appeals were not just the next stage in proceedings, but an extraordinary judicial remedy. The Supreme Court could not review the whole case, but only the accusations filed by the defence against the previous hearings. A broader examination of the case would only be possible if it turned out that Langer had had accomplices not included in the cassation appeal or if there were absolute grounds for an appeal against the previous judgement. But neither of these options applied in this case, which left only one possibility: to prove that the legal assessment of the case had previously been flawed.

It was a hard nut to crack, but not impossible.

What sort of result could they expect? Again, there were few possibilities. The court could reject the appeal, uphold it or overrule the previous judgement, either partially or entirely.

If the appeal was accepted, the case would be handed over to another court to be reheard, and that was what Oryński and Chyłka were counting on.

There was also one more possibility, highly optimistic and highly unlikely. The court could discontinue the proceedings or even acquit the accused. It would take a miracle. And the light at the end of the tunnel seemed very faint indeed.

After Chyłka's visit to the prison, the two lawyers had filed a request to suspend Langer's prison sentence—everyone filing for cassation had the same right. Chyłka had argued that Langer's stay in prison was causing him irreversible change, and also that in the light of recent discoveries regarding the Grey-Haired Man, there was a possibility that he was being manipulated. Unfortunately, their arguments did not convince the Supreme Court, and the application was rejected, giving a clear signal that they couldn't count on the power of the media.

Kordian was not especially surprised. It would take an immense dose of altruism to believe Piotr had not murdered those people. If he was one of the five judges deciding Langer's fate, he'd have suspected the lawyers were bending the rules. Playing intellectual games, as Radwański put it.

All the evidence was against Langer. His behaviour, and the sheer impracticality of all other scenarios, meant he must surely be the perpetrator; also, his fingerprints were all over the murder weapons, and he had never denied his guilt, either to the police or the courts. The fact that someone had kidnapped and threatened the two lawyers proved nothing, at least as far as Langer's case was concerned. Without a convincing chain of cause and effect, to the court these were unrelated events.

Oryński stopped spinning the chair when he started to feel dizzy. He spun the other way a few times, then, still in the chair, rolled towards his desk. He leaned his elbows on the surface and stared blankly at a Supreme Court ruling he was trying to get through. It didn't look particularly useful at first glance, but he needed to kill time somehow.

"Zordon!" called the only other person on that floor. Other employees also worked long hours, especially in the newbie-burrow, but by two in the morning, Chyłka and Oryński were the only ones left. Deadlines usually expired by midnight, so anyone who stayed after that needed their heads examined.

"Zordon!"

Oryński turned the chair around and jumped off it. He walked down the empty corridor and turned to the open door of Chyłka's office. He entered slowly and calmly, and was met with a disapproving look.

"At the sound of my voice you should be scurrying here like a rabbit!"

"Yes, but . . ."

"Quiet," she interrupted him, rising from her chair. "Look at this," she said, turning her laptop round to face Kordian then tapping the monitor.

"What's that?"

"A revelation. One brilliant fucking revelation. A breakthrough."

He looked at the screen, where the video player window was maximised. The image was of an interior; it looked like a visiting room."

"What's that?" repeated Oryński, leaning to take a closer look. Joanna pressed the space bar to set the recording in motion.

"Don't you recognise it, dumbass? It's the visiting room in Białołęka holiday home."

Sometime later, Chyłka appeared in the picture. In a dignified manner she made her way around the small metal table and sat down opposite the entrance. Then she spread a pile of documents on the table. The date in the bottom right corner indicated that the recording was made shortly after the police had arrested Piotr.

After a while, the star of the show appeared. Langer sat down opposite Joanna, and then it was as if time stood still. They both sat motionless.

"At first, you may remember, he wasn't very talkative," said Chyłka. "Then towards the end of the recording he proposed that I do something for him up against the wall."

"Why the hell are we watching this?"

"Just watch."

He watched the next several dozen minutes of recordings. Kordian had no idea whether Chyłka had coerced the detention centre to give her the recordings, they'd been given to her out of goodwill, or if she had obtained them illegally. One way or another, he was sure her determination and wiliness had played a significant role.

"Are you watching it?" she asked when the next recording started.

He was, but he didn't spot anything interesting. Chyłka pulled out a packet of cigarettes, and handed one to Oryński. With another, she pointed to Langer.

"The eyelids," she said. "Can you see what he's doing?"

"He's blinking like a madman. But that's not all that strange. We knew about his tic from the start."

Chyłka replayed the first recording. There was no nervous blinking. "The blinking started later," she said before Kordian could light his cigarette.

"Yes, but what has that . . ."

"Look at his eyes, dumbass," she said, playing the next recording. "Three short blinks, three long ones, and then three short ones. SOS. Di-di-dit, dah-dah-dah, di-di-dit."

"What?"

"SOS in Morse code."

"Are you trying to tell me that Langer . . ." began Oryński, but then paused. For a moment he wondered whether Chyłka was pulling his leg. Then he took another look, and realised she wasn't.

Without thinking, he took a drag of his unlit cigarette.

"How on earth did you notice that? And all the time he was giving signals in Morse code?"

"Yup," she confirmed, stopping the recording. "We were both completely blind to it. He even drew our attention to the camera in the corner of the room, and we interpreted it in our own way," she said, lighting her cigarette. Kordian kept looking at the laptop screen.

"How did you notice it?" he repeated.

"By accident. I've been watching these recordings over the last few days. I know them by heart. An hour ago, I was browsing some stupid news website and came across an item about someone whose door intercom could be opened using Morse code. And the rest you can imagine. Sudden revelation, total enlightenment."

Oryński looked at the frozen image, and replayed it. Yes, Langer was definitely signalling SOS.

"Could it be a coincidence, maybe?" he asked, trying not to get too excited.

"Maybe," she conceded. "But Langer is a sailor, he sails yachts and other boats, so he must know Morse code. It all makes sense," she said, switching to the browser. She opened a tab and found a tool for decrypting Morse messages.

It took them ten minutes to decipher the next phrase.

"Long, short, long, short, long," said Joanna. "Start of transmission."

"OK," said Oryński. "Now what do we do?"

She looked around the office, and thought for a moment. Deciding that any more attempts at deciphering the messages by themselves would be futile, she picked up her phone and rang Kormak.

15

"I'VE NEVER THOUGHT of you two as normal people, but calling me at this time of night exceeds the limits even of my tolerance," was how Kormak greeted them when he arrived at the Skylight building.

It was coming up to three in the morning, and if it hadn't been Chyłka calling, Kormak would probably not have answered the phone at all. She had used her powers of persuasion to make him get dressed, order a taxi, and turn up at the office.

"Sit down and shut up," said Joanna, pointing to her chair. "Thanks, but I'd prefer to work in the McCarthy Cave."

"So *raus, raus, Schneller*," she ordered.

"Less of the *raus*, I need to copy the files . . . oh, OK." Kormak took the SD card that Joanna waved in front of him.

When Chyłka called him, Kormak had no idea what to expect, but now in the office, she summed everything up from start to finish. Kormak looked at the screen and started analysing the recording.

"How come you know Morse code?" asked Kordian.

"It's an alphabet rather than a code," Kormak answered, stopping the recording. "I know a few codes, not least the GA-DE-RY-PO-LU-KI cypher."

"The what?"

"Weren't you ever a scout?" asked Kormak. "Or perhaps you were in that poor substitute for real scouting, the ZHP?"

"Er . . ." was all that Oryński could say. He had no idea about the differences between the two scouting organisations, let alone the disputes between them.

"Er? Is that all you can say?" snapped Kormak. "If I hadn't been a proper scout, you wouldn't have your own personal code-breaker here with you today. And another thing . . ."

"OK, OK," interrupted Chyłka. "Keep your honour shining bright, be loyal in the hardest fight—and get to work right now."

"What?"

"Isn't that how your scouting hymn goes?"

Kormak shook his head, took out an A4 sheet of paper and drew a diagram similar to the one Joanna had found on the internet. He worked for a solid hour watching all the recordings. In that time, his two guests managed to smoke half a packet of cigarettes, and Kordian once again firmly resolved to give up smoking and to take up sports training. At least once a week.

"OK," Kormak said finally, putting down his fineliner and flexing his back on the chair. "Allow me to read it."

"Do the honours, Scoutmaster," said Chyłka encouragingly.

"I shall ignore the SOS at the beginning, because it was only meant to draw your attention—rather ineffectually as we can see, because you dimwits don't know the first thing about how to behave in a crisis and thought that the bloke was (a) paranoid about having eavesdropping devices everywhere, (b) a weirdo who sat in silence for minutes on end, and (c) a nervous delinquent who felt a compulsion to blink like crazy during his moments of silence."

"So he gave the SOS message," said Joanna, hoping to close the subject.

"Yes. Then he gave the 'start of new message' signal, as you discovered yourselves. Though I wonder why he wasted time on the Morse prosign nonsense, it needs more patience than a Buddhist monk. On the other hand, when you're stuck in prison with not much to do, I suppose arranging and repeating Morse signals in your head helps to kill time. And for that he deserves . . ."

"Get to the point, Kormak."

The thin man turned the page and pointed to the first series of signals. Oryński and Chyłka simply saw an incomprehensible series of dots and dashes.

.- -.—— -. .. / .— .— .- - . . . . -. ..

"What does it say?"

"It says 'Antoni Wansel.'"

"What?" Oryński blurted out.

"I have no idea who he is, but that's the name Langer signalled in the second recording.

Joanna wrote down the name and looked at Kormak's A4 sheet of paper.

She now had tangible evidence that Langer had been communicating with them all along. Admittedly, she'd been getting used to the idea, but now it was beginning to sink in.

"And on subsequent visits?" asked Oryński.

"During the second visit, he signalled, "I am innocent," and I assume that was still before you managed to establish any meaningful verbal contact. Next, he signalled various instructions and warnings, such as 'Beware of the Grey-Haired Man'" and 'Find Gorzym.' Nothing that's useful to you now. He devoted the greatest amount of time to signalling the address of your grey-haired friend. Unfortunately, all that trouble went to waste because we deciphered the message long after the fact."

"And the last visit?"

"He repeated the name 'Antoni Wansel,' and then silence. That was it."

Joanna had been hoping for more. After her breakthrough, her expectations had skyrocketed, and she saw herself finding a new, key piece of evidence. In her mind's eye she saw herself and Zordon sitting opposite Rejchert, waiting for the right moment to roll out the heavy artillery and crush him.

"Find out who that Antoni man is," she said.

"Already done it." Kormak turned from his sheet of paper to the monitor. "Google hasn't found anything much other than a mention on Zumi that someone by that name runs a patisserie in Lubusz province, near Świebodzin."

"Excellent."

"Hold on, there's more." Kormak narrowed his eyes. "I also looked at a list of the deceased buried at Bródno cemetery. And bingo! The date indicate that this man was buried there very recently. Soon after Langer landed in Białołęka."

"Are they allowed to disclose that sort of thing?" asked Oryński.

"I don't know," replied Kormak, looking at the data giving the exact location of the grave. "This is a page from an amateur site. In the introduction, they say that their catalogue isn't exhaustive, and more detailed information is available from the Cemetery Board."

Kordian felt it was rather strange that a bunch of people should wander around graveyards writing down the names of the deceased and the dates of their departure to the Kingdom of Heaven, but on further consideration, there was nothing wrong with it. After all, who doesn't read the inscriptions on tombstones when they visit the cemetery?

"Give me the coordinates, sector, alley and so on," said Chyłka.

Kormak provided the required information, and turned the monitor round, pointing to the exact location of the recently dug grave.

"Go through the fourth gate, from Chodecka Street."

"What? Are we going to the graveyard?"

"I assumed that's why you went to all this trouble. And why you woke me in the middle of the night when I should have been sleeping off the previous night, which I spent playing *World of Warcraft*. I also thought there must be some reason you wanted a dead man's exact resting place."

"God rest his soul." Kordian looked at the other two. Now no one wanted to speak.

"Seriously?" Kordian finally asked. "Are we going to dig him up?"

The three Żelazny & McVay employees exchanged looks. There was no good answer to that.

"First we have to check what's in there," said Joanna. "Then we can think about what to do next. I have no ambitions to be a B-movie horror film star, so don't count on me as far as pulling corpses out of coffins is concerned."

"I'm a bit worried that you're using the plural and looking at me," said Kormak.

Chyłka shrugged her shoulders, and he had to accept that the subject was closed and resistance would be futile. He'd known he'd get involved the minute Chyłka had asked for the location of the grave.

"Let's go," she said, getting out of her chair.

With a combination of modest night-time traffic and the X5's impressive horsepower, they were parking outside Bródno cemetery just over ten minutes after leaving the Skylight building.

It was four in the morning and still dark. The graveyard looked as if it was ready to claim anyone who passed through its gate.

16

O NLY ONE STREETLIGHT was working by the cemetery wall where they had parked the car. It emitted a weak and uneven light, hardly enough to pierce the surrounding darkness, but it was enough to show them that the gate was firmly locked. None of them had thought of that.

Chyłka opened her boot, rummaged around, and took out a torch.

Her companions looked at her with approval.

"You look like your eyes are about to pop out," she remarked. "There's nothing weird about having a torch in your car. What if, heaven forbid, you need to change a wheel in the middle of the night?"

They nodded gravely. Joanna directed the beam at the gate, and then at the closed side entrance. She sighed loudly.

"Either of you happen to have a skeleton key?"

"Drive your car right up to the gate," suggested Kormak. She looked at him in disbelief, as if she was about to burst out laughing. "I'm serious," he said. "Drive up to the gate. If we climb onto the bonnet, it'll be easy to jump over the wall."

"Are you mad?"

"But your paintwork is fu—"

"There are some benches over there, Kormak," she said, pointing to some stone seats by the wall. "We're not going to trample all over my X5. And now to work! Lead the way, Scoutmaster."

"Why me?"

"Because you have a scout merit badge for jumping over cemetery walls."

He glared at her.

"Don't panic, lead the way," she said encouragingly, then saw from the corner of her eye that Zordon had decided to take the initiative.

Oryński turned on the torch in his phone and made his way over to one of the benches. He stood on it, pulled himself up onto the wall and jumped down the other side. Chyłka and Kormak joined him.

Finding the grave was not a problem. Although they only had the light from their torches and any memorial candles that were still burning on the graves, Kormak proved to be a very competent guide. Within minutes, they were standing in front of a temporary wooden plaque on a fresh grave that looked pretty much like all the others.

The name and the date of death on the black plaque were the ones they were looking for. Below it only a brief epitaph: "Memorabilis." No religious symbols, no "Rest in Peace." The grave of an atheist and aesthete.

"OK," began Kordian. "We're here."

"Bravo, Zordon. You're becoming ever more perceptive," remarked Chyłka.

"You know what I meant."

"Nonverbal question?"

"More or less."

"I have no answer."

Kormak shifted from one foot to the other, his fingers thoughtlessly picking at his lip. Their own silence made the cemetery silence seem deafening.

"We all know what we came here for, right?" asked Kormak. "We've checked. The grave is just where we thought it was."

"Well, put your gloves on, pick up your spade and get to work!" said Chyłka.

"I was thinking more along the lines of arranging an exhumation order . . . or something like that."

"No chance," she replied. "You'd need permission from the grieving family and the health and safety authorities, and on top of that, we'd have to do it during the right season, because you can't dig up human remains all year round. I don't remember the exact dates because I have as much to do with funeral law as Zordon does with Mensa. You could apply to the court or the prosecutor's office, but I'm positive we wouldn't get all the formalities done before the trial."

"So what do we do?"

Oryński's question hung in the air like a bad smell. All three of them were aware that the only option was to start digging up the body with their bare hands.

"Out of the question," said Kormak. "Stop behaving like some idiot who'll do anything to win a case. Fuck it, even I have my limits." He looked at the grave. "Besides, how do you intend to open the coffin? It's not just about digging a hole in the ground."

The three of them exchanged looks again, then two of them looked at Kormak.

"No," he repeated.

"But you can find people to do all sorts of jobs," she reminded him.

"Not for robbing graves."

"We have no choice," said Joanna.

"How do you find these people?" asked Kordian, crouching next to the grave.

"Via the web," explained Kormak. "An ad on Gumtree usually works OK."

"OK."

"Sometimes that's all you need. You can find anyone on Gumtree. A fortune teller who'll predict your future from your sperm—literally anyone."

"So what are you waiting for?" asked Chyłka.

"I won't get someone for tonight." Kormak spread his arms. "Tomorrow night, perhaps. There are places I can find even weirder stuff too, if you know what I mean."

Oryński didn't know, but he could imagine that Kormak didn't mean the Gumtree kind of site. He made the sign of the cross and stood over the grave, fixing his gaze on the name. Antoni Wansel. Spending the next twenty-four hours waiting for answers would be torture, but there was no alternative.

They returned to the Skylight office with heads hung low, full of guesswork and speculation.

They all reckoned that whatever was in that grave, it wasn't Wansel. If they could trust what the plaque said to be true, there would be no point in digging up the body. There was no chance they could do an autopsy—they didn't even have a way to transport the body, and a cursory examination would be of little use. They had to assume Langer had directed them to the grave for some other reason.

Kormak managed to find the workmen he required fairly quickly, and the trio from Żelazny & McVay reconvened at the cemetery at one the following night. Kormak's offer of an easy 5,000, no tax and no questions asked, was accepted by one Henryk Wach, a gravedigger who normally worked in Bródno cemetery. With his pale complexion, deep shadows under his eyes, and sunken cheeks, Henryk was a dead ringer for the Grim Reaper. He fitted the cemetery landscape like a glove.

Assisted by Kormak and Oryński, he dug up Antoni Wansel's last resting place, and the three of them lifted the coffin onto the surface. So far everything was as it should be. The complications began when

Henryk opened the lid on the world of the dead. Such a hideous stench billowed out from the coffin that Kordian began to heave, while a bit further on Kormak fell to the ground, and Chyłka felt her strength draining away. She was, however, the only one of the three to remain standing, looking at the corpse inside the coffin.

"Close it," she said.

The gravedigger mumbled something in response, then stuck his spade into the ground and leaned on it.

"What did you say?" she asked, covering her mouth.

The stench was so unbearable, she couldn't think of anything to compare it with. At best, it could be a combination of rotten food and sewage.

"I said that we haven't gone to all the trouble to dig up the deceased only to . . ."

"Shut the coffin!" interjected Joanna.

Henryk glared at her, but slammed the head panel shut.

"I'm not going to bury this on my own," he said. "We'll wait until your mates finish puking and we'll do it together."

"Another five thousand says you'll do it on your own," replied Chyłka.

She didn't think Kormak and Oryński would recover quickly enough to get anywhere near the corpse.

She had been convinced that they'd find something—anything—in that coffin other than an actual corpse. Perhaps the missing murder weapon, a cinema ticket providing an alibi, an item incriminating someone else . . . Meanwhile, everything seemed to indicate that they had uncovered an ordinary body that had already had time to decompose very thoroughly.

"Wait!" she signalled to the gravedigger to stop by raising her hand. Henryk, who had found the 5,000 argument very persuasive, was already getting ready to bury the coffin.

"Well?"

"We ought to open it properly."

"What? So I have to open it again?"

"Yes."

Chyłka had recovered from the initial shock and was beginning to think more clearly. She thought Langer wouldn't have sent them here if it wasn't important. If there was nothing useful in this grave, it could only be because they had exhumed the wrong Antoni Wansel.

"All right," said Henryk, sticking the spade into the mound of earth. "But I'm not going to search any pockets. Or any other nooks and crannies."

"Five thousand says . . ."

"Oh, give it a rest, woman," said the gravedigger. "I wouldn't rummage through his underwear, even if you gave me 10,000. The dead are best left alone."

"Are you superstitious?"

"No, but it's just like you wouldn't touch an anthill or a beehive," said Henryk, looking disapprovingly at the corpse. The stench did not seem to cause him any serious discomfort. "Do you know how many vermin there are lurking under there? Move the coffin, and it'll all crawl, hatch or fly out, straight into your face. If you want to have a go, be my guest, I'll just take two steps back."

"What's going on?" Kordian joined them, standing next to Chyłka. She noticed that he was struggling not to run away again.

"The gravedigger has chickened out."

"What? Nothing of the sort," protested Henryk, though the expression on his face showed that he wasn't sure himself if he had indeed "chickened out." "I simply don't touch parasites. I don't mind being around dead people, but that crap I don't touch."

"Do you want to pull him out?" asked Kordian in disgust.

Chyłka shrugged her shoulders. "Have you got a better idea? We've come this far; we've pulled out the coffin, so the next logical step would be to check whether there's anything under the corpse which might be the actual reason for our visit."

"You'll only find a sea of shit and vermin, I can assure you," muttered the gravedigger.

His paymasters ignored him.

"And if there's nothing there?" asked Kordian. "If Langer is referring to the actual body, how on earth could it be useful after we've moved it? Even if the court accepted the corpse as evidence, they'd see immediately that we've tampered with it."

"And in your opinion, why would any court be interested in . . ." began Joanna, and then suddenly stopped. She and Oryński exchanged looks which said more than a thousand words, and both leaned simultaneously over the coffin. If Langer had led them to that corpse, there could only be one reason. That corpse would prove his innocence.

Trying hard not to retch, Kordian took a closer look at the distorted face. It wasn't difficult to recognise the human features, because apart from the visual post-mortem changes on the skin and the decomposing fat, the corpse was still distinctly human. It would take some five or six years to become a skeleton. Even ten, depending on the soil.

Chyłka pointed to the dead man's temple. With some difficulty, Oryński spotted the small, circular indentation.

"It looks like the mark of a hammer."

"Do you think that this chap—"

"Was killed in the same way as the two in Langer's apartment?" confirmed Joanna. "You gave me the idea yourself."

Perhaps he had, though Kordian had not managed to verbalise it. However, if Langer had led them to this corpse, it had to have some bearing on the case.

The mark on the temple seemed to confirm their theory, although there could only be any certainty once the corpse had been autopsied. Suspicion of a violent death would be enough reason for the prosecution to have the grave opened, but they simply didn't have time to deal with all the formalities. The trial was due to start in two days' time, while the process of exhuming Antoni Wansel's body would probably last a month if not longer.

"We have to delay the trial," Oryński concluded.

Joanna remained silent, still looking at the corpse and wondering whether this discovery would be of any use. Eventually, she decided that if they informed the prosecutor's office, they could lose their only advantage. Their only chance was to go for the highest stakes. In her mind, she already had some ideas how they could play it.

"Chyłka?"

"Calm down, Zordon."

"I am calm."

"Go home and prepare for the trial."

"What?"

"You only have tomorrow, make use of every moment."

"But what about Wansel?"

"Don't worry about him, I'll deal with it," said Joanna, looking away from the contents of the coffin. She turned to Kordian and added, "And put on a white shirt with a black tie. We'll dress in black and white."

"OK," he replied. At least one dilemma was resolved.

17

W<small>HEN</small> O<small>RYŃSKI</small> <small>ENTERED</small> the courtroom, the rush of adrenaline was so great that it seemed to paralyse him. Had it been a little milder, it would have been motivating, pleasant even. But nervousness overwhelmed him. His mouth was dry, his hands were shaking and his knees were weak.

Their seats were to the left of the adjudicating panel. Oryński glanced at the public gallery and saw that attendance was at record levels. Joanna stood beside him, watching the five judges—the two women and three men who would decide whether the complaints contained in the cassation appeal were valid and justified.

Piotr Langer was sitting right behind them. Kordian glanced over his shoulder, hoping to give him an encouraging smile, but the prisoner's head was bowed. His gaze was fixed on the chains restraining his legs.

Oryński turned to Chyłka and saw that she, too, did not look overly optimistic. It seemed that the Antoni Wansel evidence had not led to any major breakthroughs.

The judges looked like pilgrims, halfway through their long pilgrimage from the Hel Peninsula to the shrine at Jasna Góra, but already at the limit of their physical capabilities. Without divine intervention, they would have no hope—a fitting analogy for the many hours the two lawyers had spent wading through volume after volume of notes, documents, and case studies.

Judges aside, the courtroom was most impressive. The building was awe-inspiring, and the largely glazed interiors brought to mind the high-profile trials broadcast from Strasbourg or The Hague. Kordian had once seen the room they were assigned to on television, and its post-communist feel, complete with ill-fitting wooden floor panels, had irritated him. But the place had been refurbished, and now its majesty was in keeping with its esteemed purpose. It was spacious and decorated in subdued colours. An elegant silver eagle adorned a milk-white glass screen. There were large Polish flags on either side of the judges' bench and at least several dozen seats. All this was very stirring, so much so that Oryński's legs were scarcely able to provide a stable support for the rest of his body. "Do you know them?" he asked Joanna when they finally sat down.

"More or less," she replied evasively. "Starting from the left: judge number one, Dublicki, an outstanding straight-A student and know-it-all. He wrote the commentary to the Penal Code, and that's probably all he's known for, and only among diehard enthusiasts of this area of law. I'm pretty sure you haven't heard of him."

"No, never."

"The second is Judge Sydoń. Gives lectures at the University of Warsaw, a smart woman, though she likes to pontificate. Next is Judge Bazan, who sat in the Contract Sejm as a representative of the United People's Party and has published a thousand and one insignificant works. Next to her is Judge Marendziak, whom you probably know from the lectures he gave at your faculty, although you'd actually have to have gone to those lectures to recognise him. And the presiding judge is Gołdyn, whom I don't need to introduce."

Adam Gołdyn was the only one of the five judges that Oryński recognised. He was president of the Criminal Law Division and often appeared on television. He looked OK, by and large, which was more than could be said for the others. The rest of the panel looked like teachers' pets and school swots who would slit your throat if you didn't agree with their point of view.

The start of the trial was announced through speakers. The judges looked up from their papers and took off their glasses. They looked disdainfully at the defence lawyers and the public prosecutor.

Oryński averted his eyes to avoid their gaze. Langer was still contemplating the chains around his ankles, while behind him there was a forest of cameras and microphones from all the major television stations.

"Good morning," said Judge Gołdyn, and started by going over the usual formalities.

Neither party submitted any requests, the presence of cameras was noted and recorded in the minutes, then the judges sat down and took off their head coverings. The presiding judge cleared his throat and said:

"The defendant is present, as are his defence lawyers and the witnesses: Maciej K., Krzysztof S., Katarzyna S., and Wojciech M. I call the first witness, Maciej K., to come forward."

No nonsense, to the point. Oryński liked it.

A man in police uniform got up from his chair and walked slowly to the witness box opposite the judges.

"In the witness box: Maciej K.," continued the presiding judge, giving time for the court reporter to tap in his words for the electronic record. "Police officer, forty years old, residing in Warsaw. His relationship to the defendant: unrelated. Do you understand why you have been called as a witness?"

"Yes," replied the policeman, and then fell silent.

The judge encouraged him to continue with a hand gesture.

"I was the first to arrive on the scene, about a quarter of an hour after one of the neighbours phoned," he said. "I found the defendant . . . that is, the prisoner . . . in the flat. Along with him, there were also two bodies, one of a man and one of a woman. I called for backup. Later, we identified the pair as Daniel Relichowski and Agata Szylkiewicz, and then . . . that is, the following day, the relatives of the victims confirmed it."

"What state were the bodies in?" asked the judge.

"Massacred. It looked like . . . like a still from a gore movie. That's a kind of horror movie where . . ."

"The court knows what a gore movie is," interrupted Gołdyn. "Please continue."

Kordian decided that the judge's interruptions could mean one of two things: either Gołdyn was all right or he couldn't care less about the case and couldn't be bothered to make a song and dance about it. So far it had more of the casual feel of a regional court than the pomp of a high-profile trial before five judges of the Supreme Court.

"At first glance I could assess that the victims had been tortured to death," continued the policeman. "The murder weapons were within my sight. I saw a bloodied hammer, knives, some skewers, and a wrench. I am not a specialist in forensic medicine, so I do not know what the exact injuries were. It seemed that the defendant . . . that is, the prisoner, did not leave any part of the body untouched. If he did not crush or pulverise the flesh, he pierced it with a sharp object. A terrible sight . . ."

The policeman broke off, and Gołdyn nodded.

"I will now read out to the court the statement you gave during the pre-trial proceedings," he said. "You may sit down while I read."

"Thank you."

It took a while for the judge to battle his way through the long, chaotic statement, in which the policeman described in detail everything he saw during his visit to Piotr Langer's apartment.

"Do you uphold what you said in your statement?" asked Gołdyn, once the torrent of words was over.

"Yes."

The judge nodded and looked at Rejchert, who was sitting to the right of the adjudicating panel. He looked relaxed, which was hardly surprising.

"Prosecutor?"

"Thank you, I have no questions," declared Rejchert, rising only briefly.

"Counsellor?"

Joanna smiled faintly at the judge, then slowly and gracefully rose from her chair. She looked into the eyes of the policeman in the witness box and raised her chin very slightly.

"In your statement, you say that my client tortured his alleged victims, is that correct?"

"Yes. And I uphold it."

"I understand," replied Chyłka, lowering her head so that now she appeared to be glaring at him. "Could you tell the court what professional police duties you were called to carry out at my client's home that day?"

"I was there to detain him."

"After the event?"

"Let's not waste time determining obvious facts," interrupted Judge Bazan, the former deputy of the United People's Party.

"Of course," conceded Joanna without a shadow of resentment. "This leads me to my next question: How much time passed between the death of the victims and your arrival on the scene?"

The policeman was silent.

"It's not a difficult question," she said.

"Everyone knows that it was more or less ten days."

"Exactly. That is what the forensic medicine experts have established," said Chyłka with a small smile. "Therefore, let us sum up: you arrive at the scene ten days after the murders. In the apartment you find my client, and then you notice the corpses."

"Yes," confirmed the policeman. "Piotr L. opened the door for me and calmly walked through to the kitchen to pour himself some water."

"Are these questions leading to anything relevant?" interrupted Bazan again.

Chyłka nodded. "On the basis of the wounds on the bodies, the murder weapons, and the presence of my client, you have concluded that Piotr L. took the lives of these people with premeditation. He tormented these people, tortured them, and repeatedly inflicted wounds until they both died."

"That is how I believe it happened, but—"

"So you have assessed my client's intentions on the basis of the wounds you saw. I am not surprised, because this is the logical conclusion we can draw from the situation. The same mistake was made by other professionals dealing with the case, including the courts of the first and second instance."

"Counsellor . . ."

"I am trying to show that even at this preliminary stage, my client's direct intention to murder had already been assumed."

"The time for final speeches will come later, Counsellor," said Gołdyn. "Please focus on your questions to the witness."

"I am, Your Honour," replied Joanna calmly. "What I am trying to do is to find out how it was determined that my client had acted with direct intention."

"That was a question?" asked Judge Bazan.

Chyłka nodded, looking directly at the witness. The policeman scratched his hand and looked at the judges, as if searching for help. After a moment of silence, the presiding judge gestured for the witness to give his answer.

"Sorry, could you repeat the question?"

"Of course," replied Chyłka. "You have determined a direct intention—that is, my client's intention to commit a crime, the direct intention to take the lives of these people—on the basis of their wounds, is that correct?"

"Yes."

"Can you please explain by what miracle you can look into someone's head and determine their motive when you've only seen the results?"

"As I have said, the victims were—"

"Yes, yes, massacred. You stressed that point repeatedly. But at the time you didn't know when those wounds were inflicted. Perhaps they were inflicted post-mortem?"

"That's possible, but it doesn't change anything."

"It doesn't change anything?" said Chyłka, pursing her lips and look-ing at the presiding judge. "If the wounds were inflicted after the murder was committed, then you have based your conclusion on a quite irrel-evant premise."

"That's absurd."

"Why?" asked Chyłka quickly, before any of the judges managed to react.

"Because you could see what had happened at first glance."

She had him.

"So in your opinion, there is no possibility that the victims could have died in any way other than through the deliberate actions of my client? And you base this certainty on the existence of wounds that could have occurred post-mortem?"

"Well, yes."

"Let me remind you that you are testifying under oath."

"Reminding witnesses of this fact is not your responsibility," interrupted Bazan.

Joanna raised her hands slightly and took a step back to show her acquiescence. But she already knew she had no chance of placating this ex-political-deputy. The old crone probably saw her presence in the courtroom as a punishment and wanted to return home as soon as possible to her cat, hamster, chinchilla, or whatever it was. The only creature that could put up with her.

"So?" asked Chyłka, looking at the policeman. "Have you based all your conclusions on deeds that could have occurred after the fact?"

"You're twisting everything. . . ."

"Please answer the question." It was Judge Gołdyn speaking this time.

"Your Honour," interjected Rejchert, rising from his chair. He felt the cold stares from the whole panel, but he didn't back down. "We are looking at a pantomime that has no place in this respectable institution."

"Please sit down," said the presiding judge. "Your chance to ask questions came earlier. You did not take advantage of the opportunity."

Rejchert lowered his head and looked towards Judge Bazan. He saw a flash of understanding in her eyes, which only confirmed his feeling that already, at this early stage in the proceedings, he was leading 1–0. He only needed two more judges on his side and he could go and light a cigar.

"I shall therefore repeat my previous question," said Chyłka. "Is it not possible that those people could have died for some reason other than the wounds you saw?"

"I don't know," admitted the policeman before he could think how to get out of the trap. "That is . . ."

"Therefore, could it be the case that the victims had already died, and my client inflicted all the wounds later?"

"Well, maybe it could. From what I know, the bodies were in such a state that it was difficult to determine when most of the wounds were inflicted. But what you are suggesting is nonsense. Why would he want to do that? Out of anger that they were dead?" the policeman asked with a foolish smile, looking at the judges.

"Thank you. I have no more questions," said Joanna, returning to her place.

"Thank you for attending," said the presiding judge to the policeman, using his eyes to show the witness which way he should go after leaving the witness box.

18

THE SECOND PERSON in the witness box was Katarzyna S. The presiding judge introduced her as a policewoman, aged thirty-four, residing in Warsaw and unrelated to the defendant. It was she who first exchanged a few words with Langer, and she arrived at the scene shortly after backup was called. She briefly described the moment she entered the apartment, expressing her thoughts much more efficiently than her predecessor. Next, the judge gave the floor to Rejchert.

The public prosecutor got up, and, looking at the policewoman, took a deep breath. Chyłka suspected that the two of them had got together outside the courtroom on more than one occasion.

"What was your first impression of the defendant?" asked the prosecutor.

"I thought he was very peculiar," replied the policewoman, narrowing her eyes. "As I have said, he was in the kitchen and the bodies were in the next room. I thought he must be under the influence of drugs, but toxicology tests didn't show anything. I'm not a psychologist, so I cannot provide a better answer."

"Of course. I am only interested in an ordinary human appraisal."

"Well, the defendant was sitting at the kitchen table, drinking water and looking at us as if we were there, but also, at the same time, as if we weren't there."

"Was he in shock?"

"No, he didn't seem to be," she answered. "He wasn't disoriented, he didn't seem nervous, but neither was he in a stupor. He was sipping water, and when I sat down at the table, he looked at me calmly."

Rejchert waited a while, frowned, and then thanked the witness.

"Counsellor?" said Gołdyn.

Joanna put aside her pen and the paper she had been writing on and looked up.

"Did my client admit to you that he had killed the victims?"

"No, but—"

"Thank you," interrupted Chyłka, and the court had no alternative but to also thank the witness.

Next in the witness box was an expert called to assess Langer's mental state. Joanna wasn't expecting any new revelations, and she was not disappointed. It was a repeat of the scenario from earlier hearings and upheld the opinion that the accused was sane at the time he committed the crime. The final witness was a forensic technician who recounted facts they knew already: the owner's fingerprints all over the murder weapons, along with his hair and other biological traces on the bodies of the victims, Chyłka pointed out that Langer could have used the hammer and knives in his flat for purposes other than committing murder, as she had done in previous trials. Judge Bazan was quick to object, which Joanna saw as a sign that the adjudicating panel was starting to get bad tempered.

These were the people chosen to determine the legitimacy—or lack thereof—of the allegations raised by the Żelazny & McVay lawyers. So far Joanna's performance might have convinced a lay jury, but not a panel of experienced veterans like these.

"Counsellor," began Bazan when Chyłka had asked the witness her last question and was intending to thank him. "We all know that you are seeking to demonstrate that the rule of law was incorrectly applied in the last adjudication; in a more or less circuitous way you are trying to suggest the lack of direct intention. But I appeal to you to respect our time and kindly request that you present concrete evidence."

The presiding judge cleared his throat, and the other woman on the panel rolled her eyes. In groups of elite judges, these reactions were not uncommon. They disagreed with one another in academic papers, they argued in corridors and liked to show who was more important in the courtrooms. After work, their relationships changed, and many of them were firm friends. Unfortunately, none of the other judges on the panel had any particular liking for the judge who was McVay's friend.

Joanna smiled at the judge who had rebuked her and sat down next to Oryński.

It was time for a break, and Langer's lawyers eagerly took the opportunity to go downstairs. They lit their cigarettes and inhaled the smoke deeply and with pleasure.

"What do we do now?" asked Kordian with a Davidoff in his lips.

"We'll summon Langer as a witness," said Joanna.

The trainee said nothing. That would be like pushing water uphill with a rake. So far, their client had avoided giving evidence like the plague; there was little chance he'd agree to go to the witness box, let alone say anything while he was there.

"You just have to give him a piece of paper," said Chyłka. "I'll summon him, and you'll turn round to hand him a slip of paper with the name 'Antoni Wansel' on it. That should be enough to make him think twice before he refuses to give evidence."

"Don't think so."

"We'll see," said Joanna, stamping out her cigarette with the sole of her shoe. "Come on, time to hot things up."

"What?"

"Let's give them hell."

Kordian knew that despite her ebullient tone, she realised their chances of winning the case were slim.

As for him, he'd already reached a point of deep pessimism. The judges on the bench weren't here to play cat-and-mouse games, and it was thanks to their goodwill that the cassation appeal was being heard at all. They wouldn't be prepared to re-examine the case so thoroughly that they'd find the defendant innocent. Not the slightest chance. At best, Chyłka and Oryński could hope to convince the presiding judge, as he seemed open-minded. But the rest of the bench were clearly hard-hearted opportunists.

There was no chance of overturning the previous judgement, he could see that now; but this had been the only route open to Chyłka to get the case before the Supreme Court. And if she didn't have some sort of ace up her sleeve he didn't know about, they should prepare to tell Piotr he'd be spending the rest of his life in prison.

Oryński sat back on his seat, unable to shake the feeling of impending doom. The judges were calmly whispering about something, and the trainee was sure it didn't have anything to do with the case—more likely they were deciding where to go for lunch or discussing some forthcoming new regulation. Langer was of only marginal interest to them.

They perked up when Chyłka called Langer as a witness. There followed a deafening silence, then the metallic clanking of chains indicated the protagonist had moved.

Rejchert glanced at Joanna to show delight. This was something he could only have dreamed of. Langer's silence would be the crowning moment in the fall of the Żelazny & McVay lawyers.

Kordian handed their client the piece of paper with the name on it. He didn't reckon it would change anything. The sacred right of the defendant in any criminal trial was to keep their mouth firmly shut.

Yet Piotr stood up. All the cameras were focused on him, and the judges were fully awake. He shuffled slowly to the witness box.

"The accused Piotr L," announced the presiding judge, more than a little surprised. And the court recorder entered his words in the minutes.

Langer stood quite still in the middle of the courtroom, not even moving his eyes, staring blankly at the Polish emblem on the wall just above the presiding judge.

"Prosecutor," said Gołdyn.

Rejchert drummed his fingers on the table, staring at Piotr.

"I have no questions," he announced.

Joanna frowned. She had been convinced that the Kim Jong-un of the Polish Bar would not miss this opportunity to finish off his opponent. With Langer in the witness box, the prosecutor could have grilled and cross-questioned him, even tried a little manipulation. With a bit of luck, he could even have closed the case immediately. Clearly, however, Rejchert had decided that the defendant could not be manipulated. Or that he might even compromise him as a prosecutor.

"Counsellor."

Chyłka felt a pleasant tingling in her hands. Her moment had come. She had Langer to herself, and the judges were fully focused on the two of them. All signs of weariness and boredom were gone—they were curious to see how this would play out.

She rose.

"Can you tell me how the victims lost their lives?" she asked in an impassive tone.

"No comment," replied Piotr, looking at the presiding judge.

"That is your right," confirmed Judge Gołdyn.

"Thank you for the information," said Langer disarmingly, and looked at the other judges, who stared at him in astonishment.

"Neither are you obliged to tell the truth," said Judge Dublicki. "As the defendant, you would not be criminally liable. We could hardly expect you to knowingly incriminate yourself."

"I don't think this is the time or place to give legal advice," said Bazan.

All the other judges looked at the presiding judge, who nodded his head to signal an end to the discussion.

Chyłka had watched the judges' reaction to her client's words carefully, and had to admit it wasn't too bad. His "thank you" had been a bit odd, but at least he no longer looked like a silent psychopath.

"Why can't you answer my question?" she asked.

"No comment."

"Did you kill those people?"

"No comment."

"I remind you that you are not criminally liable. You don't even have to tell the truth," said Joanna. "Did you kill those people?"

"No comment."

Chyłka looked at the judges. By this stage, a normal person would have thought up some sort of alibi. It wouldn't necessarily convince anyone, but at least they'd try.

"Can you say anything about the murder of these people?"

"No comment."

"Did you know the victims?"

"No."

"Did you see these people before they were killed?"

"No comment."

Rejchert got up and spread his arms. If ever there was a time to use this ploy he'd learned from American TV, this was it.

"Your Honour . . ." he pleaded. "This is absurd."

"Sit down please," said Judge Gołdyn. "If you wish to take the floor, please wait until Counsellor Chyłka has finished questioning her client."

Rejchert remained in his theatrical pose for a few moments longer, then bowed his head and sat down. Joanna cleared her throat. It was time to roll out the heavy artillery.

"The other party claims that you directly and deliberately murdered those people. Have you any comments to make about their accusations?"

"No comment."

"Counsellor," said Bazan. "Is this strictly necessary? The witness clearly won't answer any of your questions."

"He said he didn't know the victims," replied Chyłka to set the facts straight, and shifted her focus back to Langer before the judge could respond. "Did you ever use a hammer, a wrench or Fackelmann knives in your apartment?"

"Yes."

Joanna placed her hands on the desk and looked at the judges. Their academic achievements might not have been overly impressive, but they weren't ignorant fools either. They must have seen what was happening and realised that Langer was either under pressure not to speak or had some sort of sophisticated strategy. But it was hard to believe that the silence he had maintained throughout the first two trials, and minimal interaction with his lawyer, were also part of his game. Any sane person would end the farce at the Court of Appeal rather than risk spending the rest of his days behind bars.

"Why are you not defending yourself?" asked Joanna, folding her arms.

"No comment."

"Counsellor . . ."

"Please bear with me, Your Honour," said Chyłka, turning to Judge Bazan, who gave her a petulant look. Joanna turned her attention back to Langer. "Could you tell the court who Antoni Wansel is?"

Silence. Piotr looked away from the wall at last and glowered at his defence lawyer. This did not escape the judges' attention, Chyłka noticed. If ever he looked like a psychopath, this was it.

"I'll repeat the question."

"I heard it," he interrupted. "No comment."

"Thank you. I have no more questions," said Chyłka, and returned to her place.

The presiding judge cleared his throat and adjusted his sitting position. He had spent many hours reading the court documents, but did not recall seeing the name Wansel in any of them. If he'd delegated the reading of the documents to one of his juniors, he would assume he had simply missed it; but as presiding judge, he had taken the time to read everything himself. He was tempted to ask Chyłka who this person was, whose name she had brought into the proceedings in a roundabout way. He was certain that was exactly what Chyłka wanted.

"Prosecutor?" he asked, looking at Rejchert.

"I would only like to point out that the questions to the defendant have nothing to do with the case, and the defence has failed to show the significance of the answers. Moreover, I should add that silence is no defence," said the prosecutor, rising from his seat. "However cunningly this tactic is used, this does not—"

"Please do not instruct the court," said Judge Sydoń, who so far had been more interested in the court's interior décor than the case itself.

"Of course," replied Rejchert. "I merely wanted to emphasise that these tactics may be effective in the media, but not before such a distinguished group of legal experts."

The judges pretended not to hear the cheesy compliment, and Chyłka felt she could notch up a not inconsiderable success. She had piqued the interest not only of the judges, but even the public prosecutor. The iron was well and truly hot, and she was about to strike it by calling the next witness, who had not been on the list but was present in the courtroom, not by coincidence. Gołdyn gave his consent, and Rejchert had no objections.

After two policemen had escorted Langer away in chains, Kormak stepped into the witness box. The new witness's personal details were entered into the court minutes, and Kormak took the oath. This was not obligatory, but Gołdyn decided to apply it in this case.

"Do you know why you have been called to give evidence in court?" asked the judge.

"Yes," said Kormak. "I am an employee of the law firm Żelazny & McVay. I provide technical support for cases conducted by our lawyers."

Kordian nodded approvingly. That was a concise description of his job.

"Together with Ms Chyłka and her assistant Mr Oryński, we analysed recordings from the visiting room at Białołęka prison. These showed that the client was trying to communicate with his defence lawyers by blinking messages."

"What?" blurted out Rejchert.

"I'm sorry?" reiterated Bazan.

"Quiet please," ordered the presiding judge, then turning to the witness, asked him to continue.

"As I was saying, I participated in analysing the recordings. Ms Chyłka discovered that Piotr L was blinking messages in Morse code, and recognised the SOS message. As someone who knows Morse code, I was able to decipher the rest."

Kormak paused. The judges looked both flummoxed and delighted. Not often did they experience such a dramatic turn of events.

"According to my findings, Piotr L transmitted a number of messages in this way."

"What messages?" asked Gołdyn. In response, Kormak launched into a long monologue. Naturally, the most important piece of information Langer had given them was the address of the Grey-Haired Man who was responsible for a brutal assault on one of the defence lawyers and later for unlawful imprisonment of both lawyers. These crimes hadn't actually been proven, but the public prosecutor was too confused to react.

Then Kormak mentioned Antoni Wansel. The judges were fidgeting in their chairs. They were dying of curiosity.

"Were you able to determine who that is?" asked the presiding judge.

"We found his grave in Bródno cemetery."

"And?"

"And I would like to exercise my right under article 183, paragraph one of the Criminal Procedure Code."

This was the right to refuse to answer a question if it made the witness or their relatives criminally liable for an offence. Every judge, even those who had difficulty remembering numbers, knew this regulation so well they'd recognise it when woken in the middle of the night. Again, the adjudicating panel was astir.

"Your Honour . . ." began Rejchert, plastering on an oleaginous smile. "Perhaps the witness does not realise that anything he might have done to find that grave will not result in criminal proceedings against him. It would be a misdemeanour at most. And therefore, he is not entitled to refuse to answer questions."

Kormak started to feel hot. Chyłka had assured him that everything would go smoothly, but the prosecutor's words didn't sound good. If the presiding judge agreed, Kormak would find himself in a very perilous situation indeed.

This was a typical bluff, a rudimentary legal equivalent of the "I know, but I'm not telling you" ploy. Yes, we have found the man. Yes, we have located his grave. No, I can't tell you what we've found there, because of article 183.

"Your Honour?" asked Rejchert. He was not looking at the presiding judge, but at Judge Bazan. It was from her that he was seeking help, presuming that Chyłka had put all her chances on one card. If the boy was lying under oath, then perhaps they had indeed found the grave but not opened it, or, if they had, they hadn't found anything. The prosecutor concluded that it had to be a ruse.

Judge Bazan had already opened her mouth when the presiding judge raised his hand. The woman refrained from speaking—defying the presiding judge was a contravention of court procedure.

"It is not the role of the court to evaluate the grounds on which the witness is declining to answer," said the presiding judge.

"But Your—"

"There is no room for discussion here, Prosecutor," said the presiding judge. "The witness decides whether or not they should answer questions. It would be a different matter if the testimony could bring someone or something into disrepute, then the decision belongs to the adjudicating panel. But here, reference was made to consequences of a legal nature."

"Yes, but—"

"The Supreme Court has frequently emphasised that the witness has no responsibility to explain why they are declining to answer questions. It is generally enough to say that it concerns a criminal offence."

"Of course," replied Rejchert, realising he was getting nowhere.

"I feel that we should all take a deep breath," continued Gołdyn. "The defence has given us a surprise, no doubt deliberately, and is now reaping the benefits of our consternation. I see nothing wrong with it; it does not break any regulation known to me. It is a legal technique, perhaps not particularly sophisticated, but effective nonetheless. You have introduced new circumstances which cannot now be overlooked. You should remember, however, that they may only be considered if the cassation appeal is justified."

"Your Honour, if I may speak?" said Chyłka, rising from her seat. The presiding judge slowly lowered his head. A sign of approval? Or resignation? After a moment of silence, Joanna decided it was tacit consent. "In this case, I would like to say that according to the Supreme Court judgement of sixth September 1996, reference number II KKN sixty-three, the Supreme Court has jurisdiction not over the factual findings but over how they were obtained." She held up a piece of paper. "May I approach the bench?"

It was hugely risky, but she had done what she could not to sound pretentious.

"Of course," Gołdyn gestured with his hand. He took the printout of the judgement and looked at it briefly, then passed it on to Judge Bazan, who was sitting next to him.

"What are they trying to prove?" asked another judge on the bench.

"To see how the factual findings of the courts of the first and second instance had had a direct influence on how my client was judged," she replied.

"As I have tried to explain in the appeal letter, it was assumed *a priori* that all the wounds on the bodies of the victims were inflicted before their deaths."

Gołdyn looked at her.

"The officer who testified first emphasised that he had used this alone to conclude that the crime was premeditated, with direct intent and exceptional brutality. The same conclusion, based on the same premise, was also reached by the courts of the first and second instance. And yet despite this, I have not seen any expert testimony that would confirm the wounds were not inflicted post-mortem. *Manifestum non eget probatione* was assumed, that what is manifest does not require proof. Except in my opinion, nothing is as manifest as it seems."

Bazan sighed theatrically.

"And yet you still insist that Piotr L massacred the bodies out of rage. Because of what? Because he was angry they were dead?" she asked.

"No," replied Joanna. "In my opinion, Piotr L didn't touch those bodies. But that is quite irrelevant, just like your question."

Chyłka knew her emotions were starting to get the better of her, but there was not much she could do about it. That Bazan woman was getting on her nerves, and there was only so long she could stop herself from answering back. "The task of the court in these proceedings is to determine whether the factual findings made by courts of both instances were correct," she added. "Nothing more and nothing less. It does not concern the merits of the case."

Bazan snorted and looked at her companions. But they all seemed to be familiar with judgement II KKN 63/96. Judges at every level, especially this one, didn't like smart alec lawyers, even if they used accessible language and did not throw arguments straight in their faces. But in this case, the adjudicating panel had to swallow its pride and consider what Chyłka had said.

"All right," said Gołdyn with a thin smile. "You have made your case very clearly, even if it is not yet time for a final speech."

Joanna too responded with a smile, and returned to her place. She was relatively pleased, though it was still hard to believe there might be a miracle. The court thanked the witness, and around an hour later the final speeches began. Chyłka did not have much to say. She summed up her findings and stressed that a number of questions remained unanswered, including the cases of the Grey-Haired Man and Antoni Wansel. The fact that Langer referred to both those people in his covert messages was evidence enough that there was a connection between them.

Rejchert stuck to his strategy of minimal participation. He had no intention of giving lengthy speeches laying out arguments that had already been raised and were known to the judges. He'd had a much better starting position in this confrontation than the defence, and had endeavoured to give the impression that the appeal was far-fetched. He hadn't had to try especially hard, because Chyłka knew herself that the case for cassation was weak. Nonetheless, she had done everything she could—and more, if you considered her gambit with Kormak and Antoni Wansel's grave.

19

THE LAWYERS SPENT the next break downstairs, accompanied by Kormak. One cigarette wasn't enough to relieve the tension and stress, so the legal duo smoked frantically, and greedily managed two cigarettes in the allotted time.

"I think it went well," said Kormak. "They bought it."

"They bought nothing," replied Joanna. "Those people had already seen this sort of thing a hundred times when you and Zordon were learning how to use a potty. They saw through everything, and know we're just playing tactics."

"So there'll be no *hemos pasado*?" asked Kordian.

"There's still a chance. We've definitely aroused their curiosity."

"Certainly not Bazan," noted Oryński. "That old battleaxe is only interested in when she can go home."

"Never mind her," Chyłka said, sighing. "You could tell from the start she's not worth the trouble. Besides, we don't need her for anything. Let her rot."

Her companions nodded.

"And what about the factual findings thing? Is that true?" asked Kormak.

"Yup," confirmed Joanna. "The Supreme Court is not just another court. The judges can't waste time trying to determine once again whether or not it was Langer who thrust the knife into the woman's eye socket. Their task is to determine whether or not errors were made during earlier trials."

"And there were errors," said Kormak, not entirely sure whether he was asking a question or making a statement.

"It depends."

"What depends? Either there were or there weren't."

"In law, everything depends," said Oryński, stubbing out his cigarette. "It's the first thing we learn at university, and then we hear it
repeated everywhere; it's the universal answer to all questions. In negotiations and mediations, you need to constantly ask why, and in talks
with clients or opponents in the courtroom, it's always good to say that
it depends."

"Huh?"

"For example: Is there a punishment for killing a person?" asked
Kordian, looking at Chyłka.

Joanna shook her head, not wanting to play games. But then she saw
Kormak looking at her expectantly, so she sighed and replied.

"It depends," she said, rocking her head from side to side for theatrical effect. "It depends on how old the perpetrator is, whether they are
sane, whether they did it deliberately, whether it was direct intent, etc. It
all depends, Kormak. That also holds true in this case."

"Depends on what? Do you mean the judgement?"

"On a whim," murmured Oryński. "It depends on the mood of the
judges. The law is the law, regulations are regulations, but it all comes
down to their subjective evaluation."

"That's right," confirmed Chyłka. "My favourite legal brain, Ron-
ald Dworkin, who has now sadly departed to a better place, always said
that the judge is the key element in the legal system. Not any regulation, just the judge. The judgement depends on what kind of person
the judge is. Admittedly that makes greater sense in Great Britain,
because there, if there's a 'hard case,' the judge can refer to general
rules governing the system. But even here, in our country, this is also
true to some extent. We also have rules, that Dworkin would call standards. They are based on morality and general social mores, and they
are the basis on which laws are written. The thing is that they are also
the basis for adjudication."

"Er . . ." said Kormak, not really understanding what she had just
said.

"I'll put it another way," said Joanna. "Adjudicating on the basis of
general principles of morality and justice may lead to many different
decisions. That, in my opinion, is the quintessence of the thought of
Dworkin's predecessor, a chap called Hart. In a single case, ten judges
may issue ten different judgements, each of which would be acceptable
because they would all be in accordance with the law and also in accordance with current standards. But which one is best? Well, the one made
by the judge with the best character. That's why the law is the law, but it's
the person who turns that law into a decision that really counts."

"OK," replied Kormak. "That's enough for one day. In fact, it's enough for the next several weeks. It would be better if you could tell me what happens now," he said, looking at the glass wall.

"Well, what do you think will happen?" asked Chyłka. "At the moment, the judges are conferring. They're brainstorming, considering each issue separately, and later they'll vote. They'll scribble their signatures on a piece of paper and that'll be that, the case will be done and dusted."

Kormak hopped from foot to foot, looking inquiringly at Joanna. But she didn't want to speculate on the outcome of the trial. She could barely gather her own thoughts, let alone work out what the judgement was likely to be.

Common sense told her that the case was straightforward, but the court could make a number of different decisions, and each of them would be acceptable; though not necessarily from Langer's point of view.

"You're an old courtroom hand, Chyłka," said Kordian. "You should at least know what kind of judgement to expect."

"It depends."

Kormak rolled his eyes. "On what?"

"On how many Herculeses there are."

"Huh?"

"Dworkin distinguished two types of judge."

"Oh please," said Kormak. "Not Dworkin again."

"Two types of judge," she continued, undeterred. "Judge Herbert and Judge Hercules. Herbert was rather pedestrian; he was subservient to the legislature and scared to make any creative interpretations. He respected the will of the majority and did not take into account his own opinion during adjudication, if it differed from the majority viewpoint. Judge Hercules was different. He did not wish to play the role of legislator, but at the same time he felt he had a special ability to interpret the law in terms of justice and morality. Therefore, he adjudicated on the basis of his own assessments and not the will of the majority expressed in accordance with statute law."

Kormak mimed tying a noose around his neck.

"In order to win, we need three Herculeses," added Joanna, ignoring him. "Unfortunately, they are so rare in the wild that they should be a protected species."

The defence lawyers returned to the courtroom with gloomy faces, as if they were going to their own execution. Langer looked up and gazed at them blankly. They took their seats, looking at the empty chairs soon to be graced by the backsides of the five judges responsible for the defendant's fate.

"What do you think?" asked Kordian.

"Gołdyn and Dublicki have taken the bait. Bazan definitely hasn't, like-wise most probably Sydoń. That leaves Marendziak, who looked as if he was about to nod off throughout the trial. Now everything depends on him."

"Perhaps we can count on male solidarity?" asked Oryński with a foolish smile. Chyłka just looked at him, which was enough to make him wish he hadn't said anything.

"Will we take the case further if the need arises?" he asked a while later. "To Strasbourg?"

"I reckon we'd have a better chance over there than here. Especially in the light of . . ."

Chyłka broke off mid-sentence, as the gong sounded, at that very moment signalling to everyone in the courtroom that they should rise to honour the majesty of the judiciary. On TV, someone in the courtroom usually made the announcement, but in the Supreme Court the judges' arrival was heralded by a sonorous beep, similar to that announcing the approach of an underground train. The beep was followed by a grave silence, broken only by the sound of footsteps.

The five judges in their purple jabots and collars processed into the courtroom, proudly led by a man wearing the chain of justice, at the bot-tom of which dangled the Polish eagle. Everyone had risen from their seats and remained standing until the judges sat. The adjudicators removed their caps and placed them on the desks in front of them. Gołdyn took a breath and looked straight ahead, his gaze impenetrable.

"Ladies and Gentlemen, before I announce the judgement, I would like to say a few words," he began. "The case we have been deliberating is extremely complex. It is disturbing in ordinary terms and fascinating from the legal point of view. It cannot be denied that much has been left unexplained, and some previously unknown facts are yet to be con-firmed. Counsellor Chyłka has rightly drawn our attention to a number of problems that could, but will not necessarily, turn out to be relevant to the case. In particular, we should consider the question of the per-son who, according to the police, was responsible for your abduction." Gołdyn looked at the two lawyers, but there was nothing in his gaze that could be construed as a good omen.

Quite the opposite. Oryński felt that the judge was looking at them with compassion, as if he wanted to help but couldn't. Perhaps he was not up to the task, and had turned out to be just another Judge Herbert? It didn't look good.

"Using Morse code, Piotr L tried to draw your attention to a person whom, for data protection reasons, we will call the Grey-Haired Man. This was before the abduction, and even before trainee Oryński was bru-tally assaulted, which leads me to think there is a connection between that man, Piotr L, and the incidents in question. By a process of logic, this implies that the defendant's silence is in some way imposed by a third party. With this, I end my suppositions. Because these are only suppositions. As far as the facts are concerned, I can only say that new facts have certainly emerged in the case."

Chyłka nodded, because this time the judge was looking her straight in the eye.

"These facts could have changed the decision of the court if the defence had requested to reopen the case. However, they decided not to do this."

Oryński would happily have told the judge that when they decided to submit a cassation appeal, they didn't know about Langer's messages. What's more, they didn't even know about the Grey-Haired Man. But all that was irrelevant now.

"A cassation hearing re-examines the proceedings of lower instance courts, but only with respect to the law," stressed Gołdyn. "And it rules only on the grounds for appeal as given in the cassation statement."

Kordian swore profusely in his mind.

"Hence, compulsory representation by a lawyer. Only an experienced lawyer has permission to file a cassation appeal. The grounds for appeal have to be expressed extremely precisely, as they alone determine the court's decision."

Gołdyn could have ended there. But judges were not known for delivering short speeches.

"Having said that, I must emphasise one thing that might seem contrary to our sense of justice: unlike the court of appeal, we have no room here to adjudicate beyond the scope of the appeal, even in the event of a gross injustice. I might be of the opinion that the judgement in Piotr L's case is grossly unfair, but it is not in my competence to change it."

Oryński was afraid to look at Chyłka. He was afraid to see the expression of utter defeat on her face.

"To recap, the Supreme Court examines the cassation appeal only within the bounds of the charges it contains, and therefore, even with the best intentions, we could not go beyond the indictments of the appeal."

Kordian started to feel hot. When the judge paused towards the end of his speech, it seemed to mark the beginning of a funeral eulogy—over the joint grave of their legal careers.

"One of the exceptions, however, is a norm in article 455 of the Criminal Procedure Code concerning appeal proceedings. This may, in certain circumstances, be applied in cassation appeal proceedings before the Supreme Court."

Oryński shifted in his chair, feeling shivers running down his spine. He looked at Chyłka, but she maintained a stony expression, her gaze fixed on the presiding judge.

"In accordance with this norm, the court may re-examine the case with a broader scope, if there are grounds to believe that the original judgement is flawed. It is the opinion of the court that this has happened in the case of Piotr L."

Kordian felt his mouth fall open and his lips arrange themselves into a grin of satisfaction. Joanna, however, still appeared impassive, so he forced himself to stay calm. Even with the presiding judge on their side there could be several possible outcomes, and most were disadvantageous to their client. Oryński turned around to look at him, and saw something that could be construed as a glimmer of hope on Langer's face. He still looked apathetic, and every inch the prisoner, but he was no longer contemplating his chains.

"And that said, I shall now read the decision of the court," continued the judge. He adjusted his chain, looked at the sheet of paper in front of him and took a deep breath. "Judgement on behalf of the Republic of Poland," he began, and then read the date, the names of the judges and the subject of the case. "Following the Criminal Law Division hearing of the cassation appeal submitted by the defence lawyers of Piotr L regarding the judgement of the Court of Appeal in Warsaw, upholding the judgement of the District Court in Warsaw, the Supreme Court . . ."

Now, thought Oryński and closed his eyes.

". . . overrules the ruling in its entirety, and also the ruling of the court of the first instance, and remands the case for retrial in the court of the first instance."

Chyłka and Kordian didn't even hear the court order regarding reimbursement for the cassation appeal fee, so overcome were they with wild excitement; all the greater because it would have been inappropriate to show it. Almost imperceptibly they shook their heads with disbelief, and Langer, sitting behind them, slowly began to realise that he had been given a second chance. A new life.

CHAPTER

20

THE SUN SHONE lazily on the city centre streets, bathing them in an orange glow, as the young man in his shell suit and Decathlon sweatshirt jogged another kilometre towards the Saxon Garden.

He had originally planned to play squash once a week, but jogging turned out to be much more his style.

The area was not particularly well suited to it, especially when you did ten kilometres in the morning—the hard surfaces weren't great for the knees. Living in the city centre, however, had its advantages, and undeniably saved on commuting time.

Previously, he had had to spend almost two hours trundling back and forth between work and Żoliborz; now Oryński lived just a stone's throw away from the Skylight building. He was renting a small studio flat in a block in Emilia Plater Street, paying one thousand five hundred a month. Daylight robbery, but he wasn't concerned. As a Junior Associate at Żelazny & McVay he earned enough that he could also afford the occasional salmon at the nearby Hard Rock Cafe.

He had just passed kilometre five of the course. It was always a breakthrough point in his morning jogging routine, after which he felt ready to run a marathon. That was a bit of an exaggeration, although in recent months he had built up enough stamina to maybe manage a half marathon. However, he never ran more than ten kilometres, because that was all he had time for. He began his run at six and was back home before seven, so that by eight he could be at work, in office attire and briefcase in hand.

He no longer worked in the newbie-burrow; as a Junior Associate he was now entitled to his own office. Somewhat smaller than the McCarthy Cave, but that didn't bother him in the least.

The new job title sounded good, but in reality, it was not all that much of a promotion. Every lawyer in full-time employment at the firm started out as a Junior Associate. After two years, he could become an Associate, and later, after completing his training and ruining an appropriate number of companies in court, he could hope to become a Senior Associate.

A salary of six thousand gross a month was not staggering compared to what other lawyers were getting, but perfectly adequate. Oryński was satisfied with the direction in which his career was heading.

Professional life flourished, and even his social life was not too bad, bearing in mind the limited number of acquaintances he had. Everything was in good order, apart maybe from the fact that all the full-time employees referred to Żelazny & McVay as "the firm" and constantly used English expressions, even in private conversations. It was a trend all legal firms seemed to encourage. To this day Kordian could not understand what was wrong with the Polish expression "*młodszy wspólnik*," Junior Associate. The worst was the commercial law division, with that quintessentially English title of "Mergers and Acquisitions."

At the ninth kilometre, Kordian picked up the pace and stopped thinking about mergers, trademarks, and other English language loan words. A few minutes later he was back home. He ate his standard breakfast—natural yogurt with a banana and oats. Then a shower, a suit, a spray or two of aftershave and he was ready for work.

Getting to the Skylight building took less than a minute. Refreshed and pleasantly geared up by the running, he passed the interns smoking outside the building and winced. For several months now, he'd hated smoking.

"Good morning," said one of the interns. They were more or less the same age, but now there was a gulf dividing them.

Kordian raised his hand, smiled warmly, and entered the building. He was on time, so he expected to meet his mentor by the lifts. He wasn't mistaken. Chyłka was wearing a tight graphite skirt, noticeably tapered at the hem. It was hard to ignore.

"Hi Zordon," she greeted him.

"Hi Chyłka," he replied, before they entered the cabin.

"Couldn't you find anything tighter to wear?" he asked looking back and trying not to ogle her behind.

"I chose this so you could at least get a look, because that's all you're getting."

After they had won the Langer case, their relationship had remained essentially unchanged. Maybe it would have been different if not for the mentor–mentee status; traineeships lasted three years, and Kordian hoped that when that time elapsed, they would be able to have another look at it.

Or perhaps not. He was unsure what he really meant to her.

"I have a case," announced Joanna. "A doctor carrying out illegal abortions. Pretty messy."

"Want me to help you?"

"Know anything about placenta, other than in the botanical sense?"

He shook his head and shuddered at the thought.

"Besides, you have your own case," Joanna added a moment later. "What about your Bald Man?"

"He was the killer, no doubt about it."

"I can tell that just by looking at him. Can you prove that he didn't do it?"

"Maybe," replied Kordian, moving his hand to and fro as if the matter of "yes" and "no" was still fluid.

Initially, he had felt that he would be reluctant to defend people who were clearly guilty. However, he soon came to the conclusion that once he started treating his efforts simply as work and not as a morbid mission, it was much easier to avoid getting emotionally involved. So his work lost some of its initial passion and charm, but at least he felt more comfortable with himself. He was doing his job, and nothing beyond his statutory duties.

The Langer case, however, was different, because Langer had been the innocent victim of a series of unfortunate events that cast a shadow over his entire life. Not only was he innocent of the crime, but he hadn't deserved to be in that particular swamp in the first place. He had been in the wrong place at the wrong time: a hackneyed expression, but applicable in this particular case.

The legal duo, on the other hand, were exactly where they should be.

After winning the case at the Supreme Court, it was the turn of the district court to reassess Langer's guilt. This time the Żelazny & McVay lawyers were in a better position, having a clear statement from the court of the highest instance that earlier courts had failed to step up to the plate.

A few weeks later, their advantage was so great that Rejchert himself asked for a meeting and made a deal whereby their client would get a suspended sentence in return for confessing to inadvertently causing death.

The advantage was that they could include the Grey-Haired Man and an autopsy of Antoni Wansel's body in the retrial. The first of these two had gone underground so the hearing had to be conducted in his absence, but this didn't prevent him from being found guilty and receiving a sentence. Wansel had been identified as a member of a climbing group to which Daniel Relichowski and Agata Szylkiewicz—Langer's alleged victims—also belonged. It turned out that the murder of Wansel had been a slip-up, and the body had to be removed fast so as not to cast doubts on Piotr's culpability.

Antoni Wansel was murdered with the same hammer as the one in Langer's apartment. A court expert for God-alone-knows-what—Chyłka maintained he was probably a stock keeper at Castorama, Praktiker, or some other DIY outlet—identified it as a locksmith's hammer weighing approximately 1,500 grams, with a 145 by 43 millimetre steel face. The marks on Wansel's body were identical to those on the bodies in Langer's flat; the difference was in the DNA found on Wansel's body, which corresponded with that found on Oryński after he had been assaulted. Wansel was killed by Gorzym, there was no doubt about it.

Everything came together neatly and logically, and they had no difficulty defending Langer. The trial was a mere formality, and there was no real need to make a deal with Rejchert. The case inspired the prosecutor to move to the private sector. He qualified as a legal counsellor, and in all probability was rather content with his decision.

Piotr Langer was acquitted, and the local police chief resigned, praying that the news media would leave him alone. For them this was a brilliant story, shedding light on how the Polish justice system and law enforcement agencies worked. The problems were of course exaggerated, which further publicised the case. Żelazny & McVay were besieged by clients who were particularly interested in working with the lawyers who had dealt so proficiently with Langer's case—that is, either Joanna Chyłka or Kordian Oryński.

The firm's partners could not have been more pleased. All the disagreements with Artur Żelazny were now quite forgotten, and he was prepared to shower his two lawyers with gold. Contrary to McVay's suspicions, Żelazny was probably not involved with the Grey-Haired Man, although no one could be absolutely certain.

"Lunch as usual?" asked Chyłka, distracting Oryński from his thoughts.

"Sure," replied Kordian, and turned left down the corridor, allowing Chyłka to walk to her office alone. At this time, the corridor was already packed, and without advanced skills in elbowing your way through, it was difficult to reach your destination.

An hour later, Chyłka entered Oryński's room. Without knocking, she opened the door and slammed it loudly behind her.

"What was that?" Kordian managed to say before Chyłka placed her laptop in front of him and opened it.

"Watch."

"But what?"

"Kormak."

"Kormak, what? Did he die?"

She clearly wasn't in the mood for joking. He had never seen this expression on her face before, so the joke was maybe not a joke at all. Joanna shook her head, and a moment later Oryński could see for himself what she meant. A group of thumbnail pictures appeared on the screen; looking at the first of them drained the blood from Oryński's face, and he began to feel faint.

"Who took these?" he asked. Not the best question, but with the shock, nothing else came to mind. Chyłka ignored it. Instead, she took a chair and sat at the desk. Her hands were shaking.

Oryński looked at picture after picture and couldn't believe his eyes. Kormak must have had a very good lens, probably even better than the telescopic one he used to take photos of the Grey-Haired Man on his estate. This time the photos were of a shopping centre car park.

It was the ideal hiding place—crowded, constant comings and goings, and teeming with people quite oblivious to the rest of the world. It must have been the weekend because there were so many cars. One of the pictures even showed a traffic jam at the exit.

"When did he—"

"Last Friday," said Chyłka.

"And since then . . . how did it happen? Didn't he say anything?"

"Nothing," she replied and instinctively reached into her jacket pocket, where a few months ago she was certain there was a packet of cigarettes. If she'd found the cheapest, most mangled cigarette on earth right now she'd have happily smoked it, and to hell with all that rubbish about cleansing the body of nicotine. "He was instructed by McVay and Żelazny. Directly."

"He could have told us, for God's sake."

"Yes, he could," agreed Joanna. She still couldn't quite process what she'd seen. "No doubt I got this email because Rusty and the Old Man already know everything."

Kordian stared fixedly at the monitor. There was a long, heavy silence. He looked at the photos again and again, hoping it was all some terrible misunderstanding.

He stopped at a picture of a smiling Piotr Langer patting the Grey-Haired Man on the back.

It wasn't a friendly gesture. These people weren't chums. Langer looked like the godfather, and the Grey-Haired Man like his henchman.

They both looked like people pleased with a job well done.

CHAPTER

21

A<small>N HOUR LATER,</small> Chyłka and Oryński were sitting in the conference room, along with Artur Żelazny, Harry McVay, and Kormak. The door was closed and the windows were soundproof.

"I take it you've seen our findings," said Artur.

Langer's former defence lawyers didn't answer.

"It's a painful and uncomfortable matter for us all," said Harry. "Perhaps it would have been less troubling if Langer had been less refined in his methods, if he had actually tried to convince people of his innocence. But we have no option, we have to face the truth. We were the ones who did all his work for him."

"Don't get us wrong," said Żelazny. "You had a duty to do that work, and you did it to the best of your abilities. You deserve applause and presidential awards regardless of whether Langer is guilty or not."

"That's patently obvious," muttered Kordian.

"Never mind that," said Joanna. "It's not important. Langer could have killed two people or two dozen and we would have defended him with the same tenacity. I'm more worried about how he managed . . ." She paused for a moment and shook her head. She really wanted a cigarette. "How he managed to be so two-faced?"

Żelazny looked at McVay, while McVay turned his head to look at Kormak. It was Wednesday. The photographs had been taken on Friday, so Kormak had had enough time to do some serious research. But he said nothing, so Chyłka took the initiative.

"Tell us what you know."

"Or first, how much you know," added Oryński.

"A lot," replied Kormak, fixing his gaze on the light wood conference table. He ran his hand over its rough surface, took a deep breath, and looked up.

"Recently, we started getting information that Langer, well, that he was planning something on the side," said Żelazny rather than Kormak. "As one of our most valuable clients, he should have informed us to give us enough time to prepare."

"Don't give them a lecture on our little investigation," said McVay, raising one hand and placing the other on the table. "We sent out our bloodhound, with the most powerful surveillance equipment money can buy."

"With it, I was able to track down Langer and the Grey-Haired Man," said Kormak. "And then I found out the details of their . . . joint venture."

"Joint venture?" exclaimed Kordian.

"Did you bug them?" asked Joanna. The three of them slowly lowered their heads, effectively confirming that they had.

"I managed to gain access to Langer's computer. You won't believe how much information he got on it the moment he became a free man and came back from the prison underworld."

"Get on with it!" said Chyłka.

Her tone made Kormak want to stand to attention and salute; it had a similar effect on the owners of the firm.

"I hate to say this," began Kormak, "but we've been well and truly had. Do you want me to tell you in chronological order, or the order in which I pieced it all together?"

"Chronologically," decided McVay.

Kormak nodded obediently, took another deep breath and launched into the monologue for which the duo had been waiting.

"Piotr Langer did kill those people," began Kormak, all but withering under Chyłka and Kordian's gaze, as if he felt guilty for not discovering the truth earlier. "All three of them, together with Antoni Wansel, met at the climbing wall in Mokotów. They laughed together, climbed together, and then Langer suggested that they should have a drink together. It started off quite well at the Opera in Theatre Square, in the VIP section, and ended tragically in Langer's Mokotów apartment. At one point he had suggested the party move to his place, and all three eagerly agreed. And everything would have been all right if Langer hadn't started coming on to Agata Szylkiewicz. She was no prude, but she wasn't up for it, especially not with him. A scuffle ensued. . . ."

"I don't believe this," growled Oryński. It all sounded surreal, quite unrelated to the reality they'd been living over the last few months.

Kormak started nervously stroking the table top again.

"Keep going," said Chyłka.

"Langer, who was completely drunk, started touching her up anyway. She was actually the girlfriend of someone else in that group, Daniel Relichowski. However, it wasn't Daniel but Antoni Wansel who was first to react. And that was the greatest mistake of his life. He rushed to intervene, but Piotr knocked him out, presumably with his bare fists. Then he used one of the murder weapons on Relichowski; the hammer or the knife, I don't know which came first. I haven't been able to find out either what was happening with the woman at that time, because neither Langer nor the Grey-Haired Man mentioned her in their conversations, and there are no other clues. I assume she was in shock, or perhaps begging for her life."

"Either way, she didn't scream, because Agnieszka Powirska would have heard her," said Oryński.

Kormak looked at him, and then turned to Żelazny for help.

"My guess is Agnieszka Powirska heard everything," said Joanna, looking absently into the air. "She never really intended to testify. That's why she disappeared. The Grey-Haired Man drove her somewhere far away on Piotr's instructions."

"Was she in league with them?" asked Oryński.

"I think so," said Kormak. "She clearly wasn't the airhead we took her to be."

"And clearly she was closer to Piotr than we assumed," added Joanna, and swore under her breath. "She talked about him in such a familiar way. It should have made us think. She knew his habits, and it seemed like she'd known him for a long time."

"And maybe she was scared," suggested Kordian. "She knew Piotr would be released sooner or later."

Kormak nodded and took a deep breath.

"After the fact, Langer cleaned himself up, and left his apartment with the three bodies inside. He bought a prepaid phone at the supermarket, then contacted the Grey-Haired Man and told him the situation. Then after ten days he came back unnoticed."

"But how did they manage to . . ." began Kordian, but eventually gave up trying to verbalise his question. Kormak knew what he was trying to say anyway.

"That's quite important. I'll explain it at the end," said Kormak. "But to continue the narrative: Langer calls the Grey-Haired Man and causes quite a bit of consternation. Suffice to say, the last thing they needed at that stage was three corpses. There was no way to get them off the estate, because firstly there was CCTV; secondly, there were security guards all over the place; and thirdly, there were residents milling around. On top of that, dead bodies are always discovered. The Grey-Haired Man suggested they should set it up to look like murder."

"They didn't have to make it look like murder, it was fucking murder," said Joanna.

"Well yes, but you know what I mean. They wanted it to look like straightforward murder at first glance, but on closer inspection to look as if it had been a set-up. They knew Langer could end up in prison, they even devised the strategy of him staying silent. He was told not to defend himself and to create the impression that he was being blackmailed and that those responsible for the crime were holding a relative of his hostage: a lover or an illegitimate child. It didn't get to that stage because you didn't read his Morse SOS in time. The Morse bit was Langer's own idea, because he sailed."

"All right, spare us the bloody Morse code," said Oryński.

"OK. The two of them knew they had to arrange everything in such a way that it would take a very thorough investigation before anyone realised things were not as they seemed. It couldn't be too immediately obvious, because no one would believe it. Have you heard of passive aggressive methods?"

"Stick to the point, and tell us what you know," said Chyłka this time. She'd had enough, and wanted concrete facts. Kormak nodded, and stopped stroking the table.

"Initially, they thought that they could manage without having to single out a specific culprit. The investigators would eventually realise something was not right and that that would be enough. The court would conclude that a third party was responsible and acquit Langer. But they soon realised that this wouldn't work, and they needed to find a scapegoat. First, they tried to incriminate Langer Senior, but unfortunately for them, he wasn't long for this world. Then they decided it should be the Grey-Haired Man, and he was ready to do it. But you didn't pick up the Morse Code signals that Langer, who was already in prison at the time, was sending you. Beating up Zordon was the first decisive move they made to give the impression there was a conspiracy against Langer. And you have to admit, their ploy worked. But you still hadn't managed to track down the Grey-Haired Man, which is why they had to arrange your meeting with him."

"And the whole business about not submitting the cassation appeal . . . all that coercion not to file it in time?" asked the trainee.

"The Grey-Haired Man's lawyer knew the deadline would be extended. That was the plan from the start," replied Kormak. "All of it was to make the idea of a third-party conspiracy all the more plausible."

"And it actually did exist," said Chyłka thoughtfully. "Except that it wasn't against Langer, but for his benefit."

"Yes."

"Why?" she asked. "Why was the Grey-Haired Man ready to sacrifice himself?"

"Because the Langer empire that we see on the tax returns and balance sheets is just the cherry on the cake. The real revenues come from Piotr's unofficial activities."

"In league with the Grey-Haired Man," said Joanna.

"Not exactly. The Grey-Haired Man was his most trusted man, more of an employee than a partner. Their relationship was hierarchical . . . or rather, still is."

"What do they do?" asked Oryński.

"Chiefly smuggling young Ukrainian, Belarusian, and Lithuanian women across the eastern border."

"Human trafficking?"

"To a large extent, but there's more to it," said McVay. "They trade not only live goods, but also anything of value, that's worth the risk. Langer laundered his illegal revenues through charities and his father's firm. Even now, when we have gathered quite a bit of information, everything still looks pretty clean."

"Do the police know about this?" asked Oryński.

"Or the prosecutor's office?" added Chyłka.

"No," replied Kormak, feeling as if someone had stolen his microphone. He glared at his boss, and continued. "The police are aware of the activities, but so far they have been unable to put a face or name to the information at their disposal. Now they have the Grey-Haired Man. And Langer has come out of it very well. Firstly, all the charges against him have been dropped, and secondly, he has practically guaranteed that the police will leave him alone for the rest of his life. Now, everyone believes that he is the victim, and if he had anything to do with the Grey-Haired Man, it was only because the latter had tried to frame him for a double murder with exceptional brutality."

"Why the brutality?" asked Kordian, shaking his head.

"I don't know. I assume he did it out of blind fury or to give the case publicity. And so that he would initially be seen as a monster, because now, by contrast, he has become a hero, a man wrongly accused and sent to prison, where he suffered brutal treatment, only to be cleared of all charges. Moreover, a person with enough loyalty to Poland not to appeal to the European Court of Human Rights in Strasbourg for wrongful conviction or whatever you call it."

Kormak paused to draw breath.

"That explains why he was still pretty much OK after allegedly being assaulted in prison," he added. "If a gangster in prison wanted to bring someone down a peg or three, he'd just do it."

Chyłka closed her eyes and hung her head. At the time, her client indeed did not look as if he had been through the wringer in prison. In fact, the markings and bruising on his face could have been self-inflicted.

"How did they get Wansel's body out?" she asked. "And why?"

Kormak ran his hand through his hair.

"I presume he didn't die in the flat," he said. "Langer knocked him unconscious, then Gorzym or some other thug got him off the estate. The autopsy showed that Wansel died of a drug overdose. No one suspected murder."

"Did they force him to take the drugs?"

"Yes, or injected him with them. There are so many possibilities."

"And family, friends? No one reported him missing, even though two of his friends had been murdered by the Sadist of Mokotów?"

Kormak shook his head. "Wansel had moved here from Łódź two weeks before his death. He got to know Daniel Relichowski and Agata Szylkiewicz soon afterwards."

"So why was he buried in Bródno?" asked Joanna.

"Because he was originally from Warsaw. He had moved away a few years earlier, because of a girl, or work, or God knows what."

Silence descended on the conference room again. From time to time, it was broken by someone moving on their chair or Kormak clearing his throat.

"So what can we do about it?" asked Kordian. It may not have been a particularly insightful question, but it was probably at the back of everyone's mind. It was met with two stern looks of disapproval.

"Nothing," said Żelazny.

"And I don't think it needs to be explained," added McVay.

Even a novice lawyer knows they have a statutory duty to act in favour of their client, but never against them. Of course, you could decide to ruin your own career and take the story to the media, but by doing so you would also risk sinking the whole firm. And not only the firm, but all its employees, who would become a collective *persona non grata* in the legal community.

"Is that clear?" asked Żelazny.

The lawyers nodded.

"Well, that's all from us," he said, then he and Harry stood up. "If you want to keep tormenting Kormak with questions, go ahead."

"He's all yours," added McVay, and the firm's owners left the conference room.

Chyłka supposed they were able to leave without worrying because they'd hidden a tiny microphone somewhere and were recording every word they said.

"Anything else to tell us?" asked Joanna.

"No," replied Kormak. "That's all we've managed to find out, and the rest we can only assume. One thing is certain: Langer hoodwinked us big time."

"Bastard," Chyłka seethed. "We went to so much trouble to defend that arsehole."

"But just think how much trouble they went to," said Kormak. "It was an ingenious plot, and it must have taken a hell of a lot of effort."

"Have you tracked down the Grey-Haired Man?" asked Kordian.

He had no intention of talking about Langer, it was pointless. Piotr had manipulated them, and the fact that the courts had been duped too was meagre compensation.

"No," said Kormak. "He disappeared soon after the business at the shopping centre. Langer has probably sent him abroad somewhere, out of gratitude for taking the rap and being prepared to risk going to prison."

"Why didn't he do it immediately?" asked Oryński, more to himself than to the others. "He could have said straightaway that he had done it."

"That wouldn't have been credible, and the police would have suspected collusion," said Joanna. "And the way they did it, that son of a bitch could pretend to be the victim."

The three of them fell silent; there was nothing more to add.

CHAPTER

22

After such a hard blow, it was difficult to function normally again. It wasn't about morality, justice, or any other lofty ethical concept. Chyłka and Oryński were troubled by the fact that they had been beaten at their own game. They had danced obediently to Langer's tune, and it hadn't even crossed their minds that it was all an elaborate game to give him a permanent alibi for his criminal activities.

The defendant in the high-profile trial no longer attracted any attention from the police; in fact, he probably deterred them. He represented the defeat of the justice system, and if anyone wanted to prosecute him, they would have to make damn sure they'd be able to get a conviction.

Two days after Kormak's presentation, Joanna decided it was time to do something she'd been meaning to do for a while. Admittedly, she didn't attach much importance to her duties as mentor, but she and Oryński had grown close. She felt that it would be good to take his mind off their defeat.

So she asked him to dinner. This was neither an especially time-consuming nor labour-intensive undertaking. She just had to dial the right number and say a few sentences. For Kordian, she ordered salmon with greens, and for herself, an extra-large meat feast pizza. It didn't really matter what she ordered because the main item on the menu was two bottles of four-year-old Georgian wine.

"Are you planning anything?" asked Oryński at one point.

"If you want to start an office romance, you're going about it the wrong way."

"I had a less dangerous plan in mind."

"The Langer case?"

Kordian nodded and poured them some more wine. "Is there any possibility at a—"

"No," she cut in quickly. "It's very simple. You're not a prosecutor, and even if you were, you wouldn't be able to use the information you had acquired defending Langer. It couldn't be clearer, Zordon. Accept it."

He took a sip of wine. His first taste told him it was medium dry, but he wasn't especially interested in the grape variety or even the taste. The only thing that mattered today was that the alcohol content would soon bring on the desired blissful effect.

"What would you have wanted, Zordon?"

"I don't know," he grunted.

"Justice? In this world, the only justice we can expect is the justice we got. Everyone has their own part to play in the system: the prosecutor exaggerates everything, we play it down, and the judge searches for the middle ground. And before that, someone sets down the legal norms, around which we all dance like fucking marionettes, pushing and shoving, each trying to trip the other up. That's justice in its democratic form."

He nodded, because maybe she had a point.

"Instead of adjudicating on the basis of how it should be, courts struggle within the narrow range of possibilities provided by statute law. The law has become unreal, divorced from reality. It's no longer about serving the public good. It's not an instrument for improving the lives of citizens. It has become the instrument of lawyers, the means by which we pay for our houses and cars. And at the same time, we forget that no single law has a monopoly on justice, let alone any judge."

"Did you start drinking before I arrived?" he asked, smiling. She responded in kind. For a while they looked at each other in silence while their food got cold.

"Eat your salmon."

"OK." Oryński cut himself a piece.

Joanna reached for the remote control, saying that the king of TVN would be on soon. The boy turned to look at the screen, and started eating. Perhaps this wasn't the most exciting way to spend an evening, but he felt comfortable. He felt as if he'd come home, and that was the main thing.

And Langer? Kordian had no intention of worrying about him. Some things couldn't be changed. There was a high probability that Piotr would kill again. He was a monster. He had to be, to abuse those bodies the way he had. And if he was slightly less careful, he'd get caught.

"Do you think we'll defend him if he kills again?" asked Oryński.

"Quiet. Wojewódzki is about to begin."

"But what do you think?"

"Yes, we would," replied Chyłka. "But this time we'd only do it to lose and have the last laugh."

They looked at each other, smiled, and then looked at the TV screen.

"You know that I've done your task?" said the trainee after a while.

"What task?"

"The one you set me on my first day. I checked which historical figure Iron Maiden sing about for eight minutes straight. Alexander the Great."

"Congratulations."

Kordian shrugged as if it was no effort. "*Hemos pasado.* We have passed," he said with a smile. "And here's to the next *no pasarán.*"

AFTERWORD

I'D LIKE TO start by expressing my thanks. First and foremost, to my parents, without whom this book—or any other, for that matter—would not have been written. My dedication is absolutely sincere; I hope they don't just see it as an author's empty words.

I would also like to thank:

- Dagmara, who endures my notorious disappearances for large parts of the day without complaint; I spend them in the company of characters like Chyłka and Zordon.
- Karolina, the excellent editor who patiently tweaked this book and maintained the highest level of vigilance, despite the self-imposed speed at which we had to work.
- Monika, the publishing miracle worker, who took care of everything connected with the book.

All mistakes, unfortunate wording, and ambiguities are exclusively my illegitimate offspring. And since we're talking of such things, I have tried to move within the limits of the law, not allowing myself any deviations; but I haven't always succeeded. Here and there, I've stretched reality a little, although in the most important issues, those concerning the cassation appeal, I have remained almost completely within the confines of the law. I hope that in the rare cases where I have stepped outside them, I have not offended anyone who holds the literal meaning of the regulations close to their hearts.

So what comes next? It's hard to say.

But it seems that this will not be the last case for the legal duo.